"Elizabeth's signature artistry as a s_____
the Moonlight. Brimming with imp_____
a book to remind us all that we can honor the past ___
embrace the future."

—Susan Meissner, bestselling author of *The Nature of Fragile Things*

"Elizabeth Musser's beautifully written novel *By Way of the Moonlight* brings to life a little-known piece of WWII history. The characters in this touching double story stayed with me long after 'the end.' One of the best novels I've read this year."

—Lynn Austin, author of *Long Way Home*

"Elizabeth Musser fans will not be disappointed as she delivers yet another emotional escape. This split-time story reminds us that the past can come back to the surface just when we least expect it. But it also assures us that no problem is too big for God's grace. A powerful message no matter the era."

—Julie Cantrell, *New York Times* and *USA Today*
bestselling author of *Perennials*

"Elizabeth Musser gives us another beautiful story with a lush setting on the Golden Isles off the southern Georgia coast. The fascinating equestrian thread and compelling characters weave through both the contemporary and historical facets of this novel, making this one you won't want to miss!"

—Deborah Raney, author of *Bridges* and the CHANDLER SISTERS

"Steeped in horses and Southern charm, *By the Way of Moonlight* is a delightful split-time romance that explores the history of the mounted beach patrols protecting Georgia's barrier islands from Nazi U-boat attacks. Readers who grew up with *The Black Stallion* and *Misty of Chincoteague* will love the grown-up action of Musser's book."

—Janyre Tromp, author of *Shadows in the Mind's Eye*

"The pull of the past, her grandmother's secrets, and the power of love. Elizabeth Musser's *By Way of the Moonlight* is a can't-put-it-down book. I highly recommend it!"

—Ane Mulligan, bestselling author of *Chapel Springs Revival*
and the award-winning *In High Cotton*

By Way
of the
Moonlight

Books by Elizabeth Musser

By Way of the Moonlight
The Promised Land
When I Close My Eyes
The Swan House
The Dwelling Place
Searching for Eternity
The Sweetest Thing
Two Crosses
Two Testaments
Two Destinies
Words Unspoken
The Long Highway Home

NOVELLAS

Waiting for Peter
Love Beyond Limits from *Among
the Fair Magnolias* novella collection

By Way of the Moonlight

ELIZABETH MUSSER

BETHANYHOUSE
a division of Baker Publishing Group
Minneapolis, Minnesota

© 2022 by Elizabeth G. Musser

Published by Bethany House Publishers
11400 Hampshire Avenue South
Minneapolis, Minnesota 55438
www.bethanyhouse.com

Bethany House Publishers is a division of
Baker Publishing Group, Grand Rapids, Michigan

Printed in the United States of America

Library of Congress Cataloging-in-Publication Data
Names: Musser, Elizabeth, author.
Title: By way of the moonlight / Elizabeth Musser.
Description: Minneapolis, Minnesota : Bethany House Publishers, a division of Baker
    Publishing Group, [2022]
Identifiers: LCCN 2022004584 | ISBN 9780764238802 (paperback) | ISBN
    9780764240140 (casebound) | ISBN 9781493437313 (ebook)
Subjects: LCGFT: Novels.
Classification: LCC PS3563.U839 B92 2022 | DDC 813/.54—dc23/eng/20220203
LC record available at https://lccn.loc.gov/2022004584

This is a work of historical reconstruction; the appearances of certain historical figures are therefore inevitable. All other characters, however, are products of the author's imagination, and any resemblance to actual persons, living or dead, is coincidental.

Cover design and back cover illustration by Paul Higdon
Cover image by Mzorin Photography

Author is represented by MacGregor Literary, Inc.

Baker Publishing Group publications use paper produced from sustainable forestry practices and post-consumer waste whenever possible.

22   23   24   25   26   27   28   7   6   5   4   3   2   1

To three of my favorite people:

Ashlee Winters Musser, my beautiful new daughter-in-law, who stole our son's heart and then all the family's. You are the answer to the prayers I've been praying for Chris since he was born: a wife who is bright, kind, courageous, and godly. You've become like a daughter to me, and I love you.

Jere W. Goldsmith IV (1934–2022), my beloved father, who lived on Nancy Creek Road for over fifty years and put up with a barn filled with horses for most of that time. Thank you for your love, good humor, and generosity of spirit that richly blessed the lives of your family and many others, most of all mine.

Barbara Goldsmith (1938–2016), my mother and the real Barbara Dale, who was every bit as feisty as her namesake in this novel and whose love for God, family, horses, and Hickory Hills inspired so much of this story.

"A dreamer is one who can only find his way by moonlight, and his punishment is that he sees the dawn before the rest of the world."

—Oscar Wilde

1

Allie

Atlanta, Georgia
Thursday, March 5, 2020

Dinosaur Bones Found in Buckhead Backyard

It was the silliest of presuppositions, only the alliteration worthy of notice, and I loved alliteration. And yet . . . dinosaur bones.

When I read it online in the *Atlanta Journal-Constitution*, I normally would have laughed out loud. Instead, I burst into tears because I knew exactly whose backyard it was and exactly who those bones belonged to. And it wasn't a dinosaur.

It felt like death to me. I wanted to scream that some crazy backhoe was unearthing my whole life—my history and my future—and would it please, please stop?

My cell beeping a familiar tone pulled me out of my morbid mood.

"Hey, sis. I guess you saw the article in the *AJC*."

"Yep."

"I blinked about a thousand times when I read it. Those were almost your exact words from twenty years ago! Remember? 'Someday someone's going to dig up the ring and think they've found dinosaur bones in Nana Dale's backyard!'"

"Of course I remember! It was funny back then. A joke. Now reality is crashing in, and I hate it!"

"Hey, don't go down that road of self-incrimination. This is *not* your fault. You put up a fight worthy of a T. rex."

"Ha. Thanks, bro." But my words sounded flat. I knew that Wick was staring at the article from his computer screen somewhere in France. I thought of my months' long fight and of his frustration at being far away.

Wick had loved genealogy since he learned he was named after our maternal great-grandfather, Jeremiah Wickliffe Butler. He had recently gotten his master's in historic preservation and combined the two skills in many unusual ways, the most recent being a twelve-month contracted job at the Louvre in France. He had already come back to the States for Nana Dale's funeral and the reading of the will back in December. He couldn't leave again.

Nevertheless, I said, "I wish you were here. You could help me straighten out this huge mess."

"It was all straightened out in January. This is not your problem anymore."

"But that's just it! Not being my problem *is* my problem. It was my dream, my life's ambition. Everything." I let out a muffled sob because I did not want to cry on the phone with my brother. "More important, it was *her* dream too. She commissioned me to keep it."

"Hey, I'm sorry. Yeah, I know it stinks, but there's nothing you can do about it. Have you finished cleaning out the house?"

So much for sympathy.

"Almost," I lied. I had yet to pack the first box.

But Wick knew me too well. He gave an exaggerated sigh. "Sis, if you don't go through and pick out what we want, everything will get sold or given away. Please."

"I will. I promise."

"And let the estate-sale agency help you, for heaven's sake."

"I don't trust them."

"It's not their fault. Or our lawyer's. You know that."

Silence on my part.

"C'mon. Let someone help you."

I was thankful he didn't bring up Austin.

"I'm going to see the bones!" I snapped, desperate to change the subject.

"What?"

"The dinosaur bones." I gave a dry chuckle. "I'll bet they haven't found half of them yet."

"For crying out loud, just leave it all alone. You've got enough living things to worry about without . . ." He hesitated, suppressing his deep chortle. "Without helping the *AJC* reporter solve the mystery of the dinosaur bones."

I shut out the thought of childhood games and the muggy summer days when our parents dropped us off at our grandparents' estate while they gallivanted around the world. "Gotta go," I said.

"You behave yourself, sis. Promise me that?"

I didn't answer, and I knew Wick wasn't surprised.

I set down my cell phone and stood up abruptly, dislodging my cat, Maggie, from my lap. She glared at me, green eyes intense, fluffy white fur leaving its residue on my black leggings. On purpose.

I grabbed the keys to my Hyundai, left my eleventh-floor studio apartment in Buckhead that overlooked Peachtree and East Paces Ferry roads, and drove ten minutes down West Paces Ferry to Nancy Creek Road and the neighborhood that housed so many memories and so many dreams.

The people who used to live in my grandmother's Buckhead neighborhood had built their homes with their bare hands when Atlanta was still recovering from the Civil War and the roads were made of dirt. They'd worked hard, scraped by, and loved their neighbors. But now it was a mishmash of old wealth and new wealth and weasel-eyed contractors destroying perfectly beautiful homes so they could plant cluster mansions on land that used to boast of columned manors and horse stables.

I slowed down in front of my grandparents' house, the one that was supposed to become *my* house. It sat far back from the road, tall hickories blocking the view so that one had to peek through an abundance of new spring leaves to see the redbrick-faced beauty just over a small hill of manicured fescue. I passed the rock driveway and the house on my right and turned into a second rock driveway.

My little Hyundai bumped down a steep descent that eventually headed back up the hill, old hickories and dogwoods and oaks lining the road. *These woods are lovely, dark, and deep.* I quoted Robert Frost in my mind as a squirrel dashed across and up a tree, fat gray tail swishing as it climbed frantically to a waiting limb. My stomach lurched. How I loved these woods and the wildlife that happily inhabited the property.

"For heaven's sake, don't let them cut down the healthy trees!" my grandmother had ordered—so the story went—when an ice storm had knocked down a dozen of them, along with power lines all over the city, in 1973, long before I was born.

"They're gonna level it all now, Nana Dale," I whispered as I parked the car in the clearing. I shook away the anger, choosing instead to get out and take the path on the left, back up the hill, an acre or two farther behind the house, instead of veering to the right on the flat rocky path that led to the barn.

I arrived in the riding ring, where a backhoe stood, its steel-cage mouth gaping empty beside a mound of Georgia red clay. I stared at the flattened expanse where the wooden fence and the jumps and the paddocks and the trees used to stand.

Dinosaur bones, indeed.

The driver of the backhoe paid me no attention. Dressed in mud-caked overalls, his back to me, he was stamping out a cigarette in the clay. And as his smoke swirled lackadaisically in the air, I heard Nana Dale's umpteenth warning: *"Never ever carry a match near the barn!"*

"How dare you smoke here!" I shouted. "When the whole thing could go up in flames!"

He turned slowly, looked over at me with a smirk, lifted his bushy gray eyebrows, and motioned all around him to the red clay that went on for yards and yards around us. "Ain't much chance of that, Miss Allie."

I caught my breath. "Barnell!"

I walked over and threw my arms around his hunched shoulders.

"Miss Allie," he repeated, a smile spreading across his face, the wrinkles interspersed with a thick gray beard. "You ain't s'posed to be traipsing around here, you know."

"I know, and I don't care. How'd you get to be the one to dig everything up? Do you know the contractor?"

Barnell made a nasty face. "Everyone knows that contractor and his reputation." He shrugged. "I was real sorry to hear your grandmother sold it to that scoundrel, Miss Allie. Figured the least I could do was be the one to dig it up."

"Thank you for being here. What a nice surprise on such an awful day. Came out of retirement to do it, didn't you?"

He gave me a sympathetic nod. "I'm real sorry about all of this," he repeated.

"Have they taken the bones away?" The question came out harshly, but when I turned to look at Barnell, he was laughing, his beard moving up and down with the rhythm of his chuckle.

"Dinosaur bones! Of all the inane things to say."

I shrugged back tears. Funny how I felt like giggling and bawling at the same time.

"How many of them did you bury back here, Barnell? Three?"

"Yes, ma'am. And my papa buried two others. And I ain't dug up but the one."

We grinned at each other.

"Can I see the bones?"

"C'mon," he said, motioning with his head as he swiped his tanned face with a ratty bandanna, then wiped the back of his neck, bright red from the sun.

We walked to the center of what used to be a riding ring, with an outside track that was one-quarter of a mile around. I closed my eyes and saw myself as a teen cantering around the periphery on my mare, then cutting diagonally across, where she and I jumped effortlessly over the brick wall—made of plywood and painted red and white—and then took five strides before going up and over the white coop. Then we'd weave between several tall pines and canter around a thick oak before heading back across the ring in another diagonal, leaping over a row of green and white poles, all the jumps that had made up my childhood and teenaged years.

Now the whole thing was a flattened bed of red clay, except for where it looked like a crater had fallen from the sky, creating a mammoth indention in the ground.

Barnell and I walked over to the gaping hole. "Had three reporters over here yesterday morning," he said with a chuckle.

I glanced up at him. "How'd they find out about the bones?"

He shrugged, then threw his head back in his robust laughter. "You called it in, didn't you?"

"I couldn't help it, Miss Allie. I remember all them times when I was over here repairing a fence or fixing the waterline or something else and you and your big brother would be tearing around this ring playing that you were the Flintstones and chanting about burying dinosaur bones. Thought it was worth a good story."

"And they actually believed you?"

Forensic experts will be examining the bones in the next days to determine their age, the article in the *AJC* had stated.

I took a seat in the clay, beside the hole.

"Any idea which one this is?"

"It's No-No Nicotine," he said, reaching for another cigarette, which I found delightfully ironic.

"Sweet Nicky," I whispered. "She was the last one to be buried here, wasn't she?"

"Yep, she was."

"Who was the first?"

"It was your Nana Dale's pony. . . . Can't remember his name, but he was buried up here before I was born. And then there was a mare called Krystal, I believe. My papa buried her up here when I was about ten or eleven. And of course, there was that beautiful dappled gray mare, the one she called Essie. I helped my daddy bury her. Like near ripped all our hearts out, that one."

Essie. Oh yeah. Of course. I'd heard plenty of larger-than-life stories about my grandmother and her prized thoroughbred. In the house were numerous black-and-white photos of my grandmother on that mare, soaring over jumps, or standing together, Nana with her fresh-faced smile wide, holding a silver trophy. My grandmother used to serve homemade biscuits or a hock of ham on silver platters engraved with things like *Chastain Park Shriners Hunter Show, Champion, 1947.*

Nana Dale had told me stories about her beloved mare from the time I was small. *"Most striking markings I'd ever seen on a horse,"* she'd say. *"Steel gray with dapples as white as snow, a flaxen mane and tail, and white legs, every one but her right back leg, which was pitch-black up to the hock."*

I hadn't known what *flaxen* meant, but when I looked it up, I was disappointed to find it basically meant "off-white." I'd imagined a much more exotic color.

Barnell peered down in the hole, then knelt and retrieved a bone bigger than any human specimen. "Yep. Still can picture your grandma out here, yelling at me to get that hole dug for Nicky faster, 'before the police come around and arrest us for burying horses in the Atlanta city limits.'"

I remembered it too. I was no more than six or seven when I had sat, much like I was sitting at the moment, in a pile of red clay that Barnell's backhoe had dumped to the side of the hole. I'd walked over and peered in before he could grab me by my ponytail. The body of a bay mare lay in the hole.

"Why's Nicky sleeping like that?" I'd asked, even though my mother had explained to me the night before that my grandmother's ancient mare was dead.

Now I reached into that same hole and let my hands wrap around a thick bone. "It's been over twenty years, hasn't it?"

"Yep. 'Bout nearly killed your grandmom, burying that one, almost as bad as when she buried Essie."

Every horse my grandmother buried had cost her dearly. Nana Dale had been one of the feistiest, most stubborn women on the planet. Hard like steel. Except about her horses.

And now the legacy she had wanted me to prolong, the property that had been part of the family since right after the Civil War, was sold, and the back acres were being cleared so that the rocky road from the street could be paved and three new houses planted in the riding ring, where so many of my memories were made.

"Thought ya might want to keep this, though."

Barnell handed me a metal box, and as I opened it, my eyes clouded over.

When my grandmother buried her beloved horses, she sent each into the ground with a small metal box. Nicky's body had long since decayed, but the metal box, covered in clay, was intact.

I opened it and saw four rusted horseshoes. For reasons that made no sense to anyone but Nana Dale, she would have a blacksmith remove the horseshoes before burying each horse. *"Wouldn't want them to be uncomfortable up there in eternity"* was her odd explanation.

I stared at the horseshoes. "We never did figure out why she buried these separate from the horses, did we?"

Barnell tilted his head and almost looked embarrassed. "Truth is, Miss Allie, long time ago, your grandmom told me, 'Barnell, if I ever lose Hickory Hills, promise me you'll dig up the bones.'

"Thought your grandmom had suddenly lost more of her marbles till she explained it." Here Barnell's eyes softened again as he pointed to the tin box. "She said she wanted you to have the horseshoes. Said you would put 'em to good use, Miss Allie, like she used to. Said it would be her gift to you. She was mighty insistent. Made me swear on Essie's grave that I'd do it." His grin was bittersweet.

I swallowed twice, cleared my throat, and took a deep breath as the memories cascaded around me. One summer when I was about twelve, I had watched as Nana Dale nailed old horseshoes to wooden plaques so that each shoe stuck out at a right angle, allowing us to hang a bridle or a lead shank or a halter from it. Before the nailing, she'd allowed me to stain the wood and burn each horse's name onto a plaque with the woodburning kit she'd given me for Christmas that year.

After that, whenever a new horse came to board at the barn, we'd repeat the same ritual. Nana Dale kept a stash of old horseshoes in the tack room just for that purpose. Then the plaques would be attached to the wall beside each horse's stall.

"Jeff Jeffrey was the first one to give me the idea when I was a girl not much older than you," Nana Dale had explained. "I think it's mighty appropriate that we continue what was started so long ago."

I stared down at the four horseshoes and the yellowed piece of monogrammed stationery where Nana Dale had written in her lovely cursive script *No-No Nicotine (1962–1995).*

"Horseshoes are for good luck, Allie," she'd often remind me as we worked. "In this life, we need all the luck we can get." The first time she'd said it, she'd stared out the window in the tack room where we were working and said, "I don't like to call it luck, though. I call it faith."

I'd never thought of my grandmother as especially religious. She attended church, as did most people her age. But Nana Dale was filled with secrets and surprises, not the least of which was barnyard wisdom that often included phrases that sounded a lot like they came from the Good Book.

I lifted the horseshoes out of the box and cradled them in my hands. How many times had I stood outside the barn area down below watching as the blacksmith shod one of the horses or ponies?

"Thanks," I said, trying to push past the knot that had lodged itself in my throat. "Thanks for convincing the contractor to let you be the one to dig them up." Then, staring straight at him, I asked, "You'll call me when you unearth the other ones, won't you?"

He met my gaze with his dark brown eyes still twinkling. "Don't you narrow those perty turquoise eyes at me, young lady. I knew you'd read it in the paper, Miss Allie. I was just waiting for you to show up." Then he shrugged again. "But yeah, I'll call you when I bring up them other bones." He fished in his overalls and brought out an ancient cell phone. "I got your number in here somewhere." He let his eyes roam the whole expanse. "Might take me a while to do all the diggin'."

"Taking your time, aren't you?"

"They hired me as the expert to dig up them trees, which I done. Now I can take all the time I need. I hinted that we might find a passel of other bones. Keeps me busy and keeps that weasel away from the barn."

"He's gonna tear it down in a blink."

"I know."

"When will they implode the house? Has he mentioned a date?"

Barnell fiddled with another cigarette. "Believe they've set the date for March twenty-eighth."

His eyes bore into me.

Three weeks away. Three weeks, and there'd be no going back. Three weeks, and my family could let out a sigh of relief. *"Thank goodness she's finally got to give up! It's about killed her, trying to save it. Nothing worth saving now."*

Barnell interrupted my thoughts. "Where's that fiancé of yours gone off to, Miss Allie?"

"He's not around anymore." *Couldn't save that either*, I reprimanded myself silently.

"Sorry to hear that. What, don't he have no sense in his head?"

"I think he has way too much sense," I mumbled. *"Allie, sweetie, sometimes it feels like you love the land more than you love me."* "He got real tired of me spending all my time trying to save the house and the property."

"Know how much this place means to you. To all of you."

"Yeah."

I'd wanted to argue with Austin when he said it, but then I admitted that perhaps he was right.

And now I'd lost the land and the house and the guy I loved. All of it was gone.

I drove away, the rusted horseshoes sitting on the seat beside me, taunting me with thoughts of good luck when I knew all my luck had run out right when Barnell's backhoe opened its mouth and started to chew.

2

Dale

The filly came into the world the same way as the girl, with great difficulty. Dale stared from across the box stall at the gray mare lying on her side, her rounded belly matted with sweat. Greta groaned with every breath, occasionally lifting her head from the shavings to glance behind her, where Dale could see a translucent sac, like a milky balloon, protruding from below her tail.

Dale yawned and shivered with cold and drew the horse blanket around her shoulders. She'd been sitting in the corner of the stall for hours, it seemed, cradling a horseshoe in her small hands like an icon and praying as Greta paced back and forth, glancing at her flank, then lay on the fresh shavings with a heavy plop. Up and down, the mare struggled and groaned.

Since it was happening on a special day, Mama had said she could watch the birth. Dale shook with chill and strange fascination as the mare's labor continued long into the night. She heard her mother's voice trying to encourage the horse, that same voice

20

that whispered to Dale when she came howling from a splinter or skinned knee.

When the vet showed up, he found all thirty-three pounds of Dale curled in a corner of the stall on fresh hay, her nearly frostbit fist clamped around the horseshoe while her mother's voice changed from soothing to panicky and frantic. "The foal's in the wrong position. I think it's stuck. Greta's suffering terribly."

Their voices moved to a whisper so that all Dale heard were the groans coming from Greta. Then Mama was removing the horseshoe and gathering Dale in her arms. "Come on, sugarplum. Dr. Horner's gonna take good care of Greta. You'll get to see the foal in the morning when you wake up."

"No!" Dale said, jutting out her bottom lip. "You said I was old enough to watch!"

Dale stared into her mother's pale blue eyes. Mama was dressed in stained dungarees, and wisps of hay and shavings were in her thick blond hair where she'd been lying next to Greta, trying to soothe the anguished mare. Dale had never seen her mother in such a state.

Dale stamped her rubber boot, her foot wiggling around inside. "I won't go! I won't!" Everything about horses enchanted her. She wanted to watch the birth.

"You're as stubborn as the day is long," her mother whispered in her slow drawl, setting Dale on a bench outside of Greta's stall.

Mama said that often.

When Mama returned to the stall, Dale slipped the cumbersome blanket from around her shoulders and tiptoed to the half-cross stall door. She was barely tall enough to peek over, but as she did, she heard Dr. Horner.

"There you go! Good girl, Greta!" the vet cooed. Dale watched him pull the milky bag from between Greta's legs. Greta gave a final groan as the vet broke the bag and released a scrawny foal. Or at least the head. The rest of the body was still encased in the milky bag.

Dale stared, fascinated, as the foal lifted its head, tiny wet ears pinned against its head, disoriented.

"Mama, the baby's stuck in the bag," Dale whispered.

Mama turned, pushing a strand of hay from her hair as she gave Dale a weary smile. "Shh. Everything's okay now, sugarplum. You'll see."

Greta turned her head toward the struggling foal, and pricking her ears forward, gave a gentle nicker. It looked to Dale as if Greta wanted her baby to hurry up and get out of that bag. When Greta's nicker turned into a deeper whinny, the foal, legs splayed in all directions, gathered itself and wiggled out of the sac.

A few minutes later, Greta pulled herself up to a stand and made her way to the foal. She began to lick its wet gray coat.

"Got yourself a pretty little filly," Dr. Horner said. Dale heard laughter in his voice and felt relieved. She remembered not so long ago when his voice had sounded all cracked and scratchy. Lady had died that time.

Dale giggled. "She's welcoming her baby to the world, isn't she, Mama?"

Mama's eyes were shining through tears. "Yes, she sure is."

The filly scrambled in the straw, long, skinny legs skewed at funny angles. Every time the filly tried to stand, she'd only manage to get her front legs braced in an awkward upside-down V that lifted her head and neck and chest. Then she'd collapse back in the straw.

"Is she okay, Mama?"

"She's just fine. She's had quite a time being born. It'll take her a little while to get those long legs under her. She's got to figure it out."

After Greta had licked the filly clean and nickered several more times while gently prodding the filly with her muzzle, the foal struggled to her feet, shaking. She stood, swaying on her scrawny, unstable legs.

"She's a fighter, just like you, sugarplum," her mother pronounced, coming to the stall door and ruffling Dale's tangled auburn hair. Dale had overheard the story of her birth enough times to be thankful, even proud. *The cord wrapped around her neck, and a snowstorm kept the doctor stranded. Baby came out as blue as a wilted hydrangea and didn't breathe for a whole minute. . . ."*

But tonight, Dale beamed. The filly had been born in the early morning hours of her sixth birthday, just as Dale had prayed. "She's yours, sugarplum," her mother proclaimed.

———— ♘ ————

Dale named her Silk Stockings because the grayish brown filly had three white spindly legs, with the right hind one solid black. "Can't be sure she'll keep that gray color as she gets older," the vet said. "But she'll be a beauty."

Sure enough, as the filly grew, her color changed. At eight months, she was steel gray with white dapples. Her mane and mop of a tail were flaxen, and her forelegs, up to the knee, perfectly white, as was her left hind leg. But the right hind leg remained completely black. Her ears were perfectly white, too, and they pointed forward and back, flashing mischief, as did her nubby tail. Her slender head was the same steel gray as her barrel, except for a white blaze that started out thin under her forelock and gradually encased her muzzle in startling white with a pink flush at the tip. And she had a black spot right under her left nostril. Dale thought it looked like the beauty mark on actress Jean Harlow.

Dale spent her days watching her filly and petting the soft muzzles of the other horses and ponies that lived in the stable behind the house. That was how Dale described their home, but she knew what the society magazines called it. She'd seen the photos. She knew how to read, and she even knew what some of those big words meant in the captions underneath: *The magnificent estate of Mr. and Mrs. Jeremiah Wickliffe Butler V, fourth-generation Atlantans and quite the striking couple, with their fifteen-room mansion and state-of-the-art stable housing prized ponies and horses.*

One photo showed her parents posing in front of the stables. They did make a handsome duo, her mother a petite blue-eyed, blond-haired beauty wearing a ballroom gown and her tall, lanky father with his dark brown eyes and wavy auburn hair combed back just so, dressed in a tuxedo.

She loved spending time at the stable and skipping back across the velvet lawn on summer evenings, lightning bugs flashing along the path back to her house that was often glimmering from every window, as if lightning bugs had taken up residence inside too.

On the top floor were two giant bedrooms "with enough room to board three ponies in each," her nursemaid, Mrs. Hughes, used to say with a grin. Each room had a walk-in closet and a private bath. The main floor housed two more equally large bedrooms on opposite ends, each one with a private bath.

Sometimes Dale wondered why they needed so many bedrooms, since only three of them lived in the house and Mama and Daddy shared one. She wished she had a little brother or sister, but every time she'd begged her mother for a sibling, Mama's eyes had filled with tears, and she'd looked sadder and more fragile than usual. So Dale stopped asking.

In between the bedrooms on the main floor were a kitchen, breakfast room, study, dining room, living room, and paneled den with a little bar area and a wall of picture windows that overlooked the backyard and the barn.

Mr. Jeffrey and Mrs. Hughes worked for her parents, caring for the house, the property, and the horses. And for Dale. Mama spent her days at her "special functions." Dale didn't know exactly what that meant, but her mother usually left the house wearing cashmere and pearls. "These are a woman's best friends," Mama would often whisper as she brushed Dale's thick auburn mane.

Mr. Jeffrey tended the stable—or so her mother put it. Mr. Jeffrey was a thin, wiry man, with a perpetual red neck, curly black hair, bushy eyebrows, and chocolate brown eyes that filled with mischief. He knew more about horses than anyone else, and Dale delighted in traipsing behind him as he fed the horses and ponies, repaired a fence or a water spigot, or cleaned the horses' saddles and bridles with Neatsfoot oil. She'd sit beside him on a bale of hay as his tanned arms worked the oil into the leather. "Keeps it from getting brittle, Dale," he'd instruct.

When her mother came back from riding Greta, the horse lathered in sweat, she'd swing off the mare's back and toss the reins to Mr. Jeffrey. "You be sure to cool her down good, Jeff," she'd say every time. Then she'd walk away in her riding jodhpurs and high black leather boots, her blond hair netted under a velvet riding cap.

Why her mother had to repeat those instructions every day, Dale didn't know. Mr. Jeffrey kept everything at the barn spick-and-span, but he especially cared for the horses, all fourteen of them, the ones that belonged to her mother, and the ones that were boarded at the stable.

The barn sat back from the house with a manicured yard in between, tall hickories and oaks and dogwoods lining the perfectly tended grass and the pristine swimming pool. A wooden plaque with *Hickory Hills* hung on the front of the gray-green barn with big white Xs on its doors. Dale would open the white gate and walk down the aisle as horses and ponies nickered at her and reached their heads over the half doors of their stalls, ears pricked forward, anticipating the apples and carrots the tiny girl hid in her dungarees and handed out to each animal, her hand opened wide so that none of those huge horse teeth would accidentally nip her fingers.

Then, at the other end of the barn, she walked out to the fenced-in paddock, where the horses could stand in crossties to be brushed and hosed off and fitted with shoes.

Horseshoes were Dale's favorite decoration. She'd carry off the old shoes and save them in a shoe box. One day, she'd get Mr. Jeffrey to attach the shoes to a plaque on her wall so she could hang all the ribbons she'd win onto them, just like her mother did with her ribbons.

While Mr. Jeffrey tended the stable, Mrs. Hughes tended Dale. She had lived in the downstairs apartment ever since Dale was born, and Dale loved her like a second mother. At three, she began to call her Husy, and the name stuck. Often, Dale would visit Husy in her apartment before breakfast, and inevitably, she'd find her nursemaid on her knees, leaning on a worn armchair, hands folded in prayer. Dale quietly observed the stillness of the room and the way Husy never looked up at her until after she had finished praying. "I'm talking with God Almighty, and He deserves my respect, Dale. Don't you forget that. And don't you forget that no prayer is too big or too small for God."

Although Husy didn't have children, she cared for her two nieces, whose parents had died from the Spanish flu. Until the girls went off to school, Darlene and Marjorie lived downstairs with Husy, and Husy loved on them and Dale as if they were all her own.

To Dale, Husy had always looked ancient. She wore her silvery hair in a bun at the back of her neck, and that knot seemed to blend in with the bigger knot on Husy's back, the one that made her walk with her head bent toward the ground.

"Why does Husy walk like that and wear a ball under her dress, Mama?"

"Shh! Barbara Dale! What a question. We don't talk about those things," her mother reprimanded.

But that night, her father explained, "Mrs. Hughes has a hunched back. She was born with a condition called congenital kyphosis." Daddy touched Dale's back. "Her spine, this part here, is curved, sweetie. Sometimes it causes her pain. She can't straighten up. But she's strong. She can take care of you just fine, Barbara Dale."

Dale had no doubt Husy was strong. She was also kind and good, and Dale knew just how to "wrap her around her little finger," as her mother said.

—— Ω ——

When Dale turned seven and Silk Stockings—whom she'd nicknamed Essie—turned one, her mother let her sit bareback on the filly, who twitched her ears back and forth at the tickling weight and turned her head to the side to gaze at her miniature rider. Dale leaned forward over her neck, wrapping her arms around the warm dappled coat.

"I love you, Essie. Someday we'll be champions together. Just like Mama and Greta."

While Dale waited for Essie to mature—Mr. Jeffrey said she couldn't be broken to the saddle and bridle until she was three—Husy would bring Dale to the barn and tack up Mr. Jinx, a fat bay pony who seemed ageless and demure. Husy would lead the pony and little girl through the barn and up the hill to the riding ring, where Mama's trainer taught Dale to ride hunt seat.

One day, when Dale arrived at the barn, she sassed, "Husy, why isn't Mr. Jinx all saddled up? I asked you to do it ages ago!" She flashed her eyes, tiny hands on tiny hips.

Husy raised her eyebrows, and Dale knew the finger-wrapping had ended. Only Mama got away with talking like that.

After her lesson, she tossed the reins at Mr. Jeffrey, just as she'd seen Mama do a hundred times. "Go on and walk him out. I have a hundred things to take care of at the house!" she said, mimicking her mother.

She saw the grin flit across Mr. Jeffrey's chapped lips, but then his brown eyes darkened. "You're acting spoiled rotten, Miss Dale, and that ain't becomin'. If you're going to ride this pony, you will learn to care for him too. You never put up a pony when he's sweating like Mr. Jinx. You know about the colic. You understand?"

Dale barely met Mr. Jeffrey's eyes. She balled her fists and frowned, her cheeks flaming. "Mama hired you to help me!"

Hearing this, Husy said, "If I ever hear you talk like that to Mr. Jeffrey again, I'll take a switch to you! Mr. Jeffrey and I love you too much to watch you turn out spoiled." She never finished that sentence, but Dale saw it in Husy's eyes: *"Like your mother."*

She galloped Mr. Jinx on the back roads of Buckhead, the Georgia clay kicking up in tufts of crimson dust, wind blowing her pony's thick black mane in her face as she leaned low over his withers. But in a year or two, she'd be riding Essie on these very same roads.

One Saturday, Linda Betts came over to play with Dale while their mothers attended a society function. Dale didn't particularly like Linda. She tattled on other girls in the class at school and wore fancy dresses on school days and only played with dolls.

At lunchtime, Linda's eyes grew wide when Husy brought their lunch plates to the table. After Husy left the room, Linda whispered, "Your nanny is so ugly. How can you stand to look at her? She's a hunchback with a hooked nose and old as the hills. My nanny is beautiful and young."

Dale had just taken a bite of her turkey sandwich and tried to swallow, but she felt an uncontrollable anger lodge in her throat. She swiped Linda's plate off the table, and it crashed to the tile floor, splintering into a hundred pieces.

"She's not ugly—you are! Maybe she's not beautiful on the outside, but inside, she's perfect and kind and good, and you're dirty and ugly and mean. I want you to leave my house right now!"

When she heard about it, Mama called the incident a fiasco. "I'm so humiliated, Dale! What will people think of you?"

"They'll think I can tell who's ugly and who isn't," she sassed.

"You are going to apologize to Linda."

"I will not! She should apologize for what she said."

Later that night, Daddy came into her room, where Dale was sobbing on the bed, saying, "Linda is mean!"

Her father hugged her tightly and squeezed her hand. "Linda said something unkind. But, Dale, you reacted in an unwise way. You were right to be angry, but the way you expressed your anger was"—she thought she saw his lips curl up ever so slightly—"a bit over the top."

"I'm sorry. I'll tell her tomorrow at school." She gave an exaggerated sigh. "Linda will probably grow up to be just like your mean ole cousin, Mr. Weatherby."

"What in the world makes you say that?"

"He's making your life miserable, Daddy. He wants your lumber company to fail right in the middle of the Depression. That's what he's doing, isn't it? He's looking for a chance to ruin you so he can steal our land. And as if that's not bad enough, he's family!"

Daddy didn't say anything for a moment, just gave a shrug.

Dale had overheard a very heated discussion between Mr. Weatherby and her father two days earlier. She'd been headed to his office to show her father her latest sketches of ponies, but the door was closed, and the voices were loud.

Still, she could imagine the scene. Mr. Weatherby had been stopping by their house more frequently since something called the stock market crash. He always wore a fancy suit, and his black hair was always slicked down with hair tonic. He was probably the same age as her father, but his eyes looked hard and mean and held something in them she couldn't quite name. Something like hunger.

"Listen, Jeremiah. I'll offer you a good price. This is the prettiest little acreage in North Fulton County."

"I'm not selling the property, Weatherby."

"What about the mill?"

"Not the lumber mill either—" Her father's face was beet red, but he stopped in midsentence when Dale opened the door, feigning innocence.

"Daddy, look what I've drawn for you."

In reality, Dale saddled herself with an adult's responsibility to help her father keep their property. She'd heard her parents arguing over it too. "He won't stop until he's ruined us, Eleanor. He's obsessed with having it. Why my poor cousin Jane ever married him, I will never know."

Now she cuddled even closer in her father's lap. "Will you lose Butler Lumber Company, Daddy?"

"My, my, little Dale! When did you suddenly become a grown-up? There's nothing for you to worry about." Before he turned off the light, her father added, "There isn't any doubt that you're going to make it okay in this world, but you need to watch your temper." He was grinning as he said it. He kissed her forehead. "You've got guts, and you've got business savvy. You're going to be okay."

She knew it was a relief for him to say such a thing because she'd once overheard him worrying that her mother was incapable of being wise with money or time or most anything else.

That night, Dale thought about the day. Yes, her beloved nanny was ugly; it was true. She was the kind of person who made people do a double take and avert their eyes.

But Husy was the most beautiful person Dale had ever seen, because Dale had seen the real part, and she was not going to let anyone ever talk cruelly if she could help it, even though she might not go about it the right way.

Even at her young age, Dale understood something it would take years before she could put into words: the absolute truth of paradox.

— ☊ —

1932

Some families in Atlanta were spared the horrible effects of the Depression, but Dale's was not one of them. For three years, her father had struggled to keep his lumber business from giving in.

"Nobody needs lumber, Dale," her father admitted. "Nobody's building anything these days except a whole lot of debt and shanties made of cardboard boxes."

She watched Mama and Daddy glance over their shoulders to the life they had known, what that society magazine had called a past of "comfort and private clubs and extravagant backyard parties."

And horses.

Mama's horses were the first thing Daddy sold. In July 1932, Butler Lumber Company hit rock bottom, forcing him to fire seven employees.

Mama cried, her face all puffy and red. "Jeremiah, they're our family. We can't sell the horses."

Daddy's face became tight and hard, and he raised his voice for the first time Dale had ever heard.

"Eleanor, I just let most of my workers go. They have no way to feed their kids. Barbara Dale is our family. The horses have to go."

Daddy was rarely harsh with her mother. Dale knew the gavel had fallen when Mama accepted it with a nod and a brush of her hand across her pretty blue eyes. Dale always liked to see the sparkle in her mother's eyes, but on that day, her eyes were rimmed with red and, oh, so sad. Even sadder than when Dale used to ask for a sibling.

Dale ran to the barn and let herself into the stall where her filly was sprawled out on a bed of fresh shavings. She lay down beside her and sobbed.

"I won't let them take you, Essie! I won't!"

She spent the night in the stall with Essie, and when dawn broke outside in pastel tones, Essie nickered and licked her small hand. Dale cried at the feel of Essie's rough tongue and fished in her dungaree pocket for the last cube of sugar. She'd already dispensed nine other ones throughout the night.

Late that morning, while Mama, Mr. Jeffrey, Husy, and Dale looked on, a man came and took away the horses and ponies that belonged to Mama as well as the ones owned by the boarders. And he took her dappled filly that Mama had given Dale for her sixth birthday, the one she just knew she would ride in horse shows over big jumps, like Mama did with Greta, the one Dale would stand beside with a beautiful shiny trophy in her hands and a three-tiered ribbon attached to Essie's bridle, its long tails blowing in the wind.

As the man approached her filly's stall, Dale shouted, "She's mine! She's my filly. You can't take her away from me!"

Inconsolable, Dale clutched at Essie's halter until Husy took Dale's hand, and together, they watched the man load up each horse and pony. Husy loved the horses and ponies as much as Dale and her mother did, but she had a special soft spot for Essie. "She's as pretty and feisty as you are, Barbara Dale," Husy often said.

Dale sobbed, huge tears spilling down her face as she watched her filly being loaded into the trailer. "You're my best friend, Essie! I won't ever forget you."

31

3

Allie

Friday, March 6

I stood behind a few thick oaks and watched them prepare the house. With every movement of the workers, I felt a horrible cramping in my stomach. Surely this wasn't happening. Hadn't they promised to restore the old house? And now, in just a few moments, it would be destroyed. My whole life, my family's history, and my very own future were about to be imploded.

I stifled a sob.

I had played out back in the vast yard of my grandparents' estate, idyllic in every way, from the huge oak that offered shade and a tree swing, to the swimming pool that offered cool refreshment on the muggy, hot Georgia summer days, to the barn where horses whinnied from their stalls.

I reached out as if to touch the old house. It wore its age with quiet dignity and understated beauty. The way it sat on the property, only the ground floor with bay windows and a pitched roof showing, belied the fifteen rooms inside. Rooms that were elaborately and painstakingly decorated in every fashion, remodeled from decade to decade, while the antique furniture had remained.

I saw Nana Dale standing over the stove, dressed in jodhpurs—having just returned from riding—and her face wet with perspiration as she prepared the pot roast.

Then I saw myself leading my chestnut mare on the path behind the house up to the riding ring, while Nana Dale walked ahead, glancing back with an adoring smile at her budding equestrian.

And if I blinked again, she was wearing a stylish pants suit and strappy sandals, her graying hair wavy and short as she called out to my parents and Wick and me, "For heaven's sake, stand still so I can snap this photo."

Three months later, her Christmas card showed Mom, Dad, Wick, and me dressed in our finest and standing beside her behind the split-rail fence.

In that photo, we all wore nervous expressions—we giggled every time we saw that photo afterward—as Nana Dale pressed the self-timer button on her Nikon and rushed on high heels from twenty yards away to stand beside me. She had barely made it before the camera's red light began to flash frantically and then, whoosh! There she stood, hanging on to me, her cinnamon eyes lit up with life and mischief.

BOOOOOM!

The sound shook me from my reverie as one side of the house collapsed. I caught my breath and felt as if I were choking. *"No!"* I screamed silently. How could they take it from me now? Barnell had promised me it wouldn't be imploded for three weeks!

BOOOOOM!

I sat up straight in bed, sweat pouring off me, heart ramming against my ribs, as my cell phone jangled me awake.

"Hello?" I shook my head to clear it of the nightmare.

Someone from the estate-sale company introduced herself with a lovely French accent. "Hello, I'm Cécile." When I, still recovering from the dream, remained silent, she added, "I'd love to set up a time to come over and start pricing, Miss Massey. The sale is in two weeks."

I detected a note of worry in her voice. *Yes, I know.*

—— ◠ ——

I might have been a millennial, but I felt more like Scarlett O'Hara when she stooped down and grabbed that red clay and swore to the heavens that she'd never be hungry again. I understood the worth of the land. In our day and age, it was getting used up awfully quick. I had plans for this property.

Ever since I was young, I knew I wanted to be around horses every day. My grandmother had shown hunters until she turned seventy. But my fondest recollections were of her instructing the minuscule riders perched on a pony's back, learning to post. She'd initiated half of Atlanta into hunt seat equitation.

In fact, my first memories were of me in a playpen lodged between two pine trees near the riding ring, watching Nana Dale teach riding lessons. I didn't mind a bit being left at my grandmother's. My grandfather, Daniel Taylor, had passed away the year before I was born. I wondered if Nana Dale got lonely all by herself in that huge house. Whenever I asked, she'd say, "There's never a dull moment, Dale, with the horses and my riding students. But my favorite time is when you come over."

I loved everything about Nana Dale and the horses.

My mother would have none of it. Or rather, she'd had way too much growing up, coerced into Pony Club and then horse shows and then show jumping. When her gelding crashed into a four-foot wall and threw her over it, resulting in a broken neck—which miraculously did not paralyze her—she'd had enough.

"Allie, you do what you want," Mom often said. "But don't do it for your grandmother or me. Do it for yourself." I knew the story of her accident, and I always felt there was a look of dread or fear behind her eyes when she'd let me off at the barn behind her parents' house.

But I didn't want to compete, and my grandmother didn't pressure me into it. I suppose she'd learned her lesson with my mother. I was content to canter around the riding ring or meet a friend on her pony and ride the trails on the grounds of our private school a mile down the street from my grandmother's estate.

Before I was even in double digits, I knew that I wanted to spend my life helping people heal on a horse's back. As a teen, I read about equine therapy. Two of my brothers' friends who had been strung out on coke found healing at a ranch in Colorado. I discovered that nearby Chastain Park had the same type of therapy.

I understood the meaning of equine therapy long before I'd ever heard the term. Nana Dale was teaching a lesson up in the ring, and I, around five years old, had graduated from the playpen to sitting on my bottom with dead leaves and pine straw as my companions. My plastic horse statues galloped in a circle around me or jumped over the brittle sticks I'd stacked together to mimic the overturned trunk of an oak tree that sat in the middle of the ring and which I'd watched horse and rider jump over on many occasions.

But that day, Nana Dale was instructing a beginner.

"Up, down! Up, down!" Nana Dale hollered to the boy, about my age, the oversized hard hat bobbing on his head. He bounced around on Nicky's back, but Nicky was the world's calmest horse. She was small at 14.2 hands, barely qualifying as a horse. I didn't remember her age, but Nana Dale had said she was well over thirty, which, in pony and horse years, was nearing one hundred.

Despite being the gentlest animal on earth, she frightened children at first sight. Nicky only had one eye, and where her left eye should've been, there was an empty gray socket where she'd lost the eye to cancer. Nicky also had an ugly ragged scar under her right foreleg where she'd been speared by barbed wire. The horse literally had nine lives, and Nana Dale could tell ten times more stories about those lives. Her official name was No-No Nicotine, so dubbed because when she came into the world, born to Nana Dale's mare Essie, Nana Dale had told Barnell, "You'll catch your death from smoking, you know that, don't you?"

While Nicky endured the uncontrolled bouncing of this child, I concentrated on the "Up, down! Up, down!" of Nana Dale. Her voice, usually hoarse by the third lesson of the day, nonetheless felt reassuring. I'd first mounted Nicky as a toddler, and at four, Nana Dale had let me sit in a saddle, hold the reins, and walk around the ring with Nicky beneath me. I was hooked. I caught on to posting quickly, and at five, I cantered the small mare around the ring and begged to jump over the log, which Nana Dale categorically refused. "Your mother would have my hide!"

Mom lived in perpetual fear that something like what she'd experienced would happen to me. But since my mother never came up to the ring, Nana Dale gradually let me move from the walk to the trot to the canter.

So I couldn't quite understand why little Carter could not get the hang of posting. This was his fifth lesson—I'd counted them—and he still bounced around in the saddle like a rag doll.

And though my grandmother surely grew exasperated with him, she never let on, just kept yelling out, "Sit up straight. Tighten your thighs! Use your reins, Carter, to make her turn. Don't let her take advantage of you. That's right. Easy!"

"I don't think Carter will ever learn to ride," I said after the little boy had skipped away, holding his mother's hand as if he'd mastered the canter. "A waste of time and money."

Nana Dale squatted down in the dirt to my height and looked me straight in the eyes. "In a way you're right, Allie. He won't ever learn to ride like you. And so it could be seen as a waste of time and money. But Carter was born different from most children. He won't ever be able to control his movements like you can. But being on Nicky gives him confidence. You can tell he isn't afraid of her anymore, right?"

I'd nodded.

"His mother is very smart. She knows that being around the barn and the horses and sitting on Nicky's back, well, it's opening up a new world for him."

"Is that why you have to put the stairs by Nicky and help Carter climb them to get on her back?"

"Exactly. And yes, we've been working on the same few things for many weeks now. But I've seen him progress." Nana Dale got a look in her eyes that I would see many times in the following years.

"You're remembering something, aren't you?"

She turned to me. "You don't miss anything, do you? Yes, I'm remembering a friend of mine, Tommy. He was a show jumper who won all kinds of competitions. Then he got real sick. The doctor told him he'd never ride again. But I didn't believe it. I knew he had guts and determination. But Tommy had to start over, and his body didn't work like it used to. He'd bob around on the horse like little Carter. Until he learned how to make his limitations work for him."

After that, I always made sure I was up in the ring when Nana Dale taught Carter. Those lessons went on week after week, year after year, until one day, Carter and I rode together around the ring and on trails and even in Pony Club.

Nana Dale didn't have special training in equine therapy or any of its many derivatives. But she was a great equestrian with a great big heart—a bit tough on the outside but determined to help any child find confidence and pleasure and love on a horse.

I wondered if equine therapy could help my mother.

It had certainly helped Tommy. When Nana Dale told stories about her growing-up years with Tommy and horses, they seemed almost fabricated, as if she'd taken them out of a Walter Farley novel with his larger-than-life black stallion.

"One time, we galloped together bareback on Tommy's horse in the middle of the night, my arm in a cast, and me holding a flashlight in my good hand to scare away the wild boars. . . ."

"We showed our horses at Madison Square Garden, way up in New York, with all the fanciest people looking on. . . ."

I always wondered if they were true, but whenever I'd ask her, my grandmother's eyes would get all liquid—and she wasn't one to cry—and she'd nod and simply say, "Why, of course they're true. Why on earth would I make something like that up?"

I didn't know. All I knew was that a lot of her stories had the ring of fantasy to them.

"There was the time during the war that I found a sailor, burned and half drowned on the beach. His tanker had been destroyed by a German U-boat. We pulled him to safety, my filly and I . . ."

But whenever she told that story, she'd stop in midsentence, look around as if someone might be spying on her, and whisper, "I'll tell you later."

Which she never did.

Anyway, my mother wanted nothing to do with horses or equine therapy, and I wondered if there was more to it than a terrible fall from her horse.

Still, I continued to ride my mare, Foxtrot, and to plan my future, dreaming of the horses, dreaming of a happy and healed mother, and dreaming of the career that I had whispered about to my grandmother.

"I want to turn your barn into a center where kids with physical and mental challenges can come and find healing." I always hesitated to pronounce the next words, "Like what happened with Tommy."

Nana Dale would inevitably pause and give a sad smile. As busy as she liked to keep, mentioning Tommy always stopped her cold. She'd simply nod and eventually say something like "You have such a great dream, Allie. Your mother doesn't want anything to do with the house or the horses." Her toughened face frowned. "I pushed Mary Jane too hard, I guess, and now she's been inoculated, but you, my dear, you have the heart and the dream."

By eighteen, the dream still alive, I had become much more realistic.

"But, Nana, it would cost a fortune to keep the estate. None of us has that kind of money!"

"The estate is worth millions. Ten acres in the middle of Buckhead!"

"That isn't the question. We know the property is worth a lot. But none of us has the money to keep it."

Nana was insistent. "I know that, but I promise you there will be plenty of money after I'm gone, money enough to keep the house and the property, if you want, and plenty for your parents and your brother too."

That seemed like an awful lot of money, but I believed my grand-mother, and I worked myself ragged getting my degree in physical therapy and going through all the accreditation with PATH—the Professional Association of Therapeutic Horsemanship—needed to open a certified center for different types of equine therapy. Six long years of study, then two years interning at Chastain Park in their burgeoning therapy program, plus mind-numbing hours working through all the paperwork necessary to launch Hickory Hills Horse Therapy—my nod to Nana Dale's estate and to our love of alliteration. All the while, Nana Dale grew older and more forgetful.

When I finally received my degrees, I asked, "Nana Dale, can we start up the business now?"

"Of course, dear!" she said.

We were all delighted, my parents and Wick and, most of all, Nana Dale. Everyone wanted the estate to remain in the family. I had purchased four therapy horses and hired two other skilled young therapists, as well as recruited several volunteers. And I had become friends with Austin, whom I'd met at school, a reflective young veterinarian and someone who shared my desire to use his skills to help others.

The boy I had fallen in love with—and him with me. We had our whole life planned out.

We were just in the process of setting up the website for Hickory Hills Horse Therapy when Nana Dale died. It wasn't exactly a shock. At ninety-four, she often said she was ready to meet her Maker, her signature twinkle in her eye.

"You know there are horses in heaven, don't you?" she was fond of saying. "Just read the book of Revelation if you don't believe me. Can't wait to be reunited with mine." She'd get a far-off look in her milky eyes. "Especially Essie, my sweet, sweet Essie."

No, the shock came a few days later.

The wind blew as we stepped inside the high-rise on Peachtree and took the elevator up to the familiar office of Ted Lorrider. He'd been our family's lawyer for decades. Impeccably dressed in a gray-striped suit, his silver hair abundant and combed back from his brow, he greeted my parents first with a smile and a handshake—"Irvin, Mary Jane"—and then shook Wick's hand and mine.

We settled into comfortable leather chairs. I was feeling excited at the prospect of getting through this last piece of paperwork so that Hickory Hills Horse Therapy could finally become a reality. That day, I couldn't even muster much grieving for Nana Dale. I knew she'd be tickled for me.

But as Mr. Lorrider took a seat behind his oversized mahogany desk, he looked worried, almost baffled. He hemmed and hawed for a moment. I'd never seen him look anything but perfectly professional. He donned a pair of glasses, took a stack of papers in his hands, and straightened them by tapping them on his desk. He cleared his throat one more time and looked at my mother. "Mary Jane, I'm very sorry, but it appears your mother, Mrs. Butler-Taylor, made a bit of a mistake when she was updating her will."

We looked at each other.

"Nana? That's totally bizarre," I volunteered. I felt the first twitter of something as Mr. Lorrider's brow remained scrunched into numerous lines.

She promised!

"She, um, sold the house," he whispered, and we gave a collective gasp. "She sold the house and the property. Everything." Mr. Lorrider's face went gray as he continued to search for appropriate words to ruin our lives.

"I've known your grandmother for years, and she wasn't one to have the wool pulled over her eyes," he continued, not making eye contact with any of us. "She was very intent on you keeping the house and property, Allie, to start your healing-horse hotel, as she called it." Here, he gave a wan smile.

"So she asked me to write up a draft for a special trust fund that would allow you to draw the necessary money for taxes and

41

repairs and upkeep of the estate. I thought this was a wise move and began creating the draft."

Now he picked up a folder, opened it, stared at the papers inside, and set the folder back down. "But sometime last fall, she apparently was contacted by another lawyer"—he glanced down at his papers—"a Mr. Mark Rawlings, who claimed I had asked him to go to your grandmother's house to draw up the document for the trust fund with her looking on. I suppose he was rather convincing. . . ." He fidgeted with his papers and did not meet my eyes.

I felt a creep of red spreading up my neck and face.

"Mr. Rawlings handed your grandmother a legal document that I assume Mrs. Butler-Taylor read over. However, what she ended up signing was not for a trust fund, but rather an addendum to her will, specifying the sale of the property and house, and signed also by a witness and a notary public."

He sat back in his chair, finally looking up at us. "In her defense, I believe Mrs. Butler-Taylor thought that Mr. Rawlings was legitimately connected to my office. The bill of sale even specifies that she envisioned her property becoming"—Mr. Lorrider stared over his thick-rimmed glasses at me—"an equine therapy center for children and their families. But somehow, she failed to understand that she was not setting up a trust fund at all, but rather, selling the property to Mr. Ralph Hightower, one of Atlanta's most infamous contractors." He cleared his throat. "I wonder if Mr. Rawlings drafted a real document for a trust fund that your grandmother read over and approved, and then he replaced it with the bill of sale. But we have no way to prove this."

Mr. Lorrider's face had turned deep crimson, and he was sweating profusely. "I think she truly believed she was creating a trust fund to provide everything you needed to keep up the house and property."

Now he pushed the thick manila folder across the desk for us to inspect.

"As you can see, Mr. Rawlings made this document an addendum to her will that supersedes what is stated in the will—that the property be left to you, Allie."

"That's absurd," I said. "No one has ever sweet-talked Nana Dale. She was a tough businesswoman!"

"Yes, I agree. I worked with her for over forty years. But she was over ninety." He said this as if that explained how my life's dream was coming crashing down.

"Evidently, Mr. Rawlings drafted this addendum to the will only a few weeks prior to her death. It stipulates that the house and property be sold to Mr. Ralph Hightower for an outrageously low sum. All of Mrs. Butler-Taylor's other holdings are to be divided up equally among each of you."

"But you have the will! You were her lawyer!" I accused.

He looked mortified. "Yes, I am very much aware of that. However, she had this addendum in her safe-deposit box. It was dated and signed and stamped by the notary." He swallowed. "And I was completely in the dark. In fact, I had called your grandmother just a few weeks before her death to tell her I had the trust-fund document ready for her inspection."

He tilted his head. "She thanked me in her typically blunt way and said that was fine. It didn't occur to me that she had already done something different."

We stared at him silently while he apologized yet again.

We knew Nana had become senile, but she wasn't suffering from Alzheimer's or severe dementia.

"It can't be true!" From me again. "When I was with her three days before she died, she looked at me and said, 'Promise me you'll keep the house, Allie. The property. If anything happens to me.'"

Mr. Lorrider was nodding. "Yes, she called me the morning before she went to the hospital, sounding very confused about the trust fund. I tried to reassure her that all was well and that I would bring the document to her immediately. But then she had the stroke."

We hired an investigator, and although we all knew that my grandmother had been taken advantage of, when the investigator pressed Mr. Mark Rawlings, the lawyer claimed that Nana Dale had sought out his expertise. The addendum was found to be completely legitimate, and the house and property were sold to horrible Mr. Hightower. My parents and my brother and I were each left with a handsome inheritance. But Hickory Hills Horse Therapy floated off into a fantasy land like the stories Nana Dale told me when I was a kid.

— ♘ —

This morning I drove to Hickory Hills, passing the rock driveway to the right of the house, then the house itself, and turning onto the rocky road that led down to the back of the house and then split into the V, one road heading to the ring, and the other to the barn. I parked again in the clearing, relieved to see that my nightmare had not been an early premonition. The house still sat at the bottom of the hill.

I got out of the car and walked up the sprawling deck to the back French doors. Because of the way the house had been built on the property, from the front it looked like a one-story brick house, while from the back, it rose three stories high. I unlocked the door and took a deep breath.

I sat down on a brightly colored couch in the sunroom and took out the letter, for I had received one other thing from Mr. Lorrider. After destroying my world, he'd looked over his glasses at me and said, "Your grandmother left you something else." Then he fidgeted with his notes and read, "'And to my granddaughter, Allene Massey, I leave the small cherrywood chest, lovingly carved with horseshoes and hearts by my father, Jeremiah Wickliffe Butler V. The other affairs in the house may be split up between my daughter and grandchildren, but the cherry box is for Allie.'"

Poor Mr. Lorrider had shrugged and admitted, "Unfortunately, I do not have this cherrywood chest."

My parents and Wick and I had exchanged baffled expressions. Honestly, I was so heartbroken that I felt no gratitude for a wooden

44

box, and neither my parents nor Wick had any recollection of having seen this particular wooden chest at Nana Dale's.

Mr. Lorrider had cleared his throat once again. "That bit about the chest was put in the will years ago, Miss Massey, so I seriously doubt it has anything to do with—" he paused and took a white handkerchief from his suit pocket and brushed it across his wrinkled brow—"with the unfortunate circumstances we now are facing."

Then he handed me an envelope with my name written on the outside in Nana Dale's unmistakable cursive. Always beautifully slanted to the right, even at her advanced age, Nana Dale's handwriting remained legible, although the letters looked as if they were quivering slightly. "She gave me this letter to include in the will several years ago now."

I had waited until I was home alone to read it, afraid I would burst into angry tears in front of my family if I opened it at the lawyer's office. Back in my studio, sitting on my tiny balcony in the December chill, I'd torn open the envelope, expecting to read an apology from Nana Dale. Instead, it was a letter filled with enigmas.

Now, seated in the old house, I took it out of my jeans pocket and read it for the hundredth time. The letter—really, just a short note—was dated September 14, 2017.

Dearest Allie,

I want you to know that everything you need to start Hickory Hills Horse Therapy is in this little chest. Your grandfather made it for me. It is my dearest treasure, and I'm leaving it to you. You'll know where to find the money, and you'll learn about Tommy and my tall tales. And remember the charm bracelet too. It holds the key to your future.

Lovingly,
Nana Dale

Shockingly, Nana Dale had added a smiley face after her name.

For the past three months, I had scoured the house, looking for a small chest, to no avail. But I remembered the bracelet. With that thought, my left hand went to my empty right wrist, where occasionally during my preteen years, Nana Dale's silver charm bracelet had dangled.

"I want you to have this, Allie. My father gave it to me for my tenth birthday, and I've been adding charms to it ever since," Nana Dale had said when she gave me the bracelet on my own tenth birthday. I'd accepted it with a knot in my throat. I was a sentimental soul, and this trinket had obviously meant a lot to Nana Dale. Only later did I realize that the charms and the link bracelet were made of sterling silver. For years now, I'd kept the bracelet in a Limoges china dish, also a gift from my grandmother, but examining the charms it held had not helped me locate the wooden chest.

And now it was well past time for me to stop looking for a small chest or hidden money and instead go through everything else before the estate-sale agency stepped in, before all the antiques and oil paintings were labeled with a tag and sold off to someone ready to pounce on the misfortune of others.

"They pounced on the misfortune of others during the Great Depression," Nana Dale had told me. *"But I had my dreams, and I had my prayers."* She'd looked over her reading glasses at me. *"Don't forget your prayers, Allie."*

I climbed the carpeted staircase from the fully redecorated lower level to the main floor, then wound through the house to another staircase, slowly climbing to the top floor and turning into one of the two thirty-by-thirty–foot bedrooms that ran off the small hallway.

"The Pink Room," I whispered to myself.

The house had four bedrooms, which we labeled by color. This one had belonged to my grandmother when she was a child and had gone through several freshening ups, as Nana Dale described them, but still held the charm of a young girl's dreamland. A white-lace canopy floated above a delicate cherry four-poster bed that overflowed with bright pink and white pillows and a frilly white bedspread. A large cedar hope chest sat at the end of the bed. *"Hand carved by my daddy,"* I remembered Nana Dale telling me on more than one occasion. Black and gray horses interspersed with bright pink roses pranced on three papered walls, and one wall was completely covered with white bookshelves, on which sat some of my grandmother's cherished children's books and knick-knacks and old photo albums.

I touched the rough wood on a painted plaque that sat on one shelf, surrounded by porcelain horse statues. I'd always chuckled when I saw that plaque. "I'll keep this, for sure," I said out loud to no one, and I plucked it off the shelf, smiling as I always did when I read what was painted under the hindquarters of a fat dappled horse: *A filly's worth depends on how she's reared.*

4

Dale

1933

A filly's worth depends on how she's reared, the little five-by-seven plaque read. Dale laughed at the caption written underneath a cartoon painting of a dappled Connemara pony whose buttocks and tail crowded the foreground and whose head was turned toward its tail, ears pricked forward and a gleam in its eyes.

"Look, Mama! Can I buy it?"

The nickel in her hand was burning to be spent at the Macon County Fair.

Her mother shrugged. "You want to spend a whole nickel on a little wooden plaque?"

Dale knew that Mama didn't think she'd caught the pun, but Dale caught on quickly to most everything, especially her parents' somber moods.

"Can't you see, Mama? The filly looks like Essie! I'll keep it forever, or at least till I get her back."

When her mother really looked at the plaque, her pale blue eyes danced, and she winked at her daughter, "She does look like

Essie." Immediately, Mama's face clouded. "You know, Barbara Dale, I'm sure Essie's got a good home with another family. We aren't going to get her back."

Dale bought the plaque anyway.

Sitting on her bed that night, eyes closed, the plaque in her lap, Dale went over every inch of her filly's body, recalling the details that she'd memorized. "With those kinds of markings, I know I'll find you again, Essie, once Daddy gets his lumber business back up and running."

She hung the plaque on a wall by her bed, and it became like a shrine for her. She'd stare at the fat gray filly and pray, "God, please let me get Essie back. Please. I'm not praying for just any filly, God," she specified. She wanted *her* filly back. According to her mother, the chances of this prayer being answered were non-existent. But then again, her mother was only human, and Dale was not praying to her.

At eight, Dale soaked up the stories that Husy told her in Sunday school whenever Mama and Daddy went out of town and Husy took Dale to her church. Seven little girls listened, mesmerized, as Husy wove her stories of clouds forming crosses or doves or some other symbol in an otherwise cloudless sky, convincing them that God was real. God was the good guy, of that Dale was sure. But the bad guy was a little harder for her to describe. She'd heard him called several things: the Depression, the Stock Market, and the Devil Himself. Even Mean Cousin Weatherby.

Whatever he was called, Dale detested him for stealing away all the horses, especially Essie.

So every morning before school and every night before she fell asleep, Dale got on her knees, like she saw Husy do, rested her hands on the bed, and prayed, "God, I know You have a lot of other things to do, but You are big, and I don't think it would be hard at all for You to find my filly and bring her back to me."

She glanced over at the plaque beside her bed: *A filly's worth depends on how she's reared.* Dale had been reared well too, she knew. Yes, by her parents, but mostly, it was Husy who taught her truth, who taught her how to pray and how to be kind, how to find what was underneath.

Essie didn't come back, but finally, horses did find their way to the house and barn again.

On a spring day when Dale was nine, Mama called her to the barn. "Look who we found," she said, teary-eyed.

Mr. Jinx lifted his head and nickered, and Dale ran to the fat bay pony, threw her arms around him, and cried.

— ♘ —

April 6, 1936

Dale stared out the picture window from her bedroom way up on the third floor as the tall hickories swayed back and forth like the people in Husy's church, their hands raised high and their bodies keeping time to the music.

In the early morning light, she could barely make out the riding ring in the distance. The mares were tossing their heads, and the fillies frisked in and out, like black bats darting through the fog. They ran in spurts, then screeched to a halt, nipped at each other, reversed, and galloped off in the other direction. The two geldings raced madly on the other side of the fence in the hilly paddock.

Mr. Jeffrey was tossing hay over the split rails, and Dale imagined him saying, like he did every morning, *"Bout feeding time, boys. Now, now, you settle down. Ladies first."*

Mr. Jeffrey was so skinny that he always slipped through the railings instead of opening the gate to the paddock. Arms laden with hay and the feed bucket hanging from one arm, he'd pass the geldings, ignoring their protests, and lumber to the ring, where mares and foals waited.

Often Dale helped Mr. Jeffrey with the morning feeding, but today, she watched from her room. She hadn't gone to school. "Croup," the doctor had said, diagnosing the cough that sounded deep in her chest, constricting till she could hardly breathe. Mama had shut her up in the bathroom with all the hot water running until steam helped clear her lungs. By the time the doctor arrived in the middle of the night, she'd started to breathe normally again. Still, Mama kept her home.

Daddy had left early for the office, and Mama had come into her room wearing silk and pearls. She'd felt Dale's forehead, brushed a kiss across her cheek, and announced, "You stay put, young lady. I've got a breakfast meeting with the Ladies Society at the club. I'll be back before lunch." She turned and added, "Rest, sugarplum. If you need anything, Husy's downstairs." At eleven, Dale cringed whenever her mother called her sugarplum.

A half hour after her mother left, Dale heard a howling sound, the wind making the trees toss and zip, no longer a slow dance but something like a frenzy. Through the trees just barely getting dressed for spring, she could see Mr. Jeffrey straining against the strength of the wind. Above its roar, she heard a terrifying splintering and watched a limb as long as two fence railings break. Strands of hay flew upward, caught on the wind, as Mr. Jeffrey collapsed under the weight of the branch.

In an instant, Dale raced down two sets of stairs, found her boots by the back door, and rushed out into the wind. The trees moaned, and the horses pranced and whinnied, the geldings grabbing mouthfuls of hay and backing away from where Mr. Jeffrey lay.

The air felt warm, even muggy—a sharp change from the prickly snowflakes that had greeted her yesterday. April weather could be like that.

Now the sky swirled with ominous gray clouds.

"Tornado weather," Husy had declared. She should know. She'd lived through a deadly tornado in her hometown of Gainesville back in 1903 and liked to talk about it.

Dale pushed against the blasting wind. "Mr. Jeffrey!" She shimmied through the railings to where he lay, the limb split three ways beside him. "Can you get up, Mr. Jeffrey?"

She saw the gash in his head, the blood soaking the ground so that the red clay turned a darker, deadlier color. She fell to her knees. His eyes fluttered and rolled back in his head.

"Shoo on now, Fudgy! Thimblefoot! Go!" she yelled to the geldings. She rushed down the hill to the barn, and ran through the wide hallway to the tack room. Picking up a bucket, she filled it with water from the spigot and grabbed one of the rags they used for bandaging the horses' legs. The sponge was covered with horsehair, but she took it too.

She sponged the cold water on the gash above his eye, but it kept right on bleeding. "Can you wake up, Mr. Jeffrey? I can't move you myself."

Limbs crackled and splintered around her, and dust and hay and bark from the trees swirled upward, forcing Dale to shield her eyes.

Mr. Jeffrey's eyes fluttered open, red rimmed, the skin on his tan face slack. She wrapped the bandage around his head, tight and neat like he'd showed her for the horses' legs, but the blood just seeped right through in scarlet rivers.

"Thank ya, Miss Dale," he coughed out. "You go on an' git in the storm shelter quick. Get Mrs. Hughes to call the doctor. Don't believe I can be moving just yet."

"It's tornado weather, Mr. Jeffrey. Gotta get you to the storm cellar too."

The wind whipped through the trees, fierce and angry, and the trees protested as their limbs splintered and broke. She needed to bring the horses into the barn. Or did she leave them out to fend for themselves? Tornado warnings happened often in Georgia, but it was always Mr. Jeffrey who handled the horses in those circumstances.

"What about the horses?"

He groaned, eyes closed under the heavy bandages. "You go on and git inside the shelter. It's too dangerous."

"I won't leave you! And the horses. Tell me what to do with the horses."

She watched his chest rise and fall. With extreme effort, he mumbled, "Stubborn girl!" Dale leaned over him to hear what he said next. "Let the other horses out of their stalls now, you hear. If a tornado comes up and rushes through, they'll fare better outside. Open all the gates too."

She opened the gate to the ring, and the mares and foals reared and cowered, scurrying in circles. Then they rushed into the paddock. When she opened that gate, the geldings reared, screaming whinnies and tearing down the long rocky driveway that led up to the dirt road in front of the house.

She hurried into the barn, where the four ponies were pacing and kicking. She opened the stall doors and pushed herself away as they careened into the hallway and then out the front gate, the hooves making a racket on the concrete. All but Mr. Jinx. He looked at her wild-eyed, but she put the halter on and grabbed two lead shanks.

"We gotta get Mr. Jeffrey to the shelter."

She led the pony up the steep embankment. Mr. Jinx never reared or bucked, but today he pulled against the shank, and her hands chapped and bled as she held on. Dale's copper hair whipped in her face, and the wind stung her cheeks. Finally, she was beside Mr. Jeffrey. "You hold on to this shank, Mr. Jeffrey. I remember how you did it for that little boy when he was hurt. Jinx'll pull you to the shelter."

"No, go . . ."

The wind howled, and lightning bolts jagged across the suddenly pitch-black sky; an eerie greenish tint swirled too. She tied the shank around Mr. Jeffrey's hands, and he held on, dragging himself beside the pony as Dale led Mr. Jinx up the hill and out the open gate. In this way, the three of them progressed slowly through the storm.

Outside the gate, Dale pulled off her sweater, tied it around Mr. Jinx's eyes, and led him down the hill. Beside the house, the storm door rested at an angle, and she yanked it hard.

Husy appeared from the back doorway, her long gray hair, normally wrapped in a neat bun, falling over her shoulders. "Barbara Dale!"

When she caught sight of them, the woman pulled herself

along the railing and down to the storm shelter. "Lord, have mercy!"

Together, they helped Mr. Jeffrey inside the door.

"Let the pony go!" Husy yelled over the wind.

Hail as large as tennis balls began pummeling them. Mr. Jinx reared and whinnied.

Dale hesitated.

"Now git in!" Husy screamed.

Dale unhooked the shank, and Mr. Jinx tore off up the hill to the dirt road. Husy pulled Dale into the shelter and shut the door as a whirling mass spun by.

— ∩ —

The tornado completely destroyed the town of Gainesville, the second time tornadoes rampaged Husy's hometown. Dale learned of the details over the next days while she and Mama went along the dirt road looking for the horses. Several wandered back, but Mr. Jinx and her mother's mare, Krystal, took three days to locate.

After thirteen stitches in his head and three days in the hospital, Mr. Jeffrey came back to work. Husy was also absent for a few days.

"Her girls were there in Gainesville," Mama whispered. "Darlene was eating breakfast at the cafeteria at Brenau College, where it struck. Marjorie was at work when it hit," Mama had explained, a shell-shocked expression on her face.

"What happened to Husy's nieces?" Occasionally, Darlene and Marjorie still visited Husy, and often one or the other would watch Dale.

Mama just shook her head.

Dale found out later from Mr. Jeffrey. "You saved my life, young lady," he said.

She ignored him, demanding, "What happened to Darlene and Marjorie?"

"Younger one was at the women's college, and she was mighty lucky. Hid under a table and got a concussion when a wall fell. But she'll be all right."

"What about Miss Marjorie?"

"She was at work, just arrived with all the other young ladies over at that Cooper Pants Factory. Plenty of kids too. Whole building collapsed on 'em. Weren't many survivors." Soft brown eyes, watery and kind, met Dale's. "Real big tragedy. Never heard of three tornadoes striking the same town at the same time. Just plain near leveled the whole place. Real pretty town too. We used ta call it the Queen City of the North Georgia mountains." Mr. Jeffrey looked off, eyes clouded. "Poor Husy."

Dale found her nanny absentmindedly sweeping the kitchen. "I'm so sorry, Husy. I wish I could have been there to save Miss Marjorie."

Her nursemaid grabbed her in a headlock hug and held on for a long time. "You're a real brave girl, Miss Dale. You ain't scared of nothin', are you? You done a real courageous thing, rescuing Mr. Jeffrey like you did."

Dale studied Husy, sniffed, and brushed away the liquid in her eyes. She wished she could bring back Marjorie for Husy. From then on, it seemed like Husy walked even more bent over than usual.

"Broken in her spirit, she is," Mr. Jeffrey said.

On her knees, Dale prayed, "Can't You help me find Essie, God? We can't resurrect Marjorie, but I know Husy would find her smile again if You'd just bring Essie back."

5

Allie

Friday, March 6

Standing in front of the white bookshelf in the Pink Room, I stared up at a framed professional black-and-white photo of Nana Dale sailing over a brush fence on her mare, Essie. Everything about the pair was perfection, Nana Dale leaning over the mare's neck, her seat out of the saddle, her boot-clad heels down in the stirrups as Essie's white ears pricked forward, her front legs tucked tight to her chest.

I sighed and plucked a thin off-white photo album from where it sat sandwiched between dozens of other albums on my grandmother's bottom shelf and traveled back in time. Leafing through this album, clearly from the 1970s, with its vinyl cover and clear plastic that stuck more-or-less well to yellowed pages, I let my fingers move over the square Kodak color photos of Nana Dale and my grandfather, Poppa Dan, and my mother, Mary Jane, as a gangly preteen with long, wavy dark brown hair. And horses. Lots of horses.

I replaced the album on the shelf. My grandmother had taped

a slip of paper on the spine of each photo album, which she called scrapbooks. On this one, she'd written *Spring 1971–Winter 1972*. The scrapbooks were shelved in chronological order, with the oldest dated *Winter 1931*. I had skimmed through some of them before, but today I wanted to examine each one carefully. Depending on the era, my grandmother had either glued or stuck under the clear plastic not only photos but also newspaper clippings and birthday cards, postcards, and other memorabilia.

Maybe I'd find another letter from Nana Dale inside one of them, a letter written to me, explaining where in the world the cherrywood box was located. It was a stretch, but I was running out of other options.

Opening the oldest scrapbook, I encountered page after page of black-and-white photos rimmed in white. Many showed my great-grandmother Eleanor astride her mare, wearing a riding coat and jodhpurs and tall black boots, her smile always mesmerizing as she held a ribbon or trophies. She looked just as Nana Dale described her: *"A true Southern belle. She even wore pearls in horse shows. I don't think she ever perspired. She was a high-society lady, but she loved horses, and she was a gifted equestrian."*

I frowned as I recalled another of Nana Dale's descriptions of her mother. *"A real Georgia peach. Soft on the outside, with a hard interior."* When she had whispered that to me, my grandmother's face had become hard as well.

There were a few photos of baby Nana Dale in her mother's arms and several of Nana Dale as a little girl with her arms wrapped around a fat pony.

"Mr. Jinx," I whispered, remembering my grandmother's stories of learning to ride on that pony.

And then Nana Dale, sporting a toothless grin, was sitting bareback on a beautiful dappled filly. Her mother stood on one side of the filly and her father on the other.

"Nana Dale and her Essie!" I said this out loud too.

The next pages were filled with newspaper clippings about the Tupelo–Gainesville tornadoes. I vaguely recalled Nana Dale telling the story. Now I scanned the clippings in the scrapbook from the *Atlanta Constitution.*

Tornadoes Rip Apart Queen City

On the morning of April 6, three tornadoes struck the Gainesville area at practically the same time. The wreckage was astounding, with debris filling the streets up to 10 feet deep. 750 houses were destroyed, and 254 were heavily damaged in the hub for manufacturing with a population of nearly 9,000.

The largest death toll in a single building for any US tornado occurred at the Cooper Pants Factory, most of whom were young women and children. . . .

I shivered with the tragedy, but I wondered why my grandmother had noted it. Then I saw the obituary for Marjorie Malor, twenty-four, and I remembered one of my grandmother's stories. "Dear Husy," Nana Dale had whispered. She always got choked up just mentioning her name. "I was afraid she would never get over losing her niece in the tornado. But when the Good Lord answered my prayers and we found Essie, something was reborn in her."

I flipped the page past the obituary to a black-and-white photo of Nana Dale with her arms around an ancient-looking woman with a hooked nose and dark eyes. She was stooped over, her gray hair pulled in a tight bun, a thin dress covering the undeniable hunch in her back. Both Nana Dale and Husy were smiling at the camera, and what I read in Nana Dale's eyes was pure ove.

"Husy and Jeff really ran the place," she told me on many occasions. "My poor father was weighed down with his business, trying to recover after the Depression. He cared for his employees. He made his fortune back eventually, but sometimes, I thought Mama was bent on spending it before the money even landed in the bank."

Then Nana Dale would get that bittersweet look in her eyes, and

I knew she was remembering the way her mother "frittered away money like it wasn't worth more than a bucket of oats."

I turned the page and read the next clipping.

Local Girl Saves Caretaker

At 8:20 on the morning of April 6, Barbara Dale Butler, 11, watched from her window as the stable hand, Mr. Jeff Jeffrey, was knocked to the ground by a tree limb while a tornado rushed through the Southeast . . .

I read with fascination about how Nana Dale had rescued Mr. Jeffrey, trying to imagine my tiny grandmother at eleven years old, rushing out into a tornado to drag the man who ran the stable to the safety of their storm cellar. And I could. Nana Dale was fearless, brave, intrepid. And she wasn't one to tell others about her bravery. "Can't rest on your laurels, Allie," she'd quip whenever I asked her about a trophy or accomplishment.

She didn't brag to others. Instead, she stored the memories safely in these scrapbooks. I was more convinced than ever that Nana Dale died with her secrets. "Why didn't you reveal them, Nana Dale? Are they tucked away in the cherrywood chest, along with a lot of money?"

But I knew part of the reason. My grandmother called herself a "carpe diem gal." The present tense was her best friend. She'd woken in the morning with a sense of adventure whirring away in her mind and went about making all those ideas come true in real time.

I set the scrapbook back on the shelf and knelt with my legs tucked under me on the hardwood floor of the Pink Room, Nana Dale's cedar hope chest beside me. Lying on top of the chest was an ancient wedding-ring quilt, handmade, I knew, by Husy. I carefully folded the quilt and placed it on the canopied bed. When I'd opened the cedar chest back in January as I was searching for the little cherrywood chest, I'd expected to find moth-eaten clothes from the 1930s or a few roaches from 2019, but instead, I'd discovered my grandmother's cashmere sweaters, well-preserved because "cedar does that, you know, Allie. Put a cedar chip in every drawer and closet and you won't get those darned moth holes. Especially with your cashmere, Allie. Moths love cashmere."

Nana Dale knew all about wood, her father having built his fortune in the lumber business. She also knew a lot about cashmere. "My mother's favorite. I inherited all of her sweaters." Then she'd smile. "Not that I mind."

I had never paid a moment's notice, nor had I ever donned a cashmere sweater, but now I stood up and lifted out the white plastic bag with a Neiman Marcus label that I had merely glanced at in January. When I unzipped the bag, a dozen soft sweaters lay stacked inside, all of them cashmere.

I raised a pale yellow short-sleeved crew neck sweater with a matching cardigan and held it to my chest, imagining my grandmother wearing the sweater set and wool trousers, a short string of pearls around her neck and pearl earrings clipped to her ears. I must have seen a photo of this: tiny Nana Dale, never quite five feet tall as an adult, tucked inside her butter-colored outfit, her short hair wavy, its auburn highlights gleaming under a sassy but feminine hat, her cinnamon eyes sparkling.

"My daddy, Papa Jeff, said she was the pertiest little brunette you ever did see," Barnell had told me a dozen times. "Sassy as all get-out; headstrong to beat the band. Never saw nothin' that scared her. And of course, I got to know her when I started going to the barn with my father. By then, she was at least twenty or so. She'd grit her teeth and haul a fifty-pound bag of feed up them steps to the hayloft or drag a coupla' bags of hay. Tough, she was." He'd chuckled. "But then, she'd go on up to the house and shower up and come down those steps lookin' like the debutante she was. Yessir, she could dress up mighty fine, but her true love was them horses, and soon as the party was over, no matter that it was late in the night, there was your grandmother with a pitchfork hauling manure outta her filly's stall and into the wheelbarrow."

I reached into the cedar chest, hearing Barnell again. "Nothing she loved better than them horses of hers. Don't believe there was a human on earth she cared for like them." His eyes crinkled and softened. "Well, an' you, Miss Allie. She loved you. Shore did. Always said you had horse sense and a good head on your shoulders. Better than the rest of the family."

"Well, she loved Poppa Dan, didn't she?"

"Well shore, she did. And your momma, too, even if they got in spats. And your brother, of course. But you know what I mean. Had a real soft spot for you." Barnell was leaning on the pitchfork, his overalls stained with the ubiquitous red earth. "And Tommy. Now, Tommy, she loved that boy. Shore did. Least that's what my daddy always told me. I never met him."

I wiped a tear from my eye, wondering for the hundredth time about Tommy. *You'll know where to find the money, and you'll learn about Tommy and my tall tales.*

I stood and, almost without thinking, pulled off my T-shirt and pulled on the cashmere sweater set. I was half a foot taller than Nana Dale, but we'd both worn a size small up top. I stood in front of the oval mirror and could almost hear her whispering to me, *"You're a spring girl, Allie. That color suits you well."*

Nana Dale loved to take me shopping, insisting on buying a few clothes that weren't meant for the barn. Now I pulled my "unruly palomino hair"—Nana Dale's description—over one shoulder. Nana Dale attributed horse colors to people. So I was a palomino, and Wick, a sorrel, and my parents were a pair of dark bays. My hair looked barely a shade lighter than the cashmere, and somehow, my jeans brought the cashmere into the twenty-first century.

"Nana Dale," I whispered, staring at myself in the mirror but wishing to see her cinnamon eyes instead of my turquoise ones staring back. "You said there was plenty of money, that I'd find everything I needed to launch the equine therapy in some obscure wooden box that you left me. But I've looked and looked, and the only wooden chest is this big one, also made by your father but filled with clothes. For some reason, you've hidden *mine* somewhere in this house. But where? And why? I need a little help, please."

I turned back to the cedar chest and lifted out three of Nana Dale's wool riding coats—plaid, navy blue, and forest green. I smiled. Not a moth hole anywhere. The tags inside the collar were faded with age, but slipping on the jacket, after removing the sweater, I once again married 1940s fashion with today. I'd never been interested in the trappings of Nana Dale's hunter/jumper life, preferring faded jeans with holes made from use, not some factory machine and costing a hundred and fifty dollars, as was the style now. But on this day, my grandmother's riding clothes made me itch—not the wool rubbing my skin, but an interior itch, a deep desire to understand where my grandmother hid her secrets.

I knew the why. She'd told me a dozen times—confided in me, actually, the first time when I was barely a teen. "They've never been wise with money, Allie. My daddy, your great-grandfather Jeremiah, tried, but Mama loved the extravagant parties and trips. I watched Daddy suffer through the Depression, but Mama, she pushed it away like a flitting idea as soon as he got his lumber business going again.

"Before Daddy died, he commissioned me to manage the business, the house, the horses. He'd been grooming me for the job before I was even an adult. When he passed away, I was in my late thirties." For a moment, her mind floated off, and I could tell she was reliving something. She had been extremely close with her father.

Then she came back to me. "I took over the accounts and doled out small amounts of money to Mama to appease her." She looked away. "It didn't work. She called me names and made all kinds of ridiculous threats. And no matter how hard I tried with your mother, she inherited the same taste." Nana Dale said this while sucking in her cheeks, her expression sour, as though she tasted a lemon.

"History repeats itself, Allie. Mama was a spendthrift, and I was a spoiled only child. Then I had Mary Jane. So much like her grandmother—except much kinder. But she was beautiful and soft and reckless with money. She became a spoiled only child too, no matter how hard I tried to prevent that."

It was true. My mother was rather spoiled, and my parents, Irvin and Mary Jane Massey, greatly enjoyed their comfortable lifestyle. My grandmother called them "high-society movers and shakers." And although my father earned a good living in real estate, Nana Dale was quick to remind me that my mother's family had the fortune, one that my great-grandfather Jeremiah had worked hard to build back after the Depression had stolen so much.

"But you, my dear, you've got horse sense," Nana Dale used to say.

The first time she'd said it, when I was thirteen, I looked it up in the dictionary, just to be sure. *Common sense, discreetness, discretion, gumption, level-headedness, wisdom, prudence, wit.*

When I didn't question her, she'd pushed back her wavy auburn hair, just beginning to be tinted with gray, and laughed. "You know what I mean without asking. Horse sense, I tell you."

"Wick is smart too, Nana Dale," I'd countered. Only fourteen months apart, my older brother and I had grown up inseparable.

"You're right, Allie. He's smart in a different way."

The memories crowded in, and I pulled out my cell phone and called my brother in France. "I've started going through her stuff for a second time," I said with no other greeting.

"Hey back," he said, the sound of his deep voice calming me. "How's it going?"

"Hard," I managed around the huge knot in my throat.

"Okay, sis. Deep breath. I'm proud of you. This whole thing sucks, but you are going to get through it."

When I didn't reply—because I couldn't get a sound out—Wick continued, "You sure you don't want to let Mom help?"

I sniffed. "You know what it does to her. She gets all sentimental and then sad and then mad and then defensive. And that drives me crazy."

"I know. I wish I could be there with you. You know that, right?"

I nodded as if he could see. He had tried for days after the will was read to help me start the packing-up process, but I'd refused, determined to find the missing box before I did anything else.

And then he'd gone back to his job at the Louvre, and he worked nonstop.

"I'll try to get off next week. Would that help?"

"No. You've got a million things going on over there. You already took all that time off for the funeral and, you know, everything else."

"True, but there are rumbles about that nasty virus going around. Coronavirus. Have you heard of it? Italy's closing its borders, and France may be next. I may be coming back a lot sooner than I'd planned anyway."

"Oh, I hope not. I don't want you to miss out on a single thing over there. I don't know much about that virus, but I'll be okay. I'll figure something out."

"What about Tricia? Could she help?" He knew my best friend had a knack for talking me off a ledge.

"She's been out of town, but she'll be back this afternoon. She basically hired the estate planner for me."

"Oh good. Then let her help." When I again couldn't reply, Wick asked the elephant-in-the-room question. "You want Austin there, don't you?"

I cleared my throat three times as tears rolled down my cheeks. Thank goodness this wasn't a video call. "It's too late for that."

"Deep breath. You're gonna get through it."

I changed the subject. "It's so awesome that Barnell's doing the backhoe thing." I had filled Wick in on that surprise via email.

He chuckled. "Yep. Good ole Barnell, loyal as the day is long."

"I'm gonna keep working now. It's good to hear your voice."

"Hang in there, sis. Love you."

I can do this, I repeated in my mind, taking several of Wick's recommended deep breaths.

I changed back into my T-shirt, replacing the sweater set and riding coat over more of my grandmother's vintage clothing in the chest. I closed the top, admiring the way the lid fit snuggly over the base, a hand-carved work of art.

I fingered the frames of two eight-by-ten black-and-white photos that sat on a shelf. In the first, tiny Nana Dale was sitting on a split-rail fence, holding the reins of a dark bay with a star on its forehead, and a boy about her age was sitting on the same railing, holding the reins of a horse with very similar markings. The horses stood in between the riders, heads held high over the fence, ears pricked forward. Nana Dale and the boy were wearing matching riding outfits: dark coats, white shirts with white ascots fitted at the neck, black velvet hard hats, white gloves, and black leather knee-high boots. The horses and the boy were staring off in the same direction, presumably at the camera, but Nana Dale was looking straight at the boy, her face a picture of pure joy, and she had a silver tray in her gloved hands. "Dale and Tommy," I whispered to myself.

In the other photo, Nana Dale and Tommy, dressed in the same clothes, were riding side by side on the same mounts, the horses trotting perfectly in stride.

"The couples class," I said out loud. As soon as I pronounced those words, I hopped up off the floor and ran downstairs to the dining room, examining the array of silver pitchers, platters, bread trays, and bowls in the hutch. I nabbed one as if I'd found gold and brought it back to the Pink Room, holding it up to the photo. Sure enough, it matched—an oval sterling silver tray with pretty scalloped detailing all around the rim and an engravement in the center.

1937 Greater Atlanta Shrine Horse Show
Atlanta, GA
Pair of Hunters Abreast

"We used to enter the couples competition as kids, take our horses to the shows up and down the Southeast coast." Nana Dale's eyes closed, and she said, "We loved it!"

They loved riding together. But I knew the truth: they loved each other. Or at least, Nana Dale had loved Tommy.

Horse love led to human love.

Austin.

Do not invade my thoughts right now, please!

The moisture on my cheeks surprised me as tears trickled down my face. At least no one else was around to see them.

I hurried down both sets of stairs and out the back French doors to clear my mind, but the puffy white morning clouds were chasing one another, just as they had on that day. It infuriated me that Austin could intrude on any and every space in my life, as if he belonged, as if he weren't the one who had turned and left.

You gave the ring back.

I stomped across the leaf-covered lawn, passing the pool—covered for the winter months—refusing to examine that unwelcome truth, and headed to the barn, staring down at my jeans and worn boots. I refused to look back up from the pebbled path to the luminous sky, refused to be reminded, to be taunted by him. The barn stood empty in front of me. I let myself in the gate and walked through the long hallway between seven sets of box stalls swept clean of wisps of hay and bits of manure. I hung my arm across one of the half doors and thought of Nana Dale watching Essie come into the world.

But that memory, recounted a half-dozen times in vivid detail by Nana Dale, could not obliterate the other memory, the one I knew because I had been there. Doggone it, if the sky didn't betray me, the barn would.

I had been leaning over a stall door at the University of Georgia's beautiful new equestrian complex, ten miles off campus.

"Hey. I've seen you hanging around the stables a lot. I'm Austin Andrews. Third-year vet school."

I'd turned to give some snide comment when my eyes met a dimpled chin. I looked up to where a young man towered over me, sporting a white lab coat and a ridiculously disarming smile. Add to that eyes the color of the bluest part of the Mediterranean, blond, blond hair—if he were a kid, he'd be called a towhead—that touched his collar, and another dimple in his right cheek, and I swallowed my comment and felt heat on my face.

"Hi, I'm Allie. Second-year physical therapy."

"Like horses, huh?"

"I sat on a horse before I could walk. Hoping to open a center for equine therapy."

"Equine therapy?"

Mortified. Why in the world had I let that slip out? "Well, maybe."

"I grew up around them too." His voice held what sounded like regret. He came beside me and leaned over the same half door. "Can't get them out of my head, so I thought I might as well dedicate my life to taking care of them."

"So you're going to be a large-animal vet?"

"I am."

I did not want to remember the rest of the conversation or how that casual, chance meeting had lasted three hours, and how, by the time we left the equestrian complex, I'd had the rest of my life planned out. With him.

And I had almost gotten it right.

I walked through the empty barn, past the paddock to where a red clay trail led up a steep incline to the riding ring and to where Barnell's backhoe sat silently today. I turned around and trudged back to the front of the barn and ran my hand over the cedar sign that hung beside the gate: *Hickory Hills Horse Therapy*.

The sign that had been delivered two days before Mr. Lorrider crushed my dreams. The death of a lifetime of dreams, one tumbling after the other, built over years on my knees in prayer and then two more years leaning over a fence, my shoulder gradually moving closer to Austin's, until we stood almost as one. And then his arm went around me, and he gently twisted a ring onto my finger.

I walked the fifty yards back toward the house. I could not wrap my mind around the truth—in three weeks, the house, the barn, the pool, the whole property would be flattened, leaving only a few large mounds of dirt. As I passed the manure pile, my lips flickered slightly. Nana Dale used to host a "feed your garden party" and invite her friends to BYOB—as in "bring your own (wheel)barrow"—and load up on manure for the flowers.

Every step across the property held a hundred memories. What I wanted was a sign of the future, something to promise me I would keep breathing, that I hadn't died with my dreams. I stared up at the billowing clouds again and thought of Nana Dale's tall tale about Husy seeing all kinds of religious symbols in them.

I used to scoff internally, but today I muttered, "Sure would be nice to have a clue, Nana Dale."

As I trudged back to the house and up the steep hill to the road, I caught a glimpse of a prism of color. I stopped, turned my face upward, and gave a small gasp. A full rainbow towered above the trees, weaving in and out of the clouds.

6

Dale

1936

She'd always remember how the rainbow announced his arrival. The sky had turned black and plummeted slicing rain on the path to the barn. Dale waited impatiently for the sky to clear so she could meet the new kid whose horse would come to the stable soon.

She fell for him the first time he walked into the barn, all bravado and charm, the only child of Thomas and Ada Ridley. "Thomas Ridley, who made his fortune in steel," her mother had whispered. "We're delighted to board their horses at our barn!"

"Hey there, kid," he said, bright chestnut eyes filled with life. "I'm Tommy."

She swallowed hard, trying not to show her surprise. He looked a lot like the dreamy boy actor Mickey Rooney.

She squared her jaw, stood up straight. "Nice to meet you, Tommy. I'm Dale. This is my barn. My mother said you might be bringing a horse over to board." She tried to feign indifference. "She asked me to show you around."

He followed her through the fourteen stalls as she commented on the horses already boarded there. "And this one's mine. Mr. Jinx. I'm going to take him to the National Horse Show next year."

Tommy reached out and stroked the forehead of the dark bay pony. "Mr. Jinx. Well, he's a beauty. Going to Nationals next year, eh?"

"Yep. I hope to, at least."

"I was there this year, and gee whiz, it was fun!"

Dale's eyes grew wide. "You rode in the show? You and your horse went up to New York City?" She tried to calm her burgeoning awe. "How old are you, anyway?"

"Thirteen. I rode in the junior class on my horse, Beau. This was my first year, and I did okay."

Dale had dreamed of going up to New York City one day, but she couldn't really imagine it.

"What's it like? I mean, riding at Madison Square Garden?"

"You've never seen so many beautiful horses, with people dressed up in their finest, all those colors, waving at you from the stands. And you're riding in this gigantic covered arena. And the jumps! Wow! They're mighty fine too. Not just striped poles and white coops, but oxers and thick wooden structures painted to look like brick and stone walls, and another that looks like a wishing well. And all those cameras flashing their fancy bright bulbs and making the horses shy and rear!" He paused, the enthusiasm dancing on his face like a kid at a carnival.

She surveyed this boy who was two years older than she and only about four inches taller, with dark reddish-brown hair and thick brown eyelashes highlighting his chestnut eyes. Over the next week, she found that his eyes had a perpetual twinkle in them, and he was quick to laugh at himself and his size.

But put Tommy on a horse, and he seemed larger than life. "Aren't you ever afraid?" Dale had asked the first time he took Beau over a three-and-a-half-foot jump. The way he careened around the ring made her heart race. He was half daredevil and half sweetheart.

"I was afraid I was going to die when I was ten. But I lived. I take every day as a gift. I mean, I should've died, you know. Guess the Good Lord looked after me."

Everyone in Atlanta knew the story of the Ridleys' beloved and reckless only child, who had tried to take their sixteen-hand thoroughbred over a four-and-a-half-foot stone wall, but instead was thrown into the wall, suffering a concussion and broken leg.

"I've heard about it. You're brave."

Tommy grinned at her. "No, Dale Butler, you're the one who's brave. I've heard the story of the tornado." He leaned in close. "I'm going to call you DB. That okay with you?"

She shrugged. "DB for Dale Butler?"

"Maybe. Or maybe DB for Darn Brave." He winked at her, and Dale blushed.

"What a beauty!" she exclaimed when Tommy's dark bay gelding arrived at Hickory Hills. He had a fine head like a thoroughbred's and tiny ears that perpetually twitched back and forth.

Tommy patted the bay on the forehead. "Yep. Beau's swell. Mild mannered and smooth to sit. And he can jump." Then Tommy added, "Maybe you could ride your mother's mare. What's her name?"

"Krystal Klear is her show name—we just call her Krystal."

"I saw your mother riding Krystal when we visited last week. That mare jumps well too. Next year, we can take both of them up to New York. We'll ride in the same classes. It'll be swell."

For a moment, she was caught up in his excitement, then deflated. "Sure. That would be swell." Except for one thing. Money. She'd seen the worry lines on her father's usually handsome face and the account papers on his desk, and she understood the pressure. Mr. Weatherby, the man she'd thought of as the devil himself when she was younger, was still there, threatening to ruin her father and the business he'd built back, tree by tree, log by log, two-by-four by two-by-four. Dale couldn't understand how a family member—even if he was only a distant cousin by marriage—could be so mean and manipulative. Or why. She felt a creeping dread that this man would find a way to steal their fortune.

She knew she wouldn't be attending the National Horse Show in New York City any time in the near future. Her mother paid no attention and went right on spending money, wearing her cashmere and pearls and ignoring the way her father's shoulders slumped, a lost expression in his dark eyes when he stared out the window at dinnertime, his fork in midair.

— ♍ —

"Did you know you can tell a horse's age by its teeth?" Tommy stood beside Mr. Jinx and pried the pony's mouth open, revealing his whitish-pink gums and his long, yellowish-brown teeth. "Wow! He's ancient, DB." He pointed to the very back molars. "See how they're worn down but still long? I'll bet he's over thirty."

Dale stuck her head right next to Mr. Jinx's muzzle, so close she could feel Tommy's knuckles on her cheek as he held the pony's mouth open. Then she kissed Mr. Jinx on his fuzzy gray muzzle. "Shh. You might hurt his feelings if he hears you talking like that."

For the next two weeks, they spent late afternoons lifting the lips of horses and ponies and guessing their ages. Tommy laid down the rules. "We pay each other a dime for every correct guess. No pay if neither of us guesses right."

"That's a stupid game," she said, but since this presented another way to be close to Tommy, Dale went along. She even kept their guesses on a piece of paper that hung from a nail in the tack room. Then she'd convince Mr. Jeffrey to show her the official papers of the purebred horses.

After she had beaten Tommy at the teeth-guessing game four times in a row, she ripped down the paper and tossed it in the trash barrel. Tommy didn't just love competition; he loved to win. She could see how even losing at such a silly game annoyed him, and she didn't want him to feel annoyed.

By the middle of August, Tommy had forgotten about the National Horse Show. "I'm going to ride in the next Olympics," he said, then cursed the Nazis.

Dale had never heard a boy swear, certainly not one who was thirteen. "You're aiming for the Olympics?"

"Sure am. 1940. I want to be the youngest rider on the US team. No way we'll let those Germans win six gold medals again, every stinkin' one in the equestrian competitions."

Dale straightened up tall. "I heard all about it. Mama said the Germans had an unfair advantage."

"Well, of course they did! That's just how they are."

"I don't see how you can be in the Olympics in 1940. I thought you had to be an officer in the military to be allowed to compete in the equestrian events."

She saw a blush creep behind the smattering of freckles on his cheeks. "I'll join the cavalry somehow. Rules can change, you know."

Dale's parents had closely followed the Olympic Games in Berlin on their radio. She'd listened along with them. As the games continued over those two weeks, she heard her father on more than one occasion say, "This is a sham, an excuse for incendiary German propaganda! Thank God for Jesse Owens. He's a brave man."

Later, her father's face grew red with anger and then pale with something else when Germany won every equestrian event.

"Unheard of," he whispered to her mother. "You watch. This is not a good sign."

"What do you mean, Jeremiah? Not a good sign for horsemanship?" she'd asked, her words lazy as she puffed on a cigarette.

Dale would never forget the way her father's eyes, normally soft and kind, hardened, and he'd clenched his hands into tight fists while the static on the radio overcame the announcer's excited voice.

"I mean for the world."

On a late afternoon, when the August sky hung thick and muggy, Dale and Tommy sat side by side on two hay bales, her feet dangling, her heart thumping as Tommy chewed on beef jerky and recounted his dreams. "Your folks have some mighty nice horses here. How high can your mama's mare jump?"

"She can jump four feet easy. Mama's won a load of ribbons on her. She won even more on Greta, before she sold her."

Tommy shrugged. "Four feet is nothing to laugh at, that's for sure. I'm gonna jump that high soon too."

She scrunched up her nose. "You sure do seem to be in a hurry, Tommy."

"Ya gotta have dreams, DB. And goals. Especially to make the Olympic team."

"Have you got a trainer?" She'd heard her mother talk about some of the best horse trainers in the country preparing a girl who lived across town for the South's finest horse shows. Mama's trainer had left when all the horses were sold in 1932, and he'd never come back.

"Of course. He'll be moving down here this winter to help me train. We'll be boarding my new horse here too, Infinity. He's white with thousands of gray flecks across his barrel and flanks. A truly infinite number of specks. Get it? Infinity?"

Dale rolled her eyes. "It's called a flea-bitten gray, Tommy."

"Yep, you're right. He's my *infinitely* flea-bitten gray gelding." He grinned. "I'll start showing him next year. Infinity can jump the moon!"

"I've got a filly who can jump the moon too."

"Which one is she?" Tommy asked.

"She isn't here. My father sold her in 1932. But I'll find her again. I know I will. And she's got a wonderful pedigree. She'll be a champion for sure."

Tommy eyed her suspiciously. "You sure have high aims. I admire that. But I'd plan on heading to New York on a real horse." Then he winked, and Dale stomped away, indignant.

Ω

1937

Every afternoon after school, Tommy and Dale rode together in the ring. On Mondays and Thursdays, Tommy's Danish trainer, Mr. Jorgensen, gave a separate hour-long lesson to each of them. After cooling down Mr. Jinx and sponging him off, Dale always traipsed back up the hill to the ring, eyes glued on Tommy as Mr. Jorgensen took him through challenging routines. On this day, Husy stood beside Dale. Her gray eyes looked rimmed with age, her face lined with a road map of wrinkles, her back more bent, her limp more pronounced.

"You're tired, Husy!"

"I'm fine, Dale. You mind your business and pay attention to that highfalutin' trainer. Hear he's from Denmark."

She watched as Mr. Jorgensen had Tommy slip his legs out of the stirrups, cross the stirrups over the pommel on the saddle, and take an entire course over fences without them.

"He likes Tommy more than me. He knows Tommy's a better rider. Just look at what he's having him do!"

"He's a fine rider, Dale. But don't you dare let jealousy come in to strangle you, young lady. Ain't becoming at all. Anyway, Tommy is two years older than you, so it's only natural that he'd be able to jump higher and be entered in stiffer competitions."

"Mama always says the same thing, and I hate it. Just because I'm younger doesn't mean I can't ride every bit as well as Tommy Ridley."

"I don't want to hear it!" Husy's eyes flashed annoyance. "Do you know how fortunate you are to be here with horses in your backyard? Don't you dare let some foolish jealousy sneak in to steal your joy, Barbara Dale. Don't you dare! You're a proud girl, and that's okay. But you use that mind of yours wisely. And sometimes, you need to keep your mouth shut."

Her tone sounded harsh, but Dale knew the wisdom behind Husy's words. Dale wasn't really jealous of Tommy. It was something else she couldn't explain. A feeling that sneaked up in her stomach, just like Husy said, only it felt warm and fluttery and confused and happy all at once whenever she was around Tommy.

She needed to change the subject.

"Someday, I'll be riding Essie up here, Husy. I believe it. Don't you?"

"You just keep praying about that, young lady. I'm not the one who's gonna be answering those prayers."

When Tommy finished his lesson, he cantered Beau over to the fence where Husy and Dale were watching and swung one leg over the saddle so that he sat facing sideways. "Mr. Jorgensen's trying to kill me. I'll be sore for a week."

He grinned at Dale, the patch of freckles across his nose inching up to his eyes in a way that made her lose her concentration. "But we're going to the show in two weeks, and we have to be ready."

"*You're* going to the show at Chastain," Dale said with a pout. "Mr. Jorgensen doesn't think I'm ready."

"Not for the jumping competition, but he wants you to enter the equitation classes."

Dale shrugged, then felt Husy nudging her. "Yeah . . . I guess."

"Look, DB, if you want to, we could do some of the classes together. You know, the couples classes. They're all the rage right now. But you couldn't ride Jinx. Has to be a horse, and the two horses should look somewhat alike, or at least have the same coloring." He hopped off Beau, took the reins over his head, and led him toward the paddock, Dale by his side. "What about Krystal? She's a dark bay like Beau. Even has a star on her forehead. Would you like to do that?"

"You're just trying to make things better. I want to show on my own."

"Have it your way," he said with a shrug. He unfastened the girth and lumbered off with the saddle in his arms and Beau following behind.

Dale raced after him. "Okay. I'll do the show. Long as it isn't too much money to enter." She frowned. "Only one problem. We don't have a trailer right now." Her father had sold theirs back with all the horses.

"We have a trailer. And my mom says we're gonna keep it parked right here at your barn."

— ♞ —

Chastain Park Shriners Show

Dale blinked at the flash of the light bulb as she and Tommy rode side by side in the couples competition. When they lined up in the center of the arena, the loudspeaker blaring their names as winners, Tommy took off his riding hat, held it high, and waved to the crowd.

"Ya gotta do the same, DB," he said out of the side of his mouth, his attention on the bleachers filled with spectators. "Play to the crowd."

Obediently, she took off her hard hat and waved just as another camera bulb flashed right in front of her. Krystal shied, and Dale slipped to the side, barely regaining her seat. The crowd chuckled, and she heard the announcer say, "Some of our best horses get a little nervous with the flash bulbs."

She felt the heat in her cheeks, put the hat back over her curls, and glanced at Tommy.

He nodded. "See? You've got the audience with you!"

That evening, with the crickets making a racket and the lightning bugs winking through the sky, Tommy sat on the bumper of the trailer next to Dale. "I heard our mothers talking, and it's settled. We're going to take Krystal and Beau to all the shows in the Southeast this summer. We're even going up as far as Virginia." He grinned at her, the freckles barely visible in the dusk.

Her heart squeezed so that she couldn't think of a thing to say except, "Gee whiz. That'll be fun."

One week later, Tommy grabbed her hand and dragged her behind the trailer. "Just look! Mama got the new nameplates for the trailer. Isn't that the best?"

Dale held on tight to his hand until they skidded to a stop behind the trailer. On the back of the two-horse trailer was a big CAUTION sign. Fastened on either side were metal plates engraved with their horses' names. She stared at the plates and then burst out laughing, reading out loud, "'Krystal Klear CAUTION Your Beau.'"

She cleared her throat. "I have something for you, Tommy." She held out a thick nail, the kind used to secure horseshoes to the horses' hooves. "I had the blacksmith make it into a ring for you. You can wear it for good luck." Then, embarrassed, she added, "I mean, if you want to."

Tommy took the thick ring from Dale and grinned. "Gee, thanks. Sure, I'll wear it. For good luck." Then he winked and added, "Good luck, a good horse, a bit of skill, and you watching me, DB. That's all I need."

Dale and Tommy traveled up the East Coast, attending shows in Atlanta, then Aiken, South Carolina; Blowing Rock, North Carolina; and Wilmington, Virginia. Her mother, Mrs. Ridley, and Husy came with them on the show circuit, along with Mr. Jorgensen.

That summer, just as Tommy had said, couples classes were the rage. The crowd cheered for Tommy and Dale on their matching bays, the favorites all along the East Coast, especially as they were the youngest riders entered in the competition. And when Tommy and Dale waved their matching riding hats to the crowd, people often murmured, "Those kids even have the same color hair!"

Dale garnered her share of blue ribbons with Tommy, but she only rode in those classes to be near him. What kind of skill did it take to have matching horses and matching outfits and to trot and canter side by side?

By now, she'd become a fine equestrian too. She saw it in Mr. Jorgensen's eyes. When he announced after their first show, "You're young, Dale, but I think you can hold your own in the junior hunter classes," she looked her trainer straight in the eyes and said, "I won't let you down."

When they weren't riding in the ever-popular couples classes, Dale and Tommy competed in the junior hunter division for riders under sixteen. Inevitably, Tommy would take the blue ribbon as he cantered Beau around the course of eight fences with a finesse and panache no other equestrian possessed. Dale didn't mind coming in second to Tommy.

"That boy can sure sit a horse! He's a born competitor," Husy said. "I do believe he can make it to the Olympics if he sets his mind on it."

"Oh, he's already done that, Husy. But he's not a military officer, so that won't happen."

"He's not one *yet*," Husy corrected, and Dale felt something strange and heavy descend on her, but she didn't know why. Husy placed her wrinkled hands on Dale's shoulders. "You're a born competitor too, Barbara Dale. You know that, don't you?"

She swallowed away the tinge of jealousy that snaked around her at times and nodded.

"Remember, you just do your best. And have fun. Don't you let competition or comparison steal the fun. Obsession is an ugly taskmaster."

"Do you think I'm obsessed with winning, Husy?" The question was sincere.

"No, darling. I don't think it's that."

She felt the sting of Husy's acknowledgment. Dale wasn't obsessed with winning. Something else occupied almost every space in her thoughts. She and Tommy competed in the show-ring. But in her heart, Dale was competing for his love, although she wouldn't have called it that at almost thirteen years old. She only knew that she wanted to follow him wherever his crazy bravery took him.

7

Allie

Friday, March 6

I climbed the stairs to the Pink Room again, the rainbow offering some small solace even as the weight of my own love story pulled me down. I took out my cell phone and stared at the screen with Foxtrot's chestnut head staring back at me. Until a month ago, the screen had boasted Austin with his arms around me as I gazed into his eyes while holding up my hand with the perfectly chiseled diamond embedded in white gold that he had slipped on my finger.

I absently ran my left thumb over my empty ring finger. For a half second, I contemplated calling him and begging him to come help me go through all of Nana Dale's stuff. He'd looked forward to it, or at least that's what he'd said. I believed him. Austin enjoyed history and antiques and family heirlooms. And he loved me. He really loved me.

And I loved him. I did. I still loved him.

I tossed my cell phone on the white comforter and then collapsed beside it, staring up at the billowing canopy, my throat tight with regret, and I let myself remember the good days.

Not long after our first meeting, Austin invited me to go riding with him at the farm outside of Athens where he boarded his buckskin gelding, Jeep. Of course I accepted.

When he came to pick me up at my apartment, I gawked at his outfit. He was wearing cowboy boots and a Stetson, Levi's—which fit him just right—and a faded blue chambray shirt.

"You ride Western!" I blurted out.

He cocked his head and gave an embarrassed grin. "Yep. Is that a problem for you?"

"No, not at all," I choked out, although my beet-red face most surely proclaimed my embarrassment. Desperate to recover, I asked, "When did you start riding?"

"I was seven; my sisters, five and four."

"So you learned to ride Western?"

He looked away, considered something, and said, "Not exactly." When I could think of nothing to say, he added, "My sisters and I learned survival riding."

He didn't volunteer an explanation.

For the next three hours, we rode the trails around the farm, Austin on Jeep, sitting tall and comfortable, while I bounced around in the Western saddle on a mare who twitched her ears, annoyed. I was mortified that it took me a half hour before I really felt comfortable in the saddle.

Austin trotted over to me wearing his signature sheepish grin. "I don't mean this to hurt your feelings, but I've always heard that riding Western is a lot easier than riding hunt seat."

I glared at him. "I am totally embarrassed to admit that I have never in my life ridden in a Western saddle. With this gigantic horn for the pommel, you can't post! You just have to—I don't know—bounce!"

He cocked his head, grin in place, and said, "Well, I don't mind. You still have a real nice seat, from what I can tell."

I opened my mouth, shocked at his slightly off-color comment.

I had not expected quiet Austin to have a sense of humor. His face was now deep crimson, and we just stared at each other for a moment, and then, as one, we burst into laughter.

One of the many things I grew to love about him was the way he didn't take himself or life too seriously. He liked to joke. And I needed someone to calm me down.

But he could be very reflective too. It was on the drive back to Athens after our riding date that he explained, "My father is not a nice man, especially when he's drinking. Before my mother divorced him, we kids had a bit of a rough time."

It turned out that "a bit of a rough time" meant Austin's father had tried to abuse his daughters, and when Austin stood up to him, he'd broken Austin's right arm so badly that, even now, he held it across his middle at times to calm the pain that still harbored somewhere inside.

"When you said you wanted to do equine therapy, I knew you were special, Allie. That saved my life, and my sisters' too."

It was our third official date, and I was already deeply smitten. We were enjoying dinner at a trendy little restaurant in downtown Athens, a rare evening when Austin wasn't on call.

He studied me for a long moment. "Allie Massey, I like you a lot." He looked a little shy with that admission, and his crooked smile showed a dimple.

"Um, thanks."

"You're fascinating. I can't pin you down."

I blushed, unsure of how to respond.

"It's a good thing." He'd reached across the table and squeezed my hand, just briefly. "You know what you want, but you care about what others want too."

"Nana Dale calls me a thoroughbred—high-strung and high maintenance."

He smiled again, dimple showing. "Complicated, creative, and kind."

"You're embarrassing me."

"I'm a little rusty around females—the human kind, at least. I'm used to high-strung mares. I can give a quick tug on the twitch, and I've got their attention."

I grinned. "Yeah, that probably wouldn't work so well with me."

This time, Austin blushed.

Reserved and quiet, he came alive when helping another student or client understand something. Austin was the one who was kind.

His phone beeped. "Sorry. I need to get this," he called over the din of the restaurant. "I'll take it outside."

He stepped away from the table for a few minutes while I daydreamed about everything Austin. When he came back, his face was drawn and even paler than usual. He sat down, straddling his chair. "I'm so sorry, Allie. It's an emergency." His eyes looked shiny. "Pony over in Alpharetta caught in barbed wire. I know the family well. And the little girl who owns the pony . . ." He wiped a napkin across his mouth and stood up. "I'll call you tomorrow and reschedule."

I could tell his mind was a million miles away.

"Of course." Then, "Or I can come with you. I've dealt with horses caught in barbed wire before."

The surprise on his face morphed into a waning smile. "Really?" Then he frowned. "I'm afraid it won't be pretty. And I may have to put him down."

"I've been there for that too."

"Okay. Well, um, then . . . that would be awesome. If nothing else, you can hold the flashlight."

He fished for his wallet, but I pushed it away. "I'll pay. You go get the truck."

He hurried outside, and a few minutes later, I met him by his red pickup.

We spent the whole night in a mosquito-infested field beside a brown-and-white-spotted Shetland pony lying on his side, glassy-eyed with pain. I held him still with the twitch on his muzzle while the distraught owner, a nine-year-old girl named Anna, looked on, and along with her mother, tried to soothe the poor beast. At first the pony tried to rise, but eventually, exhausted by the pain, he lay quietly, the barbed wire twisted almost impossibly around his forelegs, which were splattered with blood.

Austin talked lovingly to the pony throughout the night.

When we'd first arrived, Austin had shed tears. I was not used to seeing grown men cry. My father grew stoic in the face of tragedy, and the last time I'd seen my brother, Wick, cry was when he was pitching a fit about getting a tetanus shot when he was seven or eight.

"Not sure I can save this one," Austin whispered to me after he'd been working for over two hours. "It's such a tangled mess, and the wire is embedded near an artery. We've got to stop the bleeding."

Late into the night, the moon shining on us, illuminating the pony, he succeeded in removing the last of the wire. Austin spent the next hour stitching up the wounds.

He drove me back home in silence, the exhaustion heavy on his face. "You were made for this," I whispered. "You kept your calm when that kid was screaming, and we were all sure you'd have to put the pony down."

He shrugged, and before I left the truck, he said, "Thanks for being there, Allie."

——— ⛬ ———

Nana Dale was particular about many things, one of which was the kind of guys I dated. My father traveled the world for his job, and Mom often joined him, especially when I was a teen, so they happily left my dating schedule to Nana Dale. Yet I'd never fallen for a guy like I did for Austin. Most were not interested in horses, and those who were truly passionate about the horses weren't particularly interested in girls.

When I brought Austin to Hickory Hills for a meal, Nana Dale prepared pulled pork with coleslaw and corn bread. "Allie said you're a bit of a cowboy, so I thought you might like this."

I stared wide-eyed at Nana Dale.

She shrugged.

Austin laughed and said, "Well, at least your grandmother didn't call me a hillbilly. Both are accurate, actually. I'm a cowboy hillbilly vet."

I think that first comment won Nana Dale over, and she fell for him almost as hard as I did.

Austin seemed equally comfortable around my grandmother, as if they shared the same horse genes.

"Allie says your mother was quite a horsewoman," he commented after he'd cleaned his plate of pulled pork, "but that you're the real star."

"Honestly, Allie!" Now it was Nana Dale's turn to roll her eyes at me, thrilled, I could tell, with his compliment. "That girl will say anything."

To disprove her point, I kept quiet, enjoying the good-natured sparring between Nana Dale and Austin.

"Tell me about your showing days," he asked.

Delighted, Nana Dale paraded us around the house, narrating her horse history as we moved from the dining room downstairs to what we called the Ribbon Room and beyond.

"He's the real deal, Allie," she said later. "He's steady enough to help calm you. And he has a bit of dry wit behind that shy exterior. He also reminds me of my dear father, with his kind eyes. I like men with kind eyes."

Then she smiled. "And most important, he seems to like you."

"I like him, Nana Dale. A lot. But maybe we've got too much in common with the horses."

She'd looked away. "Oh, honey. If you find a man who shares your love of horses, it's a gift." By the look in her eyes, I knew she was remembering.

I was surprised at her comment, because I distinctly recalled hearing that Poppa Dan had no interest in horses. I ventured, "Tommy?"

She'd gotten that now-familiar look in her eyes, one of regret and deep caring and something else that I was pretty sure was akin to soul-mate love. Like I was beginning to feel for Austin.

— ♁ —

Some of Austin's and my favorite times were riding together on trails through Athens, Georgia, and then in Atlanta, when we'd moved Foxtrot and Jeep back to Hickory Hills. We would take the little-used trails behind the riding ring, watching for deer and coyotes. Sometimes when he was ahead of me, sitting tall in the saddle on Jeep, his hair sticking out from under the riding helmet that I insisted he wear, he'd turn around and have the silliest grin on his face.

"Shore do think you're somp'em special, my Allie Girl," he'd say, putting on his most authentic Southern hillbilly drawl. In his eyes, I read the simple truth that he really did think I was special, and my stomach would flip-flop, me smiling back with an equally infatuated and silly grin.

"We'll clear out these trails and make more, Allie, where the children can ride," he said. "We'll call them the Hickory Hills Horse Therapy Trails," and he grinned at me.

But there was never time. Instead, after our trail rides, we often ended up tucked together in his red Toyota Tundra truck, the one he'd affectionately dubbed Triple T, as a nod to my penchant for alliteration, Austin speeding down some rural road toward his next emergency.

We'd been dating for eighteen months when he got the call about an accident at DontKnockIt Farms. A pony had somehow leaped over the divider into the front of the horse trailer and hung by his lead shank in the space that was reserved for hay bales.

One look at the frenzied black pony, and I could tell his left foreleg was broken. I hurried to the bushes and vomited. But Austin stayed right by the pony's head, speaking softly and calmly looking straight into the animal's terrified eyes.

When I came beside Austin, he said, "Allie, I need you to take care of Kimmie. She can't see this."

And so while Austin spoke to the child's mother, I took the inconsolable little girl by the hand and walked her out behind the barn, where several goats were chomping on the grass in a pasture. We chased them through the tall weeds, and then Kimmie and I played hide-and-seek in the barn, until Kimmie's mother found us and whispered, "Kimmie, Blackie's going to sleep. He wants to tell you good-night."

The pony, doped up on painkillers, lay sedated by the trailer as Kimmie stroked his neck and then lay down next to him and told him good-bye.

I knew that Austin and I were made for each other and for a life with horses. We loved many of the same things, but we complemented each other well. He'd often tease me in his Southern drawl, "How in tarnation did a high-society girl like you let herself fall for an ole hillbilly like me? If that don't beat all. Don't understand it, but shore am thankful. I'm one lucky cowboy."

But I was the lucky one. Of that I was convinced. I wanted to spend my life right by his side, whether we were sipping champagne at my father's country club or crying together after a heart-wrenching night when he put a little girl's pony down.

I wanted him.

I still wanted him.

But I wanted Hickory Hills too, and Austin—kind, smart, and straightforward—needed me to be on his team, no matter the things life threw at us.

Why, dear Lord, couldn't I let Hickory Hills go and run back to him?

"You're stubborn as the day is long," he'd told me several times, and I'd nodded and laughed. Evidently, that very same expression had been used on Nana Dale when she was my age.

Stubborn as the day is long. Oh, Lord. I want him back.

8

Dale

1938

Husy gently jostled Dale awake. "Sweetie, we need to get to the barn."

Dale rubbed her eyes, pulling herself up in bed. "What?" When her eyes adjusted to the predawn light, she saw deep concern on Husy's face, foreshadowing tragedy.

"What is it?" she asked as she threw on her dungarees, pulled a jacket over her pajama top, and followed Husy down two flights of steps. She slid her bare feet into her paddock boots and stepped outside to a sky the translucent hue of early morn.

"When Mr. Jeffrey got here to feed, he found Mr. Jinx in a bad way."

A lump the size of a small orange lodged itself in Dale's throat. *Bad way.* The only other time Mr. Jeffrey had used that term was when he described Husy after the tornado.

Dale hurried into the barn and through the hallway, pausing at Mr. Jinx's stall, where the shavings lay scattered in dirty heaps mixed with red clay. Deep gashes in the dirt showed how Mr. Jinx had scrambled and thrashed with his legs, most likely rolling over and over in the night. Now her beloved pony was standing in the paddock, his eyes glazed with a mixture of terror and what looked to be excruciating pain.

"Jinx!" she cried, wrapping her arms around his neck.

"He colicked in the night, Dale," Mr. Jeffrey said. "Found him thrashing in his stall. Took a while to get him to stand up. Been trying to get him to walk it out, but he's in a real bad way. Vet should be here soon."

Ponies and horses could not throw up, so when they colicked, their natural response was to roll over and over, trying to rid themselves of the pain. Inevitably, their intestines became impossibly entwined. The only remedy was to keep a horse up and walking, preventing him from rolling.

She took the lead shank from Mr. Jeffrey. "Come on, Mr. Jinx," she coaxed. "Please, buddy. Please walk for me. I promise you're going to be okay if you'll just walk it out." The pony gave a low moan. She fiddled in her dungarees for a carrot, but when she held it out for him, Mr. Jinx paid no attention.

For the next hour, she tried to urge the pony forward. When he took a few halting steps, she felt a tiny spark of hope replace the deep dread that had lodged in her gut along with the lump in her throat.

When Dr. Horner arrived, she stood rooted in place as the vet examined her pony. He'd motioned to Husy to take Dale away, but she refused to move. He checked Jinx over, consulted quietly with Mr. Jeffrey, then came to Dale, squatting down and looking her straight in the eyes. "He's suffering awful bad, Miss Dale. You need to let me put him down."

Husy's strong arms came around her shoulders, but all Dale could think to say was "Where's Mama?"

Husy cleared her throat. "She couldn't quite bear to come over and see Jinx like this. But someone else is here."

Dale hiccuped a sob as a different set of arms came around her.

"It's okay," Tommy whispered.

She buried her head in Tommy's shirt and cried. "I can't let him go."

But Tommy pulled her close and said, "You remember checking his teeth, don't you? He's old. He's had a good life. You don't want him to suffer anymore."

Husy and Mr. Jeffrey nodded to the two of them.

"Thank you for coming," she whispered. "How'd you get here?"

"Husy fetched me," Tommy admitted.

Dale tried to picture her bent-over nanny, who hated to drive, shifting gears on the old Ford in the dim light, crawling along the roads until she reached Tommy's house.

While the vet did his duty, Tommy did his, walking Dale around the property, meandering between the hickories and dogwoods and pines on the well-worn trails behind the ring that they had created together when they'd walk Krystal and Beau out after a challenging lesson. Seven acres of woods, hidden from any streets and even the dirt road that ran in front of Hickory Hills.

"Do you think we could bury him here, Tommy?" Dale asked, sitting on a boulder that they'd often teased had broken off an asteroid millennia ago.

"Under the Meteor?" Normally they giggled when pronouncing their secret name for the rock, but today, Tommy's voice sounded scratchy with grief.

She gave a tight smile. "Somewhere on the property. I can't bear for him to leave us."

Tommy perched beside her, took her hand in his, and brushed away the tears on her cheek. "Do you remember what Husy always says about when an animal dies?"

Dale nodded. She kept hearing those words as she rested her head on Tommy's shoulder. Husy had said it first when Lady was put to sleep when Dale was four or five. She'd repeated it when Essie was taken away. And again when their cocker spaniel licked up contaminated water and died.

Now Tommy said the words out loud while she rehearsed them in her mind. "'It'll break your heart, Dale. And you'll grieve. But loving an animal and losing it, watching it die, and then getting another, well, it teaches a person she can love again.'" Tommy kept holding her hand and wiping the tears that streamed down her face.

Later that morning, Dale begged Mr. Jeffrey to remove Mr. Jinx's horseshoes. "I want him to be comfortable up in heaven," she whispered, and no one dared deny her wish. Then Mr. Jeffrey brought his backhoe up into the riding ring, unhitched two posts of railing, and dug a grave beside the Meteor, where he deposited Mr. Jinx's body and a tin box filled with the horseshoes while Dale, holding tightly to Husy on one side and Tommy on the other, watched.

<hr />

1939

The summer he was sixteen, Tommy entered both hunter and jumper classes at the local competitions. For the stadium jumping classes, he raced around a course over jumps that were taller than Dale.

"I'm going to enter the jumper classes too, Tommy."

He placed his hands on her shoulders and looked straight into her eyes. "You will do no such thing, DB. You're fourteen, and you have the best seat of any equitation rider in the whole circuit." He winked at her as a blush crept across her face. "You just concentrate on the hunter classes."

While hunter classes were judged on the accuracy, grace, and elegance of both horse and rider over a course of fences, the jumper classes were judged on how quickly a horse completed a course of fences with the fewest errors as the fences were raised higher and higher in jump-offs.

"You don't think I'm brave enough for jumper competition?" she asked in a tiny voice, all bravado evaporating with the warmth of his hands soaking into her shoulders.

"I think you're stubborn enough to do anything you set your mind to, DB," he said. "But why?"

She didn't dare tell him the truth. *So I can travel with you when you go to competitions that are only for stadium jumping and eventing.*

But she knew Tommy was right—she didn't appreciate the combination of speed with high jumping. And so far, all their competitions were available in the same shows. The bonus was that when she and Tommy weren't competing in the same classes, Dale often brought home the blue ribbon.

In March 1939 at a show in Blowing Rock, North Carolina, the weather lived up to the town's name. Her over-fences class was postponed for a few hours while the wind thrashed, and lightning and thunder entertained the riders, huddled under the bright green awnings by the practice ring. When her number was called first for the junior hunter class, she felt a twitter of apprehension. Krystal was as surefooted as they came, but the field where the course was set up was a mixture of slick grass and deep mud. She'd walked it earlier with the other competitors, carefully counting the distance between the fences.

When she turned her mare toward the three-foot, six-inch fence that was painted to resemble a stone wall, Krystal slipped on the turn, scrambled, and recovered, but Dale lost her concentration and urged the mare forward. Krystal responded to her heels, and Dale thought the mare could lift them over the intimidating jump by sheer force, but Krystal's front right hoof caught the wall, and Dale had the momentary sensation of floating as Krystal crashed into the jump. Then Dale flipped backward over the jump, landing in the mud, where Krystal rolled on top of her.

Dale remembered hearing the collective groan of the audience as Krystal nicked the jump, then the screams from the crowd as the magnitude of the fall became obvious. And then she didn't remember anything at all.

Until . . . Tommy was beside her, on his knees, his face as close as breath, though his voice sounded muffled and strained. "C'mon, Deebs, you crazy kid. C'mon now."

Her eyes fluttered open, and she blinked awake, registering Tommy's scrunched brow, the paleness on his usually ruddy face, and something like love in his eyes. At the same time, she felt a bone-crushing pain in her arm.

She howled.

He smiled.

"There ya go, my girl. Thank goodness."

He called me Deebs! He called me his girl!

He tapped her nose with his hand, and the pain melted into something altogether delightful.

"Pain and joy aren't mutually exclusive," Husy had told her years ago.

Reality came with that exquisite pain. A double break. And a concussion.

When Tommy came into her room at Hickory Hills two days later, she spat out, "Why aren't you continuing on the circuit? You better not miss the big show in Virginia!"

"Well, you're very welcome for my visit," he said, reaching down and tweaking her nose. Then he sat on the corner of the bed and looked up at the canopy. "Never been in your room before. It's very . . ." He stood and turned in a circle. "Pink."

She started to protest and then saw the twinkle in his eyes. "It's a swell room, Deebs." He fingered the porcelain horse statues on the white built-in shelves and then lifted a framed photo of the two of them off the chest of drawers. "The couples class at Chastain."

Already having Tommy in her room, sitting on her bed, had caused Dale's heart to thud. Now she nibbled her lip, embarrassed that he'd seen the photo.

"I like that photo a lot. And don't you worry. I'll go back on the circuit. But I had to check on my girl first." He bent over the bed and came so close, she could see the darker rim around the chestnut in his eyes. "You afraid?"

"No!" she said. When he stayed close and wrinkled his brow, she added, "Afraid of what?"

"You know what I'm asking. Did that fall scare the grit out of you? It scared me."

Dale shrugged, but she couldn't hide the truth from Tommy, even if, at the moment, her heart was fluttering with a different kind of nerves. "Yep," she whispered, turning her face down as the heat crept up her cheeks.

Every rider knew the adage that you didn't really know how to ride a horse until you'd fallen off one. And they knew the other adage too. The first thing you did when you fell off a horse was to get right back on.

But she hadn't gotten back on because she'd been carted off to a hospital. Fear had edged up in her mind, and Tommy knew it.

"You've got every right to be afraid. That was some splendid fall." He tweaked her nose again. "But don't you worry. We'll conquer that fear."

He'd said *we*. She held on to that.

— ♘ —

A hickory nut pinged on her window one night about a week after the accident. Then another. At first, Dale thought the hickory nut was falling from the trees that waved overhead. They often landed with such a loud thump on the roof that it sounded like something breaking. But when it happened for the third time, she climbed out of bed and walked over to the bay window that gave a magnificent view of the backyard and the barn in the distance. Tonight, the moon hung almost full, a pale orb that gleamed bright, as if it had just escaped from among the towering hickories and had floated up to safety in a plethora of stars.

Thwack!

She jumped back. Another hickory nut was being deliberately thrown at the glass pane. She opened the window and leaned out, looking down three stories to where Tommy stood below, flashlight in hand, motioning her down.

"What are you doing here?" she whispered loudly.

"I'm taking you for a ride!"

"Are you crazy? It's the middle of the night."

"Which is precisely why you can see I'm not crazy. I know you're not allowed on a horse for a month, but by then, that fear on your face will have sunk way down into your gut, and you won't be any good at all for the next horse show."

Dale loved a challenge. Still, she hesitated. "I don't know."

"If you give in now, you'll be sorry. C'mon."

She was wearing her mother's willowy nightgown, the only pajamas that fit over her cast. She grabbed a silk robe and tiptoed down the two flights of stairs, heart racing. She stood barefoot on the cool stones, her left arm in a cast up to her shoulder. Tommy surveyed her with his usual grin, one hand on his hip, the other cradling the flashlight. He motioned for her to sit on the wooden steps, knelt beside her, and fitted her leather paddock boots over her bare feet, lacing them tight. Then he drew the robe around her shoulders and buttoned it under her neck.

"Your Majesty," he teased.

"Your Highness," she countered, holding her good arm out to him. He took her hand and kissed it, and a shiver zipped down her back.

"Such fine riding attire."

Beau stood bridled but bareback beside the storm shelter. When Dale questioned Tommy with her eyes, he winked. "We're in this together, Deebs."

He'd placed a wooden block with three steps beside Beau. She climbed the steps, and he hoisted her onto Beau's bare back, then slid behind her, his arms coming around her. Dale swallowed, concentrating on the warmth of his arm around her middle contrasted with the soft warmth of Beau's smooth coat on her bare legs.

Then Tommy gathered the reins in one hand and headed up the driveway to the dirt road. Safely situated on Beau's back, they trotted through the back roads of Buckhead with the flashlight tucked in Dale's hand, scanning the black horizon for a possum or a raccoon or a deer or a wild boar.

Dale leaned back into Tommy, heart pounding as he held her tight. "You afraid anymore, Deebs?"

She shook her head, unable to speak. In truth, she wasn't just afraid, she was terrified . . . and not from falling off Krystal. It all came from falling in love.

9

Allie

Friday, March 6

In truth, I'd been afraid—no, terrified—of falling in love with Austin.

It seemed too good to be true. From my limited but unsuccessful experience with dating, when I'd liked a guy and the feeling seemed mutual, inevitably the guy would become fed up with my passion for horses. And our relationship would end.

Poorly.

But Austin was very different. He was endlessly patient with me. Even better, he encouraged all my plans for Hickory Hills. "We both know what a difference equine therapy can make in someone's life," he'd said when I'd finally gotten the courage to share my detailed plans for Nana Dale's estate. Then he'd taken my hand and said, "And I know you, Allie. More than anything, you want to make a difference. It's the air you breathe." He'd grinned. "Well, that air mixed with the fragrance of manure."

Oh, Austin. I did want to make a difference, and now the only differences are this ringless finger and a lost dream.

I scrolled through my photos and found the one of me looking up at him, right after he gave me the ring. It was no longer on my home screen, but I certainly hadn't deleted it.

In this photo, my eyes held the same expression as Nana Dale's in that black-and-white photo. How she had loved Tommy! Every framed photo in this room belied the truth of a beautiful young girl totally besotted, the perfect old-fashioned word to describe so much feeling. Had Tommy known? Nana Dale wanted me to find the cherrywood box so I'd have the money to keep the house, but she'd also wanted me to find the answer to the mystery of Tommy.

"Every time you mentioned his name, Nana Dale, you teared up. Why? What happened?" I asked out loud. "Please tell me what happened."

But she never had, and now more than ever, I found myself aching for lost love.

"You loved him, Allie. That's worth weeping over." Tricia's reprimand from two weeks ago whispered in my ear. I wished she were here now to hug me and make me laugh, like soul sisters do. But instead, I replayed the scene in my mind as I ran my finger around the frame and stared at those two cherubic faces. Nana Dale and Tommy were barely teenagers in this photo, their faces aglow with what would become, I was certain, true love.

I felt the swelling in my chest, that squeezing mixture of joy and pain.

Austin and I had ridden side by side six months ago, me on Foxtrot and him on Jeep, mimicking this photo, just for the fun of it, just because we too were young and in love. And because Austin was determined to help me take a deep breath, relax, and enjoy.

"Allie, you've done the lion's share of the paperwork. We're almost there, but we're taking today just for us."

Austin had needed the break too. Austin wore stability as a belt, but I'd worried for him with the craziness of joining a busy veterinary practice while his mother went through chemo and his estranged father had married for the third time.

"We're not going to think about bad news or good news right

now, Allie," he said. "We're gonna enjoy a real perty fall afternoon on our mounts, girl, and have us a hog-killin' time. Ya hear me?"

I grinned at his cowboy drawl.

Side by side, we let the horses meander through several acres of trails in the woods behind the riding ring, right in the heart of Atlanta.

Foxtrot was all thoroughbred, high-strung and nothing slow about her, despite her name suggesting otherwise. She skittered with the squirrels. When a doe and her fawn leaped across the trail, Foxtrot "danced on pins and needles." That was how Nana Dale had always described it.

I breathed in the crisp fall air, finally, a reprieve from Georgia mugginess.

"Hey, Allie! Come here a sec."

I looked behind me to where Austin had dismounted from Jeep and was standing beside what Nana Dale had called the Meteor—a rock about three feet wide and deeply embedded in the soil. I turned my mare back and hopped off.

"What?"

"Nice rock." Austin had a funny smile turning up his lips.

"Yeah, nice rock."

We were parodying a speech I'd heard Nana Dale recount for my whole life.

"Have a seat, Allie Girl," Austin said, deepening his voice to mimic Nana Dale's when she told the story.

I dutifully perched myself on the rock, Foxtrot's reins still in my hand. I was chuckling. I knew what came next. Always in the story, Dale and Tommy would be sitting next to each other, their teenaged legs swinging back and forth in cadence.

Then, as the story went, he took an envelope from his pocket and dropped it in Nana Dale's hard hat, announcing to her and the woods, "This, my dear, is an envelope that I just snagged from Husy, addressed to Miss Barbara Dale Butler."

In that way, Dale had learned that she had qualified for a prestigious equestrian event that she'd dreamed of attending for years.

99

And she'd jumped up and hugged Tommy so tightly that she suddenly realized she didn't ever want to let him go. At least that's what Nana Dale had let slip once in the telling, and I'd repeated it to Austin.

"So, Allie Girl," Austin continued, giving me a wink. "I have some good news for you."

I grinned, removed my hard hat, and held it out, ready for him to place in my cap the document that stated we had jumped through all the legal hoops for Hickory Hills to become an equine therapy center. We'd discussed before how I wanted that good news to come in the same way as Tommy had shared the good news with Nana Dale.

Austin reached in his jeans' pocket, pulled out a folded, unopened envelope, and placed it, as expected, in my hard hat, meeting my grin with his.

I narrowed my eyes. "You haven't even opened it!" I accused. "What if it's a rejection?"

Austin shrugged, suddenly serious. "I wanted to be with you when you opened it. No matter what."

I felt a twitter of anxiety, maybe even fear. Surely it was good news.

But when I opened the envelope and unfolded the sheet of paper, there were only four words scrawled on it in Austin's unmistakable scribble.

Will you marry me?

By the time I glanced up from the paper, he was on one knee, pressed into the damp of fallen leaves, and he was holding out a take-my-breath-away diamond ring.

The memories colliding together brought no comfort, just a stabbing grief. I glanced at my cell phone and saw, with relief, that it was time for me to head to Chastain. Someone had stolen Hickory Hills from me, and I no longer had a ring on my finger, but I still had a job to do.

During the week, I worked at Chastain Horse Park. Chastain Park had been around Atlanta for decades. Before it became a park, the property was made up of fields where slaves and former prisoners and actual prisoners worked, dawn to dusk. But nowadays and for many years, Chastain had been a sports mecca of swimming pools, tennis courts, a golf course, and sports fields. And an equestrian center. My grandmom had shown her horses there. My mom had also. In fact, it was there that the accident had happened for Mom.

I walked through the barn where my mare was boarded and came to the stall where she stood.

"Hey, Foxie," I said and reached for her soft muzzle, gray and prickly, then I worked my way up her forelock, scratching beside her ears. "Can't ride today, girl. But I'll be back Sunday for our jaunt with Tricia."

She twitched her chin and nickered softly.

On Mondays, Wednesdays, and Fridays, I worked with young students in therapeutic riding, and on Tuesdays and Thursdays, in hippotherapy. For the uninitiated, those sounded like the same thing. However, there were basic differences. Whereas therapeutic riding used equine-assisted activities to help people with disabilities improve cognitively, physically, emotionally, and socially, hippotherapy involved helping individuals strengthen their core, their balance, their posture, and their motor skills.

Early in our relationship, when I'd shared my dream of Hickory Hills Horse Therapy with Austin, he'd looked at me with what would become a familiar bemusement. "But you do all of this at Chastain. It's a great center for equine therapy. And it's only twenty minutes from Nana Dale's."

"Well, I'm certainly not trying to compete, Austin. I just . . . I just have had this dream, and I don't believe one can ever have too many avenues to help others. My colleagues at the horse park are thrilled with my project."

One day soon after he was hired on to the vet practice in Atlanta, he'd said, "You're right. Chastain is a busy place—there's so much going on there with the horse park and the baseball fields and swimming pools and on and on. Hickory Hills will be a good supplement."

But at times, he'd cock his head and say, "It's a beautiful dream, Allie. But please don't let it become an obsession."

I'd immediately get defensive. But now I sighed. Perhaps he'd been right all along.

My best friend, Tricia, wearing her signature rust-colored jodhpurs and sweatshirt, came around the corner of the barn, her curly black hair piled high on her head.

"Hey, friend," she said with a wave.

I always felt relief just hearing Tricia's voice. We'd grown up together on horses. Tricia had learned to ride in Nana Dale's backyard. Later, she'd boarded her pony at Hickory Hills. Attending the same school and spending every afternoon at the barn, she and I became inseparable. Eventually, after attending different colleges and grad schools, we'd found our way back to Atlanta and Chastain, both with a heart for equine therapy.

"Welcome back," I said and gave her a hug. "How was the visit with your parents?"

She shrugged. "Good. Mom's hanging in there. She still knows me, and we actually had a few really sweet conversations."

"It's hard though, huh?"

"Yep. But you always say hard and good can go together."

"Yeah, sometimes," I agreed. *But not this time. Not with Austin. That was just plain hard.*

"You ready for class? We've got a new kid today."

"I'm so ready. I need a different kind of challenge." I'd met this young teen, Jimmy, last week when his mother brought him to the stables. When she explained his background, I'd batted back tears. He'd been through hell.

Now I watched Jimmy, who towered beside the other six children at the entrance to one of the riding rings. I walked inside the ring where the horses were lined up by the fence, their reins looped over a rail.

"Okay, kids, you can walk over to your mounts."

I headed over to Jimmy, ready to show him his mount, but he yelled out first, completely unaware of his surroundings, his voice strident. "I want that one!"

He was pointing to one of the paddocks beyond the ring, where a palomino gelding was whinnying and rushing back and forth by the wooden fence. Without any thought of danger, Jimmy half ran, half stumbled toward the palomino, our newest acquisition, a quarter horse who'd been abused.

Like this boy.

I trotted after him, calling out, "Jimmy, not that one. He's new. Your horse is here."

But he paid no attention, circling the exterior of the ring, then cutting through one empty paddock to a field where mud and manure had mixed into deep muck.

"You can't get to him," I said, hurrying after Jimmy. "It's too messy to traipse out to the far paddock where the palomino is. The horse you're caring for is in the ring. Come on back with the other kids."

"I want that one, though," Jimmy repeated without glancing back, intent on his goal. He continued to slog through the muck until he reached the fence. There, he looked back at me, grinning and pointing at the palomino, who was approaching on the other side, his ears pricked forward, head lifted high. Then the horse gave a short whinny.

Jimmy climbed onto the wooden fence, hung his upper body over, and stared out to where the palomino paced in the paddock. To my amazement, the gelding reared, shook his head, and pawed the ground, as if he wanted to be sure he had our attention. Then he trotted over to where Jimmy leaned forward over the fence.

Jimmy looked back at me. "What's his name?"

"Angelfoot," I said, watching the scene unfold.

The wild horse started pacing beside the fence, eyeing the boy, drawing closer step by step, ears twitching, until he stopped right in front of Jimmy. Then Jimmy, giggling as if he were six instead of thirteen, reached over the fence to pat the dirty gray muzzle.

Jimmy giggled again. "It's soft, Miss Allie, real soft." He reached a little farther over the fence and rubbed Angelfoot's forehead, running his fingers up the long, bony face until he entwined them in the straggly, knotted white hairs of the forelock.

Angelfoot had been at the center for a week, but he'd never been brushed. Every time we got close, the gelding would back away, snorting at the long-haired brush or currycomb or hoof pick. But here he was now, the boy leaning over the fence, and the horse sticking his head ever closer as Jimmy rubbed his face.

The boy who had been traumatized rubbed the head of the horse who had been traumatized and looked in his eyes. I was sure I saw some kind of understanding between them. That one look brought me total satisfaction. I wanted to spend my life helping horse and human make that type of connection, one I'd seen happen dozens of times before.

Later, as Tricia and I put up the horses, I said, "Nothing can beat what we witnessed with Jimmy. Wonderful."

Tricia grinned and nodded. "Yep, you said it well."

After my last lesson, I listened to my voice mail. Cécile the estate-sale planner again, calling to book our appointment. I returned the call and suggested we meet in a week.

Cécile cleared her throat and explained in perfect English with a lovely French accent that she would need more time to set up all the details if we expected to have the sale on March twenty-first. So I scheduled a meeting at Hickory Hills for Monday afternoon, confirmed the date, and clicked off the call. I needed to get busy packing up the house. But all I succeeded in doing that night was wasting long hours on my phone, swiping through photos of Austin and me.

— ♘ —

Saturday, March 7

I awoke to a chilly drizzle that crept into my soul. I considered hunkering down with Maggie in my apartment instead of heading to Hickory Hills. But after coffee from my French press and thoughts of the impending visit from Cécile, I grabbed my rain jacket and drove to the house.

I bumped down the second driveway and parked in the clearing. "Hey," I said, greeting the old structure with a lump in my throat. I took a seat on the back porch in the Adirondack chair that overlooked the pool, the stables in the distance. I pulled my rain jacket around me and a fleece blanket over my leggings and sipped from my travel mug.

"Listen, I really need your help. I know you're not in the greatest shape and I've got to clean you out in about a week, but I need help now. You know—to find the money. Nana Dale said it was here. In you. I know it's not in a bank account. And I also know for sure it's not something that Horrible Mr. Hightower got his hands on."

I held out Nana's letter and jabbed at it. "She said so, right here. In this letter I got after she died. She promised! And as you know, I've spent the last months searching for that darn cherrywood box, and it isn't here. Or maybe it is, but I can't find it. Would you please help me?"

I stood up under the overcast sky.

"I know Hightower basically stole you, dear Hickory Hills, but I also know the money Nana Dale kept referring to wasn't simply the property and the house. It had to be something else. I was with her three days before she died, and she knew me. She still believed in our plan. She did not wither up, lose her mind, and give all her money away to some foulmouthed contractor."

Once again, I recalled the end of my last conversation with Nana Dale in early December. I'd brought us lunch from Henri's Bakery, a mainstay in Buckhead for almost a hundred years, splitting a chicken salad sandwich with her. She'd only nibbled at her food as I babbled excitedly about wedding plans and having the PATH certificate. "It's happening, Nana! It really is going to happen. I'm going to turn Hickory Hills into that healing-horse hotel with my husband!" I'd emphasized all the *H*s.

She smiled at me, reached over, and squeezed my hand. "I'm so proud of you, my dear. You'll never know how proud. How much you mean to me."

I gave her a spontaneous hug, and then she held me by my shoulders, looked me in the eyes, and said, "Promise me you'll keep the house, Allie. The property. If anything happens to me."

I rolled my eyes and laughed. "Of course I will, Nana. Didn't you just hear what I said?" Then I sobered. Her short-term memory wasn't great. So I repeated, "You know that. We've planned it for fifteen years. Anyway, we're almost ready to open, and you'll be right here beside me to cut the ribbon."

She'd looked off as if she hadn't really heard me and then repeated, "Don't give up on your dream, Allie, if anything happens to me."

"Oh wow," I said out loud to the old house. "She was trying to tell me that day that something had gone wrong. And I refused to see it."

I turned to face the house itself, studying the cherry tree in full bloom by the French doors.

"So tell me . . . what did she do with it?"

The old house kept totally silent, and I thought of an Amy Grant song from decades ago that my mother would listen to, "If These Walls Could Speak." I'd always liked the song with its haunting melody. Now I called out, "Speak!"

I guess if I had been in a better place inside my soul when I cried out to the sky, it would have been a prayer, but it wasn't a prayer: it was a dare or a threat, begging an old mansion to open its mouth and share its secret.

10

Dale

September 1939

Summer ended, Dale's cast came off, and she began riding Krystal again. And an ever-exuberant Tommy proposed, "Let's us both qualify for the Maclay this year."

"What's that?" Dale asked.

"You don't know about the Maclay Finals? Why, it's the very first big equitation competition for young riders in America. Mr. Maclay started funding it back in '33." Tommy glanced over at Dale, who was trying not to look too interested. "You do know who he is, don't you?"

She shrugged.

"He was the president of the American Horse Show Association. He created the award to inspire young riders like us to develop our horsemanship skills. You have to be a fine rider, but you also have to show respect and compassion for your horse. It'll be a great stepping-stone to the Olympics."

At Dale's nod, Tommy continued, "The first Maclay class was held in 1933 and sponsored by the ASPCA." He glanced at her again. "The American Society—"

107

"For the Prevention of Cruelty to Animals. Yes, of course. I *do* know what that is!" She flashed a frown his way.

"The first winner was a girl, but the others have all been guys." Dale just rolled her eyes at Tommy.

He paid no attention. "Oh, DB. It'll be swell. You should enter too. We'll be competing with the best riders in America and Canada too. You have to earn enough points to be invited to the finals, which are held at the National Horse Show."

The National Horse Show! That piqued her interest.

"How do you earn the points?"

"You enter the special Maclay class offered at horse shows all over the country. First place gets five points, second place gets three points. Stuff like that. Then you add up your points from those classes for the whole year, and if you get fifty points, you have a good chance of being invited to the finals. Of course, we'll have to attend a lot of shows, but I'm going to do it." He bumped her shoulder good-naturedly with his fist. "You should too."

Dale had absolutely no doubt that he would. Money grew on trees for Tommy Ridley. Nothing was going to stop him from qualifying and then taking Infinity to the Maclay Finals. But even if she managed to qualify, Dale wondered if she'd have the money to travel to New York. Butler Lumber Company had recovered from the Depression, but not as quickly as her father had hoped. Her mother still believed that money grew on trees for the Butlers, but the ledgers her father showed Dale indicated that perhaps the bough was breaking. Again.

***

Germany Invades Poland!

Dale read the headline before school.

Her mother didn't believe in thinking about negative things like war, but Dale had learned long ago to read the truth in her father's eyes.

"Did you hear, Tommy? Germany has invaded Poland."

"Yep. I told you those Nazis were no good."

"My father says it's going to be another world war."

"I don't know about that, but I do know they've canceled the Olympics. So that settles that." His face looked stormy, but then he smiled. "Now I don't have to enlist in the cavalry quite yet."

Dale didn't find the remark amusing. "Will our fathers have to go to war?"

"No, DB. You've seen the papers. America's not involved."

"Not yet. But it could happen, couldn't it?" When Tommy just shrugged, she pushed on. "Are you afraid? Will you have to go to war?"

"War? Nah. I'm barely sixteen. This'll be over soon. And it's on the other side of the ocean."

"But so was the last war, and Americans had to go."

"Don't worry about war, DB. Anyway, if I did sign up, one thing's for sure: I'd join the cavalry."

Of course you would.

He pulled her close. "This year, we're not going to worry about a war on the other side of the Atlantic. You and I are going to enter every single Maclay class on the East Coast, and then we'll head to the finals together, okay?"

"Okay," she choked out, unable to concentrate on anything except the warm feel of him so close and that look in his eyes.

———

Somehow, her father came up with enough money so that Dale could compete with Tommy in shows on the East Coast all throughout the 1939–1940 riding circuit, each time entering not only the hunter division classes, but also the Maclay class that she hoped would get both her and Tommy invited to the finals. But it was during those months that Dale recognized a change in Tommy.

He still slung his arm over her shoulder, tweaked her nose, and called her DB, but he treated her like his baby sister. In the afternoons and evenings when showing was done, he went off to smoke cigarettes with Jillian Brownlee and Annabeth Whitmore, two of the best and prettiest riders in the hunt seat division.

From the wealthiest families too, Dale fumed.

Once again, jealousy snaked up to Dale and wrapped its slimy body around her. She lived it out through anger, snide comments, and a raw determination to win. Tommy never seemed to notice. Once, she caught him kissing Jillian behind the stables after a show in North Carolina. She walked up to them, enjoying their embarrassment, and said to Tommy, "I thought we were going somewhere tonight." He blushed, shrugged, stuffed his hands in his pockets, and said, "Oh yeah. I forgot." He didn't leave Jillian, but Dale had the satisfaction of seeing true regret in his eyes.

Dale all but despised her body. Why wouldn't it develop a little more quickly? She still looked like a preteen girl when she'd just turned fifteen. She imagined attending the gala after the National Horse Show the next fall. When the other girls slinked by in their long gowns, looking sultry and sexy like Bette Davis and Greta Garbo, she'd look flat chested and childish.

Perhaps if she could win several of the Maclay classes, Tommy would be jealous of her. She wanted him to be jealous; she wanted him to notice her in a different way, and if it couldn't be in a long black gown with plenty of cleavage, she'd do it on a horse.

She trained relentlessly on Krystal, the terms for the jumps becoming engraved in her mind—the oxers, the in-and-out combination, the hogsback, the brush fence and coop and brick wall and triple bars. She worked out every afternoon with Mr. Jorgensen, flipping her stirrup leathers up over the saddle and squeezing her thighs into her hunt seat saddle as she took Krystal over the eight-fence course her trainer created. She limped through school in the days after, her legs sore but her determination strong. The pain would pay off.

Occasionally, she'd stare at the wooden plaque on her shelf and think about Essie, but she rode Krystal with pizzazz—a word that Mr. Jorgensen used. *"You've got pizzazz, my leetle wonder,"* he'd say, his accent strong and his tone affectionate.

She no longer prayed to find her filly. She didn't pray at all. Instead, she repeated a daily mantra: *Make Tommy notice me.*

Every weekend, Dale, Tommy, Husy, and Mr. Jorgensen, along with her mother and Tommy's mother, headed to a horse show, the sleek black truck pulling the two-horse trailer, the rumps of the two horses, one bay and one flea-bitten gray, peeking from the back, with an updated plaque reading *Krystal CAUTION Infinity.*

In Wilmington, Virginia, after a grueling day of showing in which Dale had only won a few third-place ribbons, Tommy asked, "Wanna come out with me tonight, DB? A few of us are going to hang out together."

Reluctantly, Dale went along the first time Tommy invited her. But watching him flirt with Jillian or Annabeth while he smoked a cigarette only tied her stomach in more knots than when she rode in the Maclay classes. After that first evening, she stayed in her hotel room, doing algebra or studying French, feeling miserable.

In Richmond, Virginia, Tommy showed in both the hunter and jumper divisions. She watched him from the sidelines, careening over four-feet-six-inch–high jumps in the stadium jumpers Grand Prix class. She counted the strides. Tommy took the turn too quickly, and Infinity missed his lead change. When the gelding went into the intimidating oxer at an odd angle, jumping from way too close, his front hooves nicked the rails as he rose off the ground, and Tommy lost his balance. Dale watched almost in slow motion: Tommy's legs coming out of the stirrups, the way he was clamping his thighs tightly and throwing his arms forward so as not to yank on Infinity's mouth with his awkward position. Infinity stumbled on the landing, went down to his knees, and Tommy somersaulted over the horse's head.

For a moment, silence. *"Get up, you crazy cowboy!"* she yelled in her mind.

Then horse and rider struggled to their feet, and Dale let out the breath she'd been holding. When he exited the ring, limping slightly, leading Infinity by the reins, he smiled at her, that same crooked smile, those same twinkling eyes.

She was there to challenge him. "You're crazy! You act like a daredevil cowboy instead of an equestrian! You'll get yourself killed one of these days, Tommy. Why are you so bent on riding in both the hunter and jumper circuits?"

"Life's an adventure. I'd rather go out with a flash than sit around and do equitation in a ring. We can jump the moon, Infinity and me. And we're fine. Don't worry so! Just like today, I'll always meet you on the other side."

He repeated that phrase each time they showed, one or the other poised outside the show-ring, waiting for the other to complete the course.

Tommy had broken his thumb in the fall, although he didn't let on. When Dale won the Maclay class later that day, and Tommy came in third, he said, "You're a wonder, DB." The admiration in his eyes carried her through the next weeks even when she learned of his injury. She reminded herself that she wasn't competing against Tommy to be the best rider. She was simply competing for his love.

Dale never said it, but in her heart, she begged him, *"I know you're not afraid of anything. But I'm afraid for you. Please be careful. Please don't get hurt again."*

Tommy won every other Maclay class they entered that season, with Dale often taking second or third. When Tommy received a letter with the ASPCA stamp on the envelope, they did what they'd agreed upon.

He took her on the trail behind the ring, and they sat on the Meteor, beside where Mr. Jinx had been buried. He handed Dale the envelope. "Well, go ahead, open it for me." She ripped it open, and he grinned, looking over at her. "Read it," he said, eyes dancing.

There inside was his invitation. "'Congratulations, Mr. Ridley. You've qualified for the Finals of the ASPCA Alfred B. Maclay Trophy. . . .'"

Without thinking, Dale threw her arms around him, hugging him tightly. "That's swell. That's really, really swell." She refused to be jealous or disappointed. It was indeed swell. "Congratulations!" she said with every bit of sincerity she could muster. She was proud of him.

"You'll come to the finals, won't you? You'll cheer me on, right?"

"Of course I'll be there."

Tommy let out a low chuckle. "You better be there. Look at this!" He dangled a second envelope before her, bringing it from behind his back and dropping it in Dale's hard hat.

"What is it?"

"This, my dear Deebs, is an envelope that I just snagged from Husy, addressed to Miss Barbara Dale Butler."

She gasped, opened the envelope, and saw the same invitation but imprinted with her name. "I qualified too?"

"Of course you did." He lifted her off the rock and swung her around. When he set her down, he kept his arms around her. His hand stroked her hair, her face buried in his chest. She felt his lips press against her hair, his hand wipe away her bangs. "I'm proud of you. Really proud."

She wished in that moment that he'd never let her go.

— ♘ —

November 1940

The National Horse Show for the 1939–1940 season took place amid growing whispers of war. None of the European or Canadian teams participated. Only teams from the United States, Chile, and Mexico were present. But no one seemed to notice amid the glamour.

The hype in New York belied any fear, with twelve thousand people attending the fanfare in Madison Square Garden. For Dale, the whole week passed in a haze of opulence. It seemed to her that all of New York society turned out. The men wore tuxes and top hats, and the women . . . Dale had attended lavish society events in

Atlanta, but this! Women in long gowns of every color, from slinky to silk to stiff brocaded dresses in deep purples and bright pinks. They wore mink coats or other furs draped over their shoulders, with elaborate corsages pinned to their gowns.

Dale spied plenty of pearls, but even more diamonds, all kinds of jewelry embedded with those glittering stones that women wore around their wrists, pinned onto mink coats, and even on their shoe buckles.

On the first evening, Mama whispered, "I've died and gone to heaven!" and Dale felt proud to have offered this luxury to her mother. She had no idea how her father was paying for this week-long extravaganza, but she was determined to enjoy it.

On the first night, the 16th Infantry Regimental Band led the parade into the arena at Madison Square Garden, followed by Squadron A and the international military teams. Army officers competed in the low-jumping contest with the crowd oohing and aahing as the horse and rider raced around the arena over strange jumps—leaping over a cannon-like structure and big metal tubes. Then the famous Black Horse Battery from Fort Myer, Virginia, performed a dazzling show.

Dale watched, mesmerized as the twenty-four black steeds presented what the overenthusiastic announcer hailed as "a spectacular series of maneuvers that call for split-second timing and daring horsemanship." Harnessed horses pulled huge cannons, six horses per cannon, two abreast, and she wondered how they didn't crash into one another.

"A truly remarkable exhibition as the caissons go rolling along," shouted the announcer over the blaring military music as the horses, riders, and cannons circled the arena.

"That's Mrs. Cornelius Vanderbilt making her appearance up there in the Paul Moore Box," Mama said, consulting her program.

Important army officials, as well as foreign diplomats and civic officials, filled the boxes at the Garden throughout the week, along with the upper crust of American society. Dale soaked it up. Glamorous parties every night at places she'd only dreamed of visiting:

the Empire Room at the Waldorf Astoria, the Persian Room at the Plaza.

The principal society affair of the week was the Horse Show Ball on Tuesday night, held in the Grand Ballroom at the Waldorf Astoria after the evening performance of military officers and high jumping.

"Darling, it's the top social event in all of New York, the formal opening of the society season for fall 1940," her mother said as she helped Dale dress.

Dale didn't care much for the nomenclature, but she was pleased to meet handsome young men decked out in tuxes, all of them eager to be introduced to the society equestrians, as they were called. Thanks to her mother, Dale had arrived in New York with an extravagant wardrobe of dresses, and Dale carefully stuffed her bra, satisfied with the resulting cleavage on her low-cut cobalt blue gown. She especially enjoyed the attention of Herman Battison at Tuesday night's ball. She'd learned that Herman was from Pennsylvania, and he too was a competitor in the Maclay Finals to be held on Thursday.

"So you're a Southern gal," he said, leading Dale by the hand through the ballroom as if he did this every day of his life.

"Yes, a Georgia peach, through and through."

"Well, I've heard Georgia grows some mighty fine riders. Have you ridden at all with Tommy Ridley? I hear he's the one to beat this year."

Dale gave a clipped chuckle. "Oh, sure, Tommy boards his horses at my barn. He's talented, that's for sure." She hoped she'd sounded nonchalant, covering up the confusing mixture of pride, jealousy, and something else fluttering way down inside.

Herman seemed duly impressed. "Would you introduce me to him?"

"To Tommy? Sure!"

Now it was Dale's turn to take Herman's hand and lead him through the array of colorful people. She'd seen Tommy over at the punch table talking with some of the young society equestrians.

"Hey there, Tommy," she said, her voice casual and uninterested. "Herman here wants to meet one of his fiercest competitors."

Tommy flashed her a question, recovered, and held out his hand. "Nice to meet you, Herman. I've seen your scores from the Pennsylvania and New York shows. Very impressive. And your gelding, he's quite talented."

She let the two boys chat while she made small talk—at least she tried, it was never her forte—with two girls from Virginia whom she'd met at some shows in the spring.

Herman danced with her three times, but Dale's delight was watching from over his shoulder as Tommy followed her every move. She lifted her white-gloved hand off Herman's shoulder and waved to Tommy. Even from a distance, she could see the blush crawl across his cheeks.

Later, Tommy made his way over to her, holding a glass of punch. "Well, who is this young beauty?" he cooed in a voice she'd heard him use with Jillian and Annabeth. "I don't believe I know you!"

Dale gave her best imitation at a trilling laugh, batted her eyes, and bent down briefly, hoping the cleavage showed. She stood back up, stuck out her hand and said, "Miss Barbara Dale Butler, from Hickory Hills in Atlanta, Georgia. And to whom do I owe this pleasure?"

Tommy and Dale bantered back and forth, oblivious to others in the crowded ballroom, his eyes taking her in, it seemed, for the very first time. Maybe at last Tommy saw her as more than a riding buddy, a companion, another equestrian. He'd noticed her as a girl. That in itself was worth more than ten trips to Madison Square Garden and the National Horse Show. When the band started playing a swing song, Tommy whisked her onto the dance floor, and Dale was sure that she, like her mother, had died and gone to heaven.

The Maclay Finals was but one of dozens of events at the National Horse Show, but when Dale brought Krystal into the arena, she felt like a princess. Mr. Maclay himself sat in box number seventeen, watching every performance of the young competitors. He shared his booth with people with last names of Pulitzer, Morgan, Rockefeller, and Vanderbilt.

"It's an amalgam of New York's elite and top civil servants and the highest military," her mother had whispered on the first evening. "I'm so thrilled that we're here, Barbara Dale!"

Dale had watched the other young riders' performances with admiration. Of the fifty-six competitors for the Maclay, many had had brilliant rounds.

She entered the arena, trotted forward on Krystal, pulled her mare to a halt, and nodded to the judges sitting in the first row at the east end of the arena. Then she moved Krystal into a hand gallop, circled once, and headed to the first fence, a wide brush. "Introducing Miss Barbara Dale Butler from Atlanta, Georgia, riding Krystal Klear. Miss Butler qualified for the Maclay with a score of . . ."

In a blur, they cantered from jump to jump, Krystal's ears pricking forward and then flattening against her mane as dozens of light bulbs flashed. Dale leaned forward over Krystal's neck, reins taut, her fingers touching the tight little black braids in Krystal's mane, the ones she'd braided herself at six that morning. She indeed felt herself flying, propelled into another world, hearing the mare's hoofbeats in the sand, feeling the heat of Krystal's neck as Dale's body leaned forward over each jump. And then the applause as she finished the course.

Tommy was waiting for her as she left the gate, all smiles, his dimples showing. "Excellent! Good job, DB." He reached up and squeezed her gloved hand. "You gave the performance I have to beat."

After two rounds of jumping, the twenty riders with the combined best scores were called back into the arena all together to be judged at the walk, trot, canter, and hand gallop. The horses spread out around the huge arena, dark bays and liver chestnuts and flea-bitten and dappled grays, several pitch-black geldings, a sorrel, a true chestnut. Beautiful horses with beautiful riders. She caught sight of Tommy across the arena on Infinity, and for one brief moment when they were asked to show at a hand gallop, Dale pulled up beside them. Once again, she was twelve, riding in her first couples class at Chastain Park in Atlanta. She glanced over at Tommy, whose deep concentration broke into a grin. Then the moment passed.

The twenty horses and riders lined up side by side in the arena as the announcer blasted in the microphone, "Ladies and Gentlemen, let's have another round of applause for these splendid young equestrians!" More bulbs flashed, along with applause and cheering—all polite, of course, as bejeweled women waved their white-gloved hands while they snuggled in their mink coats. "The National Horsemanship Championship for the ASPCA Alfred B. Maclay Trophy was initiated in 1933 by our own Mr. Alfred B. Maclay." Mr. Maclay had left his box and now stood beside the contestants in the arena. He stepped forward, waving to the crowd as they applauded.

The announcer continued, "As you have just witnessed this evening, these talented young contenders are judged on their seat and control of their mounts both on the flat and over a course of fences. The horsemanship championship is one of the most prestigious competitions for junior riders in the United States. You can be sure that these fine young riders will go on to represent our country in many international events."

Dale found herself in happy tears when the announcer called Tommy's name as champion. Herman took the reserve trophy, and Dale happily received a fifth-place ribbon.

After they had dismounted, Dale hurried over to Tommy. "You did it! I knew you would!" she said, giving Tommy a kiss on the cheek. He picked her up, swung her around, and left his hands around her tiny waist, bringing his forehead to touch hers, so close he could have kissed her lips.

But he didn't. He dropped his hands, tweaked her nose, and said, "Thanks, DB! You did swell too."

January 1941

Dale fingered the engraved silver urn: *Maclay Champion, National Horse Show, 1940, Thomas Ridley*. They were once again seated on two bales of hay outside Krystal's stall, Tommy treating her as he always had, the marvelous moment she'd swung in his arms seemingly completely forgotten by him.

He'd gotten plenty of attention for the Maclay win, and she was concerned. She'd never thought of Tommy as arrogant, but still.

"You deserve every accolade, Tommy," she admitted, turning the heavy trophy around. She set it down and thought to herself, *What a paradox. A shining silver urn sitting on a bale of hay. But both are necessary to make a champion.*

Out loud, she said, "And I'm proud of you. I am. But please, please don't let it go to your head. Don't change from the happy-go-lucky boy I know."

"Hey, DB, don't worry." This time when he said her nickname, she wanted to hear an underlying message of love. But she didn't.

Mama prattled on and on about New York, and Daddy studied the financial situation, fabricating designs for strange boxes that he hoped could be used to ship materials to Europe if America decided to join the war effort.

But Dale clutched her perpetually nervous stomach. One day, unable to hide the emotions from Husy, she admitted, "You've always warned me about jealousy, and I've tried to keep it at bay. But this feels even worse than jealousy. It's not what I have or what I don't have. It's not about winning classes and receiving awards, it's not the trophy, it's not even the boy." Here she glanced at Husy, who stood leaning on the split-rail fence, her blue-gray eyes compassionate even as her bent-over body looked as if someday soon she'd bend all the way to the ground and never get back up.

"It's the space it takes up in my mind, the way I can't get away from it. I don't even know what to call 'it.' Obsession? I've never wanted to admit it, Husy, but maybe it's true; maybe I'm obsessed."

She shifted her gaze to her paddock boots and added in a tiny voice, "With Tommy."

Husy was never quick with her replies, but eventually, she asked, "Have you ever considered, Barbara Dale, what would be enough? You say it's not being a champion or even having that boy's love. What is it you want?"

Brow furrowed and a frown on her face, Dale considered the question. "I don't know. I used to think it would be enough if I could find Essie again. I prayed and prayed about it, Husy, like you said. That didn't happen. Now I think it would be enough to know Tommy loved me. Really loved me." She peeked up at Husy. "But then I'd want to be his fiancée and his wife and then I'd want to be champions together and then . . ." Dale let out a very unfeminine sigh. "It will never be enough, will it?"

Husy closed her eyes. Seconds ticked by, then a minute—plenty of time for Dale to think about what she had just admitted. Husy always said she needed time to mull things over before she made a decision. Now she was offering Dale the same gift.

"It will never be enough, Dale, until you decide that you already have it all. You settle in your mind a grateful heart, a content spirit, and everything else will be gravy, girl."

11

Allie

Saturday, March 7

It rained all Saturday, which to me felt like showers of blessing. With this rain, Barnell could not put his backhoe to work. So the riding ring sat empty of all but the backhoe, with the woods just beginning to feel like spring.

And I sat on the floor in the Pink Room, flipping through old photo albums with my ever-present question gnawing a hole in my heart. So intent was I on my task that I didn't hear my mother come into the room until she said, "Well, there you are! I've texted you about ten times to tell you I'd help you out today."

I'd completely forgotten Mom's offer. Had I even agreed? I knew I didn't want her here with me. Her relationship with Nana Dale was complicated and, as far as I could tell, Mom wouldn't shed one tear when a gang of destroyers imploded Hickory Hills. It didn't make sense to me. Nana Dale was as hard as nails, but Mom was soft, kind, and hypersensitive. Nana Dale had often said, "*Your mother is much like my mother. She loved pretty things and pretty people and having lots of money. She wasn't nearly as fond of hard work."*

I had found that remark rather harsh. My mother had dark brown hair, wavy like Nana Dale's, though Mom wore hers thick and long. She was much taller and more well-endowed, and her brown eyes were exempt of mischief. She often said that she couldn't keep up with Nana Dale, but she certainly worked hard in other ways.

I went over to her and gave a quick hug. "Hey, thanks for coming. Sorry. I had my notifications turned off." I glanced at my phone. Yep. She'd sent ten text messages while I screamed out my angst to an inanimate structure.

"You sure haven't gotten very far in packing. What can I do?"

Mom's voice held a conciliatory tone. We didn't exactly have the conflict that Mom and Nana Dale had shared, but neither was she my soul mate.

Still, I felt overwhelmed. I shrugged. "I don't even know where to start. Everything in this room reminds me of her."

She reached out and touched my arm. "I know, Allie. You don't have to put yourself through this. You've had enough disappointment. I can go through all this with the estate planners."

"But I want to keep things, Mom!"

"Yes, of course." Her tone sharpened, a defensive edge creeping in.

I should have simply asked her to pack up another room. Instead, I picked up the framed photo of Nana Dale and Tommy riding in the couples class and asked, "Whatever happened to Tommy?"

She frowned, annoyance flickering on her brow. Then she pulled herself in, and her face went blank. "Oh, that's such a sad story. If your grandmother didn't tell you, it's because it's not worth repeating."

"How can you say that?" I set the photo down, grabbed the ancient photo album, and let the pages fall open, leafing through it until I jammed my finger at a photo of Nana Dale and Tommy.

"This isn't worth repeating? They loved each other! Even I can read it in their eyes. You must know something! Have you ever looked at these albums?"

Mom's arms were crossed, and she stood like a statue. "Of course I've seen them." Now her voice was ice. She didn't come and sit beside me, and her eyes wandered off like she was determined to end this conversation.

"Well, you haven't really looked at them," I accused. "Or maybe you've looked, but you haven't seen what was in your mother's eyes."

I uncrossed her arms and forced the opened album into them, jabbing at a photo once again. "Look! They're in love, and I want to know what happened."

Mother's eyes turned frosty. "Allie, for heaven's sake. They were just kids! He was your grandmother's first love, but young love never lasts."

But that wasn't quite right, was it? Some young loves lasted. I felt sure theirs would have lasted if only . . . if only what?

"But, Mom, do you know what happened? Did Tommy move away? Did he die young?"

"What happened? That kid got sick." She continued, her voice still hard as packed snow. "He got sick and then he died and your dear grandmother, she never talked about him to me except when she'd had too much to drink—which didn't happen all that often. At least not in my presence." Now she was glaring at me.

"So maybe he was the love of her life," Mom continued. "I've always suspected a lurid affair, but I have no proof. I do know that she never acted madly in love with your grandfather. You didn't see that because he passed away before you were born. By the time she met Poppa Dan, she was already married to the horses." Mom gave a dry chuckle. "Your grandmother was a polygamist."

"I find your remarks extremely distasteful."

"Of course you do. But you asked. The way I've always imagined it was that, after Tommy died, she lost herself up in that riding ring. When she married your grandfather and I was born, she dragged me around up there too until I couldn't stand it anymore.

"So, yes, Tommy died, okay? That's all I know."

I could barely take in my mother's anger, unable to digest her words. *Lurid affair, married to horses, polygamist.*

When I remained silent, she added, "Allie, I'm sorry to talk like that. I don't want to say anything that might cause Nana Dale to fall off the pedestal you've constructed for her."

I bristled, could almost feel hair standing up on the back of my neck like a rabid dog's. "I didn't put her on a pedestal," I seethed before Mom's words could even sink in. Then, when they did, I felt a type of punch to the gut or slap in the face or whatever happened when the truth was laid out before you clear and simple.

I had. Of course I had. Nana Dale still rested safely on the pedestal I'd made for her. It wasn't ivory white, though. It was made of bales of hay and horse bones and tough, tough love.

I wondered if bitterness had strangled Nana Dale. From all appearances, it was still strangling my mother. She had no sympathy for young love destroyed by young death. I took the photo album from Mom, unable to meet her eyes. "Maybe you could box up the kitchen stuff. That would be a good start."

Mom sighed, touched my shoulder, and said, "Yes, good idea," her voice tight. "I'm happy to do that." She turned and left the room, hurrying down the carpeted steps.

I didn't have the strength to stop her.

I tried to imagine how Nana Dale had felt when Tommy got sick, but all I could picture was the stricken look on her face when she said, *"I'm remembering a friend of mine, Tommy . . . a show jumper. . . . Then he got real sick. The doctor told him he'd never ride again. . . . Tommy had to start over, and his body didn't work like it used to . . . until he learned how to make his limitations work for him."*

Whatever his illness or handicap, my grandmother had made it sound like he recovered. At least it didn't sound like a death sentence, the end of all their dreams. I searched my memory to find a snippet of what had happened next. I doubted that Tommy ever made it to the Olympics. They were canceled, for heaven's sake, in both 1940 and 1944, thanks to Adolf Hitler and Hideki Tojo and World War II.

But I couldn't imagine Tommy sitting in bed while the world exploded around him. He didn't seem like the type of person to cave into self-pity. But then, what did I know of Tommy except for a few photos, several whispered stories, and the look in Nana Dale's eyes?

I stood in the Pink Room holding an old album with a photo of a long-lost love.

I spent the rest of that rainy Saturday closed up in Nana Dale's childhood bedroom, opening album after album. But I found nothing more about Tommy. The photos of him and Nana Dale riding in couples classes or holding up their ribbons and trophies stopped abruptly in 1940. I understood that there was a war, and that we were involved, but I found it odd that Nana Dale had been meticulous about recording so many other events up until 1940, and then almost a decade slid by before her albums started back up in 1948 with photos of her showing Essie and eventually of her wedding to Poppa Dan.

She looked tiny beside my grandfather, ten years her senior, a war hero, six feet tall, thick mustache, the traces of a smile turning up his lips. When I peered into those photos, I saw duty on Nana Dale's face. No twinkle in her eyes, no recognition of a soul mate. She looked at my grandfather with respect and admiration but not love.

At least it appeared that way. But perhaps I was simply being a die-hard romantic.

I couldn't imagine that Tommy had still been alive at the time of the wedding. Mom seemed convinced he'd died before then. I placed the albums back on the shelves and opened the cedar chest, lifting out the pale yellow cashmere sweater set. Surely, I could appease my mother and get past our stilted conversation if I offered her some of Nana Dale's cashmere. She would not be interested in the riding coats, the jodhpurs, the sleeveless cotton shirts with the separate white collars that looked like something a priest might wear. Each had my grandmother's monogram in fancy embroidery across the front and her name printed on little cotton tabs sewn into the back of the shirt.

But the cashmere! I reached into the chest and began unfolding the sweaters and the coats, laying them across the frilly white bedspread. I threw open the windows, fresh air mingling with the smell of cedar. The canopy, made of thin white fabric, swelled as the wind whipped through the room.

I could hear Mom sorting pots and pans in the kitchen. I gathered up half a dozen cashmere sweaters and headed downstairs. Mom had three cardboard boxes sitting on the kitchen counter, and she was wrapping Nana Dale's china in newspaper and placing it in a box. She glanced at me and said, "I thought you'd want to keep this set."

I nodded. "Thanks." I'd always loved her fine-bone Haviland Limoges china, sparkling white with a gold rim, simple and elegant.

I held out the sweaters like a peace offering. "And I thought you might want to keep these." A flicker of a grin caught at the corners of my lips, and I watched Mom's eyes soften.

"Oh yes, Nana Dale's cashmere. Actually . . ." She took one sweater and looked at the tag inside. "This was her mother's." Indeed, the little white rectangular tag sewn inside was printed with *Eleanor Butler*. "Well, yes, of course we'll keep all these, sweetie. I remember your great-grandmother Eleanor loved to say 'Cashmere is always in style.'" Mom's face contorted for a moment. "Or perhaps I just remember my mother telling that story. Anyway, it's in amazingly good condition."

She reached over and tucked a loose strand of my palomino mane behind an ear. "I know this is hard on you. I wish you'd let your father and me deal with the whole thing."

"Thanks. But Dad won't be home from California till Tuesday, and then y'all leave on the cruise in a week. And Cécile, the young woman in charge of the estate sale, is coming over on Monday. Just give me a few more days to look through—"

"Allie, please tell me you're not still hoping to find a stash of money that Nana Dale has squirreled away under a mattress or hidden in a trapdoor."

"Of course not," I lied. "But surely the cherrywood box is here somewhere." I couldn't meet her eyes. "I know you can't really understand why I'm insisting, Mom. Can you just accept that it's my way of grieving a lost dream?"

Her face softening, she set the cashmere sweaters on the kitchen table, and her arms came around me. "Yes," she whispered. "I'll leave you to it for right now. I just wanted to help before we left. I hate that we'll be gone for the estate sale and . . . and everything else. But then again, maybe we won't." She furrowed her brow. "Evidently a cruise ship is being detained at sea because of that virus that's in the news. I certainly don't want to be stuck out in the middle of the Atlantic for who knows how long."

Glancing at the sweaters on the table, she added, "You can put those back in the cedar chest. I know we'll be keeping that."

Heavyhearted, I watched my mother leave. I spent the rest of the afternoon sifting through kitchen gadgets, some that dated back to at least the 1950s—an ancient rolling pin, a dented tin sifter, a set of avocado green plastic measuring cups, surely from the '70s; the Revere Ware that Nana Dale bought in the '80s; the Betty Crocker cookbook. Another kitchen drawer was stuffed with coupons and used birthday candles and recipes on stained and yellowing file cards.

I moved into the dining room, where I hefted Nana Dale's silver chest onto the antique cherry dining room table that my great-great-grandfather had made in 1918.

"You'll be inheriting this silver chest, Allie," Nana Dale had said just six months ago. *"Keeps all the cutlery from tarnishing and saves you an armload of work polishing."* Then she'd looked up over her wire-rimmed reading glasses. She was perched on her four-poster spindle bed in the Green Room, the bedroom she'd shared with Poppa Dan. A wicker tray table with a round space for her juice glass sat on the bed, an open rectangle on its left-hand side for

the newspaper. Nana Dale still read a hard copy of the *AJC* every morning as she ate scrambled eggs with toast and butter and home-made jelly.

"You do want my silver cutlery, don't you? So many brides now aren't interested. But you are, aren't you?"

I was. *We* were, because Austin appreciated tradition as much as I did. I'd looked forward to using her silver alongside her Limoges china and the Waterford crystal that we'd registered for at a beautiful new bridal store.

Stop it! I reprimanded myself. Don't think about the embarrassment of closing the bridal registry and canceling the wedding invitations, and don't you dare think about how you should be walking down the aisle of the church in your strapless A-line wedding gown with Nana Dale's lace veil billowing out behind next Saturday. Instead, I would stand in the riding ring and watch Barnell dig up another layer of Hickory Hills. What awful i rony!

I shook myself back to the present. I fingered the mahogany box, no thicker than my laptop, and lifted the little gold handle to reveal my grandmother's sterling silver cutlery set, nestled in the cobalt blue lining, the kind that, as Nana Dale had told me repeatedly, prevented silver from tarnishing.

At first when I had received Nana Dale's letter from Mr. Lor-rider, I'd wondered if my grandmother had gotten confused, that the little wooden box she wanted me to find was this one and that she'd thought I could sell the silver cutlery for a huge amount of money. But the silver chest, though it could have been called a small wooden box, was made of mahogany and store-bought with no hearts or horseshoes carved into it. Twelve knives fit snugly into the velvet slits on the inside of the cover. The other cutlery was stacked in divided rows in the bottom half.

I pulled open the second drawer, where I knew Nana Dale kept the serving pieces—slotted spoons and a beautiful pie server and a cake cutter with its dozen silver prongs and delicate handle. I remembered each piece being used for birthdays and Christmas and Thanksgiving celebrations. And I remembered the brass key that was staring up at me from between the silver salad tongs.

"Key's for the bottom doors in the hutch, where I store the bigger pieces of silver I don't leave out to the mercy of the elements," Nana Dale had told me more than once.

The antique hutch, crafted by my great-great grandfather at the same time as the table, sat against the wall and held a striking display of silver. I lifted a pitcher, catching my reflection in the sparkling silver. Many pieces, like this one, were engraved either with Nana Dale's maiden name monogram, *BDB*, Barbara Dale Butler, or her married monogram, *BBT*, Barbara Butler-Taylor, or the title and date of one of her many horsemanship victories, ancient trophies from the '30s, '40s, and '50s, Nana Dale's heyday as an equestrian.

I took the brass key from the silver chest and opened the bottom door of the hutch, which concealed the larger pieces of silver, all shrouded in cloth—the cotton flannel that Nana Dale also reminded me would keep silver from tarnishing. One by one, I brought them out, unwrapping the cloth and placing each on the dining room table beside the silver chest. Two chafing dishes, one round with a domed top and the other rectangular, more trays and bowls. In the back left corner of the cabinet, I pulled out a particularly heavy piece. As the cloth fell away, I gave a little gasp to see an ornate silver urn, big enough to place a wine bottle in or perhaps a beautiful arrangement of flowers.

In fact, there *was* something inside the urn, wrapped in brittle newspaper. I lifted it out and removed the paper from around a glass Mason jar. It looked like the jar had been used as a candle. The last bit of white wax covered the bottom of the jar with the stub of the wick sticking up. Why in the world would my grandmother have stored an ugly Mason-jar candle in with her fine silver?

I had no idea.

Then I gasped as I peered at the engraving on the urn: *Maclay Champion, National Horse Show, 1940, Thomas Ridley.*

"Tommy!" I said out loud, as if I had finally reconnected with a childhood friend on Facebook. Then immediately, I wondered, *Nana Dale, why would you have kept Tommy's trophy? And basically hidden it away? Did his family give it to you after he died?*

When I carefully unfolded the brittle newspaper that had housed the Mason jar, I read the headline from the November 12, 1940, *New York Times*: *55th National Horse Show at Madison Square Garden Ends in a Blaze of Social Brilliance.*

12

Dale

Spring 1941

After he won the Maclay, Tommy was determined to succeed in stadium jumping events. In the spring of 1941, he entered a Grand Prix event in Wilmington, Virginia, with fences over five feet high.

Dale won champion in the junior hunt seat division, but even holding the silver platter with the tricolored blue, red, and yellow ribbon flowing from Krystal's bridle couldn't placate the way her gut twisted with worry.

"You're not ready for this, Tommy!" she begged before he entered the ring for the jump-off in the stadium jumping finals. "Infinity has never jumped that high! Please!"

"Aw, DB, life's an adventure. What? You think I'm going to bow out now?"

No, of course not. Tommy Ridley was the same overeager, multi-talented rider she'd fallen in love with five years earlier. Nothing would stop him, certainly not her feeble warning.

But she had walked the final course with him. The pièce de résistance was an enormous oxer, the first rails set at five feet one inch

131

high, followed by a gap of three feet, and then a second set of rails at five feet two.

When Tommy's name was called, he rode into the ring, calling over his shoulder to Dale, "Meet you on the other side, Deebs!"

Dale clutched the railing as she watched him canter to the first fence, a vertical set of yellow-and-white rails that were four and a half feet high. Horse and rider sailed over this as well as the next fence, an oxer at four feet nine inches high and six feet wide. The five-foot white wall—which looked like the entrance to a castle with its side spires—offered no real challenge. Dale let out a sigh of relief as they cleared what she felt to be the most challenging jump.

But then Tommy headed Infinity into the pièce de résistance, requiring a short turn and then straightening the gelding into the huge oxer. The courageous horse leaped into the air, front hooves catching the rail, which fell against the next railings, tripping Infinity, who went down, Tommy crashing beside him.

Like before.

Only this time, both horse and rider were badly injured. While Tommy was carted off in the ambulance, Dale watched the vet lead Infinity out of the ring, limping terribly. She silently prayed the gelding's leg wasn't broken.

"It hurts to breathe," Tommy complained when she visited him at the hospital later that day. The X-rays showed six broken ribs. He grimaced. "How's Finny?"

"The leg's not broken, thank the Good Lord." Dale couldn't hide the fury in her eyes. "He's got a ways to go to recover, though. Just like you."

"You warned me, didn't you, Deebs? Maybe I've lost my touch."

"You're a complete idiot, a crazy cowboy, but you certainly haven't lost your touch. You just tried to do something that you and Finny weren't quite ready for. You're always rushing ahead. That's just how you are."

Tommy shrugged. "Well, I'm paying for it now, I guess. Serves me right." Then he grinned.

"It's not funny, Tommy! Someday you're going to kill yourself and your horse. Can't you be satisfied with what you've achieved for a while?"

"It will never be enough, Dale, until you decide that you already have it all. You settle in your mind a grateful heart, a content spirit, and everything else will be gravy, girl," Husy's voice whispered in her mind.

Oh, Tommy, let what you've already got be enough for you too.

Six weeks later, Tommy could finally ride again, the ribs healed. After they put up the horses, Tommy asked, "Wanna come with us for a swim in the river tomorrow?"

"Not on your life, buddy. Go with your friends. I've got work."

"Aw, are you serious? Schoolwork?"

"Yes." The real reason was that she could not stand to see him flirting with other girls. "But after school gets out next week, I'll meet you up in the ring every afternoon, and we'll raise the bars three inches a day, until you and Finny sail over six feet."

"What about you?"

"Krystal and I will work toward four feet."

"It's a deal!"

Dale waited for Tommy to show up. In vain. All week long, she trudged to the barn alone, the bridle slung over her skinny shoulder and the saddle hitched above her joined hands. *Chicken,* she thought to herself when, in reality, she feared that Tommy had found something or someone much more interesting than a silly competition with her.

She'd just come in from the barn on Friday afternoon when her mother called out, "Come sit with me on the porch, Dale."

"What?" she sassed.

"Barbara Dale! What kind of tone is that to use with your mother?"

She shrugged, slumped on the loveseat, and glared at her mother. "Sorry, Mama. It's just Tommy. We had a fine competition going on this week. At least we were supposed to. But he hasn't shown up at all. The Maclay victory's gone to his head."

I'm in love with him, Mama, and I'm terrified that he doesn't care. But sometimes he truly seems to. He held me. And sometimes he calls me Deebs. And I can't say these things to you, to anyone.

Dale barely noticed her mother's frown. When she remained silent, Dale looked up and saw the stricken expression on her mother's face.

"What is it?"

"Tommy's mother called a little while ago." Mama scooted closer on the loveseat, and Dale's heart started hammering in her chest. She hadn't seen that look on her mother's face since the vet came all those years ago to put down Lady.

Mama cleared her throat and started again. "Mrs. Ridley said Tommy's been mighty sick. He went swimming in the Chattahoochee River last week."

"Yes, I know. He told me. He went with a few friends." *He invited me, but I didn't go. I was afraid there'd be other girls there too.* "So what?"

"He's contracted polio, Dale."

Dale frowned and drew her arms closer around her middle, making her face hard and batting her eyes to chase the tears away. She sat that way for a long time, mashing her lips together and swinging her legs. Finally, "Is he going to die, Mama?"

"No, sugarplum. They think he'll get better." She took a breath. "But he's got paralysis in his legs."

Dale jumped up, swiping at her eyes, and stomped off the porch, muttering, "Stupid, stupid boy!"

"Dale!" her mother called after her. "Dale! Of all the things to say . . ."

But she ran up the stairs to her room, slammed the door shut, and fell onto her bed, sobbing.

——— ♘ ———

"Three feet and eleven inches!" Dale proclaimed, sliding the wooden yardstick along the side of the stacked poles. "See if you can beat that, Tommy Ridley! Just see!" She said it to no one, except Krystal. He'd told her Krystal could jump, and they'd almost cleared four feet. But it didn't matter anymore because Tommy wasn't there to share in her victory.

Two weeks had crawled by, the thick humid air descending on her so that her wavy auburn hair clung to her forehead and neck when she removed the riding hat. Mosquitoes buzzed around the manure pile, and she wondered if they carried the polio disease just like the Chattahoochee River had. She swatted at them with a vengeance, and the fury kept her tears away.

Husy and Mr. Jeffrey followed her to the barn, tacked up Krystal for her, and watched her with Mr. Jorgensen. But inevitably, she'd quit her lesson after only fifteen or twenty minutes. "I'm sorry. I feel horrible." At times, she wondered if she were coming down with polio. Wasn't it contagious?

Husy smothered her in her sagging bosom. "It's okay to be upset, Dale. Just don't forget your prayers."

"What have prayers got to do with anything?" she snapped. "They haven't brought Essie back, have they?" She stomped behind the barn and trudged up the muddy hill to the riding ring, then slowed, turned, and called out to Husy, "Sorry."

The old woman simply nodded.

—— ⋒ ——

"When can I go see him, Mama?"

"He's at a sanatorium, sugarplum. It'll still be a while."

"Are they going to put him in one of those iron lungs? I've seen a picture of one in *LIFE*. Is he gonna be stuck in a box for the rest of his days?"

But a month later, the doctor declared that Tommy could leave the sanatorium, no longer contagious. When Dale got to his room, everything smelled of antiseptic. She screwed up her nose and said, "Ew. Stinks in here."

Tommy glared at her from his bed. "Good to see you too, DB."

"What'd you have to get polio for, you crazy cowboy? I would have let you win the bet." She looked away so he couldn't see her tears. "Anyway, Krystal and I cleared three feet eleven inches last week."

His grin lit up something inside her. "Told you so. You two are magic together."

I wanted to be magic with you. *And now look what you've done!*

She stood in the middle of the sanitized room, kicking at the floor.

"You can sit down, Deebs. I don't bite. Anyway, I can't even get out of this bed."

"What'd the doctor say? Can you move your legs?"

"Barely."

"But you can breathe on your own, right? They didn't put you in a horrible box . . . at least they didn't do that . . ."

She raced across the space between them and flung herself onto the bed, her arms tight around his shoulders. "Oh, Tommy, I'm so sorry! I told myself I wouldn't cry, and I haven't until now. Seeing you here. I'm so sorry." Then she backed up, swiping her tears. "I guess I shouldn't do that. I don't want to hurt you."

"Shh. It's okay, Deebs." He took her hand and squeezed it, but even though she tried not to notice, she could tell that there was no strength in his grip. "Thank you for caring."

"When can you get out of bed?"

"Not for a while yet."

"I'm taking you to the barn. And you're getting back on Infinity. I swear it! Soon."

His grin was forced. "Doctor says I may be able to walk with braces." He grimaced as he shifted in the bed, eyes dark. "Said I won't ever ride again, though."

She heard him pronounce the words, felt the chill start in her skull and slither all the way down her back so that she shivered. "Doctors don't know anything!"

Tommy bit down hard on his lip and held Dale's hand, this time squeezing it so tight it hurt. "Sometimes they do."

In the end, the high jumps hadn't stopped Tommy, as Dale had feared. It was something more insidious, a disease that had crawled into his body and stolen his legs. At eighteen, he walked with a limp, his legs in braces, using a cane. Sometimes Dale thought that the limp caused Tommy to read people's souls.

"It got me this time. Ironic, isn't it, Deebs? I should have died going over a fence. Now I've got to stick around with two withered legs."

"We must think of Lis Hartel," Mr. Jorgensen told Dale in whispered confidence. "No need to say anything to Tommy yet, but . . ." Miss Hartel was a Danish woman who had been a champion rider before contracting polio. Evidently, she'd just begun competing at high levels again.

But Dale could not keep the news to herself. "Look here, Tommy!" she said, perched on the side of his bed. "She's riding! She can't feel anything below her knees, yet she's on the horse. She was a champion just like you before she contracted polio. You'll be just like her. Or better. I'm warning your parents that if they won't bring you to the barn, I'll do it myself." When Tommy stared at Dale without a rebuff, she added, "Just you wait."

He shrugged, every bit of sparkle gone from his eyes.

She feared Tommy was slipping into depression. She felt that responsibility that she'd saddled herself with ever since she was a child climb on her back. She had to do something. Something.

"Don't forget your prayers," Husy used to say. *"Practice gratitude, Barbara Dale."* Her nursemaid's simple wisdom often drifted into her thoughts.

She had started praying again about Essie, and now she prayed for Tommy. Maybe he'd be healed, like in that story Husy told where a little boy's leg, shortened through polio, grew back to be the exact same length as the good leg. Or maybe it would be like Lis Hartel, who was becoming a champion dressage rider. Or maybe it would be something that only could happen to Tommy Ridley, her reckless, daredevil, softhearted friend.

Please just do something, God. Please.

Two weeks later, when Tommy balked again at her prognosis of him riding, she shouted at him. "Don't you tell me you can't ride! That you'll never ride again. Don't you dare say it to me, Tommy Ridley! You promised me you could do anything. You said it. You said you weren't afraid of anything. If taking Infinity over a five foot two inch oxer didn't scare you, then you can't be afraid of polio. I won't let you be!"

Tommy was squinting his eyes, cocking his head, and Dale thought that maybe, just maybe, she saw a tiny flicker of a smile spread over his face.

So she continued her tirade. "Don't you remember how you forced me to get on Beau in the middle of the night when my arm was in that gosh-awful cast? How dare you refuse to get back on that horse of yours. There's a lot of bad things about you, Tommy Ridley, but I've never seen you feel sorry for yourself before, and I won't let you start now. I swear I won't. So you better quit whining and get back on Finny!"

His face crumpled, and Tommy couldn't even force the dimpled grin. "The doctor won't let me." He pulled at the leather straps on his legs and cursed the braces. "DB, let me be. I've got to focus on walking and being independent so I can go to college in the fall. I don't have time to worry about the horses. We'll get someone else to exercise Beau and Finny . . . take them to the horse shows."

"You'll do no such thing! I've read lots about people who keep riding with polio," she lied. "And what do doctors know, anyway? They're always discovering new stuff that proves the old stuff is false. And Mr. Jorgensen knows this woman. He *knows* Lis Hartel! She trained with him in Denmark before he came to the States. Please. Listen to him. Please."

"You're as stubborn as the day is long, Dale Butler."

"Well, I hope so. I've got to outlast you, stupid boy. Stupid, stupid boy!"

She slammed his door, tears springing to her eyes, and rushed down the stairs, almost colliding with Tommy's mother at the bottom. Mrs. Ridley's blond hair, normally perfectly coiffed, was astray, as if she'd slept on it wrong, and she was wearing a faded day dress instead of one of her usual form-fitting linen suits.

Screeching to a halt, Dale blushed furiously, staring at her boots. "I'm so sorry, Mrs. Ridley. I . . . I didn't know you were here. I . . ."

Mrs. Ridley took her by the arm. "Dale Butler, please come into the parlor with me." Mrs. Ridley motioned with her eyes for Dale to follow her. "Can I get you a cup of tea?"

Dale prepared herself for a reprimand. She swallowed. "No, thank you. I'm sorry if I was hard on Tommy."

Mrs. Ridley drew Dale into a tight hug. She was crying. "Oh, Dale, you're right. He's so stubborn. But thank you for goading him on. You're the only one he'll listen to, the only one he respects—more than Mr. Jorgensen or us. He'll listen to you. He's always said you're the bravest person he knows. He admires you. Maybe you can talk some sense into him." She turned, her faded blue dress brushing the cushions on the sofa as she wiped a manicured-but-chipped fingernail across her eyes. "We're so worried about him."

The bravest person he knows. He admires you.

"The doctor said depression is normal after a polio diagnosis. He says we should give him time. He feels confident that, with physical therapy, Tommy can regain the use of his legs. And—" here she paused, pursing her lips, her eyes a little glassy—"he's a good doctor, but he doesn't know about the healing power of horses." She cleared her throat. "But we do, don't we, Dale?"

Dale felt the grin spread across her face until it became a wide smile. She reached over and took both of Mrs. Ridley's hands in hers. "We sure do, Mrs. Ridley! We sure do!"

———— ♘ ————

Every morning that summer, before the oppressive Georgia air had descended on them and he headed to the lumber mill, Mr. Butler drove Dale to Tommy's house, where Dale walked with him across the property, urging him to keep working through all the exercises from the physical therapist.

First, she'd say, "Tighten the braces, cowboy! How can you

forget that? You don't forget to tighten the girth on Finny's saddle before you mount, do you? It's just a habit. You'll get used to it."

Tommy would roll his eyes at Dale, fiddle with the leather braces, and then plant his cane in the grass, step forward on the right leg, pause, then step forward on the left leg, and repeat.

Twice a week, with Dale looking on, Mrs. Ridley would open the door to the passenger seat of the Ridleys' Packard Convertible Victoria while Tommy used his crutches to pivot so that he could sit down and, with his hands, lift his legs that were enshrouded in two metal strips held in place by leather straps at the thigh, knee, and ankle. Then Dale would ride in the convertible with them to Hickory Hills. Mrs. Ridley would park outside the barn, where mounds of fresh shavings were heaped under a roofed-in area. With the help of his crutches, he'd hobble through the stable, stopping at Infinity's stall, Tommy's freckled face pale, his chestnut eyes dull. "Hey, buddy," he whispered. "Good to see you."

Late one afternoon in the middle of July, when Mrs. Ridley drove down the rocky driveway, she paused where the road parted in a V, and instead of driving down the hill to the stable, she took the rocky road that led up to the ring where Mr. Jeffrey, Husy, and Mr. Jorgensen were waiting.

Tommy glanced at Dale, sitting in the back seat. "What's going on?"

"Nothing much, cowboy. Just a riding lesson."

Tommy narrowed his eyes, but she saw a brief spark cross his face. Slowly, he opened the convertible's door and got out, hobbling into the ring.

"Here you go," Mr. Jorgensen said, motioning to a wooden block that stood beside an impatient Infinity.

"What's that?" Tommy asked.

"You know what that is," Dale said. "Remember when you used this to force me on Beau? Now I'm forcing you back on Finny."

With the help of a cane, Mr. Jorgensen on one side, and Dale on the other, Tommy climbed the three wooden stairs till he stood at the top, breathing heavily. Then Mr. Jorgensen hoisted him onto

Infinity. The gelding's ears flashed back and forth as Tommy landed with a plop in the saddle.

"Sorry, old friend. I'm afraid I'm lacking my former finesse."

Dale let out the breath she'd been holding when Tommy picked up the reins while Mr. Jorgensen positioned his braced legs in the stirrups. She put her right hand on Infinity's bridle and looked up at Tommy. "I'll lead him around till you get the feel of being back in the saddle."

She felt that hollow, hopeful feeling in the pit of her stomach when Tommy barked at her, "You'll do no such thing! Finny and I are fine!"

Dale swung onto Krystal's bare back, and once again, they were walking side by side on their mounts.

"Thanks, Deebs," he whispered.

"Of course," Dale choked out through the knot in her throat.

They continued walking their horses around the ring until the sky was dusky and the lightning bugs began their magic show, flitting off and on, off and on. The incessant chirping of the crickets and Krystal's soft nickering were the most welcome sounds Dale could imagine.

13

Allie

Saturday, March 7

By nightfall, the dining room table held a large assortment of silver, which I surveyed with a pinch in my heart. Together, these precious pieces would help me piece together another story. A love story.

Maybe I'd never find the cherrywood box that Nana Dale had willed me, but at least I could figure out the love story between Nana Dale and Tommy. Or maybe I was just turning my obsession from finding the money to keep the house into another obsession of finding out about Tommy.

Or maybe, just maybe, they were related.

You'll know where to find the money, and you'll learn about Tommy and my tall tales.

Or maybe I should let it all go and beg Austin to take me back.

I moved from the dining room on the main floor, downstairs to the basement—actually, an assortment of rooms with tiled floors and white walls covered with photos and art. Years ago, these rooms had been an unfinished basement and an apartment for my grandmother's nursemaid, Husy. Now they comprised a laundry room, a pool room, a kitchenette, two dressing rooms, a full bathroom, a wine cellar, and the Ribbon Room.

Every wall in the Ribbon Room was plastered with photos of Nana Dale and her beloved Essie, winning trophy after trophy. And the trophies that weren't silver bread trays and bowls and water pitchers engraved with her name lined the shelves. But by far the best part was the ribbons themselves, which hung above my head and encircled the walls on golden thread wound through dozens of old horseshoes nailed into the crown molding. Many other ribbons were housed in narrow wooden cabinets with glass fronts, all handmade by my great-grandfather.

I'd once spent a long weekend counting the ribbons, arriving at nine hundred forty-three, then separating them into the colors. Over fifty blue-red-yellow championship ribbons, twenty-three red-yellow-white reserve championship ribbons, and more than five hundred blue ribbons, along with multiple reds, yellows, whites, pinks, and greens. But mostly the blues. Nana Dale was a blue-ribbon woman, a true Southern belle with the grit of a cowhand.

I opened a forest green trunk with her monogram on the lid, and the smell of Neatsfoot oil and leather assaulted me. I carefully lifted out the halters, five of them, each one with an engraved gold plate on the side: *Mr. Jinx, Krystal, Nicky, Essie, Infinity*. I recognized the names of the first four as my grandmother's beloved pony and mares. But I couldn't place Infinity. Was this my mother's horse, one she had never mentioned to me? Surely not!

Memories kept nipping at me as I examined the framed photos in the room of beautiful women in ball gowns and men in top hats and tuxes. I could name many of those dignified people. I'd heard their stories. Some lived right around the corner from Nana Dale's estate. Or they had. Now, if they were alive at all, they were tucked into the city's elitist nursing homes and walking with canes or using wheelchairs, the cream of the crop, reduced to their humanity. The glazed eyes, milky with age, the spotted hands, the swollen ankles. Still brave and genteel and, oh, so strong. Just as Nana Dale had been.

It brought me to tears.

Success. Wealth. Ease. Generosity.

When I drove around the familiar streets of Buckhead, I could name my grandparents' friends who lived in the different houses. Who *had* lived there, I corrected myself again. For now, they were owned by young families starting their own traditions.

But in the Ribbon Room, as in all the others at Hickory Hills, were the memorabilia and, more important, the memories of long ago. If I wandered these rooms long enough, perhaps a memory would emerge to lead me back to what I was looking for.

Just in case he was listening, I whispered, "Tommy, where are you?"

— ♘ —

Late that night, I picked up the cashmere sweaters still sitting on the kitchen table and climbed the stairs to the Pink Room, suddenly exhausted from my discoveries. I looked around the Pink Room with all its mysteries and decided I'd spend the night in Nana Dale's canopied bed.

The rain still pelted the big panes, and the trees swayed in the dusk like multifingered ghosts. What had it been like for Nana Dale to live in this cocoon of paradise, with a forest of trees as her closest neighbors, and a barn filled with prized hunters and jumpers just down the gravel road?

I remembered Nana Dale saying, *"Daddy thought he was going to lose the house and property and horses to his cousin, Mr. Weatherby. We did have to sell the horses back in '32. But eventually, we got them back. And then came the war . . ."*

From the bed looking out on the backyard with the barn and the riding ring far in the distance, I tried to imagine what Nana Dale had lived through during the Depression, and when the tornado had ripped through her yard, and then during World War II.

I washed my face in the porcelain sink with the brass handles on the spigots and dried it on the monogrammed towels that hung, as they had for decades, by the shower. I plucked a silk robe from the cedar closet, built, of course, by my great-grandfather. The clothes, decades old, were clean, free of stains and bugs. I pulled on an old oxford shirt, buttoned it up, climbed into bed, and fell asleep.

— ♘ —

Sunday, March 8

Out behind the barn the next morning, I climbed the hill up to the ring, slipping a little in the fresh mud. Several different well-worn paths were still visible as I climbed up the hillside, despite the fact that I'd moved the horses to the Chastain Horse Park a month ago. I traipsed past where the gate used to be and walked to the back of the opened area and into the woods, the leaves damp beneath my boots. Wildlife lived back here, away from humanity's touch. Squirrels scampered up trees, and chipmunks scurried beneath pine straw. In the distance I often saw a small herd of deer. They'd freeze, statuesque, sweet faces turned to my noise, their brown ears wide and attentive.

I'd had such plans for these woods!

Barnell caught sight of me and waved me over.

"What are you doing here on a Sunday morning?" I called to him. I knew Barnell faithfully attended church, unlike me. I'd stopped going in the month since I'd informed our pastor, the one who was supposed to marry Austin and me, that we'd canceled the wedding. "You getting ready to unearth another dinosaur?"

He chuckled. "I reckon so. Darn contractor's breathing down my neck, so I thought I'd better stop by and check on things."

"What do you mean?"

"He's threatening to hire someone else if I don't get moving. So I'll make as like I'm moving, in case he's watching me today." Then, glancing at the menacing sky, he said, "Figure the heavens are looking out for us, though, Allie. Can't be running the backhoe in a downpour."

"Um, it isn't raining yet."

"That's right. Not yet." Barnell retrieved a brown paper bag from the front seat of the backhoe and brought out a glaze-covered doughnut. "But it's time for a coffee break, so I best wait a few minutes."

I thought of the rainbow and listened to the rumble of faraway thunder, and I grinned at this man whose whole countenance told the story of his devotion to my family.

He took a seat on the coop jump. In between bites, he threw out, "My grandson's been after me to do some highfalutin' thing called DNA testing for some sort of genealogy project at his school." He patted the coop, and I joined him there. "So I did. Nothin' much to it. You just spit into a little test tube, of all things, and then you mail off your spittle to who knows where. And two weeks later, you get a report that tells you all the people in the world you're related to, from the beginning of time—or almost."

Barnell scratched at his beard and kept talking. "Well, my grandson got the results back yesterday and called me, so excited he was 'bout to wet his pants. Guess we've got royal blood in us. Says we're related to that little Frenchman called Napoleon."

I guffawed. "As in Napoleon Bonaparte, the emperor?"

"Yeah, that's the one. Personally, I was never all that impressed with him. Shore had a high opinion of himself, and then he went and started all them wars. I prefer Charles de Gaulle. Wish I was related to him."

"Your grandson sounds like Wick. He's our family genealogist. Do you remember that Nana Dale did that DNA test for Wick last fall?"

"Do I remember! Your grandmother like near had a heart attack when she found out she was related to that lowdown scoundrel, Mr. Hightower."

I hopped off the coop and swiveled to face Barnell. "She was related to him? You mean, *I'm* related to him?"

Barnell lifted his bushy eyebrows and frowned. "Dagnab it. Guess she didn't tell you that."

"No, she certainly didn't! You mean the same Mr. Hightower who cheated us all out of Hickory Hills is *related* to us?"

"Appears to be that way. 'Course your grandmother didn't know nothin' about him gettin' the estate back in September or October. Least, I don't think she did. I don't reckon she ever knew that. But she knew he was a scoundrel. He had a real interestin' reputation all over the Southeast, that fella. A wheeler-dealer. And she didn't wanna have a thing to do with him."

Barnell scratched his head. "She got even madder when she realized that Mr. Hightower was the grandson of a man named Weatherby—a cousin of her father's who'd made her daddy's life miserable way back during the Depression . . . or something like that." Barnell's eyes grew wide. "Lordy be! I hadn't put it together till right now. This Hightower fella is the *grandson* of Mr. Weatherby. I grew up hearing my daddy talk about that lazy cousin by marriage of Nana Dale's daddy. And here the man who's stole this property is his grandson!"

I tilted my head, puzzled. "You're confusing me, Barnell. What exactly are you saying?"

"Just that the scoundrel from the past and the scoundrel from the present are related to each other and to your family. Now, if that don't beat all." He shook his head.

Barnell poured black coffee from his thermos into a cup and took a sip as thunder rolled in the distance. "My grandson said he's gonna bring my DNA report over this afternoon. I'll git ta see for myself if I'm related to that Napoleon fella. Hope I'll find out I got some other famous family way back. All I know is what she found out upset your grandma something awful."

Barnell bit into his doughnut and took another swig of coffee. "Miss Allie, 'scuse me for asking, but whatever happened to your fiancé—to Dr. Andrews?"

My gut lurched at the quick change of subject, and I cleared my throat and mumbled, "He couldn't handle me."

"Shore gave you a perty ring. Seemed real genuine to me—the boy and the ring."

"Yeah, well, he came to see the real genuine me, and it wasn't what he wanted."

Barnell was quiet for a while, slowly chewing his doughnut, then taking a swig of coffee from the cup and setting it back on the coop before wiping his bright-red bandanna across his face.

"How do you mean? I didn't fancy him to be superficial. Seemed like a real serious guy, a kind man. Don't find those all that often."

I didn't want to continue this conversation. I gave a loud sigh. "Barnell, it was all on me. I was obsessed. That's what he said. Obsessed with finding that cherrywood chest—or at least the money—so I could keep all this." I let my arms sweep around the property.

"Yeah. I understand you, Allie. Your Nana Dale too. Shore is a shame, like I've said a hundred times." He hopped down from where he was perched on the coop jump. "But maybe you're having second thoughts about him?"

I bit my lips and felt the rush of tears. "Maybe," I scratched out.

Then the rain began to fall, big drops that splattered on the backhoe, making dots in the dust on the seat and wheels.

Barnell laughed. "Well, guess that's that for today." Then he took me by the shoulders. "Miss Allie, you've always been so hard on yourself. I'll be working up here slow as can be. But if you need that young man to help you at the house, might not be too late to give him a call."

My arms went around Barnell. "You've been such a good friend to our family for so long."

His rough hands held me close. "Seen you grow up, Miss Allie. Shore do love your family. Want you to have what's right for you." His dark eyes and thick gray brows came together in a V. "The house, the barn . . . and the boy."

I trudged back to the house as the rain intensified, the plump, disparate drops becoming smaller and more insistent.

"Obsessed," I whispered to myself as I entered the back door. I shed my muddy boots, found a towel in the changing room, and made myself a cup of coffee in the downstairs kitchenette.

I closed my eyes and could hear Austin's and my last conversation, could feel the way my stomach plummeted when Austin said the truth. His voice was chasing me again. He'd said it in a desperate way, but I heard it in my mind as another chastisement, and the guttural reaction came next, my voice calling above the slicing rain, "Go away!"

But it didn't. Instead, my mind replayed the conversation.

"Allie, I know it's a horrible disappointment, the death of a lifetime dream. But it's not the death of *us*. We still have each other."

I had answered way too quickly. "But it's all I ever wanted and planned for. It's gone without the land and the horses."

His eyes, usually soft and kind, became cloudy. "Honey, I know it's devastating. But we'll get through it. I promise all your hard work won't be wasted. We can make the dream happen another way."

Letting the anger and fear overcome me, I insensitively blurted out, "Oh yeah, sure. Like we're somehow going to magically find ten acres of land in the Atlanta city limits that we can buy and build a stable on?"

"Allie, please." His touch felt like an electric shock, and I backed away. I stabbed him with the movement, but I couldn't make myself move into his arms. "Allie, I love you. Didn't we say love was the strongest thing? We can figure this out. I'm afraid that this obsession—"

"It's not an obsession!" I interrupted. "It's looking for what has to be here. Nana Dale *promised*! It's finding an answer to what I've always wanted and dreamed about more than anything else. What I've loved with all my heart. This house, this land. I will *not* give up!"

I had swallowed hard, because I could see the way my words were turning the knife in the wound. I could actually see it, but I didn't back down. "You don't get it, do you? This was my whole *life*. This dream was everything I ever wanted. Everything I've been working for. Nothing will ever be the same."

I saw the hurt in his eyes the moment I pronounced those words.

He grew silent, nibbled his lip, then cleared his throat. My heart was ramming so hard, my head pounding, my throat raw from yelling at the world.

"I'm sorry," I whispered. "I didn't mean it. I'm so sorry." *Pound, pound, pound.*

He nodded, still silent. Slowly, he reached over and took my hand. When he looked up at me, his eyes pooled. "I think you did mean it, Allie. I think it's the truth. I think you'll find a way to move on through this huge disappointment. But it's shown you that we aren't enough."

"No . . ."

"Allie, you know I love you. But I'm afraid I could never make you truly happy. You'll always be looking for something else, just over the horizon. Just out of reach."

I swallowed hard—once, twice, three times. "No . . ."

When I looked at him, he was fighting back tears. "You're right. You do love something enough to sacrifice everything else. But it's not me. It's *this*. It's the dream. I don't know if I can be second in your heart."

I felt the blood pumping hard behind my eyes. I wanted to melt in his arms and assure him that he was wrong, that I loved him most. Was it pride or fear or love that kept me from it? Or maybe, it was the piercing sword of conviction. Austin was right. I did love him. But the way I was acting showed that I loved something else more.

I slid the ring off my finger, placed it in his hand, and left. I ran to my car and started blubbering tears he couldn't see. He wasn't going to know how much it broke my heart, and yet I cursed myself the whole time because I knew his heart was broken too.

He loved me. Austin didn't have a scrap of malice in him; he didn't have any second thoughts. He just said the truth, and oh, how I wished I could tell him the truth: that I would do anything if we could keep my dream and his alive together. But I didn't see how. I didn't see any loosening of my grip on this obsession, an obsession that was as tactile as my mare's saddle or the leather boots I used to shine with Neatsfoot oil. I couldn't let go of it, and I wasn't sure what it would take.

By the time that nightmarish scene had played itself out in slow motion in my mind, I had changed into an old pair of sweats, probably Wick's, that I found stuffed in a drawer in the boys' dressing room. My wavy blond mane had expanded exponentially from the rain and humidity. I towel dried it and climbed to the main floor and then turned to the second set of stairs.

As I examined the black-and-white framed photos hanging on the stairway wall, I thought how Nana Dale had a steel exterior, but deep down, she was as sentimental as I was, almost the opposite of her description of her mother. Nana Dale did not know how to throw things out. Here were the photos of her as a teenager with her arms wrapped around Husy and the caretaker, Barnell's father, Mr. Jeffrey.

And Tommy.

I wondered if, when Tommy got sick—whatever it was—Nana Dale's penchant for protecting the weakest had grown exponentially. Nana Dale wasn't looking for any accolades or anything to put after her name or to hang on her wall beside her trophies and ribbons. Those she loved, but the rest, the part that was down deep in her heart, that love, that caring, that fierce independence and courage and faith, she didn't care if anybody else saw it or not. It was there, and it was enough.

No one would deter her from protecting what she loved: her house, her horses, and the few people she actually thought were nice enough people to protect. And she'd taught me the same thing.

She looked straight ahead at the present and the future and the heart. She would not be deterred by something as insignificant as the Depression or a tornado or the boy she loved falling deathly ill with an unnamed illness. Or a lousy thieving contractor. And neither would I.

Back in the Pink Room, I continued emptying the cedar chest, reflecting on my mother's words, all of them. Why did I insist on persecuting myself? I thought again of calling Austin, begging him to come over.

"No one understands," I whispered out loud to the room.

That wasn't totally accurate. Tricia certainly understood and had offered numerous times to help me. Heather and Megan and Charlotte, my other colleagues at Chastain, all supported my dream. But who understood it enough to push me to keep going?

"No one understands," Nana Dale had said, *"except you, Allie. It's okay. In life, you often have to take the risk of being misunderstood. That's what I've done. I love my family, you know that. But I can't trust them with the money. And you have to be smart. My daddy's cousin tried to find a way to steal all our property back during the Depression. Gotta watch out for property hawks. And gotta be careful even with family. I've seen too many families ripped apart over inheritances."*

"So did you purposely throw it away? To protect us from affluence?" This I said out loud, my voice dripping with anger.

Maybe Nana Dale had had second thoughts and didn't even trust me.

Or maybe she knew it was too heavy a burden for me to bear.

Or maybe . . . maybe I really hadn't found what I was looking for yet.

Instead of replacing the cashmere sweaters in the cedar chest, I set them to the side, along with the riding coats and shirts. I wanted to make sure I inspected all of Nana Dale's retro wardrobe stashed inside. Riding jodhpurs sat on top of a layer of layette—fine cotton baby clothes, surely from the 1930s and '40s. Some had stains, but I recognized a lacy white smocked dress for a baby girl. My one-year-old photo, as well as my mother's, my grandmother's, and my great-grandmother's, had all been taken in this dress. We had the four photos in a frame downstairs to prove it.

My eyes welled with tears as I brought the soft fabric to my face, smelling the baby powder and lotions I imagined Mom using on me.

When I'd lifted the last of the clothes from the chest, I stared at the almost-empty interior. A much smaller wooden chest sat in the bottom.

I let out an involuntary gasp and then whispered, "Is this it, Nana Dale? Is this the chest you were talking about?"

I knew immediately that it was.

At first glance, it looked like a perfect replica of the silver chest in the dining room. But when I reached in and lifted it out, this chest felt much lighter than the one downstairs, and its sides were intricately carved with a band of alternating horseshoes and hearts. The craftsmanship took my breath away. A miniature brass lock hung from the metal hinge. When I stooped down to peer more closely at the lock, which of course didn't budge with my prodding and pulling, I saw the minuscule keyhole. It almost seemed like a toy lock or a decorative trinket. But it held the wooden box closed, and I would have to break it to get in.

With that thought, my left hand went again to my empty right wrist. *And remember the charm bracelet too. It holds the key to your future,* Nana Dale had written in the letter. Now I remembered how Nana Dale had looked at me as I'd inspected each charm when I was ten. *"You'll know what this goes to if you ever need it."* She'd winked at me that day, and I grabbed that memory too and tucked it away.

Now I needed to get back home quickly. "Oh, Nana Dale," I whispered. "Now I think I understand."

If I could only hold on to these snippets of conversation tucked somewhere in my memory, perhaps I could fill in all the gaps in her life until they led me to the truth.

But did I want to know the truth?

I carried the locked chest home, enveloping it in my raincoat as if it were indeed a hidden treasure. For one moment, I imagined opening it to find thousands, maybe even hundreds of thousands of dollars inside. Or at least something of great worth, something that made her promises of *"everything you need to start Hickory Hills Horse Therapy is in this little chest"* true.

Back at my studio, safely tucked in my fleece robe after a hot shower and having devoured a bowl of red pepper soup for lunch, I felt butterflies twittering around inside. I sat at my table—hickory, round, made by my great-grandfather—with Maggie doing figure eights around my legs. I'd fetched the silver charm bracelet from the porcelain jewelry box Nana Dale had given me. Even as I'd lifted the lid covered in tiny Wedgewood blue hyacinths, I'd feared the bracelet would be gone.

Obsessed. Yes, perhaps.

But the bracelet was now in my hands, and I leaned in to read the engravings on each charm. There were four sterling silver silhouette charms—two of little boys' heads, and two of little girls'. Three of them had our names—my mother's, my brother's, and mine—engraved across each face in pretty cursive: *Mary Jane, Wick, Allene.* The other little boy silhouette charm had no name on it. I remembered my mother telling me that Nana Dale had had a miscarriage.

"She always wanted another child, and I desperately wanted a sibling. But it wasn't to be," Mom had confided.

There was a tiny silver calendar charm with *January 1943* engraved at the top, and a pinpoint diamond embedded where the numeral 14 should have been. There were five silver silhouette horse heads, each engraved with horses' names: *Essie, Mr. Jinx, Krystal, Nicky, Infinity.* Hanging next to these was a thick nail, like a blacksmith would use to shoe a horse. It had been twisted into the shape of a ring. I could imagine Nana Dale asking the blacksmith to make her a special charm to add to her bracelet—perhaps a keepsake from the horseshoe of one of her beloved mares? And there was a tiny brass key that looked as incongruous as the nail amid all the sterling silver dangling from the chain's links. I'd thought it a charm that represented something to Nana Dale. Now I knew that it was a real key, and I knew what it would unlock.

I fiddled with the key until I held it between my thumb and forefinger, the rest of the bracelet dangling below. I slipped the key into the keyhole on the brass lock of the cherrywood chest. It fit perfectly, and when the lock popped open, I squealed like a child surveying her gifts on Christmas morn.

I carefully opened the chest, but it wasn't filled with money or jewels or anything of value. Just a few folded and yellowed newspaper clippings.

My stomach plummeted as I fought back tears. Silly tears. *Honestly, Allie*, I reprimanded myself. *What did you expect to find?*

Except . . .

When I unfolded the clippings, each of them proclaimed world news in big, bold print: *1940 Olympics canceled! Thomas Ridley Becomes Youngest Maclay champion! Polio Epidemic! America at War! Mounted Horse Patrol on St. Simons Island!* And the newspapers concealed an album that fit snugly inside the chest. Immediately, the smell of well-cared-for leather filled my senses. This was no cheap photo album with clear plastic that no longer stuck to its yellowed pages. This album's cover was made of supple tan leather that looked as if it had been fashioned from old bridles and stirrup leathers that had been woven together. The effect was more lovely than any rare leather-bound old book I'd ever seen.

As I held the leather album in my hand, I felt two simultaneous poundings—one in my head, the throbbing of the beginning of a migraine, and one in my heart, that lurching of excitement because I had at last found what Nana Dale had promised. Or at least the next clue in what she wanted me to find, like a hoofprint in the sand.

I put my hand to my mouth as chills raced up and down my spine and tears flooded my eyes again—happy, joyful, celebratory tears. I looked over to where the rain made pattering sounds on my window and whispered, "Thank you!"

14

Dale

1941

The barn was located on St. Simons Island on the Georgia coast, near Savannah, part of what was known as the Golden Isles. "I'm going to spend the year there in school," Tommy informed Dale on a boiling August afternoon after they'd finished their now daily walk around the ring, lap after lap, the flea-bitten gray carrying the polio-bitten boy beside the dark bay carrying the lovesick girl.

"Mr. Jorgensen will be working with my physical therapist to develop a special kind of training therapy at the stables there, Deebs."

"How d'you mean?"

"You're the one who told me about Lis Hartel—the Danish equestrian. Mr. Jorgensen's spoken with her trainer, who's given him some tips." Here, Tommy winked at her. "I'll be staying at my parents' vacation house and keeping Finny at this fancy uppity rich people's barn." Another wink. "Which is on the campus of a fancy uppity private college." He smiled, then scrunched up his nose. "Well, actually, the school is for rich kids who have some sort

156

of physical disability." He shrugged. "And every afternoon, Mr. Jorgensen and a team of therapists will work with me. On Finny."

"Every afternoon?" It was all she could manage to spit out. Her mouth had gone dry. Finally, "Wow, that's swell. I sure will miss you, though."

He was leaning on his crutches, the metal bars in his braces clamped to each leg. He still looked so weak, almost fragile, and Dale suddenly wondered if all her encouragement was simply wishful thinking.

"You'll bring Krystal down, and we'll gallop along the beaches together. You'll see!" His eyes were shining with their signature sparkle, the taste of adventure and risk right under the surface. "It may take a while before I'm high jumping, but we'll do just fine on the beaches."

Dale swallowed hard, fighting the juxtaposition of emotions—relief, even joy at his enthusiasm and obvious belief in healing; terror that he'd be disappointed; sadness at having him five hours away.

"St. Simons is a great place to live," she agreed. "And your house there is really swell too."

Dale had heard Tommy talk about the Ridleys' vacation home on St. Simons. She'd seen a photo of the mansion with Spanish moss draping from the trees that shielded the sprawling beach house from the road. Behind the house, a sandy path surrounded by sea oats led out to the beach. When she'd stared at that photo, she could almost hear the roaring of the waves as they crashed on the sand, froth hurrying up the beach.

Her father called the Golden Isles "the playground of the rich and famous." Those isles were made up of St. Simons Island, Sea Island, Jekyll Island, and a few others. She'd stayed at The Cloister, a beautiful hotel on Sea Island, several times, and her mother often found a way to insert into a cocktail party conversation that they'd vacationed at the Jekyll Island Club with people whose last names were Pulitzer, Morgan, Rockefeller, and Vanderbilt. The same names Dale had encountered at the National Horse Show last year.

And one other name: Ridley.

Exclusive. That was the word for the Golden Isles. It was also one of Eleanor Butler's favorite words.

A week later, as Dale watched the truck pulling the trailer up the rock driveway and away from Hickory Hills, she felt a lurching in her stomach, just like all those years ago when Essie left. Her filly had never come back. But Tommy and Infinity were just going five hours away. She knew where they'd be, and Tommy had said she could visit, right?

He leaned out the window, grinning and waving. "See you soon, Deebs!" If she hadn't known better, she'd have thought the boy in the truck was simply heading to another competition.

— ∩ —

October 31, 1941

Until that fall, breakfast had been a favorite time of day for Dale. Her mother did not rise early, so Husy made eggs, bacon, and toast for Dale and Mr. Butler. In between bites, her father educated his daughter on what was happening in the world.

Even as a teenager, Dale adored the special attention from her father, the smell of his cologne mingled with that of crisp fried bacon, how handsome he looked in his navy or gray suit, his auburn hair slicked back in style.

But with the world at war, breakfasts became one long list of catastrophes that left Dale's stomach in knots.

"A German U-boat has sunk the USS *Reuben James*, Dale." Daddy peered over the morning newspaper, his buttered toast growing cold on the plate alongside the uneaten scrambled eggs. "An American destroyer, torpedoed off the coast of Iceland."

Dale nibbled her lip. "Was it firing on the Germans, Daddy?"

"No, the *Reuben James* was an escort ship protecting the merchant ships and tankers so that supplies can get through to France. President Roosevelt will have to retaliate. Looks like America will be entering the war soon."

"Really?" She rose to stand beside him, peering over his shoulder while cradling a glass of orange juice. "Are you sure?"

"We'll see what the president says."

War.

Mama refused to hear talk of war and forbade Daddy to listen to the radio while she was in the room. "She's just worried for her friends. She can't imagine them sending their sons off to war," her father explained.

Dale understood that fear for so many of her classmates. But she also felt an opposite, competing emotion that she admitted only to herself: relief. Tommy would not qualify for the draft, nor could he volunteer for the military. Ironically, the death threat of polio would ultimately protect him from the death threat of war.

A few days later, her father said, "Congress has voted the president down. We'll not be entering the war yet."

"Aren't you thankful, Daddy?"

Her father stared out the breakfast room window to where a carpet of emerald grass was sprinkled with golden and crimson leaves. "We're just putting off the inevitable, and that means those darn Nazis'll become even more invincible."

But then he added, "Can't blame Congress for dragging its heels. Memory of World War I is awfully fresh. No one wants to go back to war, Dale."

She knew her father had turned eighteen during the last year of World War I. He'd gone to Fort McPherson right in Atlanta for training, but the war ended before he was shipped out.

Setting the newspaper down, he said, "I lost a lot of my buddies in the Great War."

When Tommy came home from school for Thanksgiving, his hobble less pronounced, Dale whispered, "Daddy thinks we'll be at war soon. Do you?"

He shrugged. "Lots of rumors going round. I think it's mighty likely."

Tommy joined them for dinner that evening, reporting, "The

president's announced that he's transferring the coast guard from the treasury to the navy."

Dale watched her mother's mouth pucker into a pout.

"What does that mean?" Dale asked, not sure she wanted to hear the answer.

"The coast guard are the specialists in shallow waters," her father said. "Our navy boys aren't trained for this. It'll be a boon for them. 'Course, the navy isn't too keen on it yet."

"Why not, Daddy?"

"The coast guard is made up of civilians," her father explained. "The navy tends to think of them like a volunteer fire department. They look down their noses at them since they're not professionals like navy men." He frowned, tilting his head. "It's too bad."

"Sure is! They know what they're doing." Tommy speared a potato with his fork. At least the strength in his arms had returned. Three months ago, he could barely feed himself. Dale busied herself with those thoughts so that she didn't have to concentrate on the conversation or the fear that had lodged inside her gut.

"The coast guard will help prevent the enemy's landing on beaches."

"What beaches, Daddy?"

"Our beaches, honey. On the Atlantic coast. Those U-boats will be coming our way."

Now her mother's eyes were sending explosive messages to her father, a very personal torpedo heading his way.

"How do you know?" Dale asked, but the grim expression on her father's face told her that, however he'd come by the knowledge, it was true.

Our beaches. St. Simons Island.

"That's what we're hearing too." Dale didn't like the excitement in Tommy's voice. "The boys who board at school have seen explosions at sea and stuff wash up on shore. And lots of oil on the sand." He glanced over at Dale and continued. "Last week, a submarine was beached a good ways south of Savannah and spotted by the coast guard. But the navy didn't believe them and ignored their signals, even when the submarine was beached for hours. Then the tide took the sub back out."

"Surely not!" Mama said.

"No, absolutely true. Me and a few other boys saw it too, with our binoculars, when we were out riding on the beach."

Her father's eyes were fiery. "Navy better start believing! Otherwise, we'll have Nazis in our backyard."

"Jeremiah!" Mama's eyes filled with fury. "I will not have all this talk at the table. With the children! Of all things!"

"Mama, we're not children. We need to know," Dale said, wiping a cloth napkin over her mouth.

Silence.

Mama threw her napkin on the table, stood up quickly, picked up the casserole dish, and took it into the kitchen.

"What does it take to be in the coast guard, Mr. Butler?" Tommy whispered after she had left the room.

Dale twisted her cloth napkin in her lap.

"Just about the same thing for the military, son. Patriotism, guts, courage, discipline."

"And two good legs?"

Her father blinked once, cleared his throat, and said, "Don't believe that's one of the requirements, Tommy."

December 8, 1941

The day before, they had heard gruesome accounts of an attack in Hawaii, but now Dale hovered around the radio with her mother, father, Husy, and Mr. Jeffrey, listening as the president began his speech. "Mr. Vice President, Mr. Speaker, members of the Senate and of the House of Representatives: yesterday, December seventh, 1941—a date which will live in infamy—the United States of America was suddenly and deliberately attacked by naval and air forces of the Empire of Japan. . . ."

Dale listened to the speech, all the while noting her mother's stricken face. When she hurried out of the den, Dale asked, "He's declaring war, isn't he?"

"I'm afraid so, Dale."

"You knew it was coming."

"I suspected it. But I thought it'd start in the Atlantic, not the Pacific."

In the end, the two oceans made little difference in the timing. America went to war with Japan the day after the attack on Pearl Harbor. Three days later, America declared war on Germany.

No sooner had Pearl Harbor happened than signs began appearing everywhere, encouraging young men to enlist and others to go to work building ships and other equipment for the US military.

School was ablaze with the news, and boys rushed to sign up.

Even her mother embraced the reality of war, and instead of attending meetings at the Garden Club, she helped Husy and Mr. Jeffrey set up a massive Victory Garden, planting the perfectly manicured lawn behind Hickory Hills with tomatoes, squash, cucumbers, corn, raspberries, and strawberries. The enthusiasm her mother had showed for parties was now transferred toward energy to help the war effort.

Once a week, they gathered around the radio to listen to the president's Fireside Chats. Dale could not get the conversation of Tommy discussing the coast guard with her father out of her mind, especially as her father continued to speak in low tones with his business friends about the threat of German submarines off the coast of the barrier islands.

She knew that the Golden Isles were part of these barrier islands. Serving as a protective layer of land between the ocean and the mainland, the islands themselves were only separated from each other by narrow tidal inlets—a bay or lagoon or sound. There were dozens of these so-called islands along a hundred miles off the coast of Florida, Georgia, and South Carolina.

And one of them was called St. Simons.

ELIZABETH MUSSER

As soon as war was declared, Butler Lumber Company was catapulted into mayhem, and her father began hiring dozens of new workers. "We're building the boxes to ship jeeps and other transports to Europe, Dale. Every hand on deck."

Dale remembered clearly the havoc caused by the Depression when nothing was being built, the way Mr. Weatherby persecuted her father, determined to take over Butler Lumber Company and their land. She could still feel her stomach lurching and the warmth of Husy's arms around her skinny shoulders as Essie was led into the trailer, white ears twitching back and forth, delicate legs bracing against the lead shank. The piercing whinny.

She thought of her father's long nights in his office after he'd returned from a formal dance with Mama, the way he never even changed out of his tux, just unbuttoned the collar and tossed the bow tie on the rug beside the studded leather office chair.

Gradually, Butler Lumber Company regained a solid structure, and now it was one of the main suppliers to ship materials to Europe. Her father was prescient, she always said afterward. He'd seen the future, the war threat.

"Genius," Mama cooed.

Mr. Jeffrey agreed. "Not many things I'd say are good about a war. Can't think of anything else. But Mr. Butler, he's going to make a fortune with that little box of his."

Tommy, home for Christmas, laughed. "Yeah, right. A 'little' box."

Dale knew her father had recently gone to Detroit to display his special wooden crates that could be used to ship vehicles from the US to Europe for the war effort.

"You've got contracts with General Motors and Chrysler and Willys-Overland. Willys-Overland, Mr. Butler! Gee whiz, that's great!"

Dale furrowed her brow, trying to match the enthusiasm of Tommy's brown eyes, shining almost like they had before polio.

"You don't know about them, Deebs?"

She shrugged.

"Well, they're only the American automobile company best known for the design and production of military jeeps! And all kinds of other vehicles too. They're really swell."

Dale wrapped her arms around her father's neck as he sat hunched over his desk late that night. "I'm proud of you, Daddy! You figured out how to keep the land. All of it. Mean ole Mr. Weatherby can't get his hands on it now, can he?"

"I don't think so, Dale. But I've traded one kind of pressure for another. I've got to keep up the production for the car companies."

She understood the pressure, saw it in the dark circles under her father's eyes. But at least Mr. Weatherby wasn't breathing down his back, whispering, *Prettiest acreage in North Fulton County. Someday it'll be mine.*

By the spring of 1942, the Butler fortune was secured as Butler Lumber provided more and more crates and boxes for supplies destined for Europe. But Dale kept hearing in her head *war, submarines, Golden Isles, St. Simons, coast guard, Tommy.*

In fifth-period history class, Dale and her classmates watched a short government-produced film called *Wood for War.* "Support the war effort. How the American military uses timber during WWII." Above the frightening music and dire statistics and footage of forest fires, the voice of the narrator proclaimed, "So protect our forests! A single match could destroy hundreds of thousands of trees that are needed to fight the enemy overseas!"

"We watched this film at school today. It almost sounded like propaganda," Dale said, tossing her books on the breakfast room table. "Informing the public of how necessary wood is, warning us about the use of matches and cigarettes that can start forest fires. They showed footage of the fires and talked about how the fires are taking men away from doing their jobs of supplying the wood for war. I think they were trying to scare us out of smoking."

She grabbed an apple from the fruit stand and took a bite. "But then it talked about how wood is important for everything from making forks and knives for us to use at home to building trucks, planes, and bridges for the war." She glanced at her father, set down the apple, took his hands, and winked. "And crates for shipping supplies and ammunition to Europe and the Pacific. When they said that, well, I knew it was true! And don't worry. I'm not interested in smoking. Mr. Jeffrey put the fear in me when I was knee-high to a grasshopper. No lighted matches or cigarettes within two miles of the barn!"

Her father gave her head a pat, distracted.

"Is all that true, Daddy?"

"Yep. It's feast or famine, Dale. The Depression dried up the need for lumber, and now with the war, I can't even hire enough help to keep up."

She worried for her father, but in her mind, she was counting the days until her high school's new spring break. Ten days away—when she would load Krystal into the Ridleys' trailer and drive to St. Simons Island to ride the beaches with Tommy, just like he promised.

From her perch in the bleachers of the small field, Dale watched Tommy go through the physical therapy. "We're flying by the seat of our pants," Mr. Jorgensen said, his accent still strong, blue eyes twinkling on his tanned face. "There are no studies or examples of this therapy in the States, but we know it has been used in Denmark, Sweden, and Germany. It is common sense, you know? And like every type of therapy, it's not so fun at first. Tommy is relearning how to sit on a horse, relearning how to communicate with Infinity. It helps that he knows the horse. There is that mutual trust. They've worked together for so long."

"So he's doing well, right?" Her enthusiasm was curbed, though. Tommy couldn't mount or dismount Infinity on his own, but astride the gelding, he looked almost as smooth as before polio. At a walk.

A walk.

Mr. Jorgensen ruffled her hair. "He has no muscle strength in his lower legs, but he's regaining a bit in his thighs. He can grip the saddle. And the stubborn boy is finally accepting my suggestions, learning to communicate more with the reins too. And it's working. Time and hard work, Miss Dale. You'll see it's improving his muscle coordination and strength."

Dale watched the pair move into a trot. She remembered the spark of jealousy she'd felt the first time Husy had said, *"He sure can sit a horse."* Now, if she let herself, she'd feel pity and anger bubbling up within. "I'm glad you think he's progressing well," she said to Mr. Jorgensen.

"You worry too much about this boy, Miss Dale. He's got grit. Last week, he almost slid off the side of this big ole bully at a trot. Yesterday, he cantered for the first time. It wasn't pretty, but he's not trying to win any classes, Miss Dale."

His tone was stern, the expression in his eyes a mixture of serious care and kindness.

"Can he go on the beach? Can we ride together?"

"Of course. But go after the crowds have left. No need to spook the horses. Just a walk by moonlight. Slow. Easy. The couples class in the sand."

She felt heat creep into her face.

Tommy came trotting over. "What do ya think, Deebs?"

"I think you're both amazing. Really swell. I think I can't wait to go on that beach ride."

"All those miserable days when good ole Coach here made me ride without stirrups, posting, and cantering, and jumping—well, they've paid off. Doc says I have rock-solid thighs." He winked at Dale when she blushed. "Everything of mine works just fine from the knees up." Another wink, and her face was burning.

"Tommy!"

"What, Deebs? Aren't you happy to hear I can still have progeny?"

Yes! All I want is for that to be with me.

They headed out on their horses after dinner, walking slowly side by side on the wide white beaches, the wind warm and inviting, the sun a crimson ball of fire that hung in suspension, casting blistering ripples on the water. She felt them in her heart too. When they stopped to admire the sunset, Dale turned in her saddle and surveyed the hoofprints in the sand. Just two sets. The couples class.

This is how we're supposed to be, Tommy. Can't you see it?

They continued along the shore for hours, talking of school and last year's National Horse Show and the Maclay Medal and the war. Finally, Dale said, "We need to get back to the barn. You're not supposed to stay in the saddle for this long."

"Let's not go back, my Deebs." He looked at her, his eyes soft, full.

My Deebs.

Maybe he did see it.

"Help me down. There's a driftwood dock a little ways off I can use to get back on Infinity." When she threw a questioning look at him, he smiled. "Trust me. I've done this before."

They tethered the horses by the picket fence behind the dunes. Tommy lay on his back, the tide receding farther and farther into the distance. Dale lay beside him, feeling the warmth of the sand as she stared up into the starlit sky. "The sky looks like Infinity . . . flea-bit beauty," she whispered. She rolled to her side, facing Tommy.

She had no idea how long they lay there, but sometime in the dark, Tommy reached across the sand and took her hand. "Thank you for being here." He cleared his throat. "My Deebs." He turned his head to her. In the dark, she could barely make out the white in his eyes, but she heard the emotion in his voice. "Wish we could just stay like this for a while. Not worry about polio and war."

Dale was afraid to breathe. Afraid the shooting star above would betray the shooting star in her heart, the way her hand grew clammy in Tommy's, the way the pinpricks of chill came not from the air, balmy and calm, but from his touch.

At length, Tommy glanced at his wristwatch. "I guess we best be getting back. It's almost midnight."

I never want to leave.

"You sure you can get back on Finny?"

He winked at her. "Just you watch."

She fetched his crutches, helped him to his feet, and led Infinity beside the little wooden platform. "You've done this by yourself?" she asked, then wished she hadn't. There was no way Tommy could maneuver back onto the horse's back alone.

"Hey." He caught her eyes, touched her hand. "Mr. Jorgensen's a good man. He's come out with me a couple of times like this." He winked. "Not quite as fun, but still . . ."

Relief washed over her, like the foamy tide the ocean deposited at her feet as she knelt to wash the sand off her hands. With the dunes at his back, the moon—now a bright white sliver—and the stars shimmering down, Tommy leaned on Dale, pulling himself onto the platform. "Now after you help me up, hand me the crutches."

"I can carry them for you."

"I know. But so can I."

Infinity stood by the wooden structure, tossing his head in the black sky, ears twitching back and forth as the tide's gentle rumble—to and fro, to and fro—drowned out the music from the restaurants and bars that lit up the coast.

It took ten minutes to get Tommy onto Infinity, and Dale was sweating profusely—*perspiring*, her mother would correct—with the effort. When she mounted Krystal and they started down the beach, she didn't dare look over at Tommy for fear he'd read every single thought that kept zipping from her head way down to her heart.

Tonight, something was different. He'd called her "my Deebs" and held her hand and said he could . . . well, insinuated something about children. She grinned to herself as heat warmed her face, she and Tommy giving the horses plenty of free rein.

So peaceful.

Until . . .

The sky ruptured above them, reverberating like splintering

thunder. From somewhere up the beach came sounds of shattering glass. At the same time, far out at sea, orange, yellow, and blue fire shot to the sky as another explosion sent ocean water gushing in every direction.

Krystal danced in circles, whinnying. Infinity reared. Dale watched Tommy slip to the side, completely off-balance, then grab around the gelding's neck, dropping the crutches in the sand as he barely held on. Another explosion erupted, and both horses took off at a mad, uncontrolled gallop. Dale clung to Krystal's neck, gradually regaining her balance, grabbing back hold of the reins, which had slipped through her fingers. It took long minutes for her to pull Krystal to a hand gallop, a canter, a trot, and, finally, a sidestepping walk.

"Whoa! Whoa, girl! Easy."

Dale felt the adrenaline calm when Tommy finally halted Infinity farther up the beach. She trotted over to him. His face was white in the moonlight, his breathing erratic, his gaze fixed out past the shoreline, where the deep orange flames continued to light the sky in the shallow waters at sea.

He cursed, breathing heavily. "I think we've just witnessed a tanker being torpedoed."

"What?" But Dale had heard him. Now crimson flames climbed higher as the continuing sounds of explosions thundered around them, and the horses reared and whinnied and bucked.

When they'd at last calmed their mounts again, Dale saw the whites of Infinity's eyes, nostrils flared, the gelding pivoting back and forth while Tommy tried to soothe him. Tommy's hands were shaking, his legs hanging from the stirrups, but he seemed oblivious. "German U-boats! Submarines attacking our merchant ships, just like your dad's been saying. The German U-boats are right here!"

Krystal danced in circles as the explosions continued. Infinity reared again, throwing Tommy off-balance. Once more, he grabbed around the gelding's neck, hanging on, shifting his weight back to the saddle.

Dale felt the shock, could almost feel the reverberations deep down in her soul. For a few long seconds, she could only stare at the scene lighting up the black sky, like a forest fire out of control. She could almost feel the heat of the flames on her face.

"What does it mean? What should we do?"

Tommy was panting, eyes squeezed shut in pain, one hand grasping where the leather braces had jabbed into his jeans. "I don't know, Deebs." This time, she heard true fear in his voice. "But I bet there are a lot of merchant sailors out there who need to be rescued right now."

Dale leaned over Krystal's neck, her arms around the mare, the heat from the mare's body bringing comfort in the midst of shock.

Tommy seemed in shock too. Then he said, "We've got to get help! I'll bet that tanker was a sitting duck, unarmed and carrying tons and tons of oil and gasoline and other combustible supplies. It was a floating fire hazard, and now it's a bonfire!"

He took off at a gallop with Dale following and watching as he careened on Infinity's back, leaning low over the gelding's withers, the sand from his pounding hooves flying up in her eyes as Krystal stayed close behind. The beach echoed with screams. Lights came on all along the shoreline as Tommy and Dale galloped back to the stables, where three of Tommy's classmates stood, rubbing sleep from their eyes and tucking their white T-shirts into their jeans.

But Tommy was wide-awake and suddenly the general, commandeering troops. "Get your horses! Come on! We've got to help the coast guard get boats out to the tankers before they sink."

"Reckon they're a ways out there in the sea, Tommy," one classmate said.

"I know. That's why they've gotta get the boats out now! And we've got to figure out a way to help."

The boys had just rejoined Tommy with their horses when another blast shook the night, and fire sprang into the air from a different point on the horizon.

Mr. Jorgensen appeared, pulling a shirt over his pajamas, and mounted a big bay. "Come on, boys! Let's go to the coast guard station! We've got to get help out there! It's shallow water, but they're still a good ways offshore. Ten miles at least."

"Can I come?" Dale asked.

Tommy turned, obviously surprised that she was still there. He hesitated, and a look that said "I'm sorry" passed across his face. "No. You go to the houses here, Dale. Go on! Wake them up!"

"Who?"

"Everyone. Tell them to go to their boats. We need boats out there to rescue the sailors. They're floating on an inferno!"

Heart in her throat, she and Krystal tore up the shore, shouting, "Help! Help!" Later, she could not recall what else she had said, only the looks of terror on the faces of people crowding onto the beach, many in their bathrobes.

"If you've got a boat, please go out to the tankers," she babbled, pointing at the two flaming pyres several miles apart on the horizon.

Throughout the night, she watched as, all along the shore, a mismatched navy of yachts and motorboats joined behind several coast guard vessels heading out toward the fiery images at sea.

A marine with a blowtorch approached her. "Ma'am, since you're on horseback, could you please ride along the shore and urge the bystanders to get back inside. It's not safe out here. Only those in the rescue operation are needed."

Fear parched her throat, but she obeyed, trotting back and forth along the shore, where residents gawked and wept. "Go back into your homes. It's not safe!"

She didn't see Tommy for the rest of the night. Eventually, she dismounted from Krystal, remembering images from the propaganda film warning of the destruction from a lit cigarette in the woods or in the hay.

But this was much worse.

They're sitting ducks, completely unarmed . . .

She vomited three times that night, barely aware of the fact that she was emptying her stomach as she stared into the expanse, watching the rescue boats go near the sinking tankers.

Hours later, she stood shivering on the beach, riveted in place as she watched the two merchant vessels sink into the shallow waters off the coast. Tears streaming down her face, she gagged at the stench of oil. In the predawn light, she could make out the tankers slowly tilting backward, their bows sticking out of the sea like the tips of a fiery iceberg. And she wondered how in the world anyone could have survived.

But the boats did bring survivors back to shore. Dale heard the coast guardsmen report, "Many are severely burned and trapped out there. . . ." "Can't imagine many men on the first tanker alive . . . most surely perished."

Dale didn't think there was anything left in her stomach to eject, but bile came up, and she gagged in the sand. She would never forget those first sounds, like a sonic boom that kept reverberating, explosion after explosion. Or the look of those sailors as the boats brought them to shore throughout the night. Burned, terrified, staring empty-eyed out at the sinking tankers—like in a real-live horror film.

By morning, the whole island was in a panic. By noon, the whole state of Georgia, and by the evening of April 9, all those inhabiting the East Coast. Fear and rumors spread almost as quickly as the fire from the explosions.

"The Germans are onshore! The war's here. Spies have landed! There are five other U-boats out there right now, aimed at our tankers. War has come to Georgia!"

15

Allie

Sunday, March 8

I sat cross-legged on my IKEA couch, Maggie snuggled beside me, the album in my lap. I opened the leather cover, which concealed a thick three-ring binder. Taped to the inside cover of the binder was an envelope addressed to me. When I opened the seal, I pulled out a letter from Nana Dale written when I was sixteen.

January 10, 2005

Dear Allie,

It's my eightieth birthday, and I need to get this down in writing in case I don't make it to eighty-one—not that I plan on kicking the bucket anytime soon, but you never know.

I'm writing to you because you have horse sense and a lovely dream, and you care about family history.

I've heard your very big dreams, and I've seen the way you look at the house and the horses. I realize your parents think that selling the house and the property would be the right way

173

to go. I imagine your mother would love to park me in a retire-
ment home and be done with me now. But I digress.

That would be the easiest and the most lucrative choice.
However, you have never been someone who looks for easy or
lucrative. I'm not suggesting that your parents are lazy, but I
don't think they "get" the worth of the land.

This is my point. If you want to keep the house and the prop-
erty and turn it into a healing-horse hotel, or whatever you call
it, there is money enough to do it. There's plenty enough to buy
out your brother and placate your parents.

I set down the letter and sniffed, my fingers tracing Nana Dale's
looping penmanship written in blue ink from her fountain pen.
I had forgotten how my penchant for alliteration had started
because of Nana Dale. She was always stringing together words
like *healing-horse hotel* and *buy out your brother* and *placate your*
parents. I could almost hear her eighty-year-old voice saying those
words out loud.

I continued reading.

Trust me—all the information you need to find the money
is here in this binder. No one else still alive has ever seen this
binder—I call it DB's Diary. (DB and Deebs were Tommy's
nicknames for me.) This diary details a very wonderful and
difficult period in my life when I was about your age. And
if you can indeed make Hickory Hills into your dream of a
healing-horse hotel, well, you need to know more about my life
. . . the part lived during and after the war and before I met
and married your grandfather, Poppa Dan. I haven't shared
this with anyone else because to share it could have hurt those
I love. I certainly didn't want to do that.

But you have grown into a beautiful young woman whom
I can trust with this part of my story, and I believe you will
know how to honor it. And yes, I've almost shared this with you
dozens of times, but I just couldn't quite do it until . . . well,

until now. And obviously, you are only reading this if I am no longer here. I prefer to share it with you this way, after I'm gone.

So there you have it. When you find the money, you can keep the house. You have my blessing to do this.

If for some reason you change your mind, or your parents and Wick pitch a fit, well then, go ahead and sell the place. It will break your heart, I know, but as you will discover in the diary, mine has already been broken so many times, it won't matter to me. I will not turn over in my grave when the house is sold, although the rest of you think I will. And yes, I do hate the idea of cluster mansions and a road—a road!—being added in, but what's to be done? Nothing at all.

Be good, dear,
Nana Dale
P.S. You may think that DB stands for Dale Butler, but it doesn't.

Tears welled in my eyes, just seeing Nana Dale's handwriting and then reading her explanation of the treasure I held in my hands, a treasure she'd been planning to give me for over a decade. And yet, a treasure she didn't want me to have until after she passed away. Why?

All afternoon, I hardly budged from my seat on the couch, so engrossed was I with the diary. The three-ring binder was filled with newspaper clippings that had each been carefully inserted in a clear protective folder. In this way, I could read both the fronts and backs. Nana Dale had underlined whole paragraphs of each article, at times jotting notes in the margins with a blue fountain pen.

I'd relived the elegance of Tommy and Dale's attendance at the National Horse Show, for the same article that was tucked around the Mason jar I'd found in Tommy's Maclay Medal silver pitcher was right here in the scrapbook.

I'd read about the polio scare in the summer of 1941 and especially the article in the society section of the *Atlanta Journal*: *Local Equestrian Champion Afflicted with Polio.* At last, I knew the name of the dreaded disease that Tommy Ridley had contracted that summer. This was the spark, the beginning of Nana Dale's foray into equine therapy. Only now I saw it as more than a desire to help her good friend, Tommy. She loved him. She loved him so much that she was determined that he'd ride again.

And he must have loved her enough to give her a special nickname. DB.

I got up, stretched, and peered out the window, where the rain still sprinkled the pane, but a glimpse of blue sky hung above the thick clouds. I fixed myself an egg on avocado toast and grabbed a La Croix from the fridge, then settled in, turning a page to reveal several clippings from April 1942 with headings *U-boat Attacks Off Coast of Georgia*, *Disaster on the Beach*, *Fire from German U-boats*.

The newspaper clippings recounted the sinking of two tankers near St. Simons Island in April 1942. Most of the articles were written during the days that followed April 8 of that year, but I was especially intrigued by one from the *AJC* in 1999. Nana Dale had underlined whole paragraphs in red ink and jotted notes out to the side in her penciled cursive.

War Comes to Georgia

Lieutenant Commander Reinhard Hardegen, skipper of the German submarine U-123, steered his submarine from its base at Lorient, France, toward the United States. Sailing southward down the Eastern Seaboard, the U-123 sank four ships before entering Georgia's waters.

The sea was quiet when Hardegen spotted the SS *Oklahoma* sailing slowly under a snippet of the moon within sight of St. Simons' faintly glowing beaches ten miles away. In those early morning hours of April 8, 1942, the tanker was silhouetted against the illuminated shoreline. Hardegen fired a torpedo and sank the 9,200-ton oil tanker *Oklahoma*. Less than an hour later, he spotted and sank another tanker, the 8,000-ton *Esso Baton Rouge*. . . .

The sinkings not only brought the seemingly distant war close to home; they helped wake up coastal communities and President

Franklin D. Roosevelt to the immediacy of the German threat during America's darkest days of World War II.

Another short article explained,

Merchant mariners were civilians employed by companies hired by the government to haul badly needed war supplies such as oil, gasoline, guns, and food. Those who weren't too old to be drafted, or classified as physically unfit, were exempt from the draft only while sailing. Though they were relatively few, the merchant mariners faced the worst odds—one out of every 32 who served died, compared with one in every 34 US Marines or one in 48 GIs—and they are considered by many experts to be a prime reason the Allies won the war. Although not well known, many more people died in the Battle of the Atlantic during WWII than the 2,400 who perished at Pearl Harbor.

I sat back in the chair, staring at all of Nana Dale's scribblings and stars beside this article. *WE WERE THERE!* she'd written in caps beside the explanation of the sinkings. I knew my family had vacationed on the Golden Isles for decades. Long, luxurious, blissful days.

But reading the different accounts reminded me of watching the film *Darkest Hour* a few years earlier, about the many different British civilian boats crossing the English Channel to rescue the stranded soldiers on the French beaches in May 1940. A microcosm of that scene had happened right in Georgia two years later, and I was pretty sure Nana Dale had been watching.

She'd made notes with exclamation marks: *It's about time they realize the sacrifice!* And *This was exactly the impetus that led to the mounted patrol!* And then *Little did I know about Essie!* And finally, beside the sentence *In those early morning hours of April 8, 1942,* Nana Dale had written *Moonlight ride with Tommy* and drawn a small heart beside it.

I wondered if Tommy had been a merchant mariner, but no, he was evidently riding a horse with Nana Dale when the sinkings occurred. Had he died in the Battle of the Atlantic?

As I was pondering these questions, my cell rang. When the name flashed across my screen, I almost didn't answer. How dare he call me on a Sunday afternoon?

He's calling on a Sunday afternoon because you've been ignoring all his other calls and messages.

I could no longer put off the inevitable unpleasant conversation. "Hello?"

"Miss Massey?"

"Yes, Mr. Hightower?"

"How nice of you to finally answer your phone! I don't wish to be difficult"—*Yeah, right*—"but I've noticed your car over at the property several times. Rumor also has it that you know the backhoe man—who, by the way, is as slow as Christmas. I can hire another worker in a flash if he can't get his rear in gear! Plenty of others would like to excavate for 'dinosaur bones.'" He snickered, the sarcasm in his voice as thick as the red mud in the ring.

"So please get this straight: The house is going to be imploded whether you empty it out or not. Make no doubt about it—you will not stop this. You've got twenty days and counting, and I happen to know you haven't even confirmed a date for the estate sale. I'm sorry for your loss, but it doesn't change the timetable."

"I am perfectly aware of your scheme, thank you very much!" I fairly yelled into my cell before clicking it off.

Good grief. How many clichés did he insert into one thirty-second phone call?

I'd often regretted the call I'd made to Mr. Hightower soon after the will was read in December, accusing him of all kinds of injustices against my grandmother—which of course, did no good. He'd figured out quickly that I was the one in charge of and cheated out of the estate, and he liked to remind me that there was nothing I could do about it. I'd stopped answering his calls a month ago. His were not idle threats.

And now, with Barnell's news that Ralph Hightower and I were supposedly related, I regretted it even more. I regretted everything to do with how the property was stolen. And my reaction.

And losing Austin.

Less than three weeks left now. My stomach churned. I finally had the cherrywood chest. *The thing* Nana Dale had bequeathed me to ensure that my dream would stay alive. Right? Surely this binder would reveal more to give me hope than something floating around in my subconscious.

Or maybe it was just obsession. But how would I know?

And how could I clean out the house? In truth, I hadn't planned to get rid of anything. I was supposed to be moving into the house as is, spending my free time slowly going through all the memorabilia, deciding what to keep and what to give or throw away.

But once I'd moved in, I knew I wouldn't have carved out space to go through all these things. I'd have been planning a wedding and opening an equine therapy center, and life would have hurled a lot of busyness my way.

I stared down at the binder on my lap, convinced it held all the clues I needed to answer my questions.

Where on earth have you stashed the money, Nana Dale?

What happened to Tommy?

And Essie?

I knew my grandmother had shown the mare and been successful. I had the photos, ribbons, and trophies to prove it. But that had not happened yet in 1942. Instead, a war and polio were exploding all of Nana Dale's and Tommy's dreams. By my calculations, Nana Dale was seventeen and Tommy a year or two older. Watching torpedoes attack tankers and riding together in the moonlight on horseback . . .

On horseback!

Riding!

I stood up quickly, dislodging Maggie from my lap. She glared at me, wrapped herself around my legs, and meandered off with a pitiful meow.

Sunday afternoons were my personal therapy time. Before losing the property, when the horses were still housed at Hickory Hills, I'd head to the barn, saddle up my mare, and ride her through

179

the trails behind the property. Then we'd walk down the street, her horseshoes making that clickity scraping sound on the pavement, until we came to Nancy Creek, where we'd trot along the well-groomed trails that paralleled the riverbed, just me and my mare, dodging the occasional joggers. Live oaks and hickories and dogwoods and pines towered over us, shading the trails. Around a bend, the trail emptied out into a wide-open field. Foxtrot's pace always quickened as we neared that turn in the trail, and as soon as her hooves stepped into the grassy expanse, she took off at a canter that morphed into a full-out gallop.

My therapy indeed—the woods with all their wonders, the sunny fields, and Foxtrot and I moving as one. Harmony and peacefulness would descend on me in those moments of solitude.

The woods are lovely, dark and deep . . .

Now I slipped on jeans and a sweatshirt and drove to Chastain, Foxtrot's new home, ever since Horrible Mr. Hightower had stolen mine.

My mare was feisty and unpredictable, but she was as pretty as any of the more expensive push-button ponies and horses. That's what we called them, the ones that the moms had paid a fortune for, the ones with the kids perched on their backs and off they went around the course over the fences, behaving perfectly.

There was nothing push-button about Foxtrot. We called her "high-strung" and "a pack of nerves," much as my grandmom used to describe each of her mares.

And me.

"You're high-strung, Allie. It's okay; it's a good thing. You've got that thoroughbred blood in you, but you have to be careful, have to rein it in like you do your horse once in a while. Life can be nerve-racking, so remember to take deep breaths."

This whole business about the house and the property, it had been nerve-racking, and I was like my thoroughbred mare, whinnying and rearing and kicking and showing the whites of my eyes and pulling away from the bridle. I wanted this estate with all my heart, and I wasn't going to give up until I'd watched the house implode.

At times, Nana Dale would look at me and nod approvingly as she said, *"You're as stubborn as the day is long."* Stubborn, yes. Obsessed, maybe. And definitely refusing to be intimidated by that no-good, in-some-way-related-to-me contractor who had cheated Nana Dale out of everything she loved.

I leaned over the stall door, where Foxtrot, rump toward me, was munching on hay, her black tail swishing from side to side. "Hey there, Foxie." She lifted her head, twisted her neck around, pricked her ears forward, and meandered to the door. "Did you think I'd forgotten about our ride? Sorry to be late. It's just that, well, you can't imagine what in the world I've gotten myself into now."

She nickered, sending a sprinkle of hay and liquid onto my waiting hand. I rubbed up and down the hard bones on her forehead, then scratched under her chin with her big dark eyes watching me, a mixture of approval and understanding in them.

"Horses understand more than humans, Allie. They can tell how your day is going by the way you rub their forehead or brush their bellies or hold the reins. They sense it."

How often had Nana Dale repeated some version of this to me?

"Oh, you know it all, anyway," I continued to Foxtrot. "I've told you the story while I mucked your stall and picked out your hooves. And no, it's not just about the boy. It's about everything. And don't tell me that you don't miss Hickory Hills! It's been your home for almost ten years too." I wrapped my arms around her neck, took in deep breaths of that familiar scent of horsehair and sweet, fresh shavings. "I can't seem to let it go."

She moved her muzzle to my jeans pocket, where she knew I had a carrot waiting. As she munched on it, I attached the lead shank to her halter, opened the stall door, and led her into the front of the barn, putting her in crossties. Fetching my bucket of brushes from the tack room, I returned and began currying her belly. Dust billowed all around as I removed mounds of caked-on dirt.

"Well, you certainly had a fine time rolling in the mud yesterday, didn't you, girl?"

She stamped her leg, snorted, shook her head, disapproving, telling me in her way to "Hurry up!"

"Hey, friend," Tricia said, leading her piebald mare, Firecracker, over to where I had mounted Foxtrot. Tricia twisted her own black mane and perched it on top of her head, securing it with her hard hat.

Since we'd moved our mares from Hickory Hills to Chastain in January, Tricia and I had often ridden together on Sunday afternoons.

"Any luck at the Hills?" Tricia asked, using her term of endearment for the place that had been a second home to her for so many years. She knew every bit of the drama.

"Yes!" I quickly filled her in on finding the cherrywood chest and the leather binder as we mounted our mares.

"That's awesome. So did Nana Dale leave you details about where to find the money?"

"Nope. I just keep falling down rabbit hole after rabbit hole till I'm completely lost. Right now, I'm smack-dab in the middle of the Battle of the Atlantic and it feels like . . ." I turned Foxtrot, heading to the ring. "Never mind."

"Hey. I know the whole story. If it helps to spit it out to an objective bystander, go right ahead."

"Ha. Objective, you are not. But thanks. It feels like I'm inching up on something that Nana Dale never got around to telling me . . . but wanted to. No, that's not it, exactly. See, over ten years ago, she wrote me a letter that she taped in the front of the leather binder. She wanted me to find out about a part of her life that she'd kept secret from everyone else. She said she didn't want to hurt people she loved, but now that she's gone, she trusts me to know how to handle the information. I've just started looking through it—sorry, that's why I'm late. But she makes it sound like the binder will explain how I can keep Hickory Hills."

"So with all the digging around and rabbit trails, I take it you're not making significant progress emptying out the house."

"Ha, again. Like zero. Or negative five."

"And explain why exactly you won't let your mom help you pack things up?"

"Mom just freaks out when I bring any of it up."

"Define 'freaks out.'" Tricia had also grown up around my mother.

"Gets all defensive and then just clamps her mouth shut and then feels bad and tries to brush it all away."

"What if you sent her into a nonissue room? Couldn't she be trusted to pack up, I don't know, tax files or kitchen pots and pans?"

"I tried that. She makes comments that make me go ballistic."

"Aha. The truth comes out." Tricia was one of only two people who could give me constructive criticism without it sending me into a spiral of self-loathing or a full-blown temper tantrum. The other was Austin, and I had finally literally blown it with him.

"What if I brought over two or three dozen huge plastic containers and threw everything you could possibly want to keep in them and carted them into storage? At least you wouldn't lose it all. You could go through those bins later and spend time now looking through the 'mysterious binder'"—she made quote marks with her hands—"while the estate planners do their thing at the house."

"Mm-hmm." I wasn't really paying attention. I nudged Foxtrot forward, but Tricia was not going to be thwarted.

She trotted up beside me on Cracker. "You are so stubborn! You're hard on yourself, and you won't let anyone else help you."

"I tried, remember. But I drove Austin crazy."

Tricia leaned over and grabbed Foxtrot's reins, pulling both horses to a halt. She pivoted in her saddle so that she faced me, took me by the shoulders, and gave me a gentle shake. "I'm not your fiancé. I promise I won't break up with you if you go all obsessive on me. And I know, he didn't technically break up. You gave the ring back. Whatever."

I pulled Tricia into an awkward hug across the space between us. "Thanks a lot. At least you and Foxtrot have my back."

"We do. Now, no more depressing talk. Let's go for a ride!"

Two hours later, I was walking out Foxtrot after having hosed her off from our afternoon frolic. Out of the corner of my eye, I caught sight of a tall, lanky young man dressed in worn Levi's and a blue button-down oxford shirt. His blond hair brushed the top of his collar.

My heart stopped. Of course Austin the vet would be at Chastain. But on a Sunday? Before, we'd spent Sunday afternoons riding together. Was he riding with someone else?

I froze, unsure of what to do.

Austin turned from where he was holding a bucket in one hand, patting a palomino with the other as he leaned against the stall door, chatting with a young woman. *A pretty little palomino herself*, I seethed inside. I wasn't sure who would make the first move, but since I could be as stubborn as Nana Dale, I wasn't at all surprised when he walked over.

"Hey, good to see you." He stopped before he used a term of endearment, but it was there, hanging between us like a firefly ready to light up the dusk.

"Making your Sunday rounds?" I asked, sarcasm dripping.

I led Foxtrot to her stall, threw the fly sheet over her back, attached the buckles, and latched the stall door. All the things I used to do when Austin and I took Sunday afternoon rides together.

"Oh, you know. I was on call. Pony colicked in the night." He shrugged, and his thin face showed deep exhaustion.

I wanted to go over to him, brush the hair off his forehead. "Oh wow. You've been here all that time?"

He nodded. Gave a tiny grin. "Yeah. But the pony's gonna make it. Was touch and go, but he's okay." He suppressed a yawn. "I didn't have anywhere else to be." He gave a soft smile, the kind that made something jump in the pit of my stomach. Then he reached over and scratched Foxtrot between her ears. He knew how much she loved that. "Glad you got to take a ride."

"Yeah. I needed a break." I stuffed my hands in my jeans.

Unconsciously, Austin did the same. That was how it had been, him mimicking me. Me mimicking him. Unconsciously conscious of the other's presence. So easy, so . . . right.

"How's the packing going?" Blue eyes, sympathetic, hesitant.

"Oh, you know. Great. Having a real blast."

He furrowed his brow, but the last thing I wanted was to see compassion on his face. "I'm sure it's not easy."

"No, it's not," I mumbled, glancing up at him. "It's all such a mess, Austin. I haven't even begun packing." My voice broke, and I nibbled my lip and willed myself not to cry.

I saw Tricia round the corner, worry splayed across her face, her eyes saying *Calm down, girl.*

"I found the cherrywood chest," I volunteered. Austin knew all about the letter Nana Dale had left me in the will.

"Wow. So you've still been searching?"

To be fair, he asked the question with no ill will intended. And I knew it. But I heard ill will just the same, and all the pent-up emotions of the past month without Austin came tumbling out.

"Yes, your obsessed ex-fiancée is still searching for a way to keep the house and the property. And I know I don't have an ounce of horse sense, even though Nana Dale always said I did, but if I did, I'd stop and beg you to come back, and I'd let the lying, thieving Ralph Hightower—my distant cousin, no less—I'd let him implode the whole thing. But instead—*instead*—I'm looking at dinosaur bones with Barnell, and I'm searching through this scrapbook that Nana Dale had hidden in the cherry box that's somehow supposed to lead me to money."

And missing you. Oh, how I'm missing you!

I burst into tears, turned—swiveled, really—and started to walk away quickly, but his hand was on my arm, and then it was around my shoulders.

"I'm so sorry for you, Allie. I don't know how to help you anymore, but I want to if there's something, anything I can do."

Don't be kind to me. I have to keep searching now that I've found something. Don't be kind.

I sobbed, swiping my hands over my eyes and across my runny nose. Finally, I managed, "There is. Leave me alone. Please just leave me alone!"

This time I did break into a run, leaving him holding a bucket of oats, a silver stethoscope draped around his neck.

My heart didn't stop hammering for an hour. By that time, back in my apartment, I'd showered again, had a cup of herbal tea, wrapped myself in my favorite fleece throw, and desperate to get Austin out of my thoughts, returned to the hidden scrapbook.

I flipped the translucent folder to the next page and read the newspaper headline: *Ladies Who Launch: Women of the Brunswick Shipyard.* The article was recent—from 2019—but it chronicled how women had been essential to building Liberty ships. And there was a black-and-white photo of a group of women dressed in welding attire, one carrying the American flag, walking out of the entrance to J.A. Jones Construction Company at the Brunswick Shipyard. Nana Dale had circled the faces of several women and written *My colleagues* beside them. Reading the article, I gathered that Nana Dale had been a welder at this shipyard. She was full of surprises.

I turned the next page in the binder to reveal a brightly colored rectangular cardstock leaflet: *World War II Home Front Museum.* On one side was a photo of two young girls watching an airplane simulation.

Discover coastal Georgia's extraordinary contributions to winning World War II. Test your skills as a plane spotter watching the skies for enemy aircraft. Train to direct fighter pilots like the officers at Naval Air Station St. Simons . . .

The reverse side of the leaflet showed two color photos, one of an exhibit from the museum, and the other of the museum itself, a two-story colonial revival house with a symmetrical facade, classical columns, and wood shingle siding. An American flag flapped on a high pole while a large sign proclaimed *Coastal Georgia Historical Society, World War II, Home Front Museum, Coastal Georgia at War.*

The copy on this side of the publicity read

The museum is housed in the historic St. Simons Coast Guard Station, built in 1936. Step back to April 8, 1942, when the crew from this station rescued survivors of two American ships torpedoed by a German U-boat 13 miles off St. Simons Island. Visitors of all ages will be inspired by the stories of ordinary Americans doing their part to win the war.

Another letter written on Nana Dale's monogrammed stationery was stuck in beside the leaflet.

September 14, 2018

Allie, I'd like you to visit this museum. It's just opened, and I hear it has a wonderful display of all that happened on April 8, 1942. I'm sure it will give you more details about that time than I have put in the diary. And there is a docent there, Dr. Cressman, who can give you more information about the US Coast Guard Mounted Beach Patrol. He's a lovely man, retired military, whom I met online in a forum and who has kept me up on the more recent discoveries relating to that time.

Then, dear Allie, please go to Hilton Head. It's such a big part of my story too. Go to Camp McDougal. And find Mr. Hampton. I can't remember his first name, but he knows the story. I don't know if anyone else is still alive, but surely he is. He was just a boy in 1943.

I wish I could go with you, but I don't have the strength for that trip. And as you know, I'd prefer you to find out about this information after I'm no longer around.

*I am so proud of all the work you've done to get your degrees
and accreditation for Hickory Hills. It's going to happen!*

*Sending love,
Nana Dale*

Now my heart was beating even harder. A quick Google search
confirmed that the museum had only recently opened, in 2018.
By then, Nana Dale could no longer travel, but why didn't she
tell me about this museum earlier if it was so important to her? I
realized as well, my heart continuing to pound, that Nana Dale
had inserted information into this scrapbook almost up until the
day she died.

I looked at the leaflet again. St. Simons Island. We'd vacationed
there probably a half-dozen times throughout the years, and I remembered stories about the nearby plant in Brunswick that made
Liberty ships during the war.

"I'm going there. I'm going to see all of it," I said out loud to no
one, except for Maggie, who was pouting underneath the couch.
Hoping to appease her, I gave my excuse. "Look, Nana Dale asked
me to go, Mags. I have to." I reached underneath the couch and
brought her out by the scruff of her neck, set her in my lap, and
began scratching behind her ears and turning her over and rubbing her tummy. She purred. "I'm going, Mags, even though the
estate planner is coming tomorrow and my treacherous cousin is
breathing down my neck."

My thoughts were racing ahead of me. Then they came to a
screeching halt, as did my hand on Maggie's stomach. She glared
up at me, but I ignored her.

Why should I go? What in the world did it matter that I visit
these places? How could that help anything at all? In that moment,
I felt like Nana Dale was sending me on a wild goose chase, one
of Austin's favorite expressions. I'd already wasted three months
looking for something that Nana Dale had evidently only buried
in her mind.

I settled back in the chair as if my mare had refused the last jump in the finals, and I'd been disqualified.

Obsessed. That word kept finding its way into the recesses of my mind, tormenting me.

Austin. Oh, Austin. If you were here, if we were together, you'd say, "You bet, Allie! Let's go!" You always understood my passion for this project. Until . . . you didn't. Until passion turned into obsession, and I ignored all the warning signs and galloped headfirst into disaster.

As I tossed and turned in bed that night, I waited for the nightmares to come.

Disqualified. Oh yeah. I'd been disqualified big-time. And now a scrapbook full of newspaper clippings was all that was left as a testimony of the past and a foreshadowing of what might have been.

16

Dale

Dale couldn't stop the nightmares, the ghoulish faces of burned men that swirled around her. At last, she sat up in bed, concentrating hard on recovering the feeling of Tommy's hand in hers. But then she saw in living color the explosions and the fire and the terrified expressions of the sailors brought to shore. Nineteen had survived the SS *Oklahoma*, but no one could reach the ship's dead. Thirty-eight sailors in all. Dale did the math. That meant nineteen had perished. Nineteen!

Most of the forty-one crew from the *Esso Baton Rouge* had escaped on lifeboats, but three of their sailors had also perished.

"I saw the captain of the *Oklahoma*, Dale," Tommy whispered two days after the explosions. "Said he was asleep in his cabin when the torpedo struck. He got in a lifeboat, but then he climbed back onto the sinking ship after hearing men's cries of distress. He waded into waist-deep water to retrieve an injured crewman who died in his arms on the lifeboat." He took a breath, eyes down. "I also heard that the rowboats that went out later could sail right through the gigantic holes the torpedo blasts made in the tankers."

Dale shivered. She didn't want to hear anything else. She could feel the terror in her gut and smell the sickening odor of burning flesh and almost taste the oil that washed ashore, fouling the beaches. But it was the rumors of Germans landing on shore that caused more panic to the citizens than the sight of the wrecked boats.

And then there were other rumors—that the government had known of the danger of U-boats but didn't want to cause mass hysteria. That because these islands were resorts and the business owners didn't want to lose tourists, blackouts had not been deemed necessary. That the official word, issued daily—*Sighted sub, sunk same*—was a lie. Tommy reported that only a few German subs had been sighted, but over eighty US merchant vessels had been sunk in the past five months.

Dale had heard about the mass hysteria surrounding the Wall Street Crash in 1929, but she'd only been four years old and had no memory of it. But this time, she felt the hysteria, tasted it in the seawater, smelled it in the stench of the thick oil that ruined the beaches, and saw it printed on the creepy posters that sprang up around St. Simons after April 8.

A poster with a black background showed a man, obviously drowning, his head barely out of the swirling water, eyes bulging, and an oversized right arm pointing forward. Giant white print above and below the gruesome image declared *SOMEONE TALKED!*

Another showed the body of a submarine, its periscope up, and the boat's tower in the form of a black Nazi helmet with menacing white eyes, the caption proclaiming *He's watching YOU!*

Dale believed it. She'd seen it herself.

Suddenly the word *blackout* was all anyone talked about. Regulations called for curtains on windows and covers on the headlights of cars.

Posted on storefronts were signs advising

What to Do in Blackouts

- **Householders**

  Stay at home.
  Put out lights in rooms not blacked out.
  Use no matches or lights outdoors.
  Let no light escape from your house.

- **Pedestrians**

  Walk carefully, don't run.
  Keep close to buildings and away from curb.
  Don't smoke.
  Use no matches or flashlights.
  Cross streets at intersections.

- **Motorists**

  Park at curb—at once.
  Put out all lights.
  Seek shelter.

- **Warning!**

  Emergency blackouts will be enforced by the police assisted by
  air raid wardens. Carelessness in observing these precautions
  may invite disaster.

Dale stared at the last sentence on the windowfront of the
grocer's and thought, *Carelessness has already invited disaster*. The
papers said it—the lights on shore made the tankers easy targets.

BLACKOUT MEANS BLACK! another poster announced,
and yet another said *When in Doubt, Lights Out!*

But it was the poster that hung on the grocery window on the
Friday after the sinkings that caused Dale's stomach to sink, plum-
meting low like the ships at sea.

This one showed billowing black smoke escaping from a sinking tanker, nose turned skyward against a blood-red sky with the
headline *Loose Lips Might Sink Ships*.

Maybe loose lips had *sunk ships*. She had seen the tankers sinking, and the images engraved in her mind were more realistic than these propaganda posters.

Every day, her mother called, shrieking through the phone lines at the Ridleys' mansion, "Come home right now, Barbara Dale! Get away from that island." Her mother sounded as hysterical as every other adult.

But Tommy came alive with nervous energy. "There's got to be something I can do."

She was terrified that he'd consider going out on a tanker himself.

"You've already done something—you helped rescue the sailors."

He tilted his head. "That was one night, Deebs. Just one night. The government isn't well prepared—now they see that they've got to get more involved here. They're going to need navy escort ships along the coast."

"Well, you can't join the navy!"

He glared at her. "Don't you think I know that?" Then his eyes softened. "I know that. But I can join something."

At the end of the week, Dale returned home to Atlanta, confused and nervous. The sensation of Tommy's hand in hers still throbbed in her pulse, but Tommy's mind had steered to the Atlantic coast and the battle raging there. What did he intend to do next? Dale hoped his plans included her.

───── ♡ ─────

Dale sat in class, wondering about Tommy. In a month, she would graduate, but so many wouldn't. Day after day, the classrooms grew sparser. She'd heard that millions of high schoolers were dropping out to join some part of the military. She tried not to show her gratitude that Tommy couldn't join, but she felt it way down in her heart, and it seeped into her bones.

Tommy would be safe.

But she knew this was not guaranteed. She'd seen the sinking tankers. Would he work as a merchant sailor? Every morning at breakfast, her father read reports of more tankers torpedoed off the Atlantic coast, from Massachusetts to Virginia to North Carolina to Florida.

And suddenly, everyone was quoting J. Edgar Hoover, the head of the FBI, who had proclaimed somberly, "The spy, the saboteur, the subverter must be met and conquered!"

"Looks like Hoover was right to cause hysteria," her father grunted one morning in between bites of eggs and bacon. He slid the newspaper across the table to Dale, where she read the report.

On June 13, a lone coast guardsman spotted four Nazi saboteurs landing on Long Island, New York. They'd come ashore and tried to bribe him, but he escaped and reported the incident, eventually leading authorities to where the men had buried explosives in the sand, disguised as blocks of coal. The authorities also found incendiary devices hidden in pen and pencil sets.

On June 17, four other Nazi saboteurs landed on Ponte Vedra Beach in Florida. These incidents in both New York and Florida make it obvious that America can be invaded. The Atlantic coast seems to face the most danger because of the strength of the German U-boats. . . .

Oh yeah. Dale had seen just what a German U-boat could accomplish, and she relived it night after night. Now Nazis had been spotted on Ponte Vedra, less than two hours away from St. Simons.

Within ten days, all eight of the saboteurs had been caught by the FBI. Six of the men were hanged, and the others escaped with life in prison because they aided the FBI with information.

Yet Dale tasted oil and fear.

—— Ω ——

Tommy finished his freshman year at the private coastal college, and Dale graduated from high school during the mayhem of the searches for the German saboteurs. A year after polio had crippled him, Tommy was as comfortable on Infinity as he had been before polio. He couldn't mount or dismount on his own, and he would likely never jump again, but he was at ease on horseback.

"I'm staying on the island, continuing my therapy, and working at the munitions factory in Brunswick," Tommy informed Dale when he came home to Atlanta for the weekend.

"Then I'm coming with you!"

He grinned at her. "Sure! Why not? They're hiring women too."

"Yeah, I've heard that they're recruiting women and Negroes at the Brunswick shipyards."

Just the day before, she'd seen the posters go up: *The more WOMEN who work, the sooner we win! Women are also needed as nurses, teachers, waitresses, taxi drivers, bus drivers. See your local US Employment Service.*

"You can live with us," Tommy encouraged, "and have the same bedroom as you did when you visited. There are enough bedrooms in this house for an army."

Later that evening, she informed her father. "Daddy, I'm going to help in Brunswick for the summer. Tommy said I can live with his family on St. Simons."

Her father nodded, not the least bit surprised. "Looks like I'll be going to work in Brunswick too, Dale."

Dale, however, was surprised. "Why?"

"Fifteen hundred miles of new telephone circuits are being placed underground in the beaches. The coast guard's hiring all my trained lumbermen to clear the land for the installation of the new telephone system."

"What's it for?"

"A beach patrol, with reporting stations at quarter-mile intervals. The coast guard is authorizing all naval districts along American coasts to organize beach patrols to act as a coastal information system. The patrols won't provide military protection—that's the army's job—but they'll have outposts and be responsible for reporting suspicious activity along the coastline. Then if there's real danger from the enemy, the army will do the fighting."

"They're not part of the military?"

"No, but desperate times call for desperate measures." She wished her father didn't sound so cynical when he used that clichéd expression. "The U-boats are still sinking tankers along our coast like they're toys. The military realizes they need more help. I guess those saboteurs in New England and Florida finally got their attention."

"And the torpedoed tankers off St. Simons."

Her father set the paper down. "Yes. Of course. That too. I'm sorry you had to witness such horror."

"It *was* horrible, Daddy. I have nightmares about it."

He reached across the table and placed his hand on hers. "I know."

"But at least I can help now."

"I'm not sure that's a good idea, Dale. It's not safe. I won't have you living on an island with Nazis about!" was her mother's response when she shared her plan.

"Mama, it's war. Everybody's helping. Why, half the boys in my class have joined the military. I've seen the posters, Mama. They're hiring girls. I'm almost eighteen, and I can live with Tommy's parents. I won't be in any danger, but I can help."

Her mother pushed a few peas around on her plate, cleared her throat, and left the table, her face ashen.

"Give her a little time, Dale," her father said. "She'll come around."

One night in early July, while the three of them were eating dinner, her father brought up the subject again. "Eleanor, you remember that I told you that in March the US Maritime Commission gave Brunswick Marine Construction Corporation a contract to build thirty Liberty ships?"

"I remember, Jeremiah."

"Well, they've constructed a new federally owned shipyard on the Brunswick River, where six ships can be assembled at one time. It's part of the Emergency Shipbuilding Program involving over a dozen shipyards across the country. The country's desperate for more cargo ships."

Dale watched her mother's face, still as stone, while her father explained what her mother already knew. "More ships are being sunk than built, by four to one—I'd call those stats pretty depressing."

"I'm already aware of this, Jeremiah." Her tone was icy.

"I think we should allow Dale to be employed at the shipyard, helping construct those Liberty ships."

Dale had read plenty about this new class of cargo ships that were designed to be built quickly and cheaply using prefabricated parts.

She saw a hint of a smile turn up the corners of her mother's stern face. "Do you know that FDR's original name for them was the Ugly Duckling? I think that's much more appropriate. They're monstrous looking!"

Then her whole face relaxed, and Dale couldn't tell if it was from resignation or relief. "Good ole FDR is a bit of a boat snob, and evidently, he offended the ship's builder with that name." Dale felt hope blossom in her gut. Her mother was softening; she could see it. "And what did the builder retort?" Now she stared at her daughter.

"'These ships will provide Liberty to many,'" Dale interjected.

"For that correct answer, I'll allow you to go to Brunswick to help build those ugly ducklings!"

Dale hopped up from the table, upsetting her water glass and spilling it all over her now-empty plate. "Thank you, Mama! Oh, thank you!"

"Who knows? I might join in too!"

As she hugged her mother, her father offered a smile and a wink.

In the end, Dale's whole family moved down to St. Simons to live in the Ridleys' mansion. Krystal came as well. Every day, Mrs. Ridley drove Tommy, Mrs. Butler, and Dale to the newly built shipyard, while Mr. Butler worked tirelessly with the installation of the phone lines along the beach. Tommy worked at the shipyard, a few buildings away from Dale's post as a welder. In fact, due in large part to the high wages being paid for the work, thousands of people from across the South invaded Brunswick to join in the shipbuilding process, so much so that the Brunswick shipyards became the area's largest industry.

Dale was thankful for the mansion on St. Simons. As people continued to flood into the region looking for work, finding housing became a problem. The increase was so rapid that Brunswick officials allowed new arrivals to sleep in one of the town squares. Mrs. Ridley even rented out two of the extra bedrooms at their house on St. Simons to four young women working at the shipyard.

"It's really swell to be here with y'all," a pretty blonde named Evelyn chimed. The other three agreed. "We don't mind sharing a room together or even a mattress on the floor. At least we each have our own beds!"

They laughed.

"What's so funny?" Dale asked.

"Haven't you heard what loads of kids are doing? Hot-bedding, it's called. One girl will come home from her shift to sleep in a bed that's just been vacated by another girl just going in to work. Seems a little creepy to me. Gee whiz, it's nice to be in this fancy house!"

Indeed, the Brunswick Shipyard's employees worked eight-hour shifts around-the-clock in what seemed to Dale like a desperate attempt to build more ships than the Germans could sink.

Dale loved the challenge of welding. Though most of the women lacked experience, as new employees, she and the others were put to work after only a few days of training. As soon as Dale learned how, she began tacking. Then she moved to flat welding, vertical welding, and even overhead welding. With her leather gloves and drop-down mask, Dale loved the adventure, the challenge of hanging on to the scaffolding with one hand and welding with her torch in the other.

One evening, Dale shared her day's work in whispers with Tommy. "This morning I was welding at the bottom of the ship, and this afternoon, I climbed to the top of the mast pole to weld."

"You're not afraid of anything, Deebs!" Tommy said.

"I am afraid of one thing. That Mama will find out that the work is dangerous and forbid it!"

"Don't worry. She and my mother are enjoying all their cooking for the employees. We won't let them know."

And I'm afraid for you, Tommy. I'm afraid I'm going to lose you to the war and that you're going to find another job far away that's more exciting than working in Brunswick.

In late August, after eating dinner with all those present at the St. Simons house, Tommy motioned Dale out onto the flagstone patio. He leaned on his cane, then pointed out to the beach. "Take a walk with me, Deebs."

Together, they walked past the dunes to the little wooden platform his parents had built so Tommy could more easily mount and dismount Infinity. But this evening, they settled into two Adirondack chairs. Dale tried to read the expression on his face, tried to squelch the hope that he wanted simply to be with her.

She tried to smile when, instead, he said, "Great news, Deebs! I've signed up to be part of the beach patrol."

The beach patrol.

She preferred to have him working in one of the adjacent rooms in the shipyard, but she attempted to muster some enthusiasm. "Daddy's men have helped set up the telephone lines for that. What will you be doing?"

"We're s'posed to do three main things: look out for suspicious water vessels of any kind, and then report and prevent any enemy landings. We'll also mess up communications between enemy ships and people on shore." Tommy's eyes twinkled. "And of course, we'll still do search and rescue too."

"Preventing enemy landings sounds dangerous. I read the story about the coast guardsman in New York."

"Deebs, relax. Basically, we'll be providing reassurance to the general public."

When Dale looked unconvinced, Tommy reached across the space between them and tweaked her nose. "Don't worry; it's simple. The army defends the land, the navy defends the seas, and the coast guard becomes the part of the navy in charge of patrolling the beaches. We'll use picket boat patrols, beach patrols, and watchtowers. Simple."

"But patrolling . . . that'll be a lot of walking for you."

Here, Tommy threw his head back and laughed. "No, that's the best part! We'll be patrolling the beaches on horseback. Horses, Deebs! Don't have to be military, just need to be able to ride. I figure I can do that pretty well."

Oh yeah. He could do that.

Dale shook her head, squinted, and then smiled. "Wow. Seriously?"

His enthusiastic nod made her laugh.

"That's perfect."

"Yep. The mounted patrol will be the eyes and ears of the army and navy."

Invincible, charismatic Tommy was back, but Dale could feel him leaving her. She wanted his hand in hers, wanted him to call her "my Deebs" again. For six years, they had ridden together up in the ring and at horse shows all along the East Coast. Maybe he'd still be staying along the coast, but now, even if he stayed nearby on Southern beaches, she feared he'd leave in another way, sucked away not by a flirtatious debutante, but by the thrill of war.

The sky was drifting from pale pink to lavender to cobalt blue, but even the romance of the night could not dislodge the disappointment that sat deep in her gut. "When do you start?" she asked through a catch in her throat.

He leaned across his chair, his freckled face close, and her heart hammered. "Not until January. And guess where I'll be stationed for training?"

"No idea."

"On Hilton Head Island. Then they'll send me out to a remote station."

Hilton Head. She'd heard of this island off the coast of South Carolina, renowned mainly for its sea pines that were especially great for lumber. The island was mostly unknown to tourists, and while not a part of the Golden Isles, was still close by.

He grinned. "I'll be in the reserves with a whole bunch of guys who know how to ride." Then he added, "And lots who don't ride yet. We'll be teaching them." His grin got wider. "The army is going to provide the horses, but the coast guard has to come up with the men. So they've been recruiting. Cowboys, jockeys, polo players, and me! All ages of men from seventeen to seventy-one, all of us in some way unable to serve overseas. It'll be swell!"

Dale had rarely seen Tommy so excited, even though he always breathed excitement. This seemed like a bigger rush to him than taking Infinity over a five-foot brick wall.

"The US Coast Guard Mounted Beach Patrol. That's a mouthful."

"We've already shortened it. We're going to call ourselves the Sand Pounders."

"The Sand Pounders. That's descriptive. It sounds like a great fit for you. But still. Getting on and off the horse. Your legs . . ."

"We always go out in pairs. Two guys, two horses, and sometimes there's even a dog."

Horses and dogs? Dale wanted to sign up. She'd much prefer that to building ships.

"So what will you do? Will you have guns and stuff?"

"Don't look so horrified! This is what I was made for. And we're not going to be shooting anyone. Like I said, we're just supposed to patrol the beaches. We report what we see, and then the army will do the rest."

"But will you have guns?" she insisted on knowing.

"We'll have rifles and flare pistols. Using the horses means we can carry more equipment than if we were just on foot. And if we need to, one of us will hold a suspect and the other can go for assistance."

"Hold a suspect!" All Dale could see were the deformed faces of the sailors and the poster of the helmeted German.

Tommy ignored her concern. "We'll only have to cover about

two miles, each watch. And they're setting up special towers with telephone boxes along the beaches every quarter of a mile."

"Yes, that's what Daddy's linemen are doing. Preparing the beaches for the patrol. I just didn't know there would be horses."

"Pretty cool, isn't it? With the new telephone boxes, we won't be out of touch even in places that are too remote for jeeps or on coastlines too dangerous for boats. And we can cover a lot more ground on horseback."

She nodded, head down.

He reached over and lifted her chin. "Hey, Deebs, like you said, it's perfect."

"Of course. It is. It really is." He didn't see. He couldn't see. He wouldn't see at all.

"It's just riding a horse on the beach. What could be better than that?"

"Nothing . . . except . . . I'm afraid for you."

She could easily imagine the U-boats attacking and sinking tankers, and the jagged coastlines filled with tree stumps and debris, ship parts, raft boats, oil-strewn sand, and bodies. Yes, human bodies. Not just sand dollars or jelly fish, but real humans. Dead.

"I'm afraid for you," she repeated.

"Why?" He reached toward her.

She relished the feel of his hand cupping her face. He hadn't held her hand since the night of the sinkings, and he'd reverted to calling her simply Deebs. She tilted her head, squinting and blinking back tears. "I couldn't stand it if something else happened to you." Then she blurted out, "I love you, you know, you silly boy. So you better not let anything happen to you."

He dropped his hand and pivoted in the chair to look directly at her. "What did you say?"

She swallowed hard, eyes flashing, furious at herself for having admitted it. "You heard what I said!"

"Well, I'll be. When I get an offer like that to come back 'cause the girl I've loved for years finally admits she loves me . . . well then, I guess I'd better pay attention."

"The girl I've loved for years."

"If you've loved me, why didn't you say anything? Why did you go around kissing Annabeth and Jillian?" Dale asked later, when they had moved to the beach and were sitting side by side in the sand, the tide whispering as it brushed against the shore.

"Maybe I wanted to make you jealous."

"Well, you succeeded. You made me miserable and jealous."

"Gee, Deebs, I'm sorry. I . . . I just didn't want to do anything to ruin our friendship, and then after the polio, well, I mean . . ."

"Oh, please, don't tell me you couldn't tell I was in love with you."

He shrugged and gave a grin. "I wasn't gonna be the first to say uncle! You'd never let me live it down."

Then he brushed his hand through her hair, took her hand, intertwined his fingers in hers, and gently laid her back onto the soft sandy rise of a dune.

"Sweet seventeen and never been kissed?" he whispered when his mouth was merely inches from hers.

"Is that any of your business, Tommy Ridley?" she whispered back, breathless.

He leaned slowly toward her. Even though she knew what was coming, she wasn't prepared for something she'd dreamed and obsessed about since she was eleven years old.

The kiss blossomed like daffodils in February, like primroses peeking from under the snow, like the crepe myrtle exploding in fluorescent pink outside her bedroom window, like that giddy feeling in the pit of her stomach when they called her name in first place at a horse show. But then, of course, none of those did the kiss justice.

They remained there, kissing, for a long time, or maybe it was the shortest time in the world. All she knew was that when she came up for air, the sky had gone dark.

17

Allie

Monday, March 9

Four days. Only four days had passed since I'd read about the dinosaur bones in the *AJC*, but I felt decades older. Instead of nightmares, I had woken from a delightful dream where Austin was about to plant a kiss—our first kiss—on my lips. I was grinning to myself when my alarm sounded. Now fully awake, I reasoned that my dream had been more of a nice nightmare. Did those exist? That delightful kiss had happened, but it would never happen again.

I let out a sigh to rival those of Husy—at least according to Nana Dale. How in the world was I going to pack up her house now that I had the scrapbook? Shouldn't all my time be spent at least going through the whole thing once? And what about that museum? I wished I could think clearly.

Cécile was meeting me at four at Hickory Hills, and I had absolutely no idea what I was going to tell her about the estate sale. Or maybe I did. I wanted to sit down on the leather couch, burst into tears, and plead, "Can't we keep it all? Please? I've spent the

204

weekend here, and all I've made it through are two kitchen drawers, the shelves of one bedroom, one cedar chest, and a hutch in the dining room."

I was preparing for my last therapy class of the day at Chastain, praying I wouldn't see Austin. I knew I owed him an apology for my complete meltdown, but so far, my fingers had not found the strength to even send a text—which was, admittedly, the worst way to apologize.

Tricia met me at the barn, surveying me with absolute disapproval. She held up her phone. "Not going to answer my texts either, Miss Hot Mess?"

I blushed. "Sorry. Really, really sorry. I was just . . . shocked to see him and—"

"You're an idiot, you know. He still stares at you in the same way, and you still get that lovesick look in your eyes when you talk about him."

I walked up to Tricia and poked her in the arm. "Agreed. But"— I gave her another poke—"I'm still obsessed with the house. Haven't you noticed? Don't you remember the whole context for our breakup? The sudden and excruciatingly painful realization that Austin was right. I love Hickory Hills more than I love him."

My voice continued to rise, and I read Tricia's eyes, *"Could you tone it down a little, please?"*

"Or maybe I just love the idea of Hickory Hills Horse Therapy more than I love him."

Tricia's hands were planted firmly on her hips, and now her eyes said, *"Don't you dare mess with me until I've said my piece."* "Or maybe you're just a complete idiot who has finally realized how much you love him and how he's a pretty awesome guy, and you're just too stinking proud to tell him that!"

I opened my mouth to reply but was greeted by four young students walking toward me. "Hey, kids!" I said instead, forcing cheerfulness into my tone. "Ready for your lesson? And remember, no classes tomorrow. The fences around the rings are being repaired. But we'll be back on Wednesday."

We tacked up the horses and led them to the ring where the children stood with their sponsors, waiting for the lesson to begin. But I'd already gotten my own lesson loud and clear from Tricia.

Jimmy and Angelfoot made a perfect pair as the boy carefully led the small palomino gelding around the paddock, clutching the lead shank like a trophy. Tricia walked beside him, her hand on his elbow. The nervous gelding had calmed dramatically over the weekend, so much so that I'd agreed to let Jimmy brush him in the crossties. The gelding had responded so well to the brushing that we'd allowed Jimmy to attach a lead shank to the halter. Now I watched, slightly dumbfounded, as Jimmy walked on the left side of the palomino, whispering to the horse and, every once in a while, stopping to stroke his mane.

Jimmy looked over at me with something akin to pride on his face. "He likes me! Angelfoot likes me, doesn't he, Miss Allie?"

"He certainly does."

"We'll be friends forever. I just know it."

Even though I had lived with horses all my life, I still marveled at the quick attachment that developed between my students and their equine partners. I observed a new confidence in the gentle, yet firm way Jimmy handled the gelding.

I loved my job.

Sometimes the hardest part was dealing with the parents. Jimmy's mother seemed particularly needy, and I imagined more of their difficult story would come out over the course of our months of therapy. That's when equine therapy moved past horses and physical therapy, and I became a volunteer therapist of another sort. But early on, I had discovered my limitations. I never wanted to go through another painful experience like I'd had with one particular boy and his parents. So I figuratively tiptoed up to Jimmy's mother, reminding myself over and over to listen, breathe, listen again, and not to offer advice too quickly.

Nana Dale had put it succinctly, quoting the Bible, *"Be quick to listen, slow to speak, and slow to anger."* She loved to give advice that she didn't always put into practice herself.

I listened as this woman tearfully shared her woes while Tricia walked beside Jimmy and Angelfoot. I tried my best to concentrate on my daily battles instead of the one that had taken place on the Atlantic Ocean in 1942 and in my heart yesterday afternoon.

Cécile Dumontel was waiting in the gravel driveway at Hickory Hills when I arrived, five minutes late.

"Hi, Cécile," I said, holding out my hand and feeling very unprofessional, dressed in jeans and a T-shirt and smelling of horses. "Sorry to be late. My lesson went over."

"No problem, Miss Massey," Cécile said with a nod. She had slick black hair, cut short and sassy, with bangs hanging over one eye, and she was dressed in a modestly low-cut white blouse and a black leather miniskirt, wearing black tights and knee-high boots. She looked exactly like the sexy thirtysomething Frenchwoman she was.

"And I'm sorry. I haven't gotten very far in cleaning things out—I mean, in taking the things that I want. I . . ." I stumbled through a long apology as I led her into the foyer.

"Totally understandable, Miss Massey."

"Allie, please."

"Of course, Allie. It's all so emotional for you." I thought perhaps this was just a meant-to-make-me-feel-good-but-actually-an-insensitive-and-flippant remark, but then she added, "It's a real shame about your losing the house and property. It makes the whole thing a lot worse."

"Exactly! I wasn't going to get rid of any of it. Not yet. I was supposed to be moving into the house with my soon-to-be husband. And now I don't have the house or the husband or the horses or Hickory Hills." I looked up to where Cécile stood, compassion written across her face.

She gave a little nod. "Let's do an initial walk-through. You don't have to decide a thing. I'm just going to make notes."

Cécile knew her stuff. She had impeccable taste and a perfect résumé and had spent years buying antiques in France and bringing them to the States. We were paying a bundle for her company to manage the sale, and as soon as she stepped through the door, I felt some sort of relief. And I felt grateful.

"Husy always told me to practice gratitude, Allie. To regularly practice telling yourself that you not only have enough but much more than you need." Nana Dale's advice zipped across my brain.

After we had walked through a few rooms, Cécile announced, "Time to take a break. An *apéro,* Allie," she said. "It will make the rest of the evening better."

An hour later, we were sipping glasses of red wine—from the Languedoc-Roussillon region of France—and enjoying the robust cheeses that Cécile had brought, along with red grapes and gluten-free crackers. "This one is my favorite," she said, pointing to a wedge of hard cheese. "Comté, aged for twenty-four months."

I had my shoes off, as did Cécile, my feet propped on Nana Dale's favorite ottoman in the formal living room, and I was halfway through my story, just having revealed to her how I'd found the cherrywood chest and the scrapbook-diary. "I think she's hidden a bunch of money somewhere in this house. But I've looked and looked with no success."

"You'd be surprised at all the things we've found while planning estate sales." Cécile gave a lovely laugh. "Once we found thirty thousand in cash stuffed in a mattress."

"You mean under a mattress," I corrected.

"No, I mean *in* a mattress. We removed the bedding and the mattress cover and saw that the mattress had been sewn together in the middle, like it had had a C-section! Curious, of course, we ripped open the stitches and *voilà*, the money."

"And?"

"And we kept it as part of our commission, of course. The owners had no idea it was there."

I could not hide my shock.

Then Cécile trilled a laugh. "We gave it to the owners, naturally!

208

I am just saying we find many things, and we always let the owners know. We're quite careful. One of our employees is a specialist in rare books. He goes through each one. He's found thousands of dollars in books, but he's also found hollowed-out pages that were filled with a knife or a gun or drugs."

"Drugs!"

"Yes, of course. I love this job. So many surprises."

"Well, I doubt Nana Dale hid drugs."

Cécile shrugged. "I doubt this also, but one never knows." She flashed another smile. "Listen, Allie. I will come with two of my colleagues on Wednesday afternoon, and we'll begin pricing everything. And searching. You'll see. We know what we're doing." She popped a grape into her mouth, then reached for the cheese knife and carved off a slice of Comté. "This is okay with you?"

I felt the tension in my neck relax. "This is perfect, Cécile. *Merci.*"

The *apéro* finished—indeed, I did feel much better—Cécile stood up and asked, "Where to next?"

"To the Ribbon Room. Follow me!"

She oohed and aahed over the trophies and ribbons and photos. "I love doing estate sales for equestrians. Such beautiful things. You will not sell these." Even as she spoke, she put little adhesive pink dots on the photos and the trophies and a few coffee-table books, explaining, "This way, my colleagues know what to leave for you, in case you don't get things packed up first." Another went on the footlocker filled with the halters of Nana Dale's horses.

In the dining room, I nodded to all the silver still spread out on the dining room table. "I'm not giving any of this away."

Cécile applied more little adhesive dots. "But you do know what you want to keep!" she purred, quickly noting things on her iPad. "You'll see. Together, this will be manageable."

We climbed the stairs and entered the Pink Room. "This is really the only room I've even started going through. And for the second time." I showed her the scrapbooks and the plaque about a filly's worth and the cedar hope chest.

When I opened the chest, she exclaimed, "Retro riding gear. It is worth a small fortune!" Then she turned and winked, "But you will keep these, *n'est-ce pas?*"

"*Oui,*" I said with a laugh. "And that's the extent of my French. I'll keep the clothes and the cedar chest. My great-grandfather owned a lumber mill. He made a fortune during World War II selling crates to ship jeeps and weapons over to Europe."

"Fascinating!"

"But he was quite the craftsman himself and built this cedar chest for my grandmother. His father built the dining room table and chairs."

"Exquisite. You will not sell the handmade items. They are worth more in your heart. But these . . ." We had moved back downstairs to the formal living room, and she let her arms sweep around the space. "There are many very lovely pieces that will bring a handsome price. And they are much too fussy for you."

She sat down on the sofa. "Louis XV rococo. Worth a fortune. Some antiques work for us millennials, but not this. And the master bedroom. It feels a bit oppressive, *non?* I have a very good client who will snatch it up for whatever price we assign it." She continued jotting down notes and placing little pink adhesive dots on anything I would keep.

I watched her in transfixed awe. How did she know? When I asked her, she replied, "*Au pif,*" tapping her nose. "It's French, you know. 'By the nose.' Or as you say, 'I've got a feeling.' Instinct. Intuition. It is my business to understand my client and help her with all the difficult decisions." She hesitated, then smiled. "And it's so much easier after an *apéro!*"

Cécile followed me out back, and I pointed to the rocky drive that split into a V. "I call the road on the left side of the V the Road Less Traveled. 'Two roads diverged in a yellow wood, and sorry I could not travel both—'" I stopped myself and blushed.

"'And be one traveler, long I stood and looked down one as far as I could to where it bent in the undergrowth.'" She glanced over at me. "I enjoy poetry too. Both French and English. I especially like Mr. Frost. He's so . . . down to earth." She knelt to grab a fistful of red dirt for emphasis and laughed again. "So which way, Allie?"

"To the right, to the Traveled Road first."

"I love it!" she said as I unlatched the chain on the three-railed white gate, and we walked into the barn. She extended her arms in the hallway, closed her eyes, and inhaled. "Fresh shavings mingled with manure. The aroma's magical." She glanced at me, and we both burst into laughter.

We walked behind the barn to the paddock, then climbed the hill up to the ring. Barnell was working the backhoe on the far right side of the ring.

"Miss Allie!" he said, cutting the engine as we came over to a new gaping hole. "I was hoping you'd come up today."

"Hi, Barnell. Um, this is Cécile. She's helping me get the house ready for the estate sale."

"Pleased ta meet ya," he said. "'Fraid my hands are awfully dirty, or I'd shake yours."

"Don't worry, *monsieur*."

"Such a shame to have to sell it all off." Then he motioned over to the new hole. "I b'lieve we've unearthed ole Krystal, if my memory serves me right. Come take a look."

We peered into the cavernous space, where I could see a few clay-caked bones.

"Here are her horseshoes," he said, shaking his head. "Your grandma was nothin' if she wasn't eccentric."

I took the metal box, opened it, and fingered the rusted shoes. Once again, Nana Dale had left a piece of her monogrammed stationery tucked between the horseshoes, inscribed with *Krystal Klear (1924–1953)*.

To my surprise and Barnell's shock, Cécile knelt in the red clay, reached into the ditch, and plucked a specimen. "Horse bones!" she trilled. "No, I am mistaken. Dinosaur bones! I read it last week in the paper. Such fun!"

Maybe it was the wine or perhaps the easy banter between the three of us as we stood around Krystal's grave, but after Cécile left,

I felt strangely peaceful about the whole process. I'd found one more person I could trust, and she wanted to help.

Tricia had told me more than once, *"You can be so stubborn, Allie. Haven't you ever heard of outsourcing? Please don't tell me that you plan to pack up the whole house alone and then tag the things you want to sell."*

Tricia had been right about it all, even down to finding six reputable estate companies online, visiting three, talking to those "in the know" in Buckhead, and picking out Cécile. "She's savvy and young. You'll love her. Oh, and she's French."

I called Tricia after Cécile left. "Thank you. She was perfect. In my better moments, I totally think we can get this thing done."

"Meaning . . . ?"

"Meaning I've just had a glass of a very nice French wine and life looks better. Thanks to Cécile and to you."

"Delighted to hear it, Allie."

Text Austin.

That thought kept pecking at me when I was back in the house alone. So I did.

> Hey. I'm sorry for my awful outburst yesterday. I appreciate your concern. I've actually met with the estate-sale gal and she's fabulous. I think all is well. I hope you're able to catch up on a little rest. You looked wiped out.

I quickly backspaced over the last sentence. Too concerned, snarky, mean, loving? Too something. I pressed send before I could second or third or fourth guess myself.

The wine, cheese, crackers, and grapes were still sitting on the glass coffee table in the formal living room, as the fussy old Louis XV couch looked on. I corked the wine bottle, covered the cheese plate with plastic wrap, stuck it in the fridge, and drove back to my apartment.

After showering, changing into pj's, and feeding Maggie, I

brought out the scrapbook, pulled up my favorite jazz playlist on Spotify, and lost myself once again in Nana Dale's past. I'd taken the leaflet for the Home Front Museum out of its plastic protection, and now it, along with Nana Dale's letter from 2018, sat on the coffee table, both still tempting me.

What if I went to St. Simons? With Cécile on my team, I felt I could spare twenty-four hours, or maybe thirty-six. And the horse park was closed for repairs all day tomorrow.

Turning to the next page of the scrapbook sealed my decision.

A newspaper clipping showed a large group of riders galloping their horses along a beach, at least fifty of each. The riders were dressed in what looked to me like navy attire, with the telltale white hats. The caption under the photo read *Horse Patrol Rides the Beach at Hilton Head, South Carolina.*

Nana Dale had circled one of the heads of the men and written *Tommy! You're famous!* beside it.

I sucked in my breath and read the article underneath the photo.

Used as a marine artillery range for the nearby Parris Island training base, Camp McDougal on Hilton Head Island was leased from the US Marine Corps on December 28, 1942, and has become the training center for the dog and horse patrol. . . . Every week, six hundred recruits arrive, and six hundred are shipped out.

I stared long and hard at the photo, a smile gradually spreading across my face. Not only did Tommy ride again, he rode in something called the mounted beach patrol.

Another page showed a photo of linemen installing telephone poles and wires on the beach. Nana Dale had scribbled *Daddy's men! Daddy trained them all.*

Why hadn't she told me about this? Why had she only hinted in a way that made it sound like her stories were fabricated?

For some reason, she didn't want me or anyone else to find out about her life during the war until after her death. But now, she had commissioned me to visit this island. I grabbed her 2018 letter, reading again, *Then, dear Allie, please go to Hilton Head. It's such a big part of my story too. Go to Camp McDougal.*

I spent the next hour on my laptop, googling about Hilton Head Island during World War II. What I discovered surprised me. I knew Hilton Head even better than St. Simons, Jekyll, and Sea Island. Not a part of the Golden Isles, it is nestled up the coast from Savannah in South Carolina and was a favorite vacation spot for many Georgia families, including mine.

But according to the articles I pulled up, the island was virtually uninhabited during the war. Except for Camp McDougal.

The next article filed in the scrapbook gave more details: *The mounted beach patrol was affectionately called "the Sand Pounders."*

"The Sand Pounders," I whispered as Maggie hopped onto my lap, completely covering the scrapbook and evidently unbothered by the three rings. "Nana Dale used to say stuff about them, Mags." I furrowed my brow, trying to remember another farfetched tale. *"Well, 'go pound sand' is not a very nice expression, but the Sand Pounders were very different. They were heroes."*

I closed my eyes, hearing once again that snippet from one of Nana Dale's stories. *"There was the time during the war that I found a sailor, burned and half drowned on the beach. His tanker had been destroyed by a German U-boat. We pulled him to safety, my filly and I . . ."*

"Wait, Mags! So Tommy must have been part of the mounted patrol, and Nana Dale must have . . . she must have followed him to an island and found a sailor? Or something?" With that memory, I jumped up, dislodging Maggie from my lap, and called Tricia.

"I'm going on a mission. Tomorrow morning, very early, I'm driving to St. Simons, and I need you to come with me. We'll go to the Home Front Museum on St. Simons in the morning and then drive to Hilton Head in the afternoon. Nana Dale asked me to go. And I've found some stuff about the US Coast Guard Mounted Beach Patrol and Tommy, and I'll bet it has to do with the sailor Nana Dale rescued and her long-lost filly. I've got to see it for myself. So will you come?"

ELIZABETH MUSSER

Long pause. Finally, she said, "Um, I have absolutely no idea what you're talking about, but sure! I'll meet you at your place. What time?"

"Six a.m."

I tried to sleep, but all throughout the night, I kept picturing images of horses galloping on a beach. When the alarm rang at five thirty, I woke feeling exhausted. I put on coffee and threw a few things in an overnight bag. Maggie meowed, and I gave her food and water, then checked the litter box. "Sorry, girl. I'll be back soon."

It was as I was locking the door to the apartment and heading down to the car to meet Tricia that my phone beeped with a tone signaling a text from Austin. A smile spread across my face as I remembered the thoughtful early morning texts he used to send before he headed out to the vet clinic. Then I glanced at the phone.

Forgiven. But I did get the message loud and clear.
Don't worry. I won't be offering any more help.
Glad you feel good about the estate-sale woman.

215

18

Dale

Fall 1942

With the arrival of thousands of workers and military personnel in Brunswick, it soon went from sleepy Southern town to social hot spot. Dale and Tommy waited in the line that stretched around the block at the Bijou Theater for *Casablanca*, a movie everyone raved about. Dale hoped they'd get seats, but part of her didn't care, because all that really mattered was that she was standing hand in hand with Tommy Ridley.

But they did get in to watch the film, Dale clutching Tommy's hand. Ever since that kiss, she felt crushing excitement; she could barely catch her breath just being near him. And when he took her in his arms, which he did quite frequently now, she felt like Ingrid Bergman with Humphrey Bogart. Only she prayed her story wouldn't end the same way.

The next evening, they attended a dance party at the new King and Prince Hotel on St. Simons Island, and they slow danced together, Tommy holding her so close, his legs steady on his braces.

For those few months before Tommy left to train on Hilton Head, the war seemed like a boon, a door to the future. Her future with Tommy Ridley.

Dale continued working at the shipyard that fall. She only rode Krystal on the beach in the afternoons and evenings. She virtually forgot about horse shows and the Maclay Medal, even though the shows and Maclay classes were still being held. Everything about her life was wrapped up in Tommy and helping with the war effort. At least he wasn't going off across an ocean. He might be on some remote island in the Atlantic, but she'd keep working at the shipyard and visit him wherever he went. She'd already planned her visit to Hilton Head Island even though Tommy did not yet have the exact date for his training. She'd figure out how to make herself essential.

"Seventeen is young to be in love with a war on the horizon," Daddy said one evening when she floated into the room after a concert put on by the USO.

Dale did not want to have that discussion and changed the subject. "Business is doing better than you expected, right, Daddy?"

"Dale"—he took her by the shoulders—"you both have a lot going for you. I just don't want your heart to get broken by Tommy."

"It's not like we're planning to get married, Daddy! We're just trying this on." Trying it on, yes, and hoping for much more.

Her mother put things more bluntly. "Dale, you cannot marry polio. I know he's from a fine family, but he'll struggle all his life. Who knows how long someone infected with this disease can survive."

For days after that remark, Dale could not look at her mother without feeling some sort of revulsion. At last, she managed. "First of all, we're not talking of marriage, Mama. And second, if we were, I would not be marrying *polio*. I'd be marrying the wildest and kindest man I've ever known, my friend since I was just a kid. How dare you talk about Tommy like that! Especially when all you care about is money. And he will have plenty of that!"

Her mother's face fell. "Jenny Green's husband contracted polio two years ago," she said in a whisper, "and she's played nursemaid to him ever since. He's dying a slow death, and so is she. It's just awful. She never gets out to social functions anymore. She never does anything, Dale. I don't want that for you."

"It would be my privilege to play nursemaid to Tommy for the rest of my life, Mama. You know I don't give a hoot about your society functions!" When she saw the stricken look on her mother's face, Dale softened. "Mama, thank you for caring about me."

She kissed her mother's brow, forcing the fury down deep inside.

— ∩ —

Dale stood with her mother, Mrs. Ridley, and dozens of other women outside the gate of the J.A. Jones Shipyard in Brunswick. The members of the waterfront production crew wore their welding gear, coveralls, and shipyard identification badges. Besides the workers, a large crowd of spectators had gathered for a special ceremony. For each Liberty ship built at their shipyard, there was a public celebration to watch the vessel slide down one of the six slipways into the Brunswick River. A small group of dignitaries had gathered on a raised platform to christen the ship by breaking a bottle of champagne on its bow.

With every completed ship, a woman worker was selected to participate in the launch in her workday attire, a symbolic representation of all the shipyard's employees. Evelyn, one of the girls lodging at the Ridleys' home, had been chosen today. Now Evelyn waved to the crowd, and Dale and her fellow workers cheered.

One of the dignitaries took the stage beside Evelyn and gave a short speech. "This is our twentieth ship launch this year! It's remarkable. Because of the proficiency of our female and Negro workers, the time it takes to build a ship here has been reduced from over a year to under two months.

"These people are playing an important part in the business of winning this war." Another cheer. "Our country was woefully unprepared for building the number of ocean vessels Great Britain urgently needed. But in the past few months, our naval architects have been able to adapt the British plan for this new design of our Liberty ship. She's quick to build and pretty cheap, and she can carry over ten thousand tons. Let's hear it for our newest wonder!" He popped the cork on the champagne bottle as the crowd cheered.

— ⋂ —

After welding during the day, Dale would read before bed from one of the many books the Ridley family had about the barrier islands. Hilton Head was located one hundred fifteen miles to the north of St. Simons, past Savannah, off Port Royal Sound, at the mouth of the Broad River. The island resembled a low boot, with the toe pointing down to the southwest and the heel up at the northeast. It was typical of the barrier islands of South Carolina and Georgia, with a swampy interior and beaches littered with stumps.

And horses. Soon, it would have horses.

Beginning late in 1942, horses and dogs were brought to the island. Tommy eagerly researched information about the training he'd be starting there in January. "We'll be at a marine training base called Camp McDougal that was set up back in 1937. Now it'll be used not only for the marines but also as the training base for men, dogs, and horses for the entire southeastern seaboard of the mounted patrol.

"The camp's already got a headquarters and barracks, a mess hall, a hospital, and a rec room. They've even figured out how to turn this big ole steel warehouse where they used to store vehicles into a barn for the horses," Tommy said.

When Tommy heard of a new load of horses being brought from Virginia down to South Carolina, he said, "Let's go watch, Dale! They're going by train to Hardeeville, then by truck to the coast, and finally, by barge onto the island."

"You think your parents will let you drive there?" The excitement of the patrol had spurred Tommy along in his rehabilitation so that now he could drive. He would always walk with a slight limp, but the need for a cane became less mandatory.

"Yep. Already checked with them."

"That's a lot of travel for the poor horses."

"Horses'll do fine." He winked. "Just like when we took ours all along the coast to the shows."

At Buckingham Landing, Dale watched as trucks filled with horses were unloaded, only for the horses to be reloaded on a huge barge that would carry them across the narrow inlet to Hilton Head Island. At least fifty horses of every color and size paraded—some placid, others nervously—from truck to barge: quarter horses and Arabians, thoroughbreds, and giant work horses.

"They're beautiful, all of them. I love seeing so many different breeds and colors," she said.

"Yep. All different, but they're coming from the army, so they're well trained."

Indeed, while she had heard whinnying and stomping as they ascended the ramp to the barge, very few of the horses seemed bothered by their travels or present surroundings.

"Why doesn't the army need them?"

Tommy shrugged. "From what I hear, they've basically shut down their cavalry branch. It's pretty swell timing too. They're just shipping all the horses to the training centers for the mounted patrol." He grinned. "But those of us who already own our horses can bring them. So Finny will be coming along with me." He added, "As long as the horses can walk, trot, and canter, they'll do."

Dale joined Tommy where he stood, leaning over a weathered fence as they stared across the sound at the barge filling with a plethora of horses. A dozen young men in blue-and-white uniforms worked with the horses, leading a recruit onto the barge, securing the horse, then turning to fetch another from land.

"You are champing at the bit to start your training, aren't you?"

"Ha-ha. Champing at the bit. Yep." Another grin. "Evidently,

I have a special way with horses." He winked, and she looped her arm through his.

"You have a special way with me too."

"Hope so. You're my best filly." He turned to face her and kissed her hard on the mouth with as much passion—or perhaps a little bit more—as he had for his new adventure.

"Eventually, there'll be six hundred horses just on this island."

"Six hundred horses and six hundred men."

"And one teenage girl," Tommy said with that familiar twinkle in his eyes.

"Yep! I'm going to stay up here for the week you're in training."

"I'm glad to hear it," he said. Then he kissed her again, holding her so close, she felt that deep desire that made her head swim. When he let her go, his brow was creased. "But are you gonna quit your welding job, Deebs?"

"I'm simply going to take a leave of absence. Other girls have done it. It's long hours and hard work, and we get three days off for every five we work. I'll combine my days off so I can have the week you're in training."

"I hope the commander will give his approval."

"He doesn't have to know. I'll keep a low profile." She was grinning with her plan. "No one will need to know. Anyway, Hilton Head isn't a tourist place like Jekyll or Sea Island. The only people who live here are the descendants of the Negro freedmen that Sherman gave land to after he'd burnt down Atlanta and marched to the sea."

Tommy cocked his head. "Well, look at you. Doing research!"

"I've been reading your father's books on the barrier islands. I'm coming with you. And if I can find a way to convince that commander to let a girl join the coast guard, I will. I'll be eighteen by the time you're in training. And they're recruiting women for the guard too. You've seen the signs."

Tommy lifted an eyebrow. "From what I recall, they're recruiting women for office work, not horseback riding."

She stuck out her tongue. "You'll be hanging out at the barracks, and I'll find a way to help. Maybe I could cook or muck out the horses' stalls. I'll make myself useful at least for that week."

He tweaked her nose. "That's one of the many things I love about you, Deebs. Once you get an idea, you won't take no for an answer." He didn't say it, but Dale knew he thought her idea was completely unrealistic.

She didn't care. She leaned over the fence rail and watched the barge groan and then move across the narrow inlet to the horses' new home on the island.

〜 ♘ 〜

January 1943

The wind whipped Dale's hair in swirls and tangles as she shaded her eyes from the blinding sun. The ocean rolled with white peaks that crashed like perpetual thunder onto the wide white beaches as seagulls screamed their gossip across the sand, and the island shimmered with wild beauty. Dale walked along Hilton Head's shoreline until she came to a fallen sea pine. She stopped to watch hundreds of seagulls lift off the sand in front of her, then lingered as the sun slipped behind a cloud, casting shadows across the water.

Though she couldn't see them now, the German subs were out there. She had seen them before.

She took a seat on the fallen pine, staring out at the deserted beach, one ear to the tide that rushed and rumbled, and one ear to the sand. Then she felt it, something that gradually reverberated beneath her until she heard the sound of hundreds of hoofbeats, pounding the sand. She stood to the side and watched as a troop of horses—fifty at least—galloped by in formation, their riders dressed in crisp blue uniforms with their captain out front. For one moment, she thought she could decipher Tommy's form leaning over Infinity's neck as they raced past, a blur of blue and white against the rippling tide.

Late that afternoon, Tommy found Dale outside Camp Mc-

Dougal. He was dressed in a dark blue uniform, wearing leather boots and a white hat, looking like a bona fide coast guardsman.

"Wow. You look swell!"

"I don't have to dress up all the time, but the commander is strict. While we're on duty, we must be dressed alike in uniforms. And during training this week, we'll be wearing our traditional winter uniforms like the one yours truly is modeling right now."

She admired the navy blue wool single-breasted coat and breeches, white shirt, black tie, and army cavalry boots as he tipped his visored hat with the gold seal of the US Coast Guard.

Dale laughed and kissed his cheek.

He squinted his eyes and lifted his face toward the sky. "I feel like I've turned into a life-sized propaganda poster, Deebs. Journalists were at camp this morning, interviewing the staff and taking photos of the barracks and the dogs and horses and men. Evidently, we'll have another photo session on the beach at the end of the week."

"Do you disagree with all the hoopla?"

"No, not at all. You and I have seen the truth. Something about it feels surreal, and a lot of the guys in training with me this week are as young as I am—but not quite as jaded, fortunately."

Dale had never considered Tommy jaded. The word leaped out at her. "Jaded?" was all she could think to say.

"Sorry, Deebs. We just heard some very distressing statistics today. Over eight thousand merchant mariners died last year. Eight thousand civilians doing their best to get supplies across the ocean to help the Allies beat those darn Nazis." He took her hand, and they walked toward the makeshift barn. "So you helping to quickly build the Liberty ships and me patrolling the coast to look for subs is essential." She'd rarely seen Tommy look so serious. "What we're doing is going to help win this war."

Dale pulled her peacoat closer as the January wind wove in and out of the barracks.

"Sorry to be a killjoy, Deebs. It's just sobering."

"Yep. And cold."

He drew her close, lifted her head, and bent down to kiss her lips. "Hope that'll warm you up."

But it didn't. She still felt chilled to the bone.

"I didn't mean to worry you." He pulled her even closer, so that she was practically tucked into his thick wool coat. "I've heard it can get awfully brisk on the beaches in the middle of the night up east."

"It's almost freezing right here. And you'll be out all night, patrolling?"

"They'll take care of us. I think I even saw long underwear in the packet we were given. It won't stay cold like this for long. Anyway, down here, it's going to be the summers that do us in."

"You think the war will still be going on this summer, Tommy?"

His look didn't need translation, and it made her stomach cramp.

"The horses are going to have to learn to deal with the environment too. Finny and I are lucky. We're used to the heat, the mosquitoes. This won't be any different from riding at the Chastain Shriners Show when it's a hundred degrees outside, and we're dressed in jodhpurs and leather boots and a coat and hard hat. Or when our fingers were freezing even with leather gloves up in Pennsylvania in December. Remember that?"

She did. She remembered it all.

But he was wrong. This was different. It was a completely different kind of dangerous.

— ♘ —

"Hey, I checked with Commander McTeer, and he said I could show you around the barracks." Tommy had something tucked under his arm.

"What's that?" Dale asked.

"This is my guidebook. I've already read most of it."

"A guidebook, huh?"

"Yep. The *Manual of the US Coast Guard Beach Patrol*. It's very comprehensive."

"You mean boring?"

"No, it's good. It explains important stuff, like how we Sand Pounders will keep a constant watch along the shores, day and night." He flipped a page in the manual. "Listen to this: 'The accurate reporting of the sighting of a periscope or submarine is one of the most vital roles of the mounted patrol. Sea and air forces can then be directed to the attack.'"

She lifted her eyebrows in mock admiration. "Very impressive. What else is in this tome?" She grabbed it from Tommy and flipped to the table of contents, glancing at topics from the care of horses to military courtesy. She shrugged. "I guess it could be very dull, patrolling a deserted beach. Until it isn't."

He squeezed her hand. "Exactly. And there's nothing to worry about that you and I haven't already dealt with."

"You said a lot of the men don't know how to ride?"

"The cavalry officers are teaching them. Lessons started today. Tomorrow, the newbies will all be walking bowlegged." He demonstrated, leaning forward on his cane, legs wide apart.

Dale chuckled. She well remembered how sore her thighs had been after thirty minutes of riding without stirrups. New riders always felt the soreness after a day or two.

Tommy limped over to her and cleared his throat. "Enough talk about my training. Would you like to visit the canine center? They've been preparing dogs for the patrol here for a while now."

"Did the army send them too?"

"Some of them, but others came from Dogs for Defense and the German Shepherd Dog Club of America."

They walked to the kennels. "As you can see, the German shepherd is the official choice for beach patrol duties."

"They're beautiful, Tommy. Will you get to take care of them too?"

"Nope. Each dog has two handlers, and they're only cared for by them. No one else is allowed to be with the dog. But we can watch the training. The dogs have to learn commands like heel, sit, down, and get him."

"Get him!" Dale shivered.

"Hey, the dogs and horses get treated really well. You don't have to worry about the animals. The staff here told us that having animals around helps with the overall morale of all the guys too." He tweaked her nose. "But we already knew that, didn't we?"

Yes, horses were good for morale.

"The dogs even have an enrollment application for the US Coast Guard Dog Patrol with the dog 'signing' with his paw print. And get this: The dogs have specially fitted shoes to protect their paws from getting cut by oyster shells on the beach."

Leaving the office, they walked outside to where a dog was being fitted with his new canvas shoes that laced up the front of the leg.

"It looks like a high-top sneaker! Does it really work?"

"Yep. Poor things were coming in with bleeding paws until one of the handlers came up with this ingenious idea."

Later, they walked to the beach, where more dog training was taking place. The shepherds stood with their ears pricked forward at attention as their handlers lay amid the dunes, each with a rifle in his arms.

Dale jumped as a pistol with blanks was fired at the dog, and the shepherd immediately grabbed the pistol arm of the "attacker," which was encased in thick leather protection. The dog held on ferociously, refusing to release the arm until his handler pronounced the words "Let go." Then the shepherd stood guard over the prisoner.

"Very impressive," Dale said to the handler. "I sure wouldn't want to meet up with you both on a dark beach."

"We're training them to be ready for unusual circumstances, ma'am. They've got to go to school just like us. And some of the dogs will graduate later this afternoon."

"The dog patrol is normally conducted at night," Tommy explained. "It's just the handler and the dog, and they patrol a mile, back and forth, throughout the night."

Next, Tommy took her to a beach tower. The building stood ten feet above the ground on wooden stilts. Twelve wooden stairs led up to a small covered room with the equivalent of a wraparound porch where the coast guardsman stood, looking through a telescope.

"These watchtowers are what the linemen who work for your dad have been building. They're being set up all along the coast. They've also installed telephone lines under the sand. Hundreds of miles of it on every US coast."

After her visit to the camp, Dale fought two colliding emotions: fear for Tommy and a desperate desire to join him in the mounted patrol.

On Tuesday, Dale watched for hours as the Sand Pounders trained on the otherwise deserted beaches. The sun had come out, and the temperature rose into the midfifties.

"We're getting another shipment of horses," Tommy told her. "I'm going to help load them on the barges."

"Can I come?"

"I don't see why not."

She leaned over the same weathered fence they'd stood behind in November, watching horses being unloaded and reloaded. Only this time, Tommy was below, doing the duties. As the afternoon wore on, Dale never grew tired of admiring the variety of horses. Tommy occasionally turned to wave up at her before leading another horse onto the barge.

It was while he stared up at her that Dale noticed something behind him. A flash of color, deep gray and snow white.

She knelt down, peering through the bars as another coast guardsman led the gray horse off the truck and recognition jolted through her.

"Tommy!" she shouted down at him. When he didn't respond, she tried again. "Tommy, look!"

He glanced up and shrugged, perplexed. She pointed to the

horse being led to the barge. He followed her indication. When he turned back to her, she yelled, "Essie! I think it's Essie."

"What?" His expression showed half excitement and half disbelief.

"Could it be?" she whispered, hope frozen on her face.

Tommy said something to another coast guardsman, who took hold of the halter of the chestnut Tommy had been leading. Then Tommy limped over to where the steel gray was being led onto the barge. Dale could see him talking excitedly to his colleague, then bending down—undoubtedly to check the gender of the horse—then running his hands along the front legs, the hind legs. Finally, his head popped up, and he yelled to Dale, "Just come down!"

She untangled herself from between the fence slats and rushed down the muddy bank, slipping and sliding until she stood beside the massive truck.

"I think I've found my filly!" she said, dazed, to the young man holding the chestnut.

He grinned at her. "Go on, then, miss!"

She wove in and out of the mash of horses to where Tommy stood at the foot of the barge amid a cacophony of whinnies, nickers, and stamping hooves.

"Look, Deebs!" The steel gray horse with a flaxen mane and tail stood with its buttocks facing toward Dale.

"It's a mare!" He didn't have to say anything else. Dale talked softly as she walked to the side and placed her hands on the mare's withers, then leaned down and stared at the mare's three white legs—two forelegs and the left hind leg. But the right hind leg was totally black.

"Essie!" she gasped. "Is it you?"

Even as she quietly pronounced the name, the mare turned toward Dale, snow white ears pricked forward. On her forehead was a slim white marking that started under the forelock and gradually covered her whole face until it muted into a soft pink muzzle.

"She's even got the black beauty spot, Tommy!" she called to him.

Dale began to tremble as she stepped onto the barge, caressing the mare.

Tommy was beside her, and together, they lifted the mare's muzzle so they could peek at the deep red gums. "How old is she, Deebs?" Tommy teased. "Do you remember all those years ago, the game we played?"

Dale was in tears. "Of course I remember! And you can see plain as day that she's about twelve."

The mare had the perfect markings, and she was the right age. "Essie!"

The mare's ears twitched, and big eyes stared at Dale.

"You look wonderful, girl! All fat and sassy." Dale let her hands caress the mare's neck, then slide down to her withers and her round barrel. Then Dale reached up and scratched underneath her chin. The mare began rubbing her forehead on Dale's arm, up and down. Then she nuzzled Dale's denims.

"She remembers me! She's looking for a carrot! I always carried carrots or sugar cubes in my pocket for her."

"It does look like she knows you, Deebs. That's amazing."

As the coast guardsmen continued loading the horses onto the barge, Dale stood with Essie on the sandy stretch of beach near the dock. She went over every marking on the mare's body, pulling from her memory those same markings she had memorized before her filly had been sold. The mare was rounder, the steel gray more pronounced, the dapples a bit more muted. But Dale had no doubt that this was Essie.

She called out to Tommy, "Can I get on her?"

He shrugged and went over to another coast guardsman. Then he nodded, a big grin on his face. She shimmied onto the mare's bare back, walking her along the shore of the narrow inlet while the barge filled with horses. She closed her eyes and imagined trotting past the barracks and the mess hall and the dormitories, all the way out onto the beach where she'd watched the horses galloping that afternoon.

As she leaned over Essie's neck, a parenthesis of ten years closed in her mind. The January air sliced across her tearstained face, and gratitude welled up inside. A forgotten prayer, repeated for years, had suddenly been answered, and Dale whispered, "Thank you."

19

Allie

Tuesday, March 10

The drive to St. Simons Island took a little less than five hours from the bumper-to-bumper traffic leaving Atlanta, even at six thirty in the morning, to the boring stretch when we entered I-16 at Macon, and then the mounting excitement as the air became thick and heavy and the foliage turned to palmetto trees and sea pines along I-95.

Tricia had conked out in the passenger's seat halfway along, so I was left with a thousand thoughts pounding in my mind like hoofbeats galloping down a beach. What exactly was I hoping to find? What did Nana Dale want me to find? Certainly not her money. But something.

Her heart and soul.

Yes, that's why she'd left me the scrapbook-diary in the first place, well before Mr. Hightower stole my dream. Somehow, the events of 1942 and 1943 had shaped her in a way that carried her through life. I could not quite decipher yet if the effects of those years had left positive or negative markings. I knew that the markings had been there in the wrinkles on her aged face and in the way her eyes got that far-off stare. She spent time remembering something, but whatever it was, she didn't feel free to share it with anyone during her life, and only with me afterward.

In the excitement and rush of leaving my apartment, I had forgotten to grab her diary. Now I reprimanded myself. I had hoped with Tricia's calming presence beside me, I could finish leafing through it and find out what happened to Tommy, maybe even discover what my grandmother had stored away in her heart and in her house.

But as soon as that thought came, I felt relief. At least for this day, I couldn't look through the scrapbook. There was a part of me that didn't want to know the truth about Nana Dale's life. Surely I would find an obituary for Tommy if I just turned a few pages, and I didn't want to know that her one love had died in the war or of a crippling disease or of something completely different.

How did people get past the horror of war? I wanted to know, yet I desperately did not want to know.

Interspersed with those thoughts, I berated myself for my grief—the grief of losing the house and the horses and Austin. True grief, yes, but how did that compare to losing the person you loved to death?

The thought zipped through my mind, *Thank God you haven't died, Austin. Maybe I haven't lost you forever.*

I knew that Nana Dale had lived with grief, but she had also lived fully. She had moved past it. No, that wasn't right. She didn't exactly get past the grief, but she learned to live with the deep regret, along with full-throttled joy.

"Life is paradox, Allie. When you learn to embrace it all, let it mix together like molasses in oats, well, the sweet fragrance comes out. Even when life stinks."

She liked to remind me of this as I was mucking out a stall, the wheelbarrow piled high with manure while she dumped buckets filled with oats into the horses' troughs.

"You rarely get to a place in life where it's all good or all bad. And you know, manure makes gardens grow."

She'd toss out her barn wisdom when I'd had a spat with my mother or done poorly on a test. Or had my heart broken by a boy.

I wished she were still here to tell me what to do about Austin.

I let that thought settle. Yes, about the house and property; yes, about her past. But also about Austin. More and more about Austin.

Forgiven. But I got your message loud and clear. Austin's last text to me crossed my mind, and just as quickly came the text I should send back to him. *No, that was completely the wrong message, Austin! I'm sorry. I'm so sorry! Please give me another chance.*

But I didn't.

Somehow, Nana Dale had embraced the paradox of life. This I believed. But I was still stuck in the shock of everything that had catapulted into my life since I sat in Mr. Ted Lorrider's studded leather high-back chair and felt my world shift.

We arrived on the island before noon, crossing the Brunswick River on the beautiful cable-stayed Sidney Lanier Bridge, the longest in Georgia. Every time I had crossed the bridge in the past, I thought back to my junior high days and the poems I had memorized by Sidney Lanier, the wonderful nineteenth-century Georgian poet. I loved his "Song of the Chattahoochee," about the river that ran through Atlanta. But as I crossed the bridge, the lines that floated back to me were from "The Marshes of Glynn."

> Oh, what is abroad in the marsh and the terminal sea?
> Somehow my soul seems suddenly free
> From the weighing of fate and the sad discussion of sin,
> By the length and the breadth and the sweep of the marshes
>   of Glynn.

I longed for my soul to seem suddenly free.

I rolled down the windows and took slow, deep breaths, soaking in the familiar sights and smells of the Golden Isles, and yes, the marshes of Glynn County. The majestic live oaks were draped with Spanish moss and resurrection ferns. I always found new hope when I spied this plant. My science teacher had explained how a resurrection fern could only live by attaching itself to a host plant, and one of its favorites was a live oak. And it could survive in extreme drought, shriveling to a brown mess that appeared dead but that came back to life again when it encountered water—thus the resurrection. But, my teacher explained with a smile, the fern never really died. That was the incredible thing about it. It could lose almost ninety percent of its water and survive, while most plants could only lose ten percent before they died.

The poetry and botanical information from my school days always haunted me happily when I came back to the islands. Today, I longed for some sort of resurrection too, for it seemed I had lost at least ninety percent of whatever I needed to move forward in my life.

Tricia stirred, rubbed her eyes, and sat up in the passenger seat, then rolled down her window and stared out at the long pointy fronds of the palms and palmettos and the magnolias with their waxy white flowers, exuberant beside equally flamboyant crepe myrtles.

"Beach weather, beach smells," she said, tilting her head back and throwing one arm out the lowered window. "I love it!"

I'd read that the Home Front Museum had opened in 2018, but the white two-story building had belonged to another era when it housed coast guardsmen. I parked in the almost empty but spacious lot that was used not only for the museum but also as one of the main access points to the popular East Beach. I imagined, come June, the lot would be packed with cars and minivans.

"Ready?" I stood shading my eyes and looking to the horizon and the ocean far in the distance.

Tricia stifled a yawn. "Yep. How fun is this?"

I squinted against the sun and felt a prick of excitement as I took in the view of the sign that I'd seen on the leaflet and the stately white building with its red roof, white columns, and look-out tower. A smaller white building stood behind it.

The day was windy, and the American flag made a whipping sound as it waved against the bright sun. How I longed to know more of what happened here for my grandmother. Perhaps this museum would help me unravel the mystery.

A middle-aged docent greeted us on the front porch. "You can purchase tickets in the back building. We suggest starting your tour there, with a short film and timeline."

We walked across the yard and into the building. By the information desk was a stack of leaflets, the same ones I'd found with Nana Dale's scrapbook.

We encountered the museum's curator at the information desk, an attractive woman in her midforties. She explained the best way to take advantage of the museum. I wondered if she could shed light on anything about the mounted beach patrol.

She shrugged. "There's a little about it in the museum. But we've never found proof that horses were stabled here on this property."

"My grandmother mentioned there's a docent here, Dr. Cressman, who corresponded with her at some point about the patrol."

The curator nodded and said, "Take a look at the display, and I'll see if I can find him. He should be arriving soon. He's a World War II historian who gives guided tours of the museum. He may indeed have more information."

On the wall by the information desk was an enormous map of coastal Georgia and its islands. In the Atlantic, the tips of two black ships marked the sinkings on April 8, 1942. The map also showed the locations of the naval air stations in Glynco and on St. Simons, as well as the shipyards in Brunswick and the coast guard station where we were standing.

Tricia and I examined a huge timeline that snaked around the next room, beginning in 1932 and continuing through the end of the war, its upper half showing world events, and the bottom half following events in Georgia's history. Then we sat riveted in place as we watched a film explaining the public's universal feeling of desperation after the April 8 attacks.

Afterward, we returned to the main house and stepped inside, entering World War II and the Battle of the Atlantic. The displays showed scary-looking propaganda posters, explaining how to ration during the war and invest in war bonds. And, as the leaflet had testified, there were interactive exhibits and plenty of information about the importance of women and Black workers at the Brunswick shipyards.

In one room was a brief explanation about the mounted patrol with a photo of a man on a horse and another with a dog:

The wartime mission of the coast guard was to protect the shoreline and perform maritime rescues. The St. Simons Station organized beach patrols on the barrier islands to detect suspicious vessels and enemy agents.

I was disappointed as I read on. That was it?

"I was hoping to find out something about the training camp on Hilton Head," I mumbled to Tricia. "For the marines and the coast guardsmen. I saw the photo of Tommy riding on the beach there."

Tricia tilted her head. "Not to be obtuse, but . . . um, who's Tommy again?" she asked a bit meekly.

"My grandmother's long-lost love."

"And this Tommy fella was fighting in the war on Hilton Head Island?"

"He wasn't able to join the military because he had polio. But somehow, he could be in the mounted patrol. They called themselves the Sand Pounders."

"Love it!"

"It was like a civilian branch that guarded the coasts during the war. You know—the Battle of the Atlantic."

Tricia shrugged. "My World War II history is a bit sketchy, but I'm learning a lot today."

"They looked for German submarines and for Germans sneaking onto shore."

We continued meandering through the different rooms, and although I did not find any other information about the Sand Pounders, Tricia and I were both enthralled with plenty of other exhibits.

My attention was drawn to a display about Liberty ships. I recalled the term not from history class but from Nana Dale. I tilted my head, as if it would help me recall what she'd said.

Yes, there she was, tiny Nana Dale, dressed in her riding breeches, saddle cradled over her joined arms, walking out to the barn with me following. Her eyes were shining as she glibly proclaimed, *"I helped build Liberty ships during the war. And you know, that sailor, the one who washed up on shore, he'd been on a Liberty ship. Gone across the ocean to take supplies to Europe. Came home with tall tales."*

Tricia pointed to another exhibit. "Hey, Allie, it says blimps were used along with convoys to protect the Liberty ships, and that the blimps along with the mounted patrol are what completely changed the tide of the war by summer of 1943."

When we reached the display of the artifacts from the sunken *Esso Baton Rouge*, one of the ships destroyed in the sinkings, I whispered, "They were there."

"Who?"

"Nana Dale and Tommy were on the beach that night—when the ships were torpedoed. They were riding horses and helped with the rescue. Maybe they even helped the coast guard crew bring the rescued sailors right here to this station."

"My word," Tricia whispered back, eyes wide.

We'd made our way back to the front of the museum, where the curator met us again, introducing me to Dr. George Cressman, an older gentleman with white hair and intelligent eyes. When I explained the letter Nana Dale had left me, he smiled. "Oh yes, of course! I so enjoyed corresponding with your grandmother." Then his face clouded. "Is she well?"

"I'm afraid she passed away last December, but she asked me

to come to the museum and meet you. She wanted me to know more about her life during the war, and specifically about the Sand Pounders."

"I'm sorry for your loss, Miss Massey. I never had the pleasure of meeting your grandmother in person, but even by phone, I could tell she was quite an amazing woman."

"Thank you," I said. "Yes, she was."

"And I believe I can help you with information about the Sand Pounders." He smiled again. "Give me a few minutes."

Dr. Cressman came back out with a stack of photocopied sheets. On the top of the pile, a black-and-white cover with the title *The Beach Patrol* showed a photo of a coast guardsman lying on the beach with a bayonet in his hands as a German shepherd kept watch beside him. Flipping through the pages, I saw numerous photos of horses, dogs, and men on beaches or at the barracks, even a photo of the camp on Hilton Head Island where the men trained.

I felt a little leap in my gut. At last!

"Thank you," I said, pumping Dr. Cressman's hand. "This is exactly what I was looking for. We're heading to Hilton Head now to see Camp McDougal."

Dr. Cressman nodded. "Good for you. As you probably know, the camp is no longer there, but these pages will help you fill in the gaps."

20

Dale

January 1943

Dale rode with the horses on the barge as it slowly swayed and dipped, crossing the inlet from Buckingham Landing onto Hilton Head. None of the coast guardsmen made any comment or complaint. In fact, they watched her in an awed silence. One young man wiped a stray tear from the corner of his eyes when Tommy told him the story, murmuring, "If that don't beat all."

When the horses arrived on the island, Tommy led Essie off the barge with Dale following behind. No one breathed a word when Dale took the lead shank from Tommy and Essie followed Dale into a makeshift stall in the old steel hangar. Nor did they report when Dale spent the night right beside her mare, both of them cuddled under a heap of horse blankets, just as she'd done before Essie was carted away.

Instead, the men on duty with the horses throughout the night would come to gawk at "the little gal who found her long-lost filly."

When Dale awoke, hair tangled in hay and shavings, she looked around, momentarily confused, then sat up in the middle of the stall. Essie walked over and nudged her, and Dale leaped to her feet, engulfing the mare's neck in a hug.

"Essie! It really is true. You're here." Once again, she ran her hand over the horse's sleek barrel, grabbed a tuft of mane beside her withers, and pulled herself onto Essie's back. She bent over backward, laid her head on the mare's rump, stared up at the tin roof, and let the tears flow.

Eventually she slid off Essie's back, kissed her muzzle, and whispered, "I'll be back soon." Dale didn't know exactly what she believed about faith and prayers, but she knew someone who did, and she hurried off to find a way to contact the one person who had to know about her discovery.

Husy.

In the predawn light, Dale made her way up the dirt road to a hole-in-the-wall tavern called The Island Intown, about a mile from the camp. The owners, Willie and Lydia Burkes, a Negro couple, had two little rooms behind the tavern, one of which Dale was staying in for the week—except for last night, when she had made her home in the steel stable instead. She had prepared her speech when she entered the tavern. Gray-haired Lydia stood alone in its main room. She placed her hands on her wide hips, eyes narrowed.

"I know I was supposed to be sleeping here last night, ma'am. I'm so sorry! I promise I wasn't carousing with any of the men. . . ."

Lydia stayed transfixed, the frown spreading across her face, so Dale continued, "I'm sorry. It's not what you think." In a flurry of words, Dale explained about finding her mare. "It's a ten-year-old answer to prayer!"

No response.

"I wasn't sleeping in the barracks, I promise. I stayed with my mare." At the look of disapproval, Dale tried another angle. "Have you ever owned a horse?"

"I own two right now."

"So you know. Horses have a memory, and she remembers me! And now, I need to borrow your phone and let my family know that I've found her."

Instead of answering, the heavyset woman took Dale in her arms, smothering her into her bosom, deep-throated laughter rumbling in her throat. "Sugar, if I've heard your story once, I've heard it a hundred times. Them boys kept repeating over and over last evening and into the morning how this pretty little lady had found her filly after praying about her for a decade!"

She finally released Dale and held her at arm's length, a huge smile on her face. "It's a good story, Miss Dale. Just the kind our boys need to keep up their enthusiasm. Hard job they're getting ready to move into. They needed some encouragement." She motioned for Dale to follow her. "Let me show you to the phone." She led her through the tavern to a small office.

Her parents were still at the Ridleys' house on St. Simons, but Dale dialed the number to her Atlanta home. When Husy came to the phone, Dale blurted out, "I found her, Husy! I found Essie!"

There was no response over the crackling phone line. "I found Essie," she repeated.

"Honey, that's incredible. Are you sure?"

"Yes! Her markings are an exact match—even the beauty spot! And she's the right age—at least that's what her teeth show. And she knows me! She seemed to recognize my voice and started searching my pockets for something as soon as I went to her. Remember how I always carried sugar cubes and carrots in my pockets when I was little?"

"Well, Lord have mercy, that is wonderful news," Husy said. Dale could hear the joy in her tired voice, could imagine her huddled near the downstairs phone, cradling the earpiece.

"You told me to keep praying, Husy, and I did. Not always, but lots of times."

"I can hardly believe it. How did you come to find her?"

Dale shared every detail from the first time she'd gone with Tommy to watch the horses being unloaded and reloaded until a few minutes ago, when Lydia mentioned how the men kept telling the story.

She could picture Husy tilting her head as she puzzled over this information. Finally, she said, "Well, that's mighty fine! And yes, ma'am, a real nice answer to prayer. Years of them."

"I'm going to talk to the commanding officer down here, see if he will let me join the mounted patrol. Maybe I can train on Essie."

"What?" Husy asked.

"I know it sounds strange, and please don't breathe a word to my parents, but if it works out, I'll get to be with Essie again."

"And Tommy?"

"No, he's in training right now. If they accept me, it'll be for a different week of training. We wouldn't be sent to the same island."

Husy was silent for a long pause. "Dale, you have a job at the shipyard in Brunswick. You're needed there."

"I'm going back to the shipyard on Monday, Husy. I promise. But can you pray that the commander here agrees that I can join the mounted patrol? If he says yes, I'll transfer at some point and start training whenever they designate."

"My, my, Barbara Dale. If you don't get yourself into interesting situations. Are there any other girls in the patrol?"

"I haven't seen any yet. But that doesn't mean one can't join."

Husy was still chuckling to herself when Dale hung up the phone.

Dale found Lydia behind the bar at the tavern. "Can I pay you for the phone call? It might cost a bit, being long distance."

"No, that call's on us."

"Thank you, Lydia. Thank you so much." She shuffled her feet like a young girl trying to get up the nerve to ask her mother if she could wear lipstick. "I was wondering if you would rent out your room to me again if I'm allowed to join the coast guard? You see, I'm going to ask the commander if I can train for the mounted patrol, and since I haven't seen any other girls—I mean, women—here, I'd be the only one, and I can't very well stay in the barracks. If I could tell the commander that I already have lodging, he's apt to look more favorably on my request."

Lydia laughed. "Well, it's for sure you couldn't be lodged in the barracks. But what makes you think that commander will consider letting you join them horse riders?"

"I'm stubborn. And I can be very convincing. Please don't worry about that. All I need is for you to agree to house me. I'll pay you rent for the week. Name your price."

Lydia shook her head back and forth. "You're a handful, Miss Dale. If the commander agrees to let you join, the coast guard will certainly cover your housing." Her black eyes sparkled with good humor. "If you can convince Lieutenant Commander McTeer to let you in the mounted beach patrol, well, I can guarantee you'll have a place to stay while you're on the island."

By the time Dale was able to see Camp McDougal's lieutenant commander, she imagined that he, like Lydia, had heard her story recounted dozens of times, but she wasn't sure if that was a boon or a deterrent.

He was a striking man in his late thirties, and she'd heard he was far ahead of his time in his positive views about desegregation. One of the men on the training staff had told her, "He's a good man. Runs a tight ship and expects respect. He treats the Negroes on the island real well. He's the sheriff of Beaufort—least he was before he took a leave of absence to head up this camp."

She felt the eyes of a dozen coast guardsmen on her back as she took a deep breath and entered the commander's office.

"Sir, I'd like to join the US Coast Guard Mounted Beach Patrol," she stated, standing as tall as she could manage and attempting a salute.

He sat back in his desk chair and cocked his head, his white cap outlining his handsome face. "This is not the place to sign up, young lady. It's a complicated system with many regulations."

"I understand that, sir, but I know the coast guard enlists women. It says so right here."

Dale produced a flyer she'd snatched from the window of a grocery store in Brunswick before traveling to Hilton Head, just in case she had a chance to ask to join. She'd never imagined the added motivation of finding Essie.

The yellow flyer showed a coast guardsman dressed in the familiar blue uniform and white cap holding a pistol. In bold red letters, it read *Guard Our Waterfront*, and a smaller font proclaimed *Volunteers needed now to do a real exciting war job*. But it was the white rectangle insert that interested Dale and hopefully would interest the commander too. *Wear the Coast Guard Uniform: Serve two 6-hour watches a week. MEN needed for guard duty; WOMEN needed for motor corps and office duty*. Beside this was drawn the head of a woman in a blue cap.

"Are you in the habit of taking government property?" Commander McTeer asked, staring over the desk.

Dale's eyes grew wide, and she felt the blush on her face. "No, sir. No, I—"

"As you can most likely understand, the mounted patrol doesn't qualify as motor corps or office duty," he continued, standing from behind his desk and pointing to those specific words.

For a moment, she was speechless. Then, taking a deep breath, she blurted out what she'd practiced. "I know, sir. But exceptions can be made. Please let me join! I've just turned eighteen, and I know you accept boys as young as seventeen. I've been working at building Liberty ships in Brunswick. I can weld with one hand and hang from scaffolding with the other. I'm not afraid. And I've been riding horses practically since I was born." Dale tried to make herself taller, rolling onto her tiptoes. "You see, sir, it's a special case. Perhaps you've heard that I've found my filly. I mean, my mare."

He stared at her without a word, so she rushed on.

"During the Depression, my parents had to sell our horses. Amazingly, I've found her here, ten years later."

Lieutenant Commander McTeer, looking unimpressed, narrowed his eyes. "Little lady, your conduct is highly unusual. There is a strict protocol we follow."

"Yes, sir. I know. I've read the complete handbook." She held out Tommy's copy. "It's very thorough."

The commander narrowed his eyes further, but she detected a flicker across his lips as he rubbed a hand over his eyes. "Miss

Butler," he began, glancing at the sheet of paper she had filled out. "I cannot have you around these boys and men. I don't trust some of them farther than I can spit, and I get a new group every week. Six hundred of them.

"Did you see the road to the tavern—that little barbecue place up the street? The men love that place. They walk a mile to get there, and they drink themselves silly, and then they litter the whole area with broken glass on the way home. They're cleaning up now." He looked over his glasses. "If I can't trust them with property, I certainly wouldn't trust them with a pretty young woman."

"Oh, I wouldn't stay in the barracks, sir," she said too quickly. "I've already talked with the couple who keep the tavern and the guest cabins. I'm staying in one of them right now. And Miss Lydia says I can stay there again whenever I'm on the island for training. Please ask her. She'll verify what I'm telling you."

She counted to ten silently, then barged ahead again. "Please, let me join the mounted patrol. And let me train on Essie. I promise you won't be disappointed in me." She took a breath and continued. "Please, sir. I've heard you're a kind and fair man. I know the country's in desperate need—I'll go wherever you send me. Like I've said, right now I'm working at the plant in Brunswick, welding Liberty ships. I'm not afraid of hard work."

Then she prepared for her punch line. "My boyfriend, Tommy, is in training this week. He and I were there when the tankers were torpedoed off the coast of St. Simons last April. We were on our horses that very night. We saw the explosions, and we rode up and down the beaches, asking for help to rescue the sailors—the merchant mariners," she corrected herself. "And then I warned other civilians to stay inside. It's like we were doing the duty of the patrol even before it existed."

She saw his mouth twitch, hiding a smile behind his mustache. "Little lady, you are as stubborn as the day is long."

"I know, sir. I've heard that all my life. But I do want to help."

"I got that part, but, forgive me, I don't believe you'll meet the minimum height requirements for the patrol."

Dale felt stymied for a long moment, then said, "But, sir, if I'm to be the first woman in the mounted patrol, then surely there are no height requirements specified for females."

At this, Commander McTeer grinned. "You don't give up easily, do you, Miss Butler?"

Dale felt a twinge of hope. "No, sir, I don't. With all respect, of course, commander sir. And I'm strong. I can hold a saddle and a bridle and two horses and a bale of hay all at once. I've rescued a man in a tornado, and I've walked plenty of horses out of colic, and I've buried some too. I can muck half a dozen stalls in an hour, and I've won my fair share of championships in the hunter/jumper division in shows. A few years ago, I even qualified for the Maclay Medal and attended the National Horse Show up in Madison Square Garden. Please, sir. I want to serve, and I want to serve on my mare. I'll do whatever you ask, and I won't hold you responsible for whatever happens to me."

He pulled on his mustache, wiped his hand across his forehead, and gave a shrug of his shoulders, shuffling through a mound of papers on his desk. Finally, he looked up at Dale and said, "You're working in Brunswick, you said? When will you be done?"

"When the war's over. I'll stay to the end unless you agree to station me here and let me ride my horse in the patrol. If you let me come, I'll do a better job than any of your men. Please, just let me try. I'm not afraid."

He folded his hands together on his desk and leaned back in his chair. "If you will please be quiet for a moment, I have a few words to say. May I?"

Dale's eyes grew wide, and she nodded.

"I've heard about you finding your filly, Dale Butler, no less than twenty times. Seems a lot of men think it would only be fair to let you join. Not the least of whom is your boyfriend."

"Yes, sir. I mean, thank you, sir. For telling me that." She thrust her hand out to shake his, then let it fall to her side when he didn't respond. "I mean, I'm thankful that the men think I should join. And Tommy too. But it's not so that we'd be together. He's already training this week. I'll train whenever you ask, and then you can ship me as far away as you want, as long as you let me have my horse."

What she had hoped was a grin before now grew into a smile that covered his face, so she hurried on. "You're teaching boys and men how to ride. But I already know how to ride and take care of the horses. I've been doing it all my life. I'll help any way you want. Please, I want to help. I'm heading back to Brunswick on Sunday, sir, to be at the shipyard bright and early on Monday morning. But if you tell me what I need to do to get permission to join the mounted patrol, I'll start work on it right away."

Two hours later, he called her back into his office. "All right, young lady. I'll let you join as our first female. It might be kind of rough, I'm warning you. But you've assured me numerous times"—he lifted an eyebrow—"that you don't mind hard work."

Dale forced herself to remain still. "Really, sir? Thank you. Thank you!" She made a feeble attempt at a salute, and Lieutenant Commander McTeer broke into a smile.

"You can join the group coming in two weeks."

"And I'll get my horse?"

"You'll get what I give you, young lady. That's all."

"Thank you, sir! Thank you!"

Dale galloped all the way back to the barracks, where Tommy and at least thirty other boys and men were waiting. "I can join! Commander McTeer is going to let me join. And I'm sure he'll give me Essie."

A deafening cheer arose from the men with her news. Tommy picked her up, swung her around, and planted a big kiss on her lips. "I'm not one bit surprised, Barbara Dale Butler, that you talked him into letting you be a part of the patrol."

One of the young men called out, "Three cheers for Dale and Essie!"

Tommy locked eyes with her, their foreheads touching. "You are one stubborn girl, Dale Butler. And I love you for it."

She jumped up into his arms, knocking Tommy momentarily

off-balance. Then he straightened, kissed her on the lips, and slowly they twirled around together one more time. Then Dale said, "Let's go see Essie again. I've got to tell her the good news."

The mare nuzzled Dale as she slipped into the makeshift stall, offering a carrot Lydia had given her. "It's almost like contraband, girl. You be sure and tell your little filly that," Lydia had said.

Once back at the stables, Dale stayed with Essie, brushing her, sitting in the stall, giving the mare a monologue on the last ten years of her life. And throughout the afternoon, the coast guardsmen continued to parade by the stall, whispering the story of Dale and her filly among themselves.

The commander had heard the sentimental tone of their voices even before Dale burst into his office with her request. But it wasn't until after she had officially been accepted into the coast guard that she called her parents.

"I'm staying on Hilton Head for a few more days, and then I'll be coming back in two weeks. I'm training to be part of the mounted beach patrol."

Her father laughed. "Dale, don't joke with your mother."

"It's not a joke. It's real because, because . . ." She drew it out as long as she could. "I've found Essie. I found her."

Silence, then, much as Husy had reacted, a gasp from her mother and a robust chuckle from her father.

"Are you sure?"

"Yes! She's got the exact same markings, even the beauty spot, she's the right age—and she knows me. So I begged the commander to allow me to join, and he said yes. Now it's a party down here. You can't believe the celebration. The marines and coast guardsmen are almost as excited as Tommy and I are."

"But what about your job at the shipyard?"

"The lieutenant commander says I can transfer."

That night, as the men played cards, drank beer, and put on a dog show, Dale snuggled close to Tommy right outside Essie's stall. She didn't want to leave.

"Look at yourself, Deebs. You're going to be the first woman in the mounted patrol. That's amazing!"

"I know. I don't really believe that I've found Essie and that I can join."

"From what I've heard, you were fearless and totally stubborn when you talked to the commander."

She grinned. "You heard right."

"If that's true, answer me this, my darling: You're not afraid of anything; you've never been afraid of anything. You run headfirst into adventure and danger. And you stood up to the lieutenant commander and got him to let you join the mounted patrol just by your sheer will. You're not afraid, so why are you afraid for me?"

Dale felt her heart ramming into her ribs. How could she explain? "The first day I saw you, Tommy Ridley, I fell head over heels for you—a full-on, deep-down crush. Then I got to know you, and over the years, it became real love. Even better, now it's reciprocated." She stood on her tiptoes and kissed him full on the lips. "I'd always imagined we'd be together forever, imagined like a little girl dreams of becoming a princess. But I didn't dare pray for it. It was too good to be true. So I just pined away for you and got so jealous when you'd sneak off to kiss those other girls."

He tweaked her nose.

"But now that we're together, Tommy, I don't want to let you go."

He took her in his arms. "I'm not going anywhere. We're all doing our part in this war. Every guy is having to say good-bye to his girl for a time. No need to be afraid, Deebs. I'm just going to be riding Finny on a beach. No torpedo is going to get me."

"I know it's selfish to even be afraid. You're braver than I am."

"We're both brave." Then he glanced sideways at her. "I'm planning on us being together forever, you know. You do know that, don't you? Are you afraid I'm not?"

"Maybe," she admitted. "Maybe it just seems too good to be true, to be living my dream in the middle of this nightmare war."

Tommy stood up and offered his hand to Dale. "Come, walk with me."

His arm around her shoulders, they made their way out of the temporary stable to where live oaks and sea pines towered above them, and the moon peeked through the leaves.

On the porch of what was once the lighthouse keeper's cottage, Tommy pulled Dale into his arms, then tilted his head down and found her lips. Once again, Dale lost herself in the fairy-tale kiss. Eventually, they left the porch and came to the lighthouse that stood at the northwest edge of Camp McDougal. Tommy stopped, leaned against the steel frame, and pulled Dale into his arms again. They stared up into the black sky with an almost-full moon silhouetting them among the trees.

"It's magical," Dale whispered, leaning against Tommy so that his arms closed around her waist. "Like the moon is shining a secret spotlight on us." She breathed in the beauty and the silence and the sensation of Tommy's body so close to hers.

"What are you doing tomorrow?" he asked, turning her around to face him and drawing her hands into his.

"Tomorrow? You know what I'm doing tomorrow. I'm spending tomorrow and the next couple of days here with you and Essie before I go back to St. Simons on Sunday and drive with my mother and yours to Brunswick on Monday morning, put on my mask, and weld a Liberty ship."

"What if we got married?"

Dale caught her breath and looked deep into his eyes, then crossed her arms over her chest, frowned, and backed away. "What?"

"We could get the chaplain to marry us tomorrow, have a couple of days together before we each go off to our islands."

"Are you serious?" He joked so frequently, and his tone was light. Why did he have to be so maddeningly lighthearted? Especially when pronouncing the word *marriage*.

He threw back his head and laughed. "I love that expression on your face! I've surprised you. And yes, I *am* serious. If you're

250

so worried about losing me, I'll show you. I'll carry you across the threshold as your husband, and you'll never get rid of me. What do you say?"

He grabbed her hands, and when she met his eyes again, the moonlight reflected in them spoke of love. She swallowed, felt the pounding in her ears and chest, and whispered, "How in the world could you get the papers that quickly?"

Tommy grinned and kissed her forehead. "All my buddies have been running off to marry their girls before they go overseas. Might as well do it with my girl right here."

She cleared her throat, but no sound came out. Batting her eyes, she leaned against Tommy's chest. "I don't believe you."

He fell to one knee, fished in his pocket, and pulled out the curved nail from the horseshoe, the one she'd given him long ago for good luck. "I carry it with me always, Deebs. But now I want you to have it. Until I can get you a diamond." He looked up into her eyes. "Will you marry me, Barbara Dale Butler?"

Her eyes filled with tears, and she whispered, "Yes."

"That's swell!" Tommy yelled in a full-out shout as he stood up. His kiss bloomed with equal parts passion and forced restraint.

For one more day.

21

Allie

Tuesday, March 10

We grabbed a sandwich at a fast-food restaurant during the two-hour drive north on I-95 from St. Simons to Hilton Head. In between bites, Tricia read me snippets from the sheets Dr. Cressman had given me.

"'Imagine standing at the ocean's door in 1942 and seeing one of your favorite show-jump riders, jockeys, or polo players galloping along the beach, scanning the horizon for enemy ships. In World War II, this was a very real possibility.' And this photo shows two military-looking guys galloping down the beach."

"I need to see proof!"

Tricia held the sheet up, and I glanced over at it. "But I seriously doubt they were galloping when they were on duty," Tricia said.

"False advertising," we said in unison and laughed.

"Actually, it all looks super legit. I mean, half of these papers are listed as classified. It says that the US secretary of the navy ordered the creation of the US Coast Guard Mounted Beach Patrol in the summer of 1942. Evidently, hundreds of new stations were set up along the coasts, at first with temporary shelters until something permanent could be built. And it says that some of the Sand Pounders"—Tricia smiled as she emphasized those words—"were even housed in private facilities. I'd definitely prefer that!" She continued scanning the pages. "The mounted patrol covered almost fifty thousand miles of coastland and peaked at twenty-four thousand officers and men."

"That would be a lot to organize in a hurry."

"Yeah, crazy—two thousand dogs and three thousand horses were in use by the end of the first year. Sounds like they were practically begging for experienced riders, or really anybody who knew how to handle a horse. Oh, and here's another photo showing a bunch of guys in uniform galloping down a beach."

Again, she held up a sheet with a very dark photocopied photo.

"That looks like the same one I saw in Nana Dale's scrapbook. Wow. It's all real."

— ♄ —

"Well, here we are," I announced as I parked my car across the street from the fifth hole of the Arthur Hills Golf Course in the Palmetto Dunes Oceanfront Resort on Hilton Head.

Tricia yawned in response, took a swig from her coffee mug, and said, "Pure luxury. This whole island gives a new meaning to *beach house*. I'd call these places *beach mansions*. Definitely not the rustic cabins my family stayed at on the few occasions we ventured to the beach."

Indeed, spacious homes built of weathered wood sat beyond perfectly manicured lawns inside a gated community. We exited the car with sunglasses and sun visors in place, as if it were July instead of March.

"See?" I called to Tricia.

She looked at me doubtfully. "And what am I supposed to be seeing?"

"Camp McDougal," I said. "Where the US Mounted Beach Patrol trained during World War II."

Tricia scanned the road to the left and right, then pointed across the street. "Looks a lot like a golf course to me."

"Yeah, it's a golf course now. But Camp McDougal used to be here. I just wanted to see where it was because Nana Dale asked me to visit it. She said it was very important to her story. Come here." I took her hand, led her across the street, and pointed. "See the lighthouse?"

To the right of the course, a white lighthouse rose behind tall sea pines and huge old oak trees and smaller palm trees, which kept it partially hidden from view.

"It's lovely," Tricia murmured. "Understated but stalwart. Unless you're looking for it, you could drive right by and miss it."

By now we had crossed the road and were walking on the paved golf path, shifting until we could get a complete view of the structure.

"How old is it?"

I pointed to a wrought-iron sign near the base with the title *Hilton Head Rear Range Lighthouse.*

"It says here that it was the island's only functioning lighthouse, first used in 1881 and decommissioned in 1932." I continued scanning the plaque.

"It's also called the Leamington Lighthouse."

"Can we go up?"

"Doesn't look like it." I answered, verifying this by tugging on the door in the brick foundation. "Padlocked."

"Bet it gives an awesome view from the top."

I nodded, only half listening to Tricia as I continued to read out loud. "'The lighthouse stands on what was once the site of Camp McDougal, an advanced training site for the US Marines, US Coast Guard, and defense battalions during WWII. Soldiers used the tower as a lookout for German ships and U-boats.'"

I swiveled and grabbed Tricia's hands. "This is awesome. My grandmother's stories were real, Tricia! She'd told me something about a camp during the war. I'm afraid I didn't pay much attention to that story." I jabbed my finger on the sign. "But Tommy trained here, and Nana Dale must have come here too."

We walked around the lighthouse, which sat between two golf greens empty of players. The air was brisk, and the only sounds birdsong. "Hard to imagine German U-boats on a day like today," I whispered.

On the way back out of the resort, I stopped at the information center. "Would anyone have any information about when the marines were here in World War II? When this was the site of Camp McDougal?"

The young man at the desk, perhaps thirty and wearing a bright turquoise T-shirt and jeans, scratched his blond head and thought for a minute. "Nope. Don't have any idea about that." From his expression, I wasn't convinced he even knew or cared about the dates of World War II.

"Well, is there anyone else around here who might know?"

He shrugged. "I'd check over at the lighthouse at Harbour Town. Someone might have some information there." He grinned. "You never know, you might even find an old geezer who lived on the island back then."

I rolled my eyes. I sincerely doubted I'd locate an "old geezer"—did anyone else still use that expression?—who had a memory of the camp. But then I recalled what Nana Dale had said in her letter. *Find Mr. Hampton. I can't remember his first name, but he knows the story.*

"Thanks anyway," I said. Then I turned, "I don't suppose we can climb the Leamington Lighthouse, can we?"

The young man looked at me with a smirk. "No, you read the sign correctly. *No Trespassing* really does mean no trespassing." Then he winked. "But I'd be glad to take you up to the top of the Harbour Town Lighthouse when I get off shift. And then go out for a beer at the Quarterdeck."

I gaped at him and felt my face redden. "Sorry, but I'm, uh . . . I'm busy."

We turned back to the car with Tricia laughing at me and saying, "Can I take you out for a beer?"

"Very funny," I retorted. "But in all sincerity, if we find out something about the camp, I'll get us two glasses of champagne!"

During the fifteen-minute drive to Harbour Town in the Sea Pines Resort, Tricia begged, "I'm starving. I barely ate breakfast this morning, and that sandwich didn't fill me up. I could really use something sweet." She grinned.

"There's a yummy bakery in Harbour Town. We can get coffee and a snack there en route to the lighthouse."

"Perfect."

The Harbour Town Bakery and Café was *the* place to get breakfast and often had a line out the door, but at five in the afternoon in March, the doors were closed.

"Bummer," I said. I stared at the small house with the American flags draped across the railing and one flying out front. Then I said, "Look at this."

I'd been to this bakery several times in recent years, but I had never paid any attention to the sign right by the stairway leading inside. Now I pulled Tricia over and read, "'Lighthouse keeper's cottage, circa 1880. This cottage was the original keeper's cottage constructed and located on The Battery in Charleston, South Carolina. The cottage was transported to Palmetto Dunes on Hilton Head Island during World War II, where it was used to monitor German submarine activity along the South Carolina coast during the war....'"

"That's, um, a little freaky. I mean, it's totally serendipitous. Or something," Tricia whispered.

I felt a tightening in my chest. "I wonder if Tommy ever looked for subs from either the lighthouse or this cottage."

Against what I considered rather steep odds, the familiar red-and-white-striped lighthouse at Harbour Town held informational gold. A middle-aged woman wearing a red, white, and blue T-shirt was selling tickets on the ground floor for those wishing to walk up all one hundred fourteen winding stairs to the deck.

"Oh, let's do it!" Tricia enthused.

So we did, both of us panting a little by the time we reached the top.

"This view is worth it!" Tricia said.

The wind whipped our hair in our faces as we walked around the deck, peering out at the magnificent yachts harbored below and the condominiums surrounding the water. The eighteenth hole of yet another golf course was visible across the entrance to the harbor and the ocean beyond.

"Can you imagine having the job of standing lookout for German subs?" Tricia asked.

"No, all I've ever looked for around this harbor were dolphins."

When we returned to the ground floor and I explained to the ticket woman my interest in the island during World War II, she pointed to several books on display beside shelves of mugs, T-shirts, and postcards, all boasting the lighthouse logo.

"Have you read *The History of Hilton Head*? There are some good photos in this one." She passed a coffee-table book to me. "Go ahead. Take a look."

I leafed through the pages and soon came to a photo of a group of military men galloping horses in formation on a beach—the exact same photo I had seen in Nana Dale's scrapbook and in the photocopied pages Dr. Cressman had given us. The caption had similar information about the mounted patrol. Another photo showed uniformed men riding horses with dogs walking alongside. Still another page gave an aerial view of the camp.

"Look, Tricia!"

We could make out in the black-and-white photo what looked like hundreds of barracks, a few larger buildings—including one that must have served as the stable for the horses—a stately looking mansion of sorts at the end of the property, and the lighthouse to the left of it. The camp was completely surrounded by trees.

It was all very real.

"Would anybody know more about what was going on during World War II?" I raised my head from where it was buried in the book and addressed the ticket lady. "Evidently there was a camp here and training?"

The ticket woman scratched her head, shrugged, and then said, "Yeah, Billy Hampton might." She jotted down a name and phone number on a scrap of paper. "He's an old geezer, but his memory's sharp as a tack."

I almost burst into laughter at her use of the same term as the guy at the previous place. But then I stopped. "Wait, Billy *Hampton*, did you say?"

"Yes, he's a bit of a rough character, but he likes to share stories about when he was a boy on the island during the war. Hilton Head was definitely not a tourist destination back then."

"Thanks so much," I enthused, pumping her hand.

As we walked out of the lighthouse, I turned to Tricia. "It's too early for champagne, but this deserves a celebration."

We each ordered a scoop of mint chocolate chip ice cream in a waffle cone at the shop beside the lighthouse and sat in red rocking chairs, licking and rocking and admiring the yachts that sunbathed in the harbor.

Eighty-seven-year-old Billy Hampton had skin like brittle leather, a cap of white hair, and piercing blue eyes. His body looked feeble, but his mind was keen, and he sure liked to talk.

Tricia and I were seated in Adirondack chairs on the lawn behind his single-story condominium that overlooked the Calibogue Sound, sipping sweet tea and dipping chilled shrimp into a spicy cocktail sauce.

"This is the best shrimp I've ever tasted," I said, and I wasn't just being polite.

"Should be. Family's been in the shrimping and oyster business for near to a hundred years."

I stopped in midbite. "Oh wow. You're from *that* Hampton family." Everyone knew Hampton's Seafood House was the best place to get seafood on the island.

He chuckled. "Yes, ma'am, I am indeed. Now, you were asking about what went on during the war," he said, transitioning without taking a breath. "I was just a boy, 'bout ten years old. Running around with a lot of Black people."

I must have flinched at his comment because he added, "At the time, the island was inhabited by about fourteen hundred Black residents and very few whites, mostly fishermen and farmers. There were a few dirt roads, deep woods, a country store or two, but not much else."

I recovered, my throat dry. "Go on."

"You said you've heard about Camp McDougal?"

"Not much. Just a little."

"During most of the war years, the camp held hundreds of marines and coast guardsmen. The commander of the coast guard detachment was J. E. McTeer, the Beaufort County sheriff. He took a leave of absence during the war and was given the rank of lieutenant commander." Billy Hampton looked off. "He was quite a man. His son was a good friend of mine. Passed away now. Most everyone I knew back then is gone."

I thought maybe that was the extent of his memory, but he leaned back in the Adirondack chair, stretching out his bird-thin legs and bare feet.

"The marines painted the lighthouse green and used it as a lookout tower. And the coast guardsmen had their own beach towers. And there were telephone lines buried all along the barrier islands where the marines and coast guardsmen patrolled. Once in a while, you can still find a piece of a line—rubber-covered and about as big around as a pencil." He made a circle with his pointer finger. "Them telephone lines was how they'd check in when they were patrolling the beaches with the horses and dogs."

"You saw the horses and the dogs?"

He looked at me like I'd lost my mind. "Of course I saw them. Every day, I saw them." He took a swig of some dark liquid in a whiskey glass.

Tricia lifted an eyebrow, impressed. "That must have been exciting."

"Shore was."

I blurted out, "Were there any women?"

"Any women?"

"On the island."

"I reckon there were."

"No, I mean . . ." I felt the heat rise to my face. "I think my grandmother came here. I think she rode on these beaches. During the war." I fought with myself, trying to decide whether to explain the rest of the story. Finally, I admitted, "Somehow, I think she found the filly her parents sold during the Depression and was riding that horse—Essie was her name—on these beaches. I'm trying to find out more about her life." I dared to look up at him. "She passed away a few months ago and left me a letter, asking me to come to Hilton Head and talk to a Mr. Hampton."

He was shaking his head, and I felt disappointment well in my chest.

Until he said, "My, my, my. I've never in all these years met anyone who knew about the woman in the mounted patrol." Then he smiled. "Mighty fine story, her finding her filly. She was the tiniest little thing, not even five feet. I was taller at ten years old. But she had guts and, boy, could she handle a horse. Used to watch her galloping that pretty mare along the beach with all the men."

I furrowed my brow. "My grandmother was *in* the mounted patrol?"

"Yep. Only woman that I ever saw too. They just came here for a week's worth of training, six hundred of 'em at a time. Then they were shipped out. And I watched every week. Never saw another woman."

I couldn't quite register this, and yet it made perfect sense. I wished I had Nana Dale's diary with me. Surely I'd find proof of this.

I realized I'd been silent for a long minute, and Mr. Hampton and Tricia were staring at me. "Sorry. I'm just surprised but also not at all surprised. And she found her filly here too? Do you know how?"

"Saw her being loaded onto a barge was the story I heard." And Mr. Hampton told us how the US Army Remount Service sent down hundreds of horses each week to Hilton Head to be part of the patrol.

Oh, why hadn't Nana Dale told me the whole story? Why did she tear up every time she tried to explain how her filly came back, so that inevitably, she'd end up saying *"It was a great big answer to a little girl's prayers, all ten years of them."*

"Go on, please," I said, shaking my head.

Mr. Hampton turned in his chair and looked me straight in the eyes, a sparkle in his replacing the milky film, and gave a cackle, like the sound of a goose. "And of course, you heard about your grandparents' impromptu wedding? It was the stuff of fairy tales. My, my, that was a story to tell."

My jaw dropped as I whispered, "What?"

We hadn't moved from the Adirondack chairs in Billy Hampton's backyard for three hours. At first as I tried to absorb the shock of his words, I thought perhaps he was confusing someone else's story for Nana Dale's. He was, after all, nearing ninety.

But as he continued, I thought how he'd also called it a fairy tale. It was fitting to be hearing this tale in such an idyllic setting. His condo was located in the part of the island known as South Beach. Besides being beautiful at sunset, Calibogue Sound was teeming with dolphins. Tricia and I sat mesmerized with the story and the setting as the dolphins seesawed playfully up and down in the calm waters.

And Mr. Hampton described Nana Dale and Tommy's wedding.

I listened, mentally fitting pieces of a puzzle into places where gaps had sat for so long. But what strange and surprising pieces they were!

"It was all a big secret, you have to understand. Just Commander

McTeer and the chaplain and a handful of men in attendance, including my daddy. Did I tell you my daddy was in charge of malaria control at the camp?"

I shook my head, wanting him to hurry on.

"And the Black couple that owned the tavern was there, Miss Lydia and her husband—can't remember his name, but the tavern was called the Island Intown. Think that's where your grandparents stayed after they was married."

Here he stopped and chuckled, as if he were still a ten-year-old boy. "And me! I was always sneaking around, watching everything and hoping one day I'd spot a Nazi sub. Instead, I spotted your grandmother and grandfather out on the beach. My, my, they made a fine sight! I can still see it in my mind. They was wearing those dark blue navy uniforms and seated on their gray horses, and your grandmother carried a bouquet of the prettiest wildflowers you've ever seen while the sun set behind them as they said their vows."

I didn't correct Mr. Hampton that Tommy wasn't my grandfather. I could barely find words for my shock.

"Are you absolutely positive they got married?"

"I snuck onto the beach to watch it. It's the kind of thing a boy remembers. Along with the guns and torpedoes and the horses, I'll never forget that spur-of-the-moment wedding." He cocked his head, fiddled with a button on his shirt. "You mean, you've never heard about your grandparents' wedding?"

"Nope. They just . . . decided to get married one day and did so the next?"

"Uh-huh. 'Least that's what I was told. You know, all kinds of couples got married before the guy was shipped off to war, my older brother being one of them. So I don't guess the speed of the wedding was surprising. And there was that chaplain at the camp who was more than happy to do the duty. But having the wedding on the beach with them dressed in their uniforms and looking so fine on those horses, it was enough to make even a boy like me think about mushy stuff.

"Fact is, that whole thing impressed me so much that when I got married, it was right at the same spot on the island. 'Course by then, fifteen years later, it was a lot tamer. No gators showed up for ours."

"There were alligators at their wedding?" Trica could not keep her eyebrows from expressing doubt.

"You'd see 'em every day around the lagoons. Usually didn't get too near the camp with so much going on, but there was just a small group of us out on the beach that day. Yeah, I saw me a big ole gator. Them German shepherds had a fit when they smelled him. Forgot to say that! Dogs were there too. Two or three of 'em standing at attention."

I was trying to find a place in my grandmother's life for this tall tale from Mr. Hampton. But I couldn't. "Have you ever seen photos of it?" I asked, my voice dripping with skepticism. "Surely there are photos?"

He looked at me over his glasses. "I believe if there were photos, you would've seen them, ma'am."

Yes. Surely I would have. But the whole story sounded ludicrous. As crazy as the other stories Nana Dale used to tell. Only this one left me with a dry mouth and a pounding headache.

Billy Hampton did not take notice but continued, "You gotta understand, that wedding was a secret. My daddy got after me real good for sneaking in to see it. Told me that I couldn't tell anybody about it. He said that your grandmother and grandfather's parents didn't even know about it. Photographers came to take pictures of the camp and the men and the horses and the dogs, you know, for publicity and such. But none of them photographers showed up for that wedding."

In a small voice, I asked, "Do you have any idea what happened after the wedding?"

He gave a low laugh and said, "Yes, ma'am, I have a pretty good idea. Didn't quite understand as a ten-year-old, but I'd heard rumors."

"Oh my gosh, that came out all wrong," I said, mortified while he and Tricia burst into laughter. "I don't mean *immediately* after the ceremony. I mean later. Were they stationed on the same island?"

Mr. Hampton shook his head. "Nope. Don't have any idea. I was asked to keep that wedding a secret, and I did. With so many men coming and going each week, I didn't keep up with anyone. You can see why I'd remember your grandparents, though. Don't even remember their names, but I shore do remember that little lady finding her filly one day and the delight on every man's face. That wasn't no secret. Everybody in the camp heard about that. It was a real morale booster for the men. Something like that was good for their souls.

"And like I said, their wedding the next day, well, it touched my heart."

The sun hung low in the indigo sky across the sound, dripping rays of fire across the water so that it sparkled like kindling. "We've kept you long enough. I can't tell you how grateful I am for your time and your memories, Mr. Hampton."

"You call me Billy now, young ladies. Been a real pleasure. Real pleasure."

I couldn't decipher the feeling in the pit of my stomach—excitement, regret, disbelief, longing?

"You be sure to text me if you come up with any other questions, you hear?" he called after us as we turned to leave.

I suppressed a smile. An eighty-seven-year-old texting? I didn't doubt it. "I certainly will."

Tricia and I sat outside at the Salty Dog Café, a stone's throw from Billy's condominium, munching on fries and hamburgers and sipping on wine.

"She *married* him. Nana Dale married Tommy." I turned it around in every possible direction in my mind. Tricia was patient as I talked it through. Ruminated, as she called it. "I've never heard from anyone in my family that my grandmother was married before she married my grandfather. I'm sure my mother doesn't know. Why would Nana Dale keep that from her? From me?"

Suddenly, I was seeing Nana Dale's charm bracelet and the little diamond stud in the miniature calendar. *January 14, 1943.* Quickly, I texted Billy.

> One last question. Do you remember what time of year it was when the wedding occurred at Camp McDougal?

A few seconds later, his answer flashed across my screen.

> Sometime in winter. January 1943, I believe.

22

Dale

January 1943

The wedding was nothing at all like her mother would have wanted, but Dale had never been like her mother. She didn't care about pearls and cashmere or fancy flower arrangements or posed photos. She cared about Tommy, and she was marrying him. The dream was coming true.

A secret ceremony on the beach at sunset, with only Commander McTeer, Chaplain Glenn Edwards, Willie and Lydia Burkes, a handful of other men, and two German shepherds who interrupted the brief ceremony with frenzied barking when an alligator slithered out from under the brush a few hundred feet down the beach.

She watched it all through a blur of tears, but when the chaplain asked her the question she'd dreamed of answering for years, about loving in sickness and in health till death did them part, she yelled out, "I will!" so enthusiastically that a ripple of laughter passed through the men. Chaplain Edwards pronounced them man and wife as they were seated on Infinity and Essie in their uniforms,

Dale's far too big for her and issued to her by special request before she had formerly joined the Sand Pounders.

"This is my favorite couples class ever," she whispered to Tommy as they leaned across the space between the horses and kissed.

"It'll be like this forever now, Deebs."

Later, Lydia whisked them away to the tavern and shooed them into the rented room where Dale was staying. They found it transformed with a dozen little votive candles flickering in the space while Maxine Gray sang her enchanting version of "Love Is the Sweetest Thing" from a turntable on the chest of drawers. So Tommy and Dale spent their first night in a little bed on borrowed sheets while six hundred coast guardsmen ate dinner in the mess hall, oblivious to what was going on behind the tavern.

———— ♞ ————

Dale had two perfect days as Tommy's wife. While he trained on Infinity with the other men, Dale cared for Essie, helped Lydia at the tavern, and counted the minutes until she'd be with Tommy again, loving and being loved by him.

All too soon it was time to return to Brunswick and the shipyard.

"When are you going to tell your parents about us, Deebs?"

"I'm not going to tell them, Tommy. Not yet, at least."

Tommy shook his head. "Well then, I guess I'd better keep quiet with my folks too." He gave a shrug, "But I'll bet our parents will figure it out. You've got that newlywed glow about you."

She wrapped her arms around his waist, her weight steadying him on his polio legs. "I don't think they will have any notion that we'd be so impromptu."

She didn't dare tell Tommy what her mother had said, but those words sneaked in to bother her way too often. *"You cannot marry polio."*

"Let me live my dream come true with you for a little while. I'll tell them eventually, but they're already having a rough time thinking about me on some remote island. You know Mama. She couldn't handle finding out she missed the wedding. No one else has to know yet."

He raised an eyebrow. "There were about a dozen other people present at the ceremony. They know, Deebs."

"Yes, but we've already told them that it's completely confidential, and they know how to keep a secret."

— ♘ —

Tommy learned that he would be stationed on Daufuskie, the island nearest to Hilton Head.

"I'll be twenty minutes away from here, staying at the Melrose House, just me and twelve other men. It's a fine spot, a real nice house. We're lucky to have it."

"That island's beaches are really wild, aren't they?" Dale had heard that Daufuskie had the reputation of being difficult to patrol because of the abundance of swamps and alligators and who knew what else.

Tommy grinned. "Like all the other islands around here. Yes, there are gators and mosquitoes and everything in between. I'll be billeted with some of the enlisted men. But a lot of other marines are being shipped off to North Africa. I'm glad to be staying right here. And we'll be patrolling with both horses and dogs. The only way to the island is by boat, and it'll bring us food and mail once a week." Then he gave his signature wink before pulling her into bed beside him. "But don't you worry. I'll find a way to come visit you at night when you're training on Hilton Head, Mrs. Ridley."

She went to sleep in Tommy's arms in Lydia's rented room with a smile on her lips. Then inevitably, she heard her mother's voice whispering in her head. *"Dale, you cannot marry polio . . . he'll struggle all his life. Who knows how long someone infected with this disease can survive?"* And though she wanted to share her joy with them, those words kept her from writing a letter to her parents or to Husy and Mr. Jeffrey.

But they'd *see* how delighted she was, how good she and Tommy were together. Soon they'd see it, and that would make everything okay. And she'd tell them the truth then.

Before she headed back to Brunswick on the public bus, Dale spent an hour with Essie, brushing her and whispering all her secrets about the joy of marriage. Commander McTeer had promised not to assign Essie to another coast guardsman, and she chose to trust him. She knew Essie would be in good hands until she came back.

Dale wondered how she could feel so light in the middle of a war, but she soaked it in. Marriage and Essie were both very good for her soul. She thought of Husy and Mr. Jeffrey. She called them once more before leaving the camp. She almost told them about the wedding, but putting that kind of secret on them seemed cruel, so she let the joy in her voice be her only declaration.

On St. Simons at the Ridley house, both her parents and Tommy's noticed her happiness, but they attributed it to the almost miraculous finding of Essie and to the time Dale had spent with Tommy and her mare.

"Daddy, I'm really excited to join the mounted patrol. I may be one of the only females to ever be part of it, but you know I'm capable, prepared, and unafraid, right?"

Dale and her parents were sitting on the back porch of the Ridleys' mansion, which gave a view of the beach and ocean, the sun bright in the January chill.

"I know, sweetie, and we're proud of you. Nervous, but proud. I believe it's the perfect place for you to serve. For Tommy to serve too. Will you be seeing each other?"

"I don't think so. He's already billeted on Daufuskie Island, right by Hilton Head. So maybe I'll see him when I'm training. But after that, it depends on where I'm sent." She shaded her eyes with her hand, watching the tide break on the shore, the sound of it loud and comforting. "I'll know more after training next week. And about how often I can visit you all here too."

"I can tell you're very happy, Dale," he said, and Dale thought that perhaps he could tell something else as well.

But her mother was not happy at all. "I've seen the reports about this patrol, Barbara Dale. It's dangerous, and I will not have you taking part in it! I'm well aware that the only reason you're signing up is because you're completely besotted with Tommy! But I've warned you already. I know you don't like to hear about the reality. If polio isn't enough, now he's enchanted you with the idea of serving in the coast guard on your horse. I won't have it!"

"Mama, please. I *want* to serve. Yes, I love Tommy, but he never tried to convince me to join up. He was every bit as surprised as you are that the military is allowing it. It was completely my idea."

Mrs. Butler grabbed her daughter's hands. "I want you to have a good life, Dale. There are dozens of young men from fine families who are interested in you. You'll be making your debut as soon as this horrible war is over, and you will attend the most lavish parties and have the most wonderful suitors from the finest families. You will get to live your dream, Dale."

Dale let loose of her mother's hands and backed up, heart pounding. "Mama, that's *your* dream, not mine. You know that. I'm not like you. Not beautiful and poised, not very good at social functions. I admire what you do, but I . . ." She struggled to find the right words that wouldn't further insult her mother. "I don't think—I mean, it's not what I want," she finished lamely.

"Barbara Dale, you must trust that I know best. I've seen a lot of life. You'll have a wonderful life without Tommy Ridley and without watching German torpedoes sink American Liberty ships! Tommy has been a bad influence on you, Dale. His parents are lovely, but he is cocky and brash and daredevilish, and I will not have you involved with him."

Dale felt herself trembling. Her heart beat frantically in her chest, and feeling her legs buckle, she grabbed onto the back of the Adirondack chair. She took several deep breaths and tried to steady herself and make her voice calm. "Mama, you're wrong about Tommy. Yes, he's brave and adventurous, but he loves me. He would never let anything happen to me."

"No! I said, no!"

"Mama, I *am* going to join the mounted patrol, and I *am* going to train on Hilton Head Island. Tommy won't be there, just me and Essie—"

"And six hundred brutes who would prey on a beautiful and naïve debutante!"

"I'll have my own room far away from the barracks, Mama. I really think this job will be less dangerous than hanging upside-down from the mast of a Liberty ship, holding my welding gun."

But she could see that there was nothing she could say to change her mother's opinion. That night, Dale wept in her room, heartsick and miserable, hearing in her mind the words her mother had flung at her as she climbed the stairs to her bedroom. *"If anything happens to you while you are in that patrol, I will never forgive Tommy Ridley! Never!"*

I married him, Mama. She practiced saying the words over and over in her mind, but she could not make them come out of her mouth as she regarded her mother's face, pinched in fury.

How could her dream-come-true be her mother's worst nightmare? It wasn't fair. It was worse than seeing tankers torpedoed by a U-boat. It was a deadly explosion in Dale's heart.

Dale stood at attention while Lieutenant Commander McTeer gave her and the rest of the new recruits the same instructions that he'd issued when Tommy had trained.

After introducing himself, he said, "Welcome to the Sixth Naval District. Our region embraces the long stretch of coastline from New Topsail Inlet, North Carolina, to Ponte Vedra, Florida. The coast along this section of the Atlantic is hard to patrol by its very nature. The vast majority of these almost six hundred miles of beach are reefs and remote and unpopulated barrier islands.

"In fact, none of the twelve other districts on the East Coast, around the Gulf, or on the West Coast have quite the same peculiar difficulties. Our own Hilton Head is a swampy, jungle-infested island. You'll come across all the hazards likely to be encountered in other areas—a broken and treacherous coast, a swampy interior, beaches littered with snags and stumps, and the water at high tide. You may also encounter poisonous insects and snakes and dangerous alligators. The training this week will be rigorous and thorough, and we expect the most stringent of discipline. If you can adjust to these challenging and varied conditions, we have every confidence that you will do well wherever you're sent."

Dale regarded the ragtag group of men, all dressed in whatever they had on when they arrived. Farmhands and cowboys mostly. Several boys barely had peach fuzz for mustaches, while some of the men had leathery skin and deeply wrinkled faces. But they all held a look of respect and solemnity as they listened to Commander McTeer.

"As you can imagine, we've spent a great deal of time in preliminary planning. Here on Hilton Head, we've seen high morale in the men and excellent personal discipline. As many of you have heard, the US Army Remount Service has provided us with the horses and tack, as well as some riding gear for all of you—cavalry boots, long rain slickers, hats, Springfield rifles, and much more. We're also grateful to those of you who have brought your own mounts and tack."

Like Tommy, many of the men from the neighboring towns and cities had arrived with their own horses. *And I've got my own mare too*, Dale thought with a smile.

"This week we've got stunt riders, jockeys, show jumpers, polo players, rodeo riders, and army reserve cavalrymen here, so those of you who are new to horsemanship will have fine instructors. We're mighty grateful for all of you who have volunteered. I believe the youngest man this week is seventeen, and our oldest is sixty-nine.

"And we've got our first-ever woman in the mounted patrol. I expect you all to be on your best behavior with Miss Butler, an accomplished horsewoman." He searched for Dale as he exaggerated *Miss Butler*.

Tommy had told her that an instant and warm camaraderie formed between the men and the animals, contributing to a very high morale at the training camp, and Dale felt it even though at first the men eyed her suspiciously.

"The coast guard is providing uniforms for all of you. Clothing will vary, but in general on the East Coast, you'll dress more formally, as we do here at Camp McDougal. But when it's very hot, some of you may want to peel off some layers."

Chuckles followed.

"And now, come meet your equine partners."

There was a palpable air of excitement among the men, especially with those who had never been around horses before, let alone mounted one. The gentleness with which the men handled the dogs and horses had touched something deep in Dale the week Tommy was in training, and now she saw it reenacted among these new recruits. She was grateful to have been allowed to take part in the mounted patrol.

Essie had seemed to recognize Dale, but she had never been truly ridden by Dale until their reunion. Once training began, it didn't take long for Dale to settle into Essie's smooth gait as she trotted the mare along the beach. Someone had broken her well, and though Essie had the feistiness of her mother, Greta, she also had a steadiness about her that came, Dale was sure, from the army's careful training.

Dale and Essie were chosen that first day of training to help in one of the squadrons with the men who were unfamiliar with horses. She loved the challenge and the ability to help.

Later in the afternoon, the tables were turned as one of the officers demonstrated the use of firearms, machine guns, peloruses, and explosives. But when they talked about fire prevention, Dale once again felt at home, remembering all the times she'd heard her father explain the dangers of forest fires.

"The mounted patrols will always travel in pairs, from dusk to dawn, and there is around-the-clock patrol in lookout towers too. You'll have sidearms and 1903 Springfield rifles. And these radio backpacks will be carried by a member of each beach patrol team."

As Commander McTeer spoke, several men demonstrated with the rifle, backpack, and radio walkie-talkies.

"Each member of the mounted patrol will have a stretch of land to attend for eight hours. When your shift is over, you will pass a medallion along to the next person on shift. In populated areas, beaches will have a curfew to keep people off them at certain times.

"Remember, your main objective is to see what's happening on and offshore and then to alert the military when necessary. You will undoubtedly be gathering up the debris that washes up from the tankers that have been bombed by German U-boats. And you will most likely encounter bodies among this debris."

He allowed that grim thought to sink in before continuing, "In case of enemy contact, you coast guardsmen will dismount and use your horses as protection. Then one man will hurry to report, and the other remount his horse."

Dale shuddered. She didn't even want to think about using Essie as protection from a bullet.

"Your work is fundamental to the success of the Allies in this war," the commander said, encouraging them. "Statistically, American coastal waters are the most dangerous, the scene of half the world's sinkings. Our task is to negate this tragedy."

— ∩ —

The boy was always sitting in the same spot on the beach, watching the dogs in training before moving to where the horses galloped along the coast. Sometimes as he perched on the drift-wood, he'd lift his hand and wave as the riders passed by. At the end of one of her training sessions, Dale trotted over to where he was sitting.

"Hey," she said. "I've seen you here every day. What's your name?"

"Name's Billy. Billy Hampton."

"You like horses?"

"Yep. Horses, dogs, and oysters and shrimp." He grinned, and a dimple appeared in his right cheek.

"Well, Billy. I'm Dale. It's nice to meet you. Real nice to meet you."

"I saw your wedding a few weeks back. It was swell. Congrats."

"Thank you kindly." Dale felt the blush cover her cheeks. "I didn't see you there."

He cowered a little. "No, ma'am. I was keeping out of sight."

"I hope you don't mind me saying, but it's a secret. Even our families don't know yet."

"Yes, ma'am. I heard the commander. It's confidential." His eyes shone with excitement. "I like keeping secrets."

"Thank you, Billy. Do you ride?"

He nodded, blue eyes solemn. "A bit, yes'm. My uncle has horses, and he lets me ride sometimes." Now he reached up to caress Essie's muzzle. "I heard the story of how you found her. It's a real fine story, and she's the prettiest horse I've ever seen."

Dale leaned over and tweaked his nose, like Tommy might do. "Well, Billy, I'll let you in on another secret. I agree with you. My Essie is a beauty."

Dale was still leaning over, chatting with Billy, when an explosion ricocheted across the water. Essie reared and bucked, sending Dale wobbling to regain her balance.

"Was that a torpedo?" she asked, eyes wide, heart pounding as she struggled to get Essie calmed.

But the young boy, no older than nine or ten, was grinning. "No, ma'am. Not a torpedo. That's just my dad, Mr. Hampton, setting off dynamite."

"Whatever for?"

"It's his job—malaria control. He's draining the ditches and ponds to kill the mosquitoes. Haven't you heard? They're afraid there could be an outbreak of malaria at the camp."

She hadn't heard this, but she did know that the coast guard was issuing special uniforms to protect the patrolling officers against mosquitoes.

Malaria. She didn't want to think about that. She had other things on her mind. Twice this week on her patrol, she and her patrol mate had found luggage washed up on shore, and once they'd found a stray boot, the kind the merchant mariners would use. She feared that one day the body of a merchant mariner would wash up.

It had happened before.

— ♘ —

Dale considered it ironic that she was being sent to Jekyll Island, right near St. Simons, another one of Georgia's barrier islands and another playground of the rich and famous. In fact, according to her mother, it was the ultimate social scene for America's elite. In the late 1800s, the island had been purchased by the newly formed Jekyll Island Club to become a retreat for the families of men who represented one-sixth of the world's wealth. It was there that the modern-day Federal Reserve was formed in secret in the early 1900s.

Her mother almost swooned when she heard the news. "I can't believe you'll be staying at the Jekyll Island Club! That was our very best vacation ever. You know it's called 'the richest, the most exclusive, the most inaccessible club in the world.'"

Yes, she had heard this several times before. From her mother. "Well, I won't be there for a vacation, Mama. Essie and I will have an important job to do."

"Of course. I know that, dear. I'm proud of you."

She grabbed on to those words and felt a flicker of hope that her mother would someday be able to accept her marriage to Tommy.

For decades, many wealthy families had spent Christmas through Easter on Jekyll Island. But with the start of World War II, the government ordered that the island be evacuated because of the impending threat of German submarines. In the autumn of 1942, the stables of the Jekyll Island Club were turned over to the mounted patrol.

Dale and fifteen other patrolmen were housed in the servants' quarters of the clubhouse. As the only woman, Dale had her own private room. Their food was bought in Brunswick and transported by road to Sea Island and then by boat to Jekyll Island. Once again, the horses were brought over by barge from Brunswick, and Dale let out the long breath she'd been holding when she stepped onto the barge and spotted Essie among the other horses.

The barge that brought food to the Jekyll Island Club each week also brought mail, and that first week, she'd received three letters from Tommy.

Hey, dear WIFE!

I miss you! How was your move to Jekyll? Seen any gators yet? How's Essie doing?

Here, I'm spending most of my time guarding the beach, looking for subs or invaders. And you don't need to worry. Just like McTeer said, we patrol in pairs, one down at the water and another about fifty yards away, up the beach. Sometimes, the one on the beach uses a dog.

Last week, my buddy Lester spotted a Nazi sub off Daufuskie and put in a call to headquarters. Right away, they set off explosions, but all that came up were some bread wrappers and other trash. We think somebody in Savannah is supplying the Germans with food. As McTeer warned too, it seems like it's a common practice for submarines to jettison oil and garbage in an attempt to fool attackers. But it was pretty exciting to be part of it.

Another letter.

Guess what, Wife (I love to call you that). Yesterday, the dogs picked up a scent on the beach that we figured was a German who'd come inland from his sub. The dogs followed the scent. Whoever it was stole a boat from one of the local fishermen and rowed to a highway. We called the information in, and the law got them. They were headed for Bluffton. Later, we found their rubber raft buried on the beach. We felt

*like they had a contact around here somewhere, but we never
found out who it was.*

Another letter.

*Sad day yesterday, Wife. We held a funeral for one of the
horses in a pasture on Daufuskie. But then today, we rescued
a mariner whose boat was in trouble—not from a U-boat attack, but we saved his life anyway. It felt awful good.*

And every letter ended with *I sure do love you, my Deebs, and I
miss you something crazy!*

⎯⎯⎯ ⍭ ⎯⎯⎯

Dale was still shivering when she returned to her room at the
Jekyll Island Club in the early morn. Her shift from midnight till
eight a.m. in the February chill left her fingers numbed under the
gloves and her whole body stiff and frozen, no matter the long
underwear and layers she'd put on.

But her almost uncontrollable shaking had very little to do with
the weather. She replayed the scene over and over in her mind,
as vivid as the night she and Tommy had watched the tankers
exploding off the coast of St. Simons. But this time, she and Essie
had been alone, walking the empty beaches, eyes peeled toward
the ocean, looking for any telltale lights out at sea, anything that
might be a signal to someone on shore.

Dale shared the shift with Leonard, a thirty-year-old farmhand
from Thomasville, Georgia. Confident and calm, Leonard's presence reassured Dale every time they met, crisscrossing back and
forth throughout the night.

On their very first shift, three nights earlier, he'd radioed Dale,
"Are you seeing what I'm seeing? Those lights going off and on
farther up the shore?"

"Yes. Do you know Morse code? Could it be a signal to a sub
out at sea?"

278

"I'm calling it in."

That "signal" had turned out to be the fault of the seven-year-old son of one of the Jekyll Island Club members. When the FBI arrived at the house at three in the morning, they discovered that the little boy had caught a turtle that day and hidden it in the bathroom. He kept getting up throughout the night, flicking the light on and off whenever he checked on it.

Dale and Leonard felt slightly embarrassed but soon were laughing along with the FBI men. They had shared the story with their crewmates, and Dale had written to Tommy about the incident.

But most of the incidents weren't so lighthearted.

Two nights later, Dale spotted footprints on shore, and the pair of mounted patrol who covered the next stretch of beach reported more flashing lights. It was feared that the enemies had come to shore and hidden in pipes.

With her light, she had flashed the new code she'd been taught that morning. *Suspicious footprints, flashing lights seen.* And she waited, heart in her throat, for instructions.

Although no one was found, the patrolmen were instructed to put up barbed wire along that section of beach to keep residents from possibly seeing bodies or other refuse that washed ashore from a sinking.

On this night, Dale had tensed as she walked the same stretch of beach, searching for footprints. Essie remained calm even though Dale knew the mare could feel the tension in Dale's hands via the reins and the bit in Essie's mouth.

"Easy, girl. Easy now," she cooed.

Essie, with her ears pricked forward and her nostrils flared, was suddenly skittish in the breeze. And then Dale saw it. A body lay splayed before her in the sand, the tide rushing over it.

As they approached, the horse reared back, snorting and shaking her head, throwing Dale off-balance. Dale dismounted, her boots sinking in the soft sand. It felt like her heart was dropping way down to the pit of her stomach. She leaned over the body, and when she saw how badly burned it was and smelled the scorched flesh, she backed away and vomited. Essie nickered and pulled away, ears flattened against her head.

Dale radioed Leonard through her tears and sent out the flare that warned a body had been found. She started shaking so hard she didn't think she could trust herself to take another step toward the corpse. When she did, she saw that it was not only badly burned but also partially decomposed from time in the sea. She had no idea if the body belonged to a German saboteur or an American merchant mariner.

She fell to her knees and vomited again.

— ♞ —

Late March 1943

Nightmares pursued her in vivid and gruesome detail, and Dale began to question her sanity in joining the patrol. She felt nauseated on her night patrols, and back in her room, when she tried to sleep during the day, she often woke with an image of the faceless body in her mind.

She'd rush to the toilet and vomit.

She felt homesick for Atlanta and heartsick for Tommy. They wrote each other daily but never knew when mail would reach the islands. Sometimes, Dale received eight or nine letters from Tommy in a single delivery. She'd read them over and over until she had practically memorized his words.

Because she roomed alone, the other mounted patrol members did not witness how sick and exhausted she felt. How she could not keep food down. How she woke from a fitful dream-soaked sleep with an excruciating headache. How she feared she might fall asleep on Essie as she patrolled the lonely beaches in the middle of the night.

She'd taken to carrying a pair of spurs in her jacket and squeezing her fingers on them until they shocked her back awake. Often, she'd nudge Essie out into the ocean, lean far over, and vomit into the water.

She wondered if she had malaria. She'd heard how horrible it could be. Finally, out of desperation, she visited the island infirmary. A middle-aged nurse, plump and serious, checked her for a fever, took a urine sample, listened to her heart, looked in her eyes, and left the room, promising to return soon.

When she did, the nurse squinted at her. "Did you say you've been staying on the island for two months?"

"Yes, that's right. I'm part of the US Coast Guard Mounted Beach Patrol. We wear protective gear, but I'm sure I've gotten mosquito bites."

"But you haven't had a fever or chills?"

"No, just fatigue and nausea and vomiting. I can't keep food down."

The nurse's face clouded. She took Dale's left hand in hers, staring down at her fingers. Then she glanced at her information sheet and met Dale's eyes. "How long since your last period?"

Dale frowned, then clutched her stomach, blinked, and burst into giggles. "Oh! Am I pregnant? That makes perfect sense! It's been at least two months. I just thought . . . with all the changes. Oh, how silly of me not to know."

The older woman raised her eyebrows and frowned.

Dale glanced at her ringless left hand. "Oh, it's okay. I'm married! I just got married in January." The woman looked unconvinced. "But it's a secret from my folks. We eloped." She fished in her pocket and held out the curved nail. "This is my ring—until the war's over and we can be together again."

The nurse's eyes turned sympathetic, and she looked relieved. "Well, I won't know for certain for a week, but I'm pretty sure that's the case. And if so, may I be the first to congratulate you!"

23

Allie

Wednesday, March 11

There was no way I was going to be able to sleep, so instead of staying at the Hilton Head Inn as planned, we drove through the night back to Atlanta, with Tricia taking the driver's seat halfway through. Time and again, after staring into the black, I'd blink and repeat, "Nana Dale found Essie, joined the mounted patrol, and married Tommy, all on Hilton Head Island. And they didn't tell their parents—at least not at first. But why would Mom never have told me about that? Or Nana Dale herself? Was Mom too embarrassed? But why?"

And time and again, Tricia listened, rubbing my back in a sisterly way.

"Maybe she wasn't embarrassed, Allie. Maybe she just didn't know. Maybe your grandmother never told anyone in her family about the marriage."

"But that's . . . that's crazy! Why in the world would she keep it a secret? Sure, it was spur of the moment, but it was legal. And he

282

was from a wealthy family, wealthier than hers. I'd have thought her mother would rejoice with the news."

"He had polio."

"So did FDR, and all of Georgia loved their president for his courage and guts and for his frequent visits to Warm Springs."

It didn't make sense.

Except some things did. The fact that she married secretly explained keeping a secret scrapbook. It also explained why Nana Dale had Tommy's Maclay Trophy and why she had that charm with their wedding date.

As I let Tricia off at her condominium, she eyed me warily. "Are you going to be okay going home alone to all that you've learned? I know you. You'll sit down on the floor with Maggie, and you'll read every last article in the scrapbook, won't you? You'll be up all night, and by tomorrow morning you'll be no good to anyone."

"I really am obsessed, aren't I?"

She took me by the hands. "You are driven and caring and strong and beautiful. But it scares me that you're going to get your heart broken again. Don't look at the scrapbook tonight. Please. Wait until I can be with you. Or someone else."

Austin.

"But not alone when you have a good idea of what you'll find. I wish . . . I wish you could give yourself some grace."

"I miss him, Tricia. You were right. Austin's the best thing that has ever happened to me, and I chased him away with this drivenness. And now what am I going to do?"

Undeterred by my non sequiturs, Tricia took me in her arms. "Grace," she whispered.

To my credit, once inside my studio apartment, I didn't touch the scrapbook but tumbled into bed at three a.m. and slept until nine. My first class at Chastain was at ten, and I wondered how I would get through it without bursting into tears. I prayed I wouldn't see Austin.

And then I prayed I would.

I needed him. I longed to pour out all the details of the past five days, to feel his arms around me as I shared my latest discovery: Nana Dale had married Tommy Ridley in 1943.

In secret.

Driving to Chastain, I tried to prepare what I would say just in case I saw Austin there. If I could memorize the words, work them out in my mind, then maybe, just maybe I could force them out of my mouth when I was standing in front of him.

"I have a confession to make to you, Austin. You've known it all along, but I need to say it out loud. I'm obsessed. And I'm so sorry for the way I've treated you. Please forgive me.

"I was wrong about us. I do want us. So much! I need you to help me figure out how to become unobsessed. Will seeing the house imploded do it? Or will I just rush to another obsession? I really want help. And I really want you to help. I need you to help me. And I love you. I love you so much."

But my only encounters at Chastain were with six eager students, one right after the other, thirty minutes at a time, each one grabbing my heart and, thankfully, helping me turn my thoughts away from myself and my problems and onto them. Somehow, it worked every time.

Seeing Jimmy leading Angelfoot around the paddock, the boy less stiff and awkward, brought tears to my eyes. At the end of the therapy lesson, he threw his arms around the horse's neck and enveloped him in a hug, his face effusive, his words also.

"I did it! Did you see that? He walked all the way around the paddock with me. I did it, Miss Allie!"

This was what I wanted in life. This filled me up.

Until it didn't.

Until, once again back in my apartment, all the images from the Home Front Museum crowded in and then images of Hickory Hills being imploded, and then I was flinging the ring back at Austin. It all swirled before me, and I felt helpless under the weight.

"Help," I said to no one, not even Maggie, who, aware of my foul mood, had scooted under the coffee table and lay there, tail swishing slowly back and forth, green eyes watching, her disapproval so evident I would have laughed out loud if I weren't so close to tears.

"Help."

Another scene came suddenly, unbidden. In my mind, I saw Nana Dale on her knees in prayer. I'd rushed into her bedroom without knocking early one morning. I was probably nine or ten, old enough to know I should have knocked. And there she was, my tiny grandmother on her knees, back toward me, dressed in her bright teal-and-pink jogging suit from the 1980s even though we'd just crossed over to the twenty-first century. Her head was bowed, her hands clasped together and resting on the velvet ottoman.

I stood perfectly still, shocked. This scene seemed totally incongruous with the feisty grandmother I knew who went about life full steam ahead. Seeing her in this posture of humility, I almost felt sorry for her—or embarrassed. What in the world could be so awful that my grandmother would be on her knees, pleading with the Almighty?

I stayed there, like a kid with her fingers in the cookie jar, just long enough for my grandmother to say, "I'll be with you in a minute, Allie. I'm busy with another Person right now. I'll join you in the sitting room."

I tiptoed out as if my footfalls might disturb this conversation. Nana Dale had not turned around or changed her position at all.

Afterward, when she appeared in the sitting room, I found that I looked at her in a new way—almost as if she had an angelic glow around her.

"Now, what did you need, my dear?"

I honestly could not remember, so intrigued had I been by the scene in her bedroom. Stupidly, I asked, "Were you praying?"

"Yes, dear."

"But why? Has something bad happened? Is something wrong?"

I would never forget the sparkle in her eyes or the trilling laugh. "Heavens no! Everything is right!" She pierced me with her gaze.

"When you start your day on your knees, well, that makes the rest of the day a piece of cake."

I didn't understand. At all.

Nana Dale could see this. "When I was a child, younger than you, I'd rush down to the basement apartment here at Hickory Hills to see Husy."

I remembered Nana Dale telling me stories of her nursemaid.

"She always fixed breakfast for my dad and me, but sometimes in the early mornings before breakfast, I'd visit her in her apartment. And I'd find her day after day, rain or shine, joyful or grieving, on her knees in prayer. Mind you, it wasn't an easy thing for Husy to be on her knees with her arthritis and her hunched back. But when I told her that I was worried that she might not be able to get back up off her knees, she'd say, 'Safest place in the world, Dale, is on your knees in front of your Maker, giving Him all the joys and worries of the day. I'll keep meeting Him here every morning till He takes me home.' And she did."

Nana Dale's eyes had misted over, and she wasn't one to cry. So I leaned in, paying even more attention. "So that's why you pray? To be like Husy?"

"I start my day like Husy did because she was right. She set the example, Allie. But it's the Lord I'm praying to."

"But you still cuss and say mean things sometimes and get in fights with Mom," I had blurted out, which of course caused my grandmother to go into a fit of laughter.

"It's like learning to ride a horse, Allie. Praying, trusting God—the more you practice, the better you get at understanding how He wants you to live. It doesn't happen overnight. In my case, He's had a rather stubborn, ornery woman to work with. Some things have changed. I'm a work in progress. Not qualified for the National Horse Show yet, but hopefully someday, I'll get my invitation."

I pondered that conversation from almost two decades ago for a while. Then without really having any idea of what I was doing, I slipped to my knees and folded my hands together, leaning them

ELIZABETH MUSSER

against the coffee table where Maggie still sulked, and whispered, "I have a confession to make to You, Lord. You've known it all along, but I need to say it out loud. I'm obsessed. I really want You to help. I need You to help me. Please. Help."

I had just showered, fixed myself a cup of herbal tea, and perched the scrapbook on my lap when my phone rang.

Barnell.

"Hey? What's up?"

"Thought you'd want to know that the contractor is snooping around. Came up to the ring and questioned me about the bones. Laid into me about how slow I am. He's back at the house now and so is that cute French lady you hired." Then he paused. "Thought you'd want to know," he repeated.

I felt heat fuming out of the top of my head.

"And I uncovered two more of the graves."

"I'll be there soon."

I changed from my robe into black exercise pants and a clean T-shirt and pulled on a pair of running shoes. Then I placed the leather binder back in the cherrywood chest, along with the charm bracelet and the newspaper clippings, and I carried the chest out to the car. I was unwilling to let it out of my sight. Tricia's request kept percolating in my mind, and I succumbed to her wish. I would finish going through the scrapbook—tonight—but I wouldn't do it alone.

I'd show it to Austin or Tricia or somebody.

Fifteen minutes later, Cécile waved to me as I turned into the gravel driveway. "I thought we had a meeting this afternoon. I'm sorry if I got it wrong." She was wearing a purple miniskirt and brightly colored top.

I winced. "I'm sorry. I completely forgot. I . . . I've had so much on my mind."

"Of course. It's not a problem. Shall we go inside?"

"I think I need to talk with the contractor, Mr. Hightower. Barnell called and said he was hanging around and threatening."

Cécile nodded. "Yes, he was." She narrowed her eyes. "But I got rid of him for you. It's not his business. He's overstepping his boundaries. We still have plenty of time. He's just being a bully." A wink. "And your mother just left too. She said she finished packing up the kitchen items. She's labeled the boxes and left them in the den."

I stared at Cécile as if she were a heavenly being. Finally, I managed, "Thank you. Thank you so much."

"*Pas de quoi*. You know—it's nothing. Now, we have quite a few things to look over before my colleagues arrive, so come on. Deep breath, Allie. We can do this." As I followed her through the front door, she glanced back at me. "And I brought another good bottle of wine. And some cheese."

Cécile and I spent the majority of our time in Nana Dale's bedroom, the Green Room, the one on the ground floor that she had shared with my grandfather and then lived in alone for the past thirty years. We were in the process of labeling everything that wasn't estate sale bound with pink dots when I came to the French armoire, the one that had caused Cécile to ooh and aah.

"I could get you a fortune for that, easy. It's a beautiful piece. But I think you should keep it, *n'est-ce pas*? It fits your taste. The French lines are timeless, not stuffy."

I agreed and opened one of the doors. It was filled with Nana Dale's clothes, and the combination smell of cedar chips and Nana Dale's own fragrance brought quick tears to my eyes. On one shelf, underneath her silk slips, lay several trophies, although not the silver ones that came from horse shows in the '30s, '40s, and '50s.

The first one, made of heavy glass in the shape of the state of Georgia, sat on a wooden stand with a gold-plated plaque that read *1978—From the grateful members of SAVE. To Barbara Butler-Taylor in recognition of her years of volunteer service with the Junior League in support of protecting the Chattahoochee River*. And another, a small cross formed by two glass nails and sitting on a clear base, featured the inscription *Inner City Award for 40 years of faithful service for the glory of God: Barbara Butler-Taylor*.

"These are lovely," Cécile remarked, her voice holding a type of reverence. "She must have been very special, your grandmother. She cared about other people. She served them."

I nodded. Yes, that was true, but . . .

Nana Dale didn't need any kind of thanks for all her service, as was evidenced by her hidden awards in contrast to her easy display of equestrian accomplishments. She just naturally served other people. It wasn't in a soft, kind way, but tough and practical. When she was helping those kids learn to post, if the parents got in the way, they'd get a talking-to. And if the kids whined and complained, especially the *"rich, uppity kids,"* as she called them, they got a talking-to also.

I didn't know how to describe it, but I thought that some of the pain I read in my mother's eyes came from Nana Dale giving her many a talking-to. My mother was as gentle as a rose, and Nana Dale had been as tough as nails, and somehow nails and roses didn't seem to fit together. Somehow, the tough things Nana Dale had said pierced Mama, but for me and for so many others, we just looked at her in wonder.

Nana Dale cared in the most practical way she knew, and if you didn't like it, well, that was fine too. I only wished my mother could have received Nana Dale's practical love without dragging all the baggage of her own emotions alongside.

An hour later, I left Cécile with her colleagues and made my way to the ring, where Barnell was hard at work. "It's looking more and more like the surface of the moon with these huge pockmarks," I commented.

Four now.

"Yep. B'lieve there's only one more grave to dig up," Barnell said as he swiped a bandanna across his face. He grinned. "That cute little Frenchwoman scared the tarnation outta Mr. Hightower. A sight to see." He chuckled. "Don't believe he'll be bothering us again this week."

"Cécile is amazing. So are you, Barnell."

He ignored that comment and said, "Before I forget," and handed me two more tin boxes, each filled with horseshoes.

"And who did these belong to?"

"B'lieve that would be the pony, Mr. Jinx, that my daddy buried up here. First one. And let me see . . ."

"Essie?"

"No, haven't gotten to Essie yet."

He glanced over at me. "You look rattled, Miss Allie. You doing okay?"

I took a seat on the coop jump and shrugged. "It's been a crazy week. Believe it or not, I just spent almost twenty-four hours on Hilton Head and St. Simons."

"Sounds tiring."

"I'm finding out a lot of really weird stuff about Nana Dale."

Barnell raised an eyebrow. "Your grandmother was one of a kind. Reckon we'll be discovering your Nana Dale's stories for a long time coming." Barnell cleared his throat and mopped his brow. Then he said, "Other grave is Infinity's. Just remembered it."

"I found a halter with that name, but I didn't know Nana Dale had a horse named Infinity."

His face clouded. "Well, technically she didn't. That was Tommy's horse."

"One more thing I didn't know. It's just that I thought she'd told me most of her stories. And they sounded farfetched. But there are other ones . . ." I looked him in the eyes. "Barnell, do you know what happened to Tommy?"

You'd have thought that I'd socked him in the stomach, the way he looked at me with panic in his eyes.

"Seriously, what happened?" I continued, thinking he was pulling my leg.

"Oh, you don't know what happened to Tommy?" He recovered, making it sound like I should and that it wasn't a big deal, but I had seen his eyes.

"No, Nana Dale never told me. She always got real sad when she mentioned his name. Except," I said, correcting myself, "sometimes what I saw in her eyes was unabashed love."

"Well, yeah, I guess she loved him, that rascal. Mighty fine horseman he was, or so they say." He started walking out of the ring area and down the hill to the back of the barn. I hurried after him and found him picking up a pitchfork, like he was going to shovel the manure out of one of the stalls. But they were all clean. Then he rolled a wheelbarrow out to the shavings shed and glanced back at me like he wished I'd just leave him alone.

I wondered why he was acting so strange. "Didn't you know Tommy?"

"No, never met him."

"But your father surely knew him." I'd heard many stories of Mr. Jeffrey, almost as beloved as Husy to Nana Dale.

"Well, yes, I 'spect he did."

"When did Tommy—you know, pass away?"

Barnell shrugged. I'd never seen him act like this. "Can't rightly say, Miss Allie, can't rightly say."

I wanted to ask Barnell more questions. He'd never been one to give me a cold shoulder. He thought I was about as good as peaches and cream, something he'd told me plenty of times, and I'd seen it in his eyes just as often: a recognition, a kindness, something almost like a grandfatherly love. At least I thought we had that connection, but he went limping through the barn, finding something to keep busy with in a way that said, *This barn door is slammed shut and locked tight, and don't you ever come ask about him again.*

Instead, I wandered around the property in a sort of daze, then back into the house where, still in a daze, I trailed behind Cécile and her colleagues, going from room to room. I wanted to get back to the scrapbook, to find out what had happened to Tommy. Surely it would tell me. But Barnell's cold eyes haunted me. Cold like fear, cold like secrets, cold like regret.

Listless and confused, I was unable to piece together the fabric of these past days, where the past and present kept colliding. I felt like I was walking through the swampy marshes on a wild Hilton Head Island completely alone.

I longed to talk to Austin about it. All that evening I rehearsed what I'd say. I'd pick up my phone, cradle it, find his number under my favorites, and dare myself to punch the icon with his wavy blond hair and winsome smile. Then I'd stick the phone into my jeans pocket and walk through the labyrinth that was Nana Dale's house until I could find Cécile.

Every time I thought of calling him, I remembered our last conversation. Or more precisely, my diatribe. *"Yes, your obsessed ex-fiancée is still searching for a way to keep the house and the property. . . . Please just leave me alone!"*

I wanted to chase the scene away, make it scamper like a squirrel up one of the hickory trees on the property. But instead, it chased me through my mind, as if I were its bushy-tailed playmate. But the words I heard when my thoughts settled were not playful.

They were loud and accusing from another conversation with Austin: *"It's not an obsession! It's looking for what has to be here! Nana Dale promised! It's finding an answer to what I've always wanted and dreamed about more than anything else. What I've loved with all my heart. This house, this land. I will not give up!"*

I loved *me*. Not *us. Me*. It scratched around in my mind, like the squirrel uncovering his buried acorn treasure. *My* dreams, *my* plans, *my* hopes, *my* future. All *I* ever wanted.

I stumbled into Nana Dale's downstairs powder room and retched. The selfishness overwhelmed me. I imagined Nana Dale as a young girl, screaming as Essie was led into the trailer, *"She's mine! She's my filly. You can't take her away from me! She's mine!"* And then her ancient eyes were searching my young face and whispering, *"Be careful what you wish for, Allie. You've got the horse sense and the determination and the heart. But you can lose the ones you love. You can end up getting what you want and being all alone."*

In some ways, Nana Dale had ended up all alone. Had I inherited Nana Dale's stubbornness, bent on having what was rightfully mine? Why was it so important to me? That was the question I needed to examine, the one I had held at arm's length, terrified of what I might find if I picked up that rock and looked beneath.

I ran out the back and toward the barn. Maybe my desire had nothing to do with altruism and faith but more to do with rescuing and enabling and fixing.

The obsession was fed through the years as I watched my mother and grandmother's stormy relationship. Somehow, I felt responsible to fix it. To help them see each other in a truer light. Past the baggage that was decades old.

Austin had said to me, "Allie, some things can't be fixed. They will never look like you want them to, but it's okay. Life is messy. You know that."

"Yes, I get that," I'd retorted. "And I don't expect immediate results or miracles. But I do expect something. And now all I have is a whole big heap of nothing. Nana Dale went to her grave with unfinished business. And my mother refuses to move forward. And I am stuck in the middle. Hickory Hills Horse Therapy was going to make sense of it all. Be redemptive. I need to see redemption, Austin. I need to glimpse hope."

That was me, demanding my way, refusing to give up.

And losing it all.

For the second time that day, I fell to my knees. This time in the manure pile behind the stable, and the irony of that was not lost on me, even as I sobbed.

I'm such a mess, Lord. I really believed I was doing all this for a higher cause. It didn't start out being about me. It started out being about them—about students who needed therapy, about the greater good the house and property could be used for. But it got twisted, and I had worked so hard, and it wasn't fair! I know life isn't fair, but I thought I could fight it and turn it around. And now I've lost everything.

"But I see it," I whispered as my hands left prints in the moist

24

Dale

May 1943

Dale spent her hours off duty in the women's restroom, heaving anything she could force into her stomach back up several hours later. She had giggled with the news of her pregnancy, but in reality, she was horrified. She knew full well she wasn't ready to be a mother. She felt deep embarrassment that she and Tommy had been reckless, running into marriage. But at least they *had* married. She wouldn't have to carry the stigma of a woman pregnant out of wedlock. She'd heard whispers of their fate in the hallways of school and church.

When she'd written Tommy about the pregnancy, he'd responded with his characteristic daredevil enthusiasm. *Why, that's just swell!* he wrote. *It's the best news ever! Our parents will really be excited about our marriage now.*

She was relieved at his joy, but she was so sick and so exhausted. And she was not at all sure her mother would receive the news well. Or Commander McTeer . . .

Everything about Dale's presence in the mounted patrol was an exception, and the military did not like exceptions. As the first, and perhaps only, woman in the patrol, she and Tommy were the only married couple who were both Sand Pounders. Only Commander McTeer and their colleagues on Daufuskie and Jekyll knew they were married, and there was no rule for giving married couples time off together. "Highly unusual" was the immediate reply when Tommy asked that his first weekend away from the island be spent with Dale. But fortunately, Commander McTeer liked Dale and proved to be an ally in convincing the higher-ups that she and Tommy should be allowed a weekend leave together.

Of course, Dale was certainly the only pregnant person in the mounted patrol. But no one knew about that yet. Except for Tommy. But they would soon. Soon, she'd tell her colleagues on Jekyll Island and Commander McTeer. And her parents.

Soon.

But not yet.

For their first weekend together, Tommy came to Jekyll Island. Dale leaped into his arms as soon as he exited the barge, smothering him with kisses. They laughed throughout those forty-eight hours, loving each other in Dale's private room in the Jekyll Island Club and walking hand in hand on the sandy beaches—the ones where tourists were allowed.

"You sure are awfully thin, my Deebs," Tommy commented as Dale picked at her food at the local restaurant. "Are you eating enough? I mean, for the two of you?"

"I've been so sick, Tommy. I can't keep anything down. But I try."

"If I didn't know it was true, I couldn't even tell you're in this delicate condition."

She blushed and kissed him again. "But you do know it's true, and you also know who's responsible for my delicate condition!"

"Does anyone else know? Have you told the guys here?"

She looked down. "I haven't told anyone but you, Tommy. I know the coast guard will make me drop out of the Sand Pounders as soon as they find out I'm pregnant, and I don't want to quit.

Not yet. And like you said, it's not obvious yet. This uniform has always been a couple of sizes too big, and I'm not filling it out any better now."

"Do you think it's safe to be riding Essie, though?"

"It's perfectly safe. It may not be considered appropriate to ride in my condition, but the baby is safe. My mother used to brag that she rode Greta until she was six months pregnant with me. And I've finally started feeling little flutters of movement." She moved his hand to her slightly rounded stomach. "Can you feel it?"

Tommy concentrated hard and then looked up, his face awash in wonder. "I do, Deebs! I do!" Then he grew more serious and squeezed her hand. "And I think it's high time we let our folks know about our condition . . . and your condition." He patted the barely visible roundness in her stomach. "You wanna write the letter, or can I?"

"We can't just write a letter, Tommy. We need to go see them in person. But it terrifies me." And Dale finally told Tommy about her mother's awful comments.

He laughed it off at first. Then seeing her stricken expression, he took her into his arms. "Deebs, I am so in love with you, and I'm not afraid of your mother. We're adults, we're married, and we're pregnant with our first child. Everything we did was legal. Yes, maybe a little rushed, but it sure was a lot of fun." Then he winked, and she blushed. "Plus, grandbabies have a way of making everything all right." Another wink and a long kiss.

"When will we tell them?" Dale asked, heady and breathless in Tommy's arms.

"We'll talk about that later," he whispered. "I've got other things on my mind right now."

She did too.

By the end of their short time together, they'd come up with a plan. On their next leave, they'd go to St. Simons and share the news of their marriage and the pregnancy with both sets of parents. Together. In that way, perhaps her mother would behave herself and at least act civil when she heard. Dale in no way felt assured of this, but she prayed for it.

"It'll be okay, Deebs. Trust me. Everything will be just fine." Then he'd kissed her bare stomach and whispered, "Hey, little one in there. Can you hear me? Your daddy sure does love you a lot."

———— ◠ ————

For many nights after she had found the body, Dale and Essie came across debris that had washed onshore from the tankers that had been bombed by German U-boats. Throughout each day, the telephone lines relayed information about U-boat sightings as far east as New Jersey and as far west as Oregon. She felt a camaraderie not only with her colleagues on Jekyll Island but also with the mounted patrol at large.

Essie adjusted well to the sand dunes and swamps, the long sandy beaches and inlets. Often Dale marveled at her dappled gray mare, her answer to prayer. Then she'd stare down at the horseshoe-nail ring. Married to Tommy. Another almost unbelievable answer to prayer. In her heart, she felt grateful beyond words, but she tried to act professional, even with her frequent bouts of nausea and trips to the restroom.

The men joked that the toilets on the beach were blue and never ending, and even Dale grew comfortable with relieving herself in the ocean. Though there were fewer people out on the beaches at Jekyll than at St. Simons, they still enforced a curfew to keep townspeople and tourists off the beaches at certain times.

Leonard was the first to notice Dale's fatigue. "You okay, Dale? You're looking awfully sallow today. You need to swap shifts with Mark?"

"No, I'll be fine. I'm just tired. The humidity is getting to me. First, I thought I'd freeze on the night shift, and now, only a month later, I think I might roast to death."

"You got plenty of water with you? I've seen you throwing up. I'm afraid you'll get dehydrated."

That night, the spurs in her hands didn't help; she could not keep herself awake even as heat lightning flashed across the sky. She felt herself slipping and finally succumbed to laying her upper body across Essie's neck, eyes closed.

The next thing she remembered was waking up in the ocean, where Essie had retreated, afraid of the lightning. The freezing water that lapped up on her legs woke her up, but she knew she needed to explain to Leonard and the rest of the mounted patrol what really was going on with her.

But not quite yet.

___ ◠ ___

June 10, 1943

Dale saw the flares coming from the watchtower that meant a submarine had been sighted. She immediately sent a flare too and galloped to the nearest phone line to call it in. "U-boat sighting!"

She watched as a tanker zigzagged far out at sea.

Then Dale heard the terrible sound of a distant explosion that took her back a year to the sinking of the ships off St. Simons. She cantered to the nearest watchtower and called out to Jerry, stationed there for his watch. "What is it?"

With his binoculars trained to the sea, Jerry surveyed. "Looks like she's been struck on the port side." He cursed and said, "Did you see that oil flying up in the air? Spewing like Old Faithful!"

Seconds later, another blast reverberated like an echo bouncing across the waves. "Fire! The ship's on fire, and so's the water!" Jerry cursed again. "That tanker's been struck three times, Dale!" He sent out flares and radio signals, and sirens sounded.

It looked to Dale like the flames spread at least a hundred feet on both sides of the tanker, and smoke billowed in the air so high that it obliterated any sight of stars or moon.

She moaned, feeling utterly helpless. They'd sighted the submarine too late.

The number of sinkings had been drastically reduced in the months since the mounted patrol had been in action, but this sinking felt like a huge failure to Dale. Over the next few days, the coast guardsmen on Jekyll learned the grim details. On June 10, the *Esso Gettysburg*, an American turbine tanker with seventy-two men on board, was hit by two torpedoes about a hundred miles southeast of Savannah. The following day, survivors floating in a lifeboat were picked up by the *George Washington*, an American passenger ship. The survivors were then delivered to Jekyll Island, where, for the next week, Dale heard their stories.

The survivors, young men and older sailors, all had a dazed look about them. In the end, only fifteen men out of the seventy-two made it. Dale couldn't hold back the tears. She knew from the past that many of the bodies would remain out at sea, irretrievable, or be so badly burned that they could not be identified. She also knew that other bodies would wash up on the beach somewhere along the coast one day.

June 24, 1943

Two weeks later, the moon full and high, Dale spotted a raft farther down the beach, looking much like what the surviving sailors had described—badly charred, but somehow seaworthy. Dale dismounted and tethered Essie, radioed Leonard, took her rifle in her hand, and slowly approached the raft.

Two bodies lay inside.

One man was obviously deceased, but the other, a weathered older man, lay on his back, eyes wide open, mouth barely moving. "Help," he uttered.

A merchant mariner. An American raft.

Dale knelt in the wet sand beside him. His breath came in wisps and muffled coughs and wheezes, his eyes glazed with what must have been intense pain, and his body was badly burned.

She radioed again. "Hurry, Leonard! Get help!"

The mariner stared straight at her, struggling for breath.

"It's okay, I've got you. Help is on the way," she whispered.

300

She took the reins from Essie's bridle and put them around the raft's handles, then hooked them to the saddle, leading Essie as they pulled the raft out of the water.

"The bag," he murmured, his eyes rolling back in his head. "The bag." He lifted one finger and pointed toward Dale. "Get the bag. . . ."

Trembling, she leaned into the raft and found a water-soaked cloth bag with a rope drawstring that reminded her of the one her mother kept clothespins in. She brought it to the man. "Is this it? I've got it."

For a bare moment, he was lucid. "Take it. Keep it." He struggled with every breath.

"No, it's yours. You're going to be fine."

"Keep it." The urgency in his voice made her shiver.

"Okay, just until you're better."

"Promise me?"

When she said, "Yes, of course," and cradled the bag to her chest, the man let his head drop back and lost consciousness.

Dale gained permission to visit him the next day at the hospital on St. Simons Island. He resembled a mummy, swaddled in white bandages, his eyes closed. She came to his side and whispered, "Hello, sir, I'm the woman who found you on the beach, and I just wanted you to know I've got your bag in a safe place."

He opened one eye, found her gaze, and gave the barest of a nod, then slipped into unconsciousness again.

She tried visiting once more that afternoon. This time, his eyes were open.

"I'm Dale. I found you on the beach. I've got to go back to my station, but I'm going to bring you your bag."

The old man spoke in a stutter so soft that she had to bend way over to understand him between the coughs. "Rescued a Jewish family on my tanker back . . . 1941. Smuggled from France on . . . Liberty ship. . . . Father gave me bag. . . ."

Dale had unwrapped the bag the night before and found a Mason jar, filled with wax, swaddled under sopping wet towels.

"Yes, I saw it. A candle, right?"

He coughed and choked and tried to clear his throat. "A candle . . . to light when I need hope. . . . Told me it was for hope."

"Well, I'll bring it back and light it for you soon. It'll give you hope that you'll be getting better."

A nurse came in, and the man asked, "My friend? We was in the raft . . . together."

The nurse frowned sympathetically and shook her head. "I'm afraid he didn't survive." Then she checked his vitals and nodded to Dale.

After the nurse left, Dale said, "I'm so sorry about your friend. Were you on the *Esso Gettysburg* together?"

"Yep, tanker got torpedoed two weeks ago . . . best I recall . . . hundred miles offshore. Made it in the raft."

Dale struggled to keep from crying. Two weeks on a raft!

"My buddy . . . Riff Raff. My buddy's gone."

"Riff Raff?"

"They say we're all rotgut whiskey," he whispered, and Dale saw a spark of life come to his eyes. "Just no-good riffraff. . . . That was my buddy's name."

Before Dale could question such a comment, he began coughing. When he finally calmed, she asked, "And what's your name?"

"Aw, perty miss . . . just call me same as everyone else does, No Pants Jones." He coughed out a laugh when she stared at him with wide eyes. "Old joke between me and my buddies . . . nothing dirty about it. I reckon they'll let me in their society now. Ever heard of the 40-Fathom Club?"

"Never."

"It's a club for any merchant mariner or sailor . . . who survives a torpedo blast to his ship." Deep breath, then coughing. "Well . . . now I can join. Lotsa members."

Dale thought perhaps he was hallucinating when he explained, "Some of my buddies, they've been torpedoed four, five, six times. . . . Heard about one sailor who got himself torpedoed ten times. Just about nuts by then."

302

"That's awful. Why would anyone keep doing it?"

His rugged face told the story. "We're considered riffraff by a lot of folks. Ya see, missy, we ain't military . . . we're civilians." He paused, caught his breath, closed his eyes.

"It's okay, Mr. Jones. You don't have to talk anymore. Just rest."

But he continued as if he had not heard. "Don't have no military training. The naysayers claim the country's so desperate for help against them U-boats, they'll take anyone—thieves, convicts, drunks. Ya know . . . the riffraff." He gave a raspy laugh. "Can't say I know that any of my buddies have killed anyone. Least not before the war. Most ain't even held a gun. Just go out on the high seas to help out. . . .

"My first time on board a Liberty ship—aw, she was fast. . . . I told you about that time, didn't I, missy? 'Bout carrying them Jews from . . .'"

Now his coughing fit caused his eyes to water, and he bent over his burnt body. Dale wasn't sure if the pain from the burns or the coughing brought the tears.

"Shh, Mr. Jones," she soothed him. "You rest now. You rest good, and I'm sure you'll be going to the 40-Fathom Club before long."

But as Dale left the room, the attending nurse shook her head. "Are you a family member?"

Dale hesitated. "No, a friend."

"Well, you best be praying for him. Poor ole fool."

Dale wanted to visit the Ridley mansion, a mere fifteen minutes from the hospital, wanted to collapse in her father's arms and tell him about Riff Raff and No Pants Jones. And Tommy and the baby. Terrible news mixed with wonderful news. She wanted to burst into tears and be his little girl. Instead, she went to the room where she'd spent the night on a cot and retrieved her few belongings and No Pants Jones's bag. She hurried to where the ferry waited to carry her back to Jekyll Island, but at the last minute, she hesitated and turned back to the hospital. She needed to give No Pants Jones his candle bag, which smelled of seawater and burned flesh. The bag that held hope for the old merchant mariner.

When she arrived at the entrance to the hospital, a dozen photographers stood out front. She tried to sneak in between the watching crowd. Some sort of reporter was interviewing a nurse and doctor when the nurse said, "Why, that's the little lady who rescued him, right there!"

Light bulbs flashed at Dale, and she instinctively held up her hand to block her face as she rushed in the doors, ignoring the reporter's voice, "Miss! Miss, could we just have a moment of your time?"

Heart pounding, she hurried to the third floor where No Pants lay. When she got to his room, the attending nurse frowned. "I'm glad you came back. He's not doing well." Her face softened. "Really weak. Your visit bolstered him for a little while."

"I brought him his affairs. He had this bag with him and was determined I keep it for him. I thought maybe if he saw it, knew it was safe, well, it'd give him resolve. You know, to keep fighting."

The nurse eyed Dale and gave a quick nod. "Go ahead. But just for a few minutes."

His eyes were closed, the bandaged side of his face turned to her, the crisp white sheets lifting light as a feather when he breathed.

"Mr. Jones." No response. "No Pants. I've got something for you."

His eyes twittered underneath the lids until he forced them open.

"I brought your bag, sir. You said it was awful important, so I brought it for you."

He winced as he turned to face Dale, then his eyes flew open in stark terror and pain. Dale choked back bile. Was he going to die in front of her? She almost rose to leave, but he gave a guttural cough and said, "You keep it," through clenched teeth.

"No! You're going to live, and you can take it back to your family."

"Ain't got no family. Just them fellas on the tanker. And now they's all gone. Even Riff Raff. And I'll be gone soon."

Dale reached out for his bandaged hand. "No Pants . . ."

With what looked to be extreme effort, he turned his head, the pain sizzling through his body evident in his eyes. "Rescued them. Gave me that bag for saving their lives." His eyelids fluttered again and closed.

Dale's legs started twitching, almost like No Pants's eyes. She needed to leave, but dread weighed her down.

"Said the candle was for good luck," he murmured. "Said to light it when ya thought hope was almost gone."

"I'll light it now!" Dale fished out the glass jar filled with white wax. "I'll light it now, and it'll burn slowly and give you hope. You'll see."

"You keep it. You saved me. 'Fraid I'm headed to see ole Riff Raff."

"No! Please, Mr. Jones, please don't leave."

She raced out of the room, crying, "I need a match! A match for this poor man, to give him hope. A match, please!"

When Dale returned to his room, the candle remained unlit, and every bit of life had been snuffed out of Mr. No Pants Jones.

25

Allie

In Nana Dale's downstairs powder room, I washed the manure off
my hands. Then I hurried to my car with the cherrywood chest sitting in the passenger seat and drove straight to Austin's apartment
before I could talk myself out of it. Two prayers on my knees in one
day filled with a lot of confession had given me enough courage to
see him in person, look him in the eyes, and tell him how sorry I
was, how wrong I was, how confused I'd been, how much I loved
him. I rehearsed it again and again as I pulled up to the apartment
complex, searching the parking lot for his red Toyota, Triple T.

Which wasn't there.

Undeterred, I hurried inside and took the elevator up to his
apartment on the seventh floor. I hesitated and looked down to
where my exercise pants were stained with manure.

Then I rang the doorbell. And waited.

Of course he wasn't home at seven o'clock on a Wednesday
evening. He was still doing rounds, probably helping a cow deliver

or pacing a field in search of a horse that had gone missing and was likely trapped in barbed wire.

Or maybe he was simply out with friends.

Or another woman.

I called his cell, which went straight to voice mail. I choked out the words "Hi. I'm sorry. Please let me say this: I get it now. You were right. You've always been right. I've been obsessed, and somehow, I see it, and it doesn't matter. Not nearly as much as you matter to me. I want *us*. That's all I want. Austin, I am so sorry. About everything. Is there any way you could give me another chance? I love you. Can we please talk?"

I waited in the parking lot for an hour, feeling lightness at having confessed yet heaviness at the prospect of Austin's negative response. Finally, I started the car and left.

On the way home, I called Wick, forgetting it was past midnight in France.

"Hey, sis!" he answered, his voice heavy with sleep. "You okay?" Now he sounded concerned.

"Oh gosh, I woke you up. I'm sorry."

"Well, I'm awake now. What's the matter?"

The emotions that had been simmering now boiled over as I blurted out, "Nana Dale married Tommy!"

"What?"

In a flurry of words, I explained my most recent findings, starting with discovering the whereabouts of the cherrywood chest and Nana Dale's letters to me promising that I had everything I needed to keep the property, as well as her desire for me to go to the islands, and my trip with Tricia.

"Wow, that's a whole lot to absorb. Especially at two a.m. Hold on a sec." He came back to the phone a minute or two later. "I needed a cup of coffee. Okay, so slow down and tell me everything again. I don't even know what to say. I just wish—"

"Please don't tell me to stop now, Wick," I interrupted. "I know I've been obsessed with this whole thing, and I'm coming to terms with that. But now I've found all this new stuff—the scrapbook, the key, the newspaper clippings. Plus, I have an eyewitness who saw Nana Dale and Tommy get married! It finally seems like I'm close to discovering whatever she wanted me to find."

I could tell Wick was stifling a yawn because it took him a moment to say "Look, sis, I get it. That's weird and upsetting and confusing. But do you really think it is going to change what's happening with the house?"

"It might, Wick. It really might. Nana Dale left me letters and notes saying I could keep the property. . . ." I trailed off for a moment, then said excitedly, "And, Wick, Barnell told me about what Nana Dale discovered when she did that DNA testing for you last fall! Do you remember that we're related to Horrible Mr. Hightower and that Mr. Hightower is Mr. Weatherby's grandson? Why didn't you tell me that Nana Dale went ballistic when she found out about that?"

"She didn't go ballistic in front of me. I . . . wow, I hadn't made the connection. That's really . . . upsetting."

"Yeah, it is. So see . . . I feel . . . I don't know. I feel like I'm getting closer to something."

Wick slurped his coffee. "Okay, okay. But please let Mom help and then let the Frenchwoman—what's her name?"

"Cécile."

"Yes, let Cécile and her crew do the rest. You said she's fabulous. Please." He was silent for several long seconds. "I'm so worried about you, Allie. I know you're heartbroken. Can I just say one thing? You're not the easiest person to live with, and you found a doggone nice man who wanted to live with you. Talk to Austin. Call him. Please."

I let out the sob I'd been holding in my throat. "I tried. I can't reach him." Then in a tiny voice, I added, "You're right. I'm a huge mess. But it's not just too late for the house. I'm afraid it might be too late for Austin. I asked him to leave me alone, and I think that's what he's doing. I completely understand why. I've blown it, Wick."

I could almost picture Wick running his hands through his

thick hair, his lips tight in a frown, puzzling over what to say next. Finally, he cleared his throat and said, "Honestly, I doubt you've given the poor guy a chance. But if you have, then call Mom. Tell her everything you've told me. See how she reacts. Please."

So I did.

When she picked up, I said, "Can I come over? Now? Please?"

"Of course, sweetheart. Come."

My parents lived in a prestigious neighborhood in Alpharetta, a good twenty minutes from Austin's apartment in Dunwoody. I drove there on autopilot, much as I'd done going to Austin's. I glanced at the miniature chest sitting in the passenger seat and decided I would look through the scrapbook with my mother. She wasn't my first or second choice, but she was someone I had shared history with.

When she opened the door, I melted in her arms, the small cherrywood chest hard between us. "I know I look crappy, and it's so confusing and . . ."

Mom took in my dejected face and dirty exercise pants and said, "Shh. You go take a shower. I'll bring you my robe. Have you eaten anything?"

I shook my head. I hadn't put anything in my mouth all day.

For the second time that Wednesday, I showered—this time in my old bathroom, letting the hot water cleanse me, trying to imagine what that would look like—me being free of this heartache, this sorrow, this deep, deep guilt. I silently rehearsed my two prayers of confession that had slipped out, unbidden. As I reached for a fluffy blue bath towel, I noticed an embroidered hand towel that hung over it on the rack, and it sent chills down my back.

When life becomes more than you can stand, kneel.

I stared at it as if God had written the words in the clouds. Mom must have recently purchased that hand towel because I'd never seen it before. My parents' house was littered with pithy little sayings like this, written on a colorful plate or a wooden plaque or a hand towel. Things like *Bloom where you're planted* and *When your day is stitched in by prayer, it's less likely to unravel.* But I'd never seen this one.

I did what it said. For the third time since that morning, I knelt, this time on a bath mat, leaning against the tub where I'd washed since childhood. Once again, I prayed.

Then I wrapped myself in Mom's plush light-blue robe and luxuriated in the softness. When she came into the room with a bowl of soup and a cup of tea, I let the tears flow.

"Thank you," I choked out.

She sat on my queen-size bed beside me as I ate in silence.

Then in between bites of chicken soup and sobs, I said, "I found the cherrywood chest," and nodded to where it sat beside the bed.

"Oh! Where?"

When I explained, Mom stared down at the chest. "But you've looked through the cedar chest in the Pink Room several times."

"I know, but I hadn't taken all the clothes out."

Mom furrowed her brow. "A few weeks before she died," she said softly, "I found Nana in the Pink Room. She didn't ever climb the stairs up there anymore, so I was shocked and worried. She had pulled out a few of her riding habits from the cedar chest, and she seemed . . . well, a bit confused.

"I think I surprised her, coming into the room like that. When I asked her what she was looking for, she got a bit flustered and said, 'Oh, nothing really. Just wanted to see these old clothes and remember.'"

Mom now cradled the little chest. "Do you think she was looking for this?" she asked.

I shrugged. "Maybe." Then slowly, almost methodically, I repeated everything I'd just told Wick, everything I'd read in the scrapbook, everything Tricia and I had discovered on the islands, everything that Billy Hampton had told us. I barely gave my mother time to digest the torrent of information before I asked, "Mom, did you know Nana Dale was in the mounted patrol, like Tommy Ridley? Did you know that Nana Dale married him at Camp McDougal on Hilton Head on January 14, 1943?"

She'd been quiet through my monologue, though her face had registered surprise several times. But with this question, she sat back on the bed, tilted her head, and looked at me as if I had truly lost my mind. A dozen emotions washed over her face, but the most prominent was what I'd call terrified concern. Like she might have to commit me to a mental institution. But she didn't say that. Instead, her eyes grew wide. "Allie!" she whispered. "Whatever makes you say such a thing?"

"Like I said, Tricia and I went to Hilton Head yesterday and met Billy Hampton. When he was a boy, he used to watch the mounted patrol. He remembered Nana Dale finding Essie and watching her ride on the beach. And he says he watched her secret wedding to Tommy."

Mom set down the chest, stood up quickly, then wobbled as if she might faint before sitting back down on the bed. "That's impossible! She would have told me. There are no pictures."

"It was a secret." I reached for the chest, opened it, and lifted out the charm bracelet. "Look. Remember when she gave me this bracelet? I never paid much attention to anything except the cameos of Wick and me and you and the horses. But there's this key, Mom, a key to this chest—this one right here—and when I opened the chest, I found this scrapbook inside." Now I removed the scrapbook and newspapers and set them on the bed. "And then look at this." I held out the charm bracelet, and I pointed to the calendar charm with the tiny diamond embedded on January 14, 1943. "That's not Nana Dale and Poppa Dan's anniversary, is it?"

She shook her head slowly.

"Billy Hampton said the wedding was in January 1943. He was a ten-year-old boy at the time, and he watched the wedding. He described it all, Mom! Just a handful of men were there with Nana Dale and Tommy astride Essie and Infinity."

She swiped a finger underneath her eyes, left first, then right. Her hands were trembling.

I scooted next to her and opened the leather scrapbook between us. "Can we please look at this together, Mom? I think we'll find more answers when we do."

"Yes," she whispered. "But not here. Let's go to Hickory Hills. Let's put it all together there."

And so I found myself traipsing once again through the labyrinth of rooms at Nana Dale's home. With my mother. Wearing clothes I'd fished out of the drawer in my old bedroom.

I set the chest on the coffee table in the den, placing the photocopied pages on top of it.

"Before we look through the scrapbook, Mom, let me show you everything I've already found in the house. A lot of it I've always known was here, but now it all seems like it's slowly revealing Nana Dale's secrets."

We started in the Pink Room, then ogled Tommy's Maclay Medal in the dining room, and stared at all the ribbons, trophies, and old photos of Nana Dale and friends in the Ribbon Room.

Without thinking, I asked, "Mom, are any of these ribbons and trophies yours?" There were several professional photos of my mother, taking her light bay mare, Annie's Song, over jumps. "These are really great."

"Uh-huh," Mom said. She reached out and touched one of the photos: Annie's knees tucked tight to her chest as she soared over a fence, Mom leaning forward, legs pressed to the saddle, heels of her black leather boots down, her back arched.

"You were a beautiful rider, Mom."

I wished I could take back my words as soon as they were out because Mom cleared her throat, let her hand drop, swiveled, and left the Ribbon Room. It hit me then, in a way I'd never really considered, that in my parents' house, the house where I grew up, there were no horse photos, no memorabilia of my mother's show days, and no ribbons or trophies, although I knew my mother won her fair share.

I followed Mom up the stairs to the main floor, and we collapsed in the den, both of us worn out from emotions. Mom fingered the leaflet from the Home Front Museum that sat on the coffee table and listened as I described everything Tricia and I had seen there. Then, with me looking over her shoulder, she flipped through the pages and pages of sheets that Dr. Cressman had given me, occasionally reading something out loud to me, in a strained—no—a pained voice.

"'The mounted service proved especially valuable in rescue activity. On several occasions, horsemen were able to locate bodies missed by the foot patrolmen.'" She glanced up at me. "Do you think Nana Dale found bodies on the shore?"

I shrugged. "She told me she did. Remember? How she rescued a sailor?"

Mom narrowed her eyes. "She told you a lot of stories she never told me." Her voice was harsh, then her eyes softened. She reached over and squeezed my hand.

At last, I passed Mom the scrapbook. She ran her hand over the supple leather cover. "This is gorgeous. I'll bet Jeff Jeffrey made this for her."

Slowly, she leafed through the pages I had already seen. When she got to the photo of the mounted patrol practicing on Hilton Head, she touched the photo of the Sand Pounders lovingly, a tear sliding down her face as her finger absentmindedly traced the red circle that Nana Dale had drawn around Tommy's face. Then she read Nana Dale's scribbled notes by the side.

"She never talked about the mounted patrol," Mom said. "Ever. Neither did Grandma Eleanor. I knew that Nana Dale's father, Grandpa Jeremiah, had been a history buff and had made a fortune in lumber during the war, but he'd died when I was just a baby. Nana Dale fairly worshiped him, and I recognized the tension between Grandma Eleanor and my mother. It was hard to miss.

"And I knew that Tommy had died young as well. But I didn't know his parents, didn't know he was in the US Coast Guard, and I certainly didn't know that he married my mother." She turned to me. "I still have quite a hard time believing that."

I reached over and covered my mother's hand with mine. "All of this is quite a shock. And she kept adding to this binder throughout the years. There's that article about the torpedoed tankers from 1999."

"Yes," Mom said, still fingering the photo of the Sand Pounders. "There were so many things she kept locked up in this little chest and in her heart. So strange."

We'd examined all the pages I had already seen in the binder, and when I turned to a new page, I held my breath for fear I'd find Tommy's obituary. Instead, there was a long article from a Florida newspaper dated in 2016. The headline read *The Merchant Marines Were the Unsung Heroes of WWII: These daring seamen kept the Allied troops armed and fed while at the mercy of the German U-boats.*

A period photo from the 1940s showed a half-dozen men with grease-stained faces and arms, a few sporting what looked like handmade gas masks. The caption read *Merchant mariners training in the boiler room.*

Mom squinted and read aloud, "'The sailor from the merchant ships was in those days known to America as a bum associated with rotgut whiskey and waterfront brawls. . . .' And look," she said, pointing, "Nana Dale has circled 'rotgut whiskey' and out to the side written 'Mr. No Pants Jones.'"

I raised an eyebrow, and a vague smile crossed my mother's lips as she shrugged, shook her head, and continued reading about U-boats devastating the merchant shipping off the US East and Gulf Coasts, attacking vessels within sight of beaches from Virginia to Florida and at the mouth of the Mississippi River.

"Like what happened on St. Simons," I interjected, and Mom nodded.

Mom kept reading, almost as if she were trying to imagine what it was like to survive a U-boat attack. She sucked in her breath and said, "Those mariners dealt with fire, explosions, icy water, sharks, and flaming oil slicks. Some of them survived for days and weeks in half-burnt lifeboats. Can you imagine that, Allie? And Nana Dale rescued one of them who turned up on shore? Could that be true?"

Mom set down the scrapbook and stared out the window to the barn in the distance. "Imagine that."

I silently pulled the scrapbook into my lap and continued reading about the high casualty rate of merchant mariners and something called the 40-Fathom Club for mariners who had been torpedoed at least once. Nana Dale had underlined almost all the article, but she had circled and written three exclamation points beside *40-Fathom Club* and circled each of the names cited as belonging to the men in the photograph: Low Life McCormick, No Pants Jones, Screwball McCarthy, Foghorn Russell, Soapbox Smitty, Riff Raff, Whiskey Bill.

"Look, Mom," I said. "Nana Dale circled 'No Pants Jones' a bunch of times and wrote beside it *My beloved No Pants finally qualified for the 40-Fathom Club.*"

"Her beloved 'No Pants Jones'? That's just shocking," Mom whispered.

But what shocked me most was that Nana Dale had written *Show to Allie* out to the side, using huge penciled brackets to indicate the whole article should be shown to me. Mom and I stared at her penmanship as if it would suddenly become an audio of my grandmother explaining her interest in these merchant mariners.

Underneath *Show to Allie* Nana Dale had written *He's the one Essie and I saved. This is his photo, taken a year before his boat was torpedoed, the year before he died.* She'd drawn a long arrow up to his name, No Pants Jones, and then another one up to the photo of the merchant mariners.

"Did you ever hear about him, Mom?"

Once again, my mother looked at me as if I were partially insane. "Never. It's almost like reading a legend about a pirate ship."

"But she did tell me, Mom! Two or three times, she'd start to tell me about a sailor she rescued with Essie. And then she'd stop and say, 'I'll explain some other time.' But she never did."

When I looked over at my mother, she had tears sliding down her cheeks. "She never talked about any of this, Allie. Never said a word. I can't . . . I can't believe it. I just don't understand why she never told us about . . ."

She stopped midsentence and covered her mouth with her

hand. She sat, lost in thought, alternately swiping a finger under her damp eyes and pulling her fingers through her perfectly highlighted hair. I internally cringed at the struggle on my mother's face, awash with regret. Deep, deep regret.

"She trusted you, Allie. Obviously she wanted you to find all of this. She knew you cared. I'd lost her trust, and she'd lost mine. But she trusted you."

With Mom's comment, I got up the nerve to ask, "What happened, Mom? I know your accident was awful, but it seems like that awful accident broke more than your neck. Like it broke your heart . . . and your relationship with Nana Dale."

Mom stared off toward the window and nibbled her lip. At length, she said, "I tried to tell her I was afraid of the higher jumps, that the competition wasn't my cup of tea. That I had other interests I wanted to pursue, that I didn't want to compete anymore. But I said it all wrong." Again, she swiped a hand under her eyes.

"And looking back, I think my telling her the truth broke her heart. Only she didn't act heartbroken. She was furious. Talked about all the money and time she'd spent on the horses, the equipment, the entry fees, everything, just so that I could become a champion rider. I knew she was right. Horse showing is one of the most expensive hobbies out there. I felt guilty for wanting to quit, and I just didn't have enough courage to insist that I was becoming miserable. And afraid."

She turned to look at me at last. "So I kept showing. And then I had the accident, and I don't think she ever forgave herself for pushing me so hard. And I guess I never really knew how to forgive her either." She gave a hiccup of a shrug. "If it had happened now, I'm sure I would have gone to counseling for PTSD and maybe worked out all my fear and anger and jumbled emotions. I'd have gone to equine therapy, Allie."

She said it as if she had never once considered this before, even though hearing of my mother's accident and watching how she lived with Nana Dale had been my impetus to begin Hickory Hills Horse Therapy.

I kept quiet, but my heart was hammering.

"But it happened in 1970, and no one talked about therapy—much less equine therapy—back then. We were all worried about our brothers being sent to Vietnam and so many other things." She cleared her throat. "But no one talked about therapy."

Mom looked haggard. I drew my arms around her and said, "Thank you for telling me. Thank you for coming here with me. I'm sorry I've kept you away. I . . . I wanted to do this myself, not drag you into it. Maybe I will still lose it all, Mom. The house, the estate . . . and Austin, but at least I understand a little more about my family, about Nana Dale and Tommy."

Mom placed her hands on my forehead and gently kissed it. "I'm so sorry, sweetie. Sorry I haven't helped you at all."

"You're helping me now," I whispered. Then suppressing a yawn, I suggested, "Mom, why don't we call it an evening, spend the night here, and look through the rest of the scrapbook in the morning before I have to be at Chastain?"

Mom had turned the page in the scrapbook while nodding and saying, "Yes, that sounds good, darling. I'm too worn out to finish tonight, but tomorrow . . ." She let the phrase dangle, then said, "Oh!" and pointed to the headline of an article in the *Brunswick News*, dated June 27, 1943. I came beside her.

Merchant Sailor Gives Homemade Candle to Woman Who Saved His Life

While riding her horse along a deserted beach at midnight, a young woman came across an injured crewman washed ashore after his tanker, the *Esso Gettysburg*, was torpedoed by a German submarine. Details of the young woman are unclear . . .

There was a black-and-white photo of a young woman in civilian attire holding her hand out toward the camera so that we couldn't see her face and cradling some type of jar in the other hand. It looked like she was doing everything she could not to be photographed, and the article did not mention her name.

"It's her! It's Nana Dale!" I jumped up and ran to the dining room and retrieved Tommy's Maclay Trophy. "Look at this!" I whispered, sitting back down beside Mom, holding out the silver urn and reaching inside, where I'd replaced the Mason jar. Bringing it out, I was about to wad up the newsprint I'd already seen about the National Horse Show when I realized another newspaper was wrapped inside that one.

The same article. This was Nana Dale, saving a merchant mariner and not wanting to be photographed. So like her. She didn't want any credit. Except this time, she really, really didn't want anyone to know this was her. Beside the article in the scrapbook, she had written, *Fortunately, Allie, my parents never figured out that the photo was of me. I was terrified that they would see the article and find out that I was pregnant before Tommy and I could tell them. But that's not what happened at all. What happened was much worse.*

26

Dale

Early July 1943

Dale kept the candle under her bed in the Jekyll Island Club, mostly out of sight, because every time she looked at it, she saw the burnt body of No Pants Jones and the plea in his half-crazed eyes. *"You keep it."* In truth, she didn't want to keep any reminders of that night.

But there were plenty. The *Brunswick News* had published a short article about a young woman who had saved a merchant mariner, complete with the photo of Dale hiding her face from the camera's flash. At least they didn't have her name. She'd begged the nurses to keep it all quiet. As they stared at her abdomen, they'd agreed on one condition: that Dale come back again in a month to make sure all was progressing normally with her pregnancy.

But the photo was there for everyone to see, including her parents and the Ridleys. What if they came to see her, to tell her how proud they were, and instead discovered her delicate condition? But when nothing happened after ten days and her parents' letters made no mention of the article, Dale let out a long sigh of relief.

Dale had felt so sick and thrown up so often during the first four or five months of the pregnancy that her clothes, already baggy, still hung on her, showing almost no sign of the small, hard ball of her abdomen. She had worried that the baby wasn't growing enough, so she rejoiced at the first feeling of movement, something deep and mysterious that brought great joy.

But by the sixth month, she could no longer conceal her protruding stomach, and she knew she would have to tell her colleagues about her situation. When she did, their first reaction after "Highly unusual" was laughter and celebration. But when Commander McTeer heard the news, he came to Jekyll Island to talk with Dale.

"I have to take you off beach duty, Mrs. Ridley," he said, staring at Dale's swollen abdomen. "We could all get in trouble if the higher-ups found out that you've been hiding your condition. The military does not believe women should be working at all when pregnant, much less riding a horse on deserted beaches in the middle of the night."

Dale swallowed. "I . . . I know. I'm sorry. I just wanted to continue with the Sand Pounders. And I was embarrassed to tell anyone—especially you, sir—since I had made such a scene, begging you to join." She closed her eyes briefly, then looked up at the commander. "Is there any way I could stay on the island for a little while longer?"

Commander McTeer pulled at his mustache, seeming a bit embarrassed too. "I'll allow you to stay on Jekyll Island and help with the cooking and cleaning until a month before the baby is due, given that you remain healthy. Then you will be discharged and expected to return to your home. Is that understood?"

"Yes, sir. Yes, thank you." She stared at the floor and said in a small voice, "Our parents don't know about the marriage or the pregnancy yet."

Commander McTeer looked at her, raised an eyebrow, and then said, "Of course they don't. Why should that surprise me, Dale Ridley?"

"But we're going home and telling our parents that we're married and pregnant—in the right order, you know. That it's all legal. We'll take our next leave together in a few weeks."

Commander McTeer eyed her. "You better write a letter to explain that you are married *before* they see you, or they certainly won't believe it was in the right order. Your condition is beginning to be rather obvious."

"I will," Dale assured him.

But every time she picked up her pen to write her parents, all she told them about was the heat and the horses and how beautiful everything was on Jekyll Island.

— Ω —

Late August 1943

The August weather was hot, brutal, unending. The baby kicked and squirmed, and each movement caused joy and pain together. At least that was normal and meant everything was fine. Dale worried about a few contractions, but the nurse who was checking in on her from the hospital in St. Simons assured her that false contractions were normal. "You'll know, Mrs. Ridley, when it's the real thing," she'd said on their most recent phone call.

By the beginning of September, Dale waddled everywhere, determined to take care of the horses, reminding her fellow Sand Pounders that she was still officially on duty for another month. The men treated her with the same care and love as they did for the horses and dogs. She was finally enjoying food again, and her tiny frame carried the baby out front like a basketball. And somehow, being with a pregnant woman made the men homesick and yet happy.

But Dale longed for Tommy.

Only twenty-three days left until she'd see him, until they'd be together, until they'd share their news with their families in person and . . . and all would be out in the open and be perfect.

It was well past time to write the letter. Still, Dale hesitated, literally feeling a cramping that wasn't a contraction as she recalled the anger on her mother's face. *"Tommy Ridley has been a bad influence on you, Dale.... He is cocky and brash and daredevilish, and I will not have you involved with him.... If anything happens to you while you are in that patrol, I will never forgive Tommy Ridley! Never!"*

"But a good thing has happened, Mama. A wonderful thing." All the same, she set down the fountain pen, closed her eyes, and prayed, "Please, God, please help Mama understand."

She almost called them instead. Almost. She practiced the words she would say as her parents huddled around the phone. But she didn't. She couldn't.

Not yet.

It's going to be too late. She felt that tug in her spirit as surely as she felt the movement of her unborn child. Dale wondered at her cowardice. Tommy called her the bravest person he'd ever known, and yet, as she imagined her mother's tears and anger and incomprehension, she lost every ounce of courage. If only she could talk to her father alone, but he was so often in Detroit, overwhelmed with the details of providing enough crates to send supplies to Europe.

So she consoled herself by writing to Tommy and reading his letters. His most recent from two weeks earlier conveyed his excitement.

> *Hey, Wife!*
> *Counting the days till we're together and sharing the same bed again! Don't blush, Deebs! And don't you worry. I won't forget to bring our marriage certificate so our parents will see it's all official.*
> *How's the baby doing? Glad that all the guys know—and McTeer too—and that you're behaving yourself and staying safe on the ground. I'm not one to worry, as you know, but you've seen a lot of hard stuff, and I'm thankful you're not riding anymore. Anybody else riding Essie? Glad you'll be staying in St. Simons with family until the wee one is born.*

No big news on my end. You're the one with all the drama! Hope you're sleeping better.

My only news is that Harry fainted and fell off his horse on his shift two nights ago. Hot as Hades around here. Horse came galloping back to the stable at Melrose. I took Finny out to look for him, and we found him all right. He almost drowned! Brought him home, and I took his shift for him. Wasn't too bright of me, but I forgot to put on the mosquito protection. Spent the whole night out there with those pests, and gee whiz, I'm bit all over. Glad all those bites will be healed by the time you see me. I won't do that again.

I sure do miss you, my Deebs, my Dale, my love. Tell our baby hello from his daddy. I'm already planning on it being a boy. Hope you don't mind. We'll talk about names when we're together, okay?

September 13, 1943

It was the end of her shift, the sky still black, the moon still high, as she led Essie around to the stables. Her colleague Fred now took the shifts she'd shared with Leonard, but he always handed the reins over to Dale when he returned so that she could bathe and brush her mare.

Leonard trotted up beside her. "You okay? I can take care of Essie tonight if you want. You look, um, a little bit uncomfortable." His face reddened with embarrassment.

Dale smiled. "Thanks, Leonard. I'm okay. A little tired, but at least I'm not still riding. Although I sure wouldn't be in danger of falling asleep anymore on this ole gal." She patted the mare and gave a grin. "The baby kicks me enough to make sure of that."

"You're almost done here, Dale. I'm real happy for you and for Tommy. But it'll be a downer not to have you around. Will they let you take Essie with you?"

"I don't think so. She'll be issued to the coast guardsman who takes my place. But Commander McTeer promised he'll save her for me. He said they'll be auctioning off the horses whenever the Sand Pounders is dissolved."

"At the rate we're stopping them U-boats, they might not need us by the end of the year. Wouldn't that be something?"

A jeep rounded the turn toward the stables and stopped, a young man hurrying out of the passenger seat and running toward them. For a brief moment, Dale thought it was Tommy. Had they let him take his leave early? But as he drew closer, Dale recognized the boy as Jacob, a young farm boy who had trained with Tommy on Hilton Head and now served with him on Daufuskie Island.

She felt a cramp of fear.

Jacob stopped in front of them, trying to catch his breath, sweat pouring off his face. "Sorry, ma'am, to bring you this news, but your husband's awfully sick." He sucked in long breaths and braced his hands on his knees. "'Scuse me, ma'am. Took a while to git here from Daufuskie."

She tried to get a sound out, but the look on Jacob's face paralyzed her. At last, she whispered, "What's the matter?"

"He's got malaria. Got bit up real bad."

Malaria! It couldn't be! In his most recent letter, the one she'd received last week, Tommy had joked about that incident.

"I . . . I think you should come. You've got permission to come with me."

Dale shook her head to stay upright, her face suddenly cold with sweat. She cradled her stomach, her throat parched as the fear that had been gone for the past six months leaped back into the front of her mind, screaming at her.

Leonard took hold of Dale's arm to steady her as she choked out, "How bad off is he?"

The boy shuffled his feet, staring at the ground. "It's pretty bad, ma'am. Doctor's awful worried."

"What do you mean?"

"Doc don't have a lot of hope for him getting better. I'm sorry to have to tell you. We best be going quick now."

Dale heard the words as if holding a seashell to her ear. She felt the baby kick and looked down at her bulging stomach. "He has to live. We're gonna have a baby. He has to live!"

Jacob stood perfectly still, misery on his face.

Leonard said, "You go on back with him, Dale, right now!" Then he took Essie's reins, and turning to Jacob, Leonard added, "You take good care of Dale. She's real tired. You understand?"

Jacob nodded. "I will."

"Praying for you," Leonard whispered, his face heavy with concern.

Jacob led Dale to his jeep while she murmured, "No hope? There has to be hope. There's always hope." She tried to steady herself by leaning on the hood but felt her knees buckling.

He reached over. "Let me help you, Dale."

She nodded without moving.

"We'd best be going, ma'am. We need to hurry."

Dale heard his voice in a fog. Jacob opened the jeep door, and she started to get in, then turned and whispered, "Hold on!" She waddled up the steps of the Jekyll Island Club to her room. With difficulty, she knelt beside her bed and reached underneath, pulling out the Mason-jar candle. *"Light it when you need hope,"* old No Pants had told her. If ever she needed hope, it was now.

On the maddingly long trip via jeep and ferry and jeep again, Jacob repeated the story that Tommy had shared with her in his last letter. "Ole Harry—you know he's nearing seventy. He just fainted from the heat on his watch. Just plain fell off his horse, and the horse went galloping back to the stables. Tommy volunteered to find him and went right out on his Finny, brought Harry back, and then took his shift. But he didn't have on the mosquito netting for protection. He saved that man's life, Dale, but Tommy . . . never seen someone with as many mosquito bites. Something awful. That was near two weeks ago."

When she arrived on Daufuskie, she found Tommy in a makeshift infirmary in one of the downstairs bedrooms of the Melrose House.

A nurse hurried to Dale's side. "We couldn't move him to the hospital on St. Simons. Doctor was pretty sure he wouldn't make the trip. He's been holding on for you, ma'am. The doctor's not sure he's going to make it through the night."

"No, it can't be true!" Dale didn't recognize her own voice, so distorted was it with anguish.

The attending nurse patted her arm. "Here, take a seat before you go in to see him."

A middle-aged man in navy attire came from Tommy's room. "Mrs. Ridley, I'm Dr. Franklin." The doctor, visibly shaken, nonetheless explained the situation calmly. "It often takes two weeks for symptoms to show. He started the fever five days ago. I'm afraid it's cerebral malaria from an infection—unfortunately, there is no more dangerous neurological complication. And the polio has weakened his immune system."

Dale shook her head. "What are you saying? I don't understand! Why didn't you call me earlier?"

"We hoped—"

"You *hoped*! You hoped what?" she shouted, unable to stop herself from raising her voice. "You hoped he'd get better, but you didn't bother to tell me, and now you say there is no hope. Well, I won't believe you."

She rushed into the room where Tommy lay on a cot, his head swollen to twice its size, his eyes shut. She felt all the blood leave her face, and then everything went black.

Minutes later, the nurse was kneeling beside her, fanning her, a cold rag on her forehead. "There now. I know it's a shock. I'm so sorry, ma'am."

Dale tried to swallow and to open her eyes, to put her hand on her swollen belly. "Tommy?" she whispered.

"He's in a coma, ma'am."

"I need to sit beside him. Please."

The nurse moved a chair beside the bed and helped Dale into it.

"Tommy! Wake up, Tommy!" she whispered. "Wake up, you wonderful daredevil! Wake up!"

She sat beside the bed, staring at his almost unrecognizable face, choking back tears, stroking his hand. She jerked back when she felt the sizzle in his skin. Recovering, she touched his arm, then brushed his face with her finger, tracing the outline of his eyebrows, his nose, his lips, and finally standing and leaning over to press her lips to his.

"Tommy, you cannot leave me! Can you hear me?" She took his hand, and he gave it the slightest squeeze.

"Tommy—you hear me! Oh, nurse, come in! He's awake."

The nurse brought cool water, and for hours, Dale sponged his feverish body, memorizing it. In the middle of the night, her head resting on the side of his bed, he whispered to her, "Hey, Deebs."

"Tommy!"

"Sorry . . . so sorry."

"Shh. Save your breath. You're going to live. It'll be okay."

Long seconds passed, and then, "I need you to be brave now. You're the bravest girl I know, the bravest human."

"No, you . . . you can't leave. Not now! We've got a baby coming!"

"You can take good care of that baby for me. You can do it, Deebs. You're brave, Darn Brave, my DB. Knew it the first time I saw you."

"I love you so much, Tommy! Please don't die! You promised me you wouldn't."

"I sure do love you. Loved you ever since I first set eyes on you. I won't leave, Deebs. I'll always be right by you. You know that." His eyes closed.

"No!"

She thought he had slipped off into a coma again, but then he whispered, "Deebs?"

"I'm here, Tommy. I'm right here, my love."

"I don't want to die in this room. Take me out to the beach where I can see the stars and feel your touch. Wanna be with you and Finny and our child. Take me, please."

"No! You sound like you're giving up. Please don't give up."

With great effort, Tommy turned his head so his red and weary eyes met hers. "I ain't giving up. Let's go to the beach. Moon'll be pretty tonight."

"But . . . but they said you can't be moved."

"Just one more time. Couples class. Just us. Side by side."

When Dale begged the attending nurse, she gave her the sweetest, saddest smile. "Let me help you," she whispered.

Together, they managed to get Tommy into a wheelchair as if they were plopping a fifty-pound bag of oats into the seat instead of her husband. Dale surrounded him with the sheet and spread from his bed and stacked the Mason-jar candle swathed in towels in his lap.

She looked over at the nurse and whispered, "Thank you," as she began to wheel him through Melrose House.

The nurse touched her sleeve. "Ma'am, please let me help you."

But Dale shook her head. "I need to do this alone." She pushed the wheelchair down a ramp and out into the pitch-black night, straining with his weight in the chair, chilled at the sight of his head bobbing to the side. "Tommy! You holding on?"

"Mm-hmm" came the faint reply.

She wondered if he'd die on her right there. They bumped along the pebbled path down to the dunes, where the wheelchair sunk deep in soft sand, and she couldn't budge it. She took the blankets and carefully helped Tommy out of the chair and onto them to lie down.

"I'll be right back. You are not allowed to die on me, Tommy Ridley. Not now!"

"I'm still here, Deebs. See? Told you the moon would be bright."

She waddled to the stable gate and fiddled with the lock, holding a flashlight between her teeth like she'd done all those years ago when she was fourteen, her arm in that heavy plaster cast, Tommy's arms around her as they galloped Beau on the back roads of Buckhead. Then she went further back in her mind to a roaring wind, Mr. Jeffrey's body on the ground, and Mr. Jinx straining against the lead, eyes wild.

She'd done this before.

The welcome scent of fresh shavings and manure collided. Pungent. Alive.

When she came to Infinity's stall, the gelding snorted and leaned over the door, nuzzling deep into her shoulder. "I need your help, ole fella. One last thing for Tommy."

She snapped the lead shank to his halter, grabbed another shank and two thick green horse blankets, laid them across Infinity's withers, and led the gelding through the stable, onto the gravel, and to the sandy trail that led to the beach. There, she snapped a shank to each side of his halter, tied the leather ends together, and sat down behind Tommy, gathering the blanket all around with the shanks around her back. At last, Dale clucked her tongue, coercing Infinity. "Come on. You know what you gotta do, Finny. Come on!"

The gelding turned his head to stare at them, then gave a groan and moved forward, slowly pulling them past the sea grass and thick sand of the dunes until the horse's hooves sank into wet sand and the ocean lapped fifty feet in front of them. The moon was high, the gulls called out, and the tide answered with its slow pull.

"Whoa, boy. This'll do."

She unsnapped the shank, and the gelding turned to look where Tommy lay on the blanket behind him. He pawed the sand, snorting, powerful legs drawing closer, eyes wide as he watched Tommy.

Dale made a pillow of sorts with one blanket to cradle her husband's head and covered him with another. Then she gathered up the tattered towels, retrieved the box of matches she kept inside the candle jar—she'd learned with No Pants to keep them close—and whispered, "I'm doing what you said, Mr. No Pants Jones. Lighting it for hope."

Her gut felt charred and empty, aching so deep inside that no lit candle would do any good. But she lit it just the same. She remembered the look in the dying sailor's eyes, the peace in his eyes when she promised to keep the candle, the way the crusty lips turned up into the faintest smile. She set the candle to the left of Tommy's head, where he could see its low flame.

Then Dale lay down beside him, gently pulling her body close to his, the fire in his skin warming her along with the balmy breeze of the night, their slow breaths matching. A taut smile broke through the pain on Tommy's face as she grasped his hand. He breathed in more deeply, his eyes closed. Slowly, his body relaxed, the strain left his face, and his breathing turned shallow. "Thank you, Deebs," he whispered.

She pushed her bulging stomach into his side. "Can you feel our baby kicking? He's telling you hello. He's telling you he loves you already."

"Mm-hmm. It's good, Deebs. It's real good."

No, it's all wrong! It's not good!

But at least he would die on this beach with his three loves: his wife, his horse, and his unborn child.

Eventually, the fiery gelding sank to his knees and rolled to his side, stretched on the sand just a few yards from where Dale and Tommy lay.

"Thanks," Tommy whispered again.

She reached for his hand and covered it with hers, the horseshoe-nail ring on her finger catching a brief glimmer of the candle's light. "You don't give up, now. You promise me that, my Deebs, my love?"

She swallowed and choked out, "I'll live every day for you, Tommy, and for our child."

He heard her and gave the faintest squeeze, a smile turning the edges of his chapped lips. "Be brave," he whispered. "I'll meet you on the other side."

She woke later, when Infinity moved, Dale's hand still clamped in Tommy's, but the warmth had turned cold. She let forth a blood-curdling scream, yelling, "No!" at the coral-streaked sky.

She placed Tommy's hand on his chest, pulled the blanket over it, and let the tears run wild. The candle still flickered in the jar. She glanced over at it, her eyes blurring. She couldn't reconcile the lurching in her stomach, the dread, the death, with the glimmering in the jar. The candle sparkled and shone, the wax a puddle of liquid now. In the blur, she felt the hope.

She reached for the jar and drew back—the glass was fire-hot from burning so long. She leaned over it and, with one breath, extinguished the flame. "Good-bye, my love," she whispered through tears.

Infinity lifted his head and neck and shifted his weight away from his owner, his rider, his friend. Then he struggled to his feet, head low, and nuzzled Tommy's back. He nuzzled Tommy again and gave a low nicker, shaking his big head from side to side, as if waiting for his master to awaken with the first pale shoots of dawn. The full moon and the rising sun competed for the beach's attention as they set the rippling ocean alight.

Dale needed to find Jacob and the doctor and tell Tommy's parents and the world of his passing. Instead, she sank back down beside him, wincing with sharp pain and cradling her stomach. She couldn't tell if the pain was physical or just the fierce ache of a breaking heart.

She glanced over at the extinguished candle, reached for the jar, now cooled, lifted it, and stared at the way it sparkled under the rising sun.

Minutes or hours later, Dale sat in a trance, clutching Tommy's hand. Infinity stood watch over them, nervous and aware of something gone terribly wrong. Dale picked up the Mason jar that had shimmered with hope, but the wax had congealed again, and the jar looked as lifeless as Tommy.

Her stomach cramped with such vengeance that she dropped the jar in the sand as she sank down again beside Tommy. As she tried to stand, a jagged pain paralyzed her, and she felt another desperate cramping in her stomach. She moaned as warm liquid washed down her legs, then fell to the ground with a shriek, calling out.

Infinity whinnied again, backing away and pawing the sand, throwing his head up and down.

"Get help," she whispered. Then she threw her head back in agony.

"Dale!" She tried to open her eyes, but the heaviness forbade it. "Dale." Someone touched her arm, and she yanked it away. "Dale, it's Jacob. We're taking you to the hospital. You're in labor. Can I call someone to come be with you?"

She stared past Jacob, past the beach to the rising sun. "Tommy. Get Tommy," she whispered.

She vaguely remembered the way the stretcher felt, the men lifting her, her head turning to see Tommy's body covered with a blanket, Infinity standing beside him. She tried to call out, but instead of words, only shrieks and moans came, and then a mask came across her face, and she floated on the water, the ferry, with horses and guardsmen and Essie and Tommy. She lifted and danced and leaned forward over the jump and crashed. She jerked awake, then floated again, side by side with Tommy.

Dale woke to the sterile white of a hospital room, a needle in her arm.

"Tommy," she moaned and tried to sit up. She remembered the beach, the candle, the pain, the bloody liquid . . .

A contraction tightened her stomach until she thought it might burst. She screamed again. Then a rag came over her mouth. "Breathe in again, honey. It's chloroform. That's right, breathe. Your baby is about to be born."

"Too early . . . baby's too early. I need Tommy," she moaned.

From somewhere across the room, she could make out the figure of her mother. "Mama!" she cried. "Help me, Mama." Or perhaps it was just a figment of her imagination. "Baby," she rasped.

"Push now, honey. Push!"

Dale clasped the bedrails and felt the lightness in her head, the way the pain lessened, then the sensation of pushing. Her body shook and trembled, and from somewhere in the fog, she heard the wail of a newborn and "A tiny baby boy . . ." and she was gone again.

"Dale . . . Dale." Her mother was leaning over her bed.

"Mama," she whispered, eyes closed. When she finally managed to open them, her mother patted her hand and said, "Oh, thank goodness! We were so worried." She glanced at the nurse and asked, "Could I please have a few minutes alone with my daughter?"

"Of course."

As soon as the nurse stepped out of the room, Mama's face fell. "Oh, Barbara Dale! How could you? I told you Tommy Ridley would be a bad influence. That he wouldn't survive. But I never imagined this." She was mashing her lips together, and her eyes overflowed with tears.

"We married, Mama," she murmured. "Tommy and I got married."

"Dale, I know you're grieving, but don't lie to me."

"Our baby. Mama, please let me see our baby."

Now her mother's face contorted, as if she were fighting back not only tears but also anger or pain or maybe even desperation. Finally, she whispered, "The baby . . ." She swallowed hard. "Your baby—oh, Dale! He was born too soon." She reached out and grabbed Dale's hand. "Your baby didn't survive."

Dale felt the room spinning, flung off her mother's hand, and reached toward the sky, grasping at air as a guttural cry escaped from somewhere dark and forbidden. "Nooo!"

She must have lost consciousness again for a moment. When she forced her eyes open once more, Dale struggled to pronounce any words; her mouth felt thick, as if stuffed with cotton. Her mother still sat by her bed, head in her hands.

"Mama?" she tried again, the words raspy. "Mama, we married. Tommy and I got married. I have to go to the funeral, Mama. Tommy was my husband."

Slowly, her mother shook her head and whispered, "How could you do this to me? To your father! He'll never know. And neither will the Ridleys. Their grief is enough without this! And you won't be able to be present at the funeral. Not like this."

Dale clutched her stomach, felt her full breasts, and grimaced. "Mama, we were married in January. It was legal." Her mother had turned away, arms crossed tight across her chest. "The commander and chaplain and other men came to the wedding on Hilton Head. Ask any of them. Let me call Leonard. He'll bring the certificate. You'll see when you gather Tommy's things." Dale tried to swallow, tried to sit up, but she had no energy. "The Ridleys have to know. This baby was your grandchild, Mama. Tommy's legacy. I'll tell them! I will!"

Eleanor Butler turned to face Dale. "No one will know about this. You'll thank me later. If word got out, you'd be regarded as damaged goods. No eligible young man would want you. I won't let anyone know what you've done."

"Daddy? I want to talk to Daddy," she called from far away, the fog so heavy, her arms so heavy. "Daddy . . . please?"

"Your father is in Detroit with those godforsaken crates. They're all he can think about. Please, Dale. I know you can't understand right now, but later, you will. Not saying anything to anyone is what's best for you."

Dale struggled to sit up, then realized she was strapped into the bed. "Let me up! Let me see my baby!" She began to shriek again. "I want to see my son. I want to hold him! Please, just for a moment."

In a fog, she heard her mother's voice, "Oh, Dale. It's too awful. . . . I'm so sorry that the baby didn't make it."

Dale watched her mother's bright pink lips move, but the sounds they made were horrifying, impossible. She reached toward her mother again. "Please." But her mother had already turned her back and walked out of the room.

27

Allie

Wednesday, March 11

We didn't leave Hickory Hills that night, nor did we sleep. All weariness evaporated with the realization that Nana Dale had been pregnant. Mom and I searched through the rest of the pages in the leather scrapbook, looking for a birth certificate or photos of a baby. But we found none.

Instead, we found the marriage certificate for Tommy and Dale.

Original Certificate of Marriage

I, Reverend Glenn Edwards, Chaplain of the 93rd Division of the Marines on Hilton Head Island, hereby certify that on the 14th day of January, nineteen hundred forty-three, at Camp McDougal,
Thomas Alan Ridley Jr. and Barbara Dale Butler were by me united in marriage, in accordance with the license issued by the Clerk of Beaufort County, Hilton Head Island, South Carolina, United States of America.

And we found Tommy's obituary:

Thomas Alan Ridley Jr., 20, of Atlanta, Georgia, passed away on September 14, 1943, on Daufuskie Island, South Carolina, after a bout with malaria. He was born March 16, 1923, the only child of Thomas Alan Ridley Sr. and Ada Ann Jenkins Ridley. Tommy was serving in the US Coast Guard Mounted Beach Patrol when he contracted malaria after saving one of his fellow coast guardsmen who had fallen ill.

A champion equestrian, Tommy won the coveted Maclay Trophy at Madison Square Garden in 1940. It was his aim to serve his country first in the cavalry and then in the Olympics, but he contracted polio. Ever the fighter, he learned to ride again and eventually enlisted in the mounted patrol, surveying the beaches of the Atlantic on his prize gelding, Infinity. Tommy was known for his daring, bravery, and kindness and will be deeply missed by many. He is survived by his parents and uncles and aunts and cousins . . .

I read it over and over, as if on some reading, the phrase *Tommy is survived by the love of his life, his newlywed wife, Barbara Dale Butler Ridley, and his infant child* would magically appear.

But it didn't.

"Did her parents and Tommy's parents never know? Did Nana Dale and Tommy really keep the secret from everyone?"

My mother studied the obituary for even longer than I did. But she remained silent.

"How awful that Nana Dale wasn't acknowledged," I moaned. "Why? They loved each other! Surely my great-grandmother wouldn't punish Dale for marrying him and force her to keep it a secret!"

My mother gave a tiny shrug and wiped her manicured nail under her eyes. She looked shattered.

I grasped her hand and whispered, "I just remembered something else about the charm bracelet." I opened the small wooden chest that had housed the leather scrapbook and brought out Nana Dale's bracelet. One by one, I fingered each charm. When I came to the unnamed sterling silver silhouette charm of a boy, I realized that, though there was no name across the front, there was a date engraved on the other side: *September 14, 1943.*

I could not stop the tears. I cradled the charm bracelet in my hands, almost like a cherished infant, held it out to my mother, and whispered through a catch in my throat, "Nana Dale was pregnant, and their baby boy was born the same day that Tommy died. How unimaginably wonderful and awful and everything in between."

A sob escaped from Mom's lips as she took the bracelet and found the charm.

"Do you think the baby died too, Mom? If Nana Dale got pregnant after they married, well, she wouldn't have been more than eight months along. Did preemie babies survive back then? And there's no birth certificate."

My mother kept clearing her throat. "I had a sibling. A brother." Then she stared at me, glassy-eyed. "Could the baby have survived, Allie? But then, where is the birth certificate?" she asked as if she had not heard me pose the same questions.

She leaned back on the couch where we'd moved, closed her eyes, and put the palm of her hand across her forehead, all familiar signs that a migraine was coming on. "My poor mother. She lived with so much grief and so many secrets."

Eventually, she said, "So many other things make sense now, Allie. I can't explain it well, but there was always a part of me that felt my mother was looking at me and seeing someone else. Almost missing someone else. And I grew up believing she wanted me to *be* someone else."

That admission or confession from my mother almost felt too personal and intimate for me to hear. So we held it there, for a small slice of time, in silence.

Finally, I asked, "Was Poppa Dan kind to her? Did they have a happy marriage, Mom?"

She must have heard the note of desperation in my voice and hesitated, deep in thought. "I'd call it more like a working partnership. They let each other live their own lives. I get the feeling that

Nana Dale pretty much laid down the law. She would be an appropriately lovely society wife if and when it fit into her riding and showing schedule. By the time my parents married in 1950, Nana Dale was quite the accomplished equestrian, as you've realized."

Mom stared again out the den window toward the barn. The moon was lighting the backyard, and a few limbs of an immensely tall hickory brushed the panes.

"They cared for each other, Allie. And perhaps my father knew the secret. I understood my mother's fierce drive. It scared me. It angered me too. But Daddy looked on her with compassion. I believe he must have known about her suffering. This big ole house was not a bad place to grow up."

On the last pages of *DB's Diary* were photos of Nana Dale in her welding work clothes, of Tommy posed beside a group of men, all different ages, dressed in coast guard uniforms, all of them astride their horses. Someone—not Nana Dale—had written on the white frame of the photograph—*Hilton Head Island, 1943, The Sand Pounders.*

And there was a photograph of Dale with Husy, both tiny—Dale because of her height, and Husy, thin, ancient, and bent over, both women smiling and holding the halters of two beautiful horses—one dappled and one flea-bitten. The date on the photo was June 1944, and Nana Dale had written *celebrating D-day with Husy, Essie, and Finny.*

I removed the photo from the binder and held it to my chest.

In a thick back pocket of the leather scrapbook were dozens of letters, tied together with string. Nana Dale had attached a sticker to the string, on which she'd written *Tommy and Deebs.* Their love letters. Beside those bound letters were three familiar pale blue envelopes addressed to me. When I reached for them, Mom shook her head.

"I think you should read those in private, sweetie. They're just for you."

I nibbled my lip, eyes filling once again with tears. "You're right. Tomorrow."

Sometime in the middle of the night, we both fell asleep, me in the canopied bed in the Pink Room and Mom across the hall in the Yellow Room with its daffodil walls and the bed from her childhood.

Mom poked her head in the Pink Room sometime before dawn. "Sweetie, I need to get home. Will you be okay?"

I squinted, trying to pry my eyes open. I found them caked with sleep, and my face stiff from where my tears had dried. "Yeah. Thanks for being with me."

I stifled a yawn, and Mom came over and kissed me on the forehead. "You sleep a little longer. We'll talk later today. Call me after work."

I must have fallen back to sleep because I was awakened by the sound of hickory nuts hitting the roof. It took me a few moments to realize that the nuts were actually hitting the windowpane— one, two, three, four, five. I slipped out of the bed and crossed the spacious room to where the picture window gave a broad view of the backyard and the paddocks and the barn.

Ping!

I jerked back, heart racing, then pressed my face against the windowpane and looked down. Austin was standing by an Adirondack chair, his arm tilted back, aiming another hickory nut my way.

I threw open the window, leaned out, and called down, "What are you doing here?"

He was grinning up at me. "Trying to get into this house. To see you!"

I blinked several times, my heart pounding, and then managed, "The key's under the blue-and-white cachepot by that chair."

I ran to the bathroom, frantically searching for toothpaste, found a half-used tube under the sink, and finger brushed my teeth, and then ran both hands through my very big hair. I was still wearing the clothes I'd found at my parents' house—a red-and-black V-neck UGA T-shirt and baggy black sweatpants.

I was standing in a befuddled daze when Austin walked into the room dressed in jeans and a lumberjack flannel shirt and gathered me in his arms. He kissed my hair and whispered, "Allie." Then he held me at arm's length, his eyes filled with kindness that swam in the deep blue. I melted into his chest.

It felt so right, so familiar, in the midst of all that was so wrong.

I held on to him, not daring to meet his eyes, only snuggling into the comfort of his shoulder. I kept repeating, "Will you forgive me? Please? I've been so wrong about everything, and I don't know what to do. I can't imagine living without you, but I can't imagine you'd ever want me back."

His hand came around my head, stroking my hair. Then his fingers, rough and calloused from work, were wiping my tears. He sat me on the bed and lay down beside me. He pulled me back into him, spooning, his plaid-covered arms tight around my sweatshirt. I grabbed onto his sleeves, then let my hands drift down to cover his. After a few moments, I realized that the sobbing I heard was not only mine but also his.

"Allie," he whispered, his breath so close I felt it in my ear, "I've prayed for this day for the past month." He squeezed my hand tightly in his. "I'm sorry for everything that has caused you such grief, but I'm thankful I can be here with you now. And yes, I forgive you. I truly do."

I rolled over so that my forehead was touching his, my arms now around his neck. From somewhere deep down, I felt a belly laugh simmer, and then it erupted in a high-pitched giggle, and then Austin was laughing too, pulling me into his arms and pressing his lips to mine for the longest time.

We lay on the canopied bed in the Pink Room, laughing and kissing and holding on to each other, the two of us lost in a world of our own. At last, Austin pulled away. "I brought us some coffee and croissants from Henri's," he whispered. Austin and I used to grab coffee and croissants at Henri's on our lunch breaks.

He sat up, held out his hand to me, and I took it. Wrapped in an embrace, we stumbled down the stairs to the kitchen. Sitting across from each other at Nana Dale's kitchen table that was piled with boxes, we munched on the buttery delicacies and took sips of coffee from the to-go cups.

My stomach twittered and jumped and clutched.

"I want to be with you forever," I whispered.

Austin met my eyes with his blue ones. He stood up, leaned across the table, and kissed my nose. "Deal." He gave his boyish grin. "So what did I miss?" he said in his best Thomas Jefferson imitation from the musical *Hamilton*.

I laughed again. "A lot. I hardly know where to begin." I glanced at my phone. "I have exactly three hours before my first student."

"I want to hear everything. In whatever order you prefer. And take your time. I don't have to hear it all right now." He gave a wink. "At least we've gotten the most important part figured out."

So I told him, both of us cradling our coffee cups as I led him through the house, narrating the story, first in the Pink Room with the painted plaque of a dappled filly and the photos of Nana Dale and Tommy riding in the couples class, then in the Ribbon Room, where I pointed out all the ribbons hanging from old horseshoes, and then into the dining room, where Tommy's silver Maclay Trophy sat on the hutch. Later, we wandered into the den, where the leather binder lay open on the couch just as Mom and I had left it in the middle of the night, the Mason-jar candle and Nana Dale's sealed envelopes beside it.

As Mom had done, Austin read every article in the scrapbook, commenting on Nana Dale's handwritten notes. "What a woman! I don't think I would have wanted to cross her when she was young." Then he cocked his head and said, "Now that I think about it, she wasn't very demure at ninety." He chuckled and said, "Remember how she questioned me about my intentions with you the first time I met her?"

"Yep. She remained feisty up until the very end."

Then I handed him the photocopied sheets that Dr. Cressman had given us, and Austin leafed through the pages, squinting at the poorly copied photos.

When I told him about Tommy proposing to Dale and them getting married the next day, he laughed. "That. Is. Perfect."

"Evidently they sat on their mounts—Infinity and Essie—while the coast guard commander, the chaplain, and a handful of other men and dogs looked on."

Of course we ran out of time, but I didn't want to leave him. "There's still so much else to tell you. You haven't even seen the dinosaur bones."

He lifted an eyebrow that hid under his white-blond hair. "True, but I've read all about them in the *AJC*."

I stuck out my tongue.

"What is your day like?"

"I'll be at Chastain until five. What about you?"

"I've got two surgeries—a horse and a calf—but I can meet you back here by six." He grinned again, towering over me, the dimple in his chin and cheek so pronounced. "And don't you dare open those letters from Nana Dale without me, understand?"

"Promise."

The whole day, I whispered and giggled my thanks to God. I grabbed Tricia after our first class and blubbered the story through tears and laughter, and she stared at me, eyes round as saucers. "Wow. Just wow."

I called Mom on the way from Chastain to Hickory Hills, and she actually gave a little shriek of joy when I told her about Austin. Then I think she started crying because she said, "Wonderful, honey. Go be with him," and clicked off her phone.

When Austin's Triple T arrived at Hickory Hills, I grabbed him as soon as his boot-clad feet touched the ground, and he picked me up in his arms, swung me around, and planted a long kiss on my lips.

Then, arms around each other, we went into the house.

Once again in the den, my hand clasped to his arm, he opened the envelope to Nana Dale's first letter and handed it to me, saying nothing as I read it.

The date on it was January 10, 2015.

Dear Allie,

I'm ninety today, and surely I won't be staying on this side of eternity for much longer. And now you know my story, or more precisely, Tommy's and my story. And yes, for a few short months, I was his wife. I know it seems tragic, but the following article explains a really good part, the happy part in the midst of all the sad parts. Before you read the newspaper article here, I need you to get Tommy's Maclay Trophy from the bottom left corner of the hutch and look inside it, where I've hidden a Mason jar. Then read on to understand what it has to do with my story. Enjoy!

I wiped away a few tears before passing the monogrammed cornflower blue stationery to Austin.

"I need you to read it with me, okay?"

So we did, huddled together on the couch with the Mason-jar candle sitting on the coffee table.

You see, Allie, old No Pants Jones left me more than a candle, although I am not sure he knew it at the time.

A newspaper article dated November 22, 2015, was folded in with the stationery, and when I unfolded it, I felt tingles as I read.

Paris Diamond Merchant's Incredible Plan

Rachel Kahn, granddaughter of the late jeweler, Jean-Frédéric Kahn, told the remarkable story of how her grandfather saved his entire family during WWII. With the help of a merchant mariner, the Jewish jeweler smuggled his family out of France on a Liberty ship. When they arrived on the shores of New York, Mr. Kahn handed the mariner a jar filled with candle wax as payment.

Ms. Kahn reported from her Paris apartment last week that "somewhere, an unnamed hero received this jar, but unfortunately, we fear that his ship was torpedoed before he was able to do what my grandfather instructed: to light the candle when in desperate need. If he had only done this, he would have become a very rich man."

Prior to the war, Jean-Frédéric Kahn lived in Paris and was a prominent diamond merchant. Desperate to get his family out of France before the Nazis deported them, he came up with an ingenious plan. Though they had to leave most of their treasures behind, he melted wax into two glass Mason jars and added hundreds of extremely valuable diamonds to each one. When the wax solidified, the diamonds were hidden.

He kept one of the jars for his family and gave the other to the merchant mariner.

Though Ms. Kahn doesn't know the exact worth of the missing Mason jar, she did reveal that "If it held even half as many diamonds as the one my grandfather kept, that jar would have been worth millions."

This is one of many stories that continue to be uncovered showing the courage and ingenuity of those escaping Hitler's horrors.

I was putting two and two together: an article about a young woman saving a merchant mariner, a photo of a young woman holding a jar . . . and an article about a Jewish diamond merchant and a Mason jar filled with treasure given to an American sailor, a ship that was torpedoed, and a sailor who supposedly died at sea.

At the bottom of the article, Nana Dale had written *As Tommy was dying, I lit that candle for hope, just like No Pants Jones told me to do.*

I opened the third envelope, dated January 10, 2019. Amazingly, despite my grandmother's advanced age, her handwriting was still legible.

My dear Allie,

Well, I'm still alive at ninety-four. Lord have mercy! Who would have thought?

I hope you've enjoyed your history lesson! And isn't this chest lovely? Your great-grandfather Jeremiah made it, and Mr. Jeff Jeffrey made the leather cover for me. But no one who is still alive has ever seen either of these: not your mother or father, not Wick, not dear Barnell, although he knows bits and pieces of my story.

By now, you've most likely read through all the newspaper clippings in the binder. Did you get to visit the World War II Home Front Museum and the lighthouse? Did you meet Mr. Hampton? He's one of only a handful of people who witnessed Tommy's and my wedding, so I hope he's still alive and can tell you about it. Yes, Tommy and I got married on Hilton Head Island in January 1943, while we were in the US Coast Guard Mounted Beach Patrol, the Sand Pounders.

Only eight months later, Tommy contracted malaria and died. After all he'd been through, why did malaria have to kill him, a young man so full of life and determination? And that very same day, I gave birth to our sweet baby son, Thomas Alan Ridley III.

He didn't survive either.

I couldn't tell you. I couldn't tell your mother either. For the longest time, I couldn't tell anyone. My mother knew, but she did not believe I had married. She thought our son was illegitimate. As you can imagine, her accusation broke my heart once again.

But my dear Husy believed me and walked with me through those tragic days and months and years. She and the Lord Almighty were enough for me. In the end, I kept the secret because I decided it would have been more hurtful to a whole lot of people if I revealed it. I hated my mother for a long time after that, but I didn't hate her quite enough to tell my father and the Ridleys and the rest of the world that she was wrong, that Tommy and I were married and that we had a son together. She would never have recovered from the way that shocking news would have damaged her reputation.

In truth, I never truly recovered from losing Tommy and our son.

But healing isn't the same as recovery, is it, dear? Healing slides way down in your heart and settles there. The longing, the anguish, the crying out still come to me even to this day almost eighty years later. But I no longer ask why; I no longer shake my fist at God.

Husy told me after I lost Tommy and the baby, "Honey, you may never get the answer on this side of life to the why, so it's much better to ask the question 'Now that I'm in this place, Lord, what in the world do You want me to do?'"

So I did.

Oh, it was brutal. But after a time, with Husy by my side, I asked.

And what the Almighty wanted me to do was to keep on living and aiming for my dreams and Tommy's. So we did, Essie and I. We soared, Allie. To the Olympics, twice, to Madison Square Garden again and again, and to the delight of a gallop along the trails of Nancy Creek. Essie and I lived out Tommy's dream. I filled up that stable again with horses and the house with love. It took a while, but love came in a different way with Poppa Dan and your mother. And I consecrated my life to teaching children to ride—all kinds of kids—seeking to instill hope through horses. A precursor to your own healing-horse hotel.

And you know the rest of my story, dear, because you've been here to witness these last thirty years. Your dreams are beautiful. You've worked so hard to make them come true. And now you have the house and the property and the diamonds. They are for you. You alone, dear Allie.

"I found the candle, Nana Dale! But there were no diamonds!" I shouted with Austin hovering over my shoulder, reading the letter with me.

I picked up the Mason jar and plunged my hand inside. The bare remnants of an off-white candle were congealed in the bottom with the burnt-out wick barely protruding. I scraped at the leftover wax and immediately felt the bottom of the glass jar.

"Let's at least light it," I said to Austin.

He shrugged as I hurried into the kitchen to find a box of matches, calling after me, "Allie, there is nothing in this jar except a little dried wax."

I knew he was right, but I lit the wick anyway. It flickered for a few seconds and then extinguished. There truly was nothing else in the jar. I clutched my stomach, feeling a deep ache at all of Nana Dale's losses. And now mine. There were no diamonds.

Quietly, I finished reading her letter.

And with your healing-horse hotel, you are continuing to redeem Tommy's and my story—our lovely, terrible, tragic, and beautiful story.

Always use the gifts you've been given for good, my dear Allie. With these diamonds, do only good. You already have all you need, but these will help keep the healing-horse hotel running for a very long time. When I was a teen, Husy once reprimanded me with wisdom I have never forgotten. I was obsessed with having "enough," and she said that I would never have enough until I decided I already had enough, until I lived with a grateful heart.

Hasn't always been easy, Allie, and I've had to come back to that in the hardest times. You'll have hard times too. So let all you've known and done and what you have right now be enough.

As you read this, I imagine Austin by your side, and you as Allie Massey Andrews. You've married the love of your life. I am so thankful to have known him. Together, you and Austin will indeed accomplish many things to make your patch of the world a better place.

And, Allie, in all the hard things in my life, I have had so much good. You are my good, dear child.

I love you, Allie,
Nana Dale

I stood up to clear my head, my eyes filling with tears, my heart filled with love. Of all of Nana Dale's stories, this was the most farfetched of all. She had willed me a jar filled with diamonds so that I could continue the legacy of Tommy, the legacy of equine therapy, the legacy of healing. But I'd found the jar, and there was nothing in it but a dried bit of wax. What had she done with the jewels?

I melted into Austin's arms, melted like the candle, imagining Nana Dale watch the wick reveal its treasure even as she saw Tommy dying, his lashes so still on his pale face.

"What a story!" Austin said, his arms wrapped around mine.

"But it's not over. Where in the world are the diamonds? She acts as if they're still in the Mason jar."

He held me tight. "We can keep looking, Allie, but I wonder. If she didn't tell you where, maybe it's because she doesn't know."

"You mean you don't believe her story?"

"No, I believe she found them, and I believe they were in that Mason jar at one time. But they're not there now. I'm afraid she may have done something with them a long time ago and forgot."

I let out a long sigh. "It's time to stop searching, Austin, isn't it?"

"I think so."

"Husy was right, wasn't she? I already have enough. I have much more than enough." I traced my finger along his jaw, feeling the scruff of his two-day-old beard, then planted a long kiss on his lips. "I have *us*. And I am so, so grateful."

We stood and walked down the stairs to the basement and out the French doors, strolling arm in arm to the barn. He cocked his head and said, "Have you heard that there's a nasty virus going around? I'm afraid things are going to get bad."

I stopped and looked up at him. "What a weird thing to say, Austin! Are you talking about that corona thing?"

"Yeah, the coronavirus. COVID-19. I've been following it. It's scary, Allie."

I'd barely paid attention to the news reports, but I'd heard them. "How bad?"

"Let's just say I've been praying for weeks that you'd come back to me before the whole world shuts down."

"What are you talking about?"

"Italy just went into lockdown on March 9."

"Wick mentioned something about that possibility last week." I really didn't want to talk about Italy or a virus.

"I think it's going to happen all over the world—the quarantine. We'll be confined to our homes."

"That's nuts!" I stopped by the front gate to the barn and placed my hands on my hips. "And what in the world does that virus have to do with us, Austin?"

Surprisingly, he grinned. "Actually, quite a lot. What are you doing tomorrow?"

I shrugged. "Being with you as much as possible. Only that."

"Sounds good. And we may never find Nana Dale's diamonds, Allie, but I have a perfectly nice one that's been waiting to go back on your finger for a while now, and I think Tommy had a great idea."

He dropped to one knee right in front of the cedar plaque for *Hickory Hills Horse Therapy* and held out the diamond ring I had given back to him a month ago. "Wanna get married this weekend?"

I choked out a sob, then covered my mouth with my hands, shaking my head. "I don't understand. You're talking about a virus and a wedding and . . ."

"Shh, I just need a simple answer, Allie."

I fell to my knees one more time and embraced him. "Yes. Yes, I do. More than anything else, I do!"

28

Dale

Late September 1943

The next time Dale awoke, she saw the humped form of her nurse-maid in the chair. "Husy," she managed through the fog and heaviness. "Help me, Husy."

The expression on Husy's face as she leaned over the bed held layers of grief, her old gray eyes rimmed in red. Her veiny hand reached for Dale's, and she tried to speak but only a sob erupted.

"Where's my baby?"

"Shh . . . shh, my Dale. You've been through a lot. A whole lot. You rest."

"But my baby? Where is he? I heard him cry." She gave a weak smile. "A little boy, Husy. Tommy's little boy."

Husy just nodded.

"Tommy?" she whispered. "We married, Husy." Then she remembered. "I have to go to his funeral."

She watched Husy's throat move up and down, her pale lips part as she struggled to speak. Then she slowly shook her head.

"Please. He was my husband. My love."

350

At last, Husy managed to whisper, "The funeral's already been, my dear Dale. They already buried your Tommy."

"No! Why?"

"You've been awful weak, sugar. You started hemorrhaging after the baby was born. You've been in the hospital for five days. The nurses had to keep you sedated for your body to start healing."

Dale reached for Husy's hand, but the movement took too much effort, and her hand fell to the side of the hospital bed.

"Tommy's parents wanted the funeral to be small and private. But they know how much you loved him."

"Do they know that we married? Do they know about our child?"

"Shh, Barbara Dale. They know you were very sick. They understood you couldn't be at Tommy's funeral." Husy stood over her, bent down, and kissed her forehead. "You rest, now, Miss Dale."

But Dale sobbed in Husy's arms. "We married, Husy! We were going to tell our parents on our leave . . . about the wedding, about the baby. And I told Mama when she came to the hospital. But she wouldn't believe me. Husy, I have to tell Tommy's parents the truth! I have to tell them about Tommy and our baby! Where is our baby?"

Husy wept beside her. "Oh, sweetie."

"Why won't they let me see my baby? I have to see him!"

Husy held her fiercely, crying with her. "Shh, now, Dale. Shh." As Husy stroked her hair, Dale could feel her nursemaid's hot tears on her shoulder.

Even before Husy spoke, Dale remembered her mother's words, as if in a deep, deep fog. *"Oh, Dale. He was born too soon. Your baby didn't survive."*

"The baby didn't survive, Dale. A tiny little boy. He didn't survive."

The wail rose up from a part of Dale she didn't know existed. It ripped through the fabric of her soul, and once again, Dale felt herself drifting far out at sea, torpedoes exploding and fire leaping all around her.

—⚞—

When Dale was discharged from the hospital, she moved back to Hickory Hills, weak and despondent. She didn't venture out of the house. She ate nothing. She lay in bed, her breasts aching, her stomach barely showing that it had once sheltered a little life. The depression hung so thick that she wanted to die.

"I don't see how you kept on living, Husy, after what happened to your sister and then to Marjorie."

"Gotta keep on living, Miss Dale. Ain't got no choice. Even when your heart is broken."

"I know, but you kept on living without seeming bitter."

"Bitterness'll rot out your soul, Miss Dale. You know we've talked about that many times. Barbara Dale, you may never get the answer on this side of life to the why, so it's much better to ask the question 'Now that I'm in this place, Lord, what do You want me to do?'"

What do You want me to do?

"Faith doesn't keep bad things from happening, does it, Husy?"

"No, ma'am, it certainly don't."

"Seems like faith doesn't work for me. Seems awfully random. I find my filly that I prayed about for years, but then the boy I love more than life itself dies. I barely had time to pray for him to live once he got sick." She gave a low moan. "And our baby . . ."

Husy's arms came tightly around Dale. "Shh, my girl. Shh." Finally, "Life ain't fair. It's brutal, sometimes, Miss Dale. And faith don't stop the horrible things. But faith helps you walk through those things, whipped and angry and screaming on the inside. Lord don't mind our screaming and raging. He's done shown us how to do it in those psalms of His that King David wrote."

"I feel like I want to give up, Husy."

"Can't give up, Miss Dale. That ain't like you. You're a fighter."

"I'm tired of fighting."

"I know you are. You just rest a spell. The fight'll come back eventually. And the surprising thing is that the Good Lord will fill up all that emptiness with good things. Won't take the pain away, but there's still good in life." When Dale didn't answer, Husy pulled her close.

"Never had a husband and never had children of my own, but the Good Lord, He gave me you, Barbara Dale. You're my good, Barbara Dale. He knew He'd keep me plenty busy with you. Can't be bitter about that."

— ♘ —

Two weeks after Tommy's death and the baby's birth, Husy called to Dale, "You've got visitors."

"I don't want to see anyone."

"I know it, but I think you'll want to see this."

Dale descended the stairs from the Pink Room to the main floor, where Husy met her, brushed her feeble hand across Dale's matted hair, and led her down the next flight of stairs and out the back door to where Commander McTeer and two members of the mounted patrol, Jacob from Daufuskie and Leonard from Jekyll, stood on the gravel clearing at the bottom of the driveway. Beside them was an army jeep attached to a horse trailer.

"Mrs. Ridley," they said solemnly and saluted.

Commander McTeer cleared his throat and turned his eyes down. "We are so sorry for your losses. Of Tommy. And your child." He wiped his hand across his face. Then he opened the trailer door and backed out Essie. "The men decided you might need this fine little filly to help you along in the grief." He cleared his throat again.

Dale walked forward, legs trembling. When Essie saw her, she began whinnying, ears pricked forward, rearing and pawing the ground, then running her head up and down Dale's shirt.

With tears cascading down her face, Dale rubbed between Essie's ears.

"We thought we'd best bring her companion too. Thought Tommy would have wanted his wife to look after his horse."

Commander McTeer turned and backed Infinity out of the trailer.

Dale could barely choke out "Thank you."

Jacob came over, blushing as he said, "We've given Tommy's personal affairs to his parents—since you wanted to keep the marriage a secret. But we thought you'd want this."

He handed Dale the marriage certificate and a stack of letters she'd written to Tommy.

Then Leonard gave Dale her small suitcase and all the letters Tommy had written to her. "And I saved one of them newspaper articles about you saving the sailor . . . and also Tommy's obituary."

Dale sniffed and nodded, leaning against Essie.

"You can be mighty proud of your husband, Mrs. Ridley," Commander McTeer said. "He served his country bravely, as did you. And your finding your filly was the highlight of these dark years for six hundred men." He gave a smile and added, "And your marriage was the highlight for those of us who were privileged to witness it."

She remained silent.

"And Mrs. Hughes relayed your request when we arrived. The wedding will remain confidential. The baby too. You have our word. None of us will ever speak of it."

She could see the doubt on their faces, their desire to protect her by proclaiming the truth, and yet their solidarity.

Leonard presented her with one more letter. "This came a few days after . . . after you left Jekyll."

Dale wobbled as she took the envelope addressed to her in Tommy's broken penmanship. She tried to swallow but couldn't. Leonard patted her hand. "It's okay, Dale. Oh, and lemme fetch one other thing." He went to the jeep and came back. "I think this is yours too. We found it out in the sand. With Tommy."

She took the Mason-jar candle and nodded. Finally, she found her voice and whispered, "I'll never forget your kindness. Never. Thank you, Commander McTeer. Thank you, Jacob and Leonard. Please convey my thanks to the others on Daufuskie and Jekyll."

As the men drove the jeep up the embankment, pulling the trailer behind, Husy took hold of Infinity's halter with one hand

and looped her other arm through Dale's. Slowly, slowly they led the two horses to the barn.

Late that night while sitting on her bed, Dale opened Tommy's last letter. She hardly recognized his handwriting, scribbled and uneven.

Hey, Wife, pretty bad off. Sorry. You take good care of our baby. You will be the best mother ever. Love you always, always, Deebs. No matter what, I'll meet you on the other side. T

She clutched her throat, hands shaking, and set the letter beside the others that Jacob and Leonard had brought her. Then she set the Mason-jar candle on the shelf in between photos of Tommy and her in the couples class and the filly plaque.

She kept all the letters between Tommy and herself hidden in her room, along with the marriage certificate and her horseshoe-nail ring, all the while planning the things she would say to her mother when she confronted her with the certificate.

But in the end, she held on to Husy and said nothing. The truth of her marriage and her son's birth were too glorious and pure to be tarnished by her mother's cruel, misdirected idea of protection.

Although her parents stayed at St. Simons with the Ridleys, continuing their jobs, her father made frequent trips back to Atlanta, where he would walk with Dale to the barn, feeding carrots to Essie and Infinity, and honoring his daughter's silence. At night, while Husy stitched on a quilt, her father carved delicate hearts and horseshoes into the cover of a small cherrywood chest. And Dale watched without uttering a word.

At the end of autumn, her father gave her the small chest. "I know you've had your heart broken again and again, my Dale. But you're my girl, you're my treasure, and you can call me any time, and I'll come." Then he tilted his head, his auburn hair now streaked with gray. "And you're going to survive, Dale. You're going to do more than survive. I knew it the first time you stood up for Husy and pulled Jeff Jeffrey to safety." He kissed her forehead.

"Thank you, Daddy," she whispered, her first words in weeks, and wrapped her arms around his waist.

Later that same week, Husy climbed the stairs to Dale's bedroom, carrying the handmade quilt, which she laid across Dale's bed. Dale followed Husy in the room and leaned over the bed.

"It's lovely, Husy," she whispered.

Husy nodded. "Wanted you to have it, Dale. It's called a wedding-ring quilt."

Dale fingered the colorful intersecting rings, and as she inspected it more closely, she realized Husy had used the material from some of her old dresses and riding coats to form the rings.

She grabbed Husy, and the old woman stroked her hair and whispered, "You and Tommy had something special and blessed. Don't you ever forget it."

Dale's mother didn't visit her, but one evening, Husy answered the door to find Mrs. Ridley standing outside. She came into the den holding the beautiful silver urn that Tommy had won as the 1940 Maclay champion.

Mrs. Ridley set it down on the coffee table and said, "I know Tommy would have wanted you to have it, Dale."

She placed a gloved hand on Dale's. Mrs. Ridley looked gaunt and ravaged, and her lips trembled. "Thank you for being such a good friend to our son. I hope you know how much he cared for you." She pressed her lips together, and her gloved hand tightened around Dale's wrist.

Dale managed a nod and whispered, "Thank you." Then she set down the trophy, threw her arms around Tommy's mother, and sobbed.

Somewhere across the span of numbness and grief, the voices of truth whispered through Dale's heart and soul.

"Now that I'm in this place, Lord, what in the world do You want me to do?"

"Bitterness'll rot your soul."

"It will never be enough, Dale, until you decide that you already

have it all. You settle in your mind a grateful heart, a content spirit, and everything else will be gravy, girl."

"You don't give up, now. You promise me that, my Deebs, my love."

"I'll meet you on the other side."

And Dale made the decision. She wouldn't show her mother the marriage certificate, and she wouldn't tell her father or the Ridleys or anyone else about her marriage or her child. Only Husy, the one who spoke truth, would know the whole truth. Dale would carry that secret, too intimate and heartbreaking, with her. She would save every last memory of Tommy and hide it away from the world in the miniature keepsake chest that her father had carved for her.

February 1964

Dale shivered with cold as she watched life ebb slowly from Essie. Thirty-three years for a horse was equivalent to ninety-nine in human terms, but she wasn't ready. The dread in the pit of her stomach felt almost as heavy as when she'd lain beside Tommy on the beach twenty years earlier.

In the black of night, hope felt so far away.

"Light the candle when you're in need of hope." The old sailor's words nudged Dale. For over two decades, the Mason-jar candle had sat on a shelf in her childhood bedroom beside the little plaque and the photos of Tommy and Dale in the couples class.

Her husband, Daniel, was good in that way. After ten years of marriage, she had finally decided to tell him the secret of Tommy and her spur-of-the-moment wedding and of their infant son who died. Somehow, it had restored hope in their marriage and given Daniel permission to share his own secrets.

And there had been healing.

She knew that Daniel was lying in their bed, unable to sleep, praying for his wife and her mare. "You need this time alone with Essie," he had said earlier in the evening. "I'll get dinner for Mary Jane. Don't you worry."

Later, Mary Jane had come to the barn in tears, thrown her arms around her mother, and knelt beside Essie. At six, she was already becoming a miniature equestrian.

Now Dale made her way to the house, let herself in the back door, and tiptoed up to her old room. She grabbed the candle and scrounged in the kitchen drawer for matches.

"Never, never, never light a match near the stables!" Mr. Jeffrey had beaten it into her head, and she had always obeyed. But not tonight. She took the match, plunged it down in the jar where the wick stood, and lit it. The glass would protect the flames from escaping.

She cradled the candle in her hands as the gentle flame showed the path to the stable and the stall where Essie lay, her swayed back resting in the fresh shavings. Dale set the jar in the stall window and watched through the night as it flickered shadows across the wooden beams and Essie's dull gray coat. With every rise and fall of Essie's barrel, Dale prayed, "Take her soon, Lord. Don't let her suffer." She knew that at dawn she would call Dr. Horner and ask him to come put Essie down.

Until then, she cradled Essie's fine head in her lap. She brushed her fingers across the soft pink muzzle as she'd done a thousand times, traced a circle around the little black beauty mark. And she remembered.

Essie's birth, her struggle, her straggly legs splayed out like a rag doll. The blissful two years of watching her filly grow, and the crushing heartache of watching her leave in the trailer, her head turned toward Dale as she mounted the plank to the trailer, her shrill whinny because she didn't understand. The terrible loneliness that wrapped around Dale, and then her determination to find Essie.

She thought of Tommy, and tears filled her eyes as her throat constricted. Tommy . . . That deep love, that camaraderie, the couples classes, the polio, their rides on the beach at St. Simons. The surprise of Tommy's love among the torpedoes, the surprise of finding Essie as part of the mounted patrol, the surprise of marrying Tommy on Hilton Head Island.

She thought of the baby she had carried, of his faint cry, of her empty arms and empty soul. For so long. And she thought of Tommy's dying wish that she live, as this candle flickered beside him on the beach.

And she remembered Husy, her beloved nursemaid and soul mate and friend, who had walked her through the best and worst of life, and who had died peacefully in her sleep just a few years ago.

So much that pierced her, so much that Dale never wanted to forget.

And now Essie lay dying too.

"But you lived a long life, my little lady. A fine life. And really, you gave me back my life too."

She thought back to the 1952 Olympic Games in Helsinki, Finland, where Dale was one of four women riding in equestrian events, the first year that women were allowed to participate.

"This is for you, Tommy," she had said.

She relived the emotional scene as she watched the silver medalist, Danish equestrian Lis Hartel, being carried from her horse to the podium by the gold medal winner, Henri Saint Cyr from Sweden. Lis, who had contracted polio as a young woman at the height of her equestrian career and who could ride like the champion she was but who could not walk, stood tall and proud beside Henri to receive her silver medal. Dale recalled how the crowd had watched in amazement—very few people knew that Lis had no sensation in or control of her legs below the knee.

Dale thought of sharing meals with Lis Hartel in the days after their events, of telling Lis the way her recovery from polio had inspired Dale, which in turn had given Tommy hope too.

Lis had reached out to shake Dale's hand. "Thank you for telling me. It is my dream to support polio survivors and to show the world the benefits of therapeutic riding."

Throughout the next ten years, Dale and Lis had often corresponded, and Dale read with interest Lis's advocacy of riding for people with disabilities. Dale was sure that therapeutic riding would become an accepted method of rehabilitation one day.

Finally, Dale thought of all the years of showing Essie internationally, and then, after she retired her filly, of breeding Essie. She thought of Essie's filly, No-No Nicotine, born three years ago. Nicky was now almost ready to be broken.

She glanced over at the candle, burning brightly. The flame glittered inside the glass, sparkling with love and hope.

She sang to Essie; she rested her head on her belly. She stroked her gently, and the flame showed the sweetness in Essie's eyes. The pain and the trust and the love.

She stroked her mare's forehead again, whispering, "We've had a good life, haven't we? I'll miss you terribly, but the Good Book says there are horses in heaven, and I know I'll see you there. One day Tommy and I will ride Finny and you in those green, green pastures. On the other side."

The candle burned down lower and lower, and Essie's breathing slowed. And then she stopped breathing altogether. The traces of dawn came across the horizon as Dale looked up through the stall window.

Essie was gone.

She noticed the glimmer and glitter in the jar, but now it appeared as if tiny pebbles were stacked inside. Shining pebbles.

She stared in wonder as she realized what was hidden there.

And Dale felt hope.

29

Allie

Thursday, March 12

We walked up the hill to where Barnell's backhoe was chewing its last piece of bones, Austin's arm around me. When Barnell looked up and saw us coming, he got a big grin on his face.

"Well, I'll be!" he chuckled. "Shore is good to see you two together."

I just smiled, and Austin reached out to shake Barnell's hand. "Thanks for looking after her while I was 'away,'" he said.

Barnell nodded, eyes still twinkling. "My pleasure. You sure got yourself a handful there, Dr. Andrews."

Austin grinned and raised his eyebrows. "Don't I know it!"

"Come on over and see the last grave. Dear, sweet Essie. Saved her for last."

Thoughts of Nana Dale riding her mare on a moonlit beach flashed in my mind as we walked over to Barnell's latest gaping hole.

"B'lieve that mare saved your dear Nana Dale's life." When I raised my eyebrows, saying nothing, he continued, "She gave your grandmother something to believe in, to work for, after a real tough patch in her life."

"I'm glad to hear it," I managed, and Austin squeezed my hand. "We've been reading some of Nana Dale's letters."

"Uh-huh," Barnell grunted as he climbed down inside the grave.

While Barnell's back was to me, I said, "We learned about Tommy. And them getting married."

Silence. Then Barnell stood up and turned around, his hand holding a metal box. "Yep. That rascal."

In a smaller voice, I said, "And Nana Dale was pregnant. And then Tommy died. And the baby was born early and died too."

I sniffed, and Austin held me around the waist with one hand and reached into the hole to help Barnell climb out with the other.

"It was all so awful, Barnell! Did you know about all that? That she married Tommy and had a baby and both of them died? And that she found diamonds in a Mason jar?"

Barnell fiddled with the metal box, set it on the ground, wiped his hands on his overalls, then mopped his brow with the bandanna. His eyes were heavy now. "I didn't know for the longest time, Allie. To be honest, I just found out some things the other day. But I had my suspicions. Little bits and pieces your grandmother would let slip. 'Bout Tommy—sounded like they'd been married. And that sailor.

"Never saw them diamonds, but I read about it in the paper a few years ago. Your grandmother showed me that article. Said it was No Pants Jones who rescued that Jewish family and that he did have that jar—that candle. She'd giggle like she knew a secret and clam up."

He scratched at his head. "You remember we talked about how upset your grandmom got when those DNA results came back showing she was related to Mr. Hightower?"

"Of course. I wish Wick had never asked her to do that test. Imagine her discovering we're related to the man who would eventually steal her property! I hate thinking how rattled it got her. How upset. Barnell, do you think that was the last straw? She died only a few weeks later."

"Yep. Was quite a shock. What she found." He took off his cap, mopped his head with it. "She went to her grave with several secrets. Her marriage to Tommy, the diamonds, and a son."

"Yes, we found the marriage certificate, and we found a charm for a baby boy born in 1943. And Nana Dale told me in a letter that their son didn't survive. Do you know about that baby?"

"I do. And I know that baby boy survived. Always a bit scrawny, but he survived."

"What?" I gasped.

Austin drew me closer. "Her son survived? Are you sure, Barnell?"

"Yep, Nana Dale's son survived, and not long ago, that man's grandson was doing a project on DNA and got his granddad to test. And just like that, Nana Dale's son found his mother."

I was staring at him, openmouthed. "What are you saying? And why would Nana Dale tell you and not my mom or me or Wick? She wouldn't do that!"

The betrayal felt excruciating, but Barnell took me by the shoulder before I could wallow for long.

"She didn't tell me." He shoved some clay around with his foot. "I'm afraid she went to her grave without knowing. No, I just found out about her son a few days ago when I studied those DNA results that my grandson brought over."

Slowly, slowly, I felt something blooming in my mind.

"I'm Dale and Tommy's son, Allie."

Austin gave a low chuckle, and my mouth fell completely open. "You. Are. Kidding!"

"Nope, telling you the truth." He mopped his brow once again. "Glad ta finally be able to tell you."

"What?" I repeated stupidly. "I don't . . . I don't understand. I mean, that's amazing, but . . . but I don't understand."

He nodded. "I'll do my best to explain. I just found out myself, Miss Allie, but I've had a few days to try to piece things together. So here goes.

"When I was about ten, I began asking my parents about my

birth parents—they'd always been open with me about being adopted. They'd never been able to have children, but as my mama described it, I was a gift from heaven they hadn't even prayed for. One day, out of the blue, she got a call from a private adoption agency. She and my father had been chosen for a closed adoption of a four-month-old baby boy.

"Evidently, I'd been in the hospital for a while. Born prematurely to a teenage unwed mother who loved me very much but couldn't keep me."

"But that's not right!" I interrupted. "Nana Dale was married, and she thought her son died! She wouldn't have given you up, Barnell! She wouldn't have."

"No, I agree. It wasn't Nana Dale. Best I can figure, it was her mother, Eleanor Butler, that did it."

Austin muttered under his breath, and I whispered, "That's beyond awful. Surely she wouldn't do something that cruel?" I started shaking my head. "No, I just read in a letter Nana Dale wrote me last year that her mother didn't believe she'd married Tommy or that their baby was legitimate. But they all knew the baby had died."

Barnell gave a sigh. "I'm afraid Mrs. Butler lied to her daughter . . . to everyone."

I stared at Barnell, openmouthed, then recovered and hugged him. "I'm so glad you lived. So glad you're Tommy and Nana Dale's son. But I can't believe my great-grandmother would do such a thing."

"You gotta understand the rules of the South back then. If Mrs. Butler thought the baby was illegitimate, letting that news get out would have stained her daughter forever. Woulda ruined Dale's chances for a well-matched union, a society marriage. Woulda been a big blot on the family name."

I felt the earth shift, like the backhoe had once again upended my life. *Barnell is Nana Dale's son!*

Austin glanced over at me. "You okay?"

I nodded, feeling lightheaded. "Just trying to absorb all this." I grabbed on to his hand. "So Eleanor was the only one who knew the baby—you—survived? Husy knew about the marriage and the baby—but she thought the baby died—and she's the one who helped Nana Dale through all the grief."

Barnell nodded. "That sounds right. I did some poking around this week. When I showed my DNA results, got me permission to access some records, and that's when I found out that Tommy was my daddy, and that it was Mrs. Butler who worked out a closed adoption with my parents. Looks like Dale was eighteen when I was born, but somehow, Eleanor must have lied about her age to the hospital staff so as she could have parental rights. I reckon she knew my parents hadn't been able to have children. But I don't think they knew it was Eleanor who set up the adoption, and they certainly didn't know that I was Nana Dale's son."

My eyes grew wide. "And they never figured it out?"

"I don't think so. Never let on to me. Don't believe anyone ever knew the truth, except Eleanor Butler. Once, when I was a grown man and starting full-time work around horses and barns, my mother told me she thought it was mighty fine that I'd fol- lowed in my father's footsteps—she meant my adoptive father. Then she'd laughed and said I didn't have much of a choice be- cause way back when I was adopted, attached to my birth records was a note requesting that I be raised around horses. She thought that was a strange request but quite easy to honor, since my dad worked at a barn."

He shrugged and lifted his eyebrows. "I imagine when Eleanor realized what a hideous and cruel thing she'd done by taking her daughter's baby away, she felt awful regret. Didn't know her real well, but she wore regret and grief on her face that no amount of makeup could cover up.

"And the way I imagine it was that she did the only thing she could to keep her sanity and to keep her grandson, her daughter's son, close. She requested that I grow up in the shadow of my birth mother and hear all the stories of my birth parents. Maybe my adoptive mother had an inkling of what was going on. Maybe Eleanor told her years later. I don't think we'll ever know that."

"But surely Nana Dale would have wondered about your parents adopting a baby boy, especially if you looked like her or Tommy." I peered into Barnell's weathered face, searching for a resemblance. "Wasn't it risky that someone, anyone, would figure it out?"

Barnell shrugged. "Can't rightly say, Allie. Tommy wasn't around anymore, and the Ridleys, I don't believe they ever came back to Hickory Hills. I don't recall ever meeting them. Real sorry for them. Wish I coulda known my grandparents. They gave Infinity and Beau to your grandmom. But, boy, do I remember how things would go silent whenever someone mentioned Tommy.

"And I don't think that Nana Dale's father ever knew about the marriage or the baby. Maybe Nana Dale guessed the truth about me at some point. She always loved me like her son. Sometimes, in her later years, she'd get a look in her eyes and call me Tommy. Sometimes, I think she knew. I hope so.

"Your grandmother didn't dwell in the past. You know that. Always said bitterness was a poison she wouldn't swallow. But I imagine she wondered about her baby. When Wick suggested the DNA testing, he didn't have any idea of what she'd find. And your grandmother was tickled to do it. She had been so excited when Wick got his master's in some kind of history thing. You know how she always said you were the only one who cared a lick about family history. So she was happy to see Wick's interest too."

He cleared his throat. "Until she realized that Mr. Hightower was her distant cousin. I wish she'd found out the truth about me instead of that. But like I said, sometimes I think she knew just by the way she'd look at me."

I was still trying to digest the information. "So, Barnell, you're mom's half brother? You're my uncle?"

"Guess so. And yep, 'bout had a heart attack when I saw them DNA results on Saturday!" His eyes crinkled and shone, and his arms came around me tightly. "Sorry I reacted so strongly when you asked me about Tommy yesterday. Wasn't sure it was my right to say anything, and I wasn't over the shock myself. But the wife, she let me have it. Said I'd better tell you the truth, and fast. So

I was fixin' to do it, and then you beat me to it. Don't think it'll help you keep the house, but might help you with other things."

Austin and Barnell and I stood arm in arm, staring around the ring with its mounds of red clay, then looking at each other and grinning.

Finally, I said, "Thank you for telling me, Barnell. Thank you, *Uncle* Barnell."

He gave a belly laugh. "Just love hearing that! Glad that secret's out. I've been thinking on it a lot. Me and my wife, we've had a few days to laugh over all the ways I was raised in your grand-mother's—my mother's—shadow, hard as I worked for her. She was feisty, that woman. I loved her something crazy."

He scratched at his head again, then replaced his cap. "I've wondered whether, if I'd have found out I was her son while she was alive . . . well, maybe we could've saved this place from that schemer, Mr. Hightower. But maybe not. We all saw that she was getting a bit confused. She was fading fast." He frowned. "And maybe it was a blessing she didn't know all the bad her mother did. 'Cause she did patch things up with her mother near the end of Mrs. Butler's life. Don't know if that'd been possible if she'd found out that her mother had lied about me and arranged for an adoption."

"This is a whole lot to take in, Barnell." I hugged him around the waist, my emotions ricocheting from heartbreak and grief to joy and delight. And everything in between.

"Shore is, Miss Allie. But you got a good man beside you to help you digest it all."

We'd been standing around Essie's grave for a half hour as we pieced together Barnell's story. I stared down into the grave again and asked, "What do you think she did with the diamonds, Bar-nell?"

"She kept insinuating to Allie that they were still here," Austin said, "or that the money from their sale would be available to Allie. But we're thinking maybe she sold them long ago or gave them away or something."

Barnell shrugged. "I've wondered that too. She inherited the house and property and had plenty of money from her father's lumber business. And then she married, and your grandfather made a handsome living too. So I guess she didn't need to sell the diamonds."

"And she didn't trust her mother or my mother with money, so she wouldn't have given the diamonds to either one of them," I added.

"Reckon you can keep lookin' for a few more days. But truth is, we've run out of time. Last grave is dug up. They'll start clearing for a real road in here, and in two weeks, the barn and the house will come down."

"Thanks for putting them off until I found out at least some of Nana Dale's secrets." Then I looked up at Austin. "And I've decided to stop looking. I'll be busy enough taking care of my husband."

Barnell lifted his thick eyebrows and chuckled. "Yore husband!"

"Yep, we're getting married tomorrow. Hope you'll come."

He threw back his head and howled with laughter. "Nothing could make me happier. Shore am glad you got your horse sense back, Allie. You and Dr. Austin will do just fine. You'll do good stuff with the kids and the animals. Mighty hard that it won't be here, but it'll be okay."

"Austin's afraid that a nasty virus is going to shut the world down, and he wants us to be confined together. That's the only reason he proposed." I winked at Austin.

He laughed, and Barnell made a face. "Oh, I heard about that corona thing. Conspiracy is all that is. The governments of the world is out ta git us. I don't believe it." He shrugged. "But if it takes a virus to git the two of you hitched, well, I'm all for it!" Then he stooped down, picked up the metal box, and handed it to me. "Here ya go."

Austin cocked his head. "What's this?"

"Didn't I tell you?" Allie asked. "Nana Dale took off the horse-shoes before she buried her horses and Tommy's, and then she buried the shoes separately in tin boxes."

Austin shook his head. "That grandmom of yours was several levels of weird."

"Agreed." And I grinned. "But I've saved all the horseshoes from the other graves, and I'm going to have them mounted on wooden plaques where our students can hang the horses' halters." I emphasized the *H*s and then stood on my tiptoes and kissed Austin on the mouth. "Because we are going to have students, even if it isn't at Hickory Hills, and they're going to need a place to hang the horses' halters."

"Yes, ma'am," Austin replied with a wink.

I opened the tin box and fingered the rough horseshoes. Beside them, Nana Dale had written the dates of Essie's birth and death—*January 10, 1931–February 4, 1964*—on a cornflower blue envelope that was thick, almost bulging. When I picked up the envelope, the bottom ripped open, and something clattered against the tin, like pebbles cascading into the box.

I looked down. Glittering among the rusted horseshoes lay hundreds of diamonds.

Epilogue

Allie

Thursday, March 12

When Austin and I called Mom to tell her about her half brother, she jumped in her car and drove straight to Hickory Hills, parked her Lexus at the bottom of the rocky drive, ran out to the barn to meet us, and hugged on Barnell for a long time.

"I've always felt like you were part of the family," she said.

His face turned beet red, and he mumbled, "Dang it, Mrs. Massey, you're embarrassing me!"

"You'll call your little sister by her first name, please, Barnell. I'm Mary Jane."

"Yes, ma'am, I'll try."

Austin had left us, claiming he had business to attend to, and Mom had looked at me and winked. She thought the impromptu revival of our wedding was a brilliant idea.

Now Barnell was sitting on the couch in the den, Mom on one side and me on the other, as we leafed through *DB's Diary* again. When he saw again the article about Jean-Frédéric Kahn, Barnell said, "Now I know why Nana Dale—why *my mother*—was so dang-blasted determined that I have those graves dug up if ever the house was to be sold. She wanted to make sure we found the diamonds."

"She was full of surprises to the end," Mom said. "Diamonds are pretty amazing, but for me, by far the best is finding out I have a big brother." Watching them there, I tried to imagine Nana Dale there too and wished—oh, how I wished—she could be sharing this moment. But maybe she was.

"And, Uncle Barnell, we'll discuss this more as time goes on, but you're her son. I know she'd want you to have part of the inheritance," I said. "Some of these diamonds."

He shook his head, "No, ma'am. Them diamonds are for you, Allie. You alone. We all know that. Just real thankful to know who my parents were and find my family. Can't say you was ever lost from me, but now it's different."

"Discussion to be continued," I said. "But at least for now, you should have this." I plucked Tommy's Maclay Trophy from where it sat on the coffee table beside the Mason jar and handed it to Barnell, whose eyes clouded over.

"Now you'll dare to eat dinner with us, Barnell. No more excuses," Mom said. It was true; Nana Dale and Mom had often invited Barnell and his family for Thanksgiving meals and other family celebrations, but he'd never come. "And you'll start by attending the wedding."

"Be my pleasure."

— ♞ —

All day Friday, Mom and I giggled and primped as I tried on my wedding gown, which Mom brought over from where she'd had it stored in a closet at my parents' house. We spent the whole afternoon together, planning the ceremony. We'd decided it would take place on Saturday. My father arrived back in town on Friday morning, and Wick flew in from France that evening.

"I had to leave the country anyway because of the pandemic. So I figured I might as well attend the wedding too," he said with a wink when I fell into his arms at the airport.

Turned out he wasn't joking. All of France went into lockdown on March 17.

So in a perfect twist of fate, of irony, of answered prayers, Austin and I got married on March 14, 2020, our original wedding date. Not at the church or the country club but in the riding ring. And instead of four hundred guests, there were just a handful.

The white-petaled dogwoods and bright pink azaleas seemed to bloom overnight, lending bountiful color to the rocky road that led to the riding ring. Barnell cut the grass behind the house and used the blower to send three months' worth of leaves into the woods between the V in the road. Tricia was delighted to have her role as maid of honor reinstated and spent all of Friday finding flowers and a photographer.

When Austin called Dr. Ramsay, our pastor who had led Austin and me through premarital counseling, and asked if he could by any chance perform the ceremony, he laughed. "Funny thing, I had the day blocked off for a wedding that was canceled, so I'm free." Then he admitted, "I was praying Allie would come to her senses."

We brought Jeep and Foxtrot over from Chastain in a trailer, and Austin and I sat bareback on our horses beside thick mounds of red clay with our few guests looking on as we said our vows. My wedding dress cascaded over Foxie's rear, and Austin wore his best and only suit with his cowboy boots.

Cécile set up a tent in the backyard and covered two tables with white tablecloths and Nana Dale's silver platters, filled with French cheeses and red grapes and gluten-free crackers. And bottles of red wine from the Languedoc-Roussillon. "For the *apéro*, after the ceremony. It's what we do in France," she explained.

Austin's mother and sisters had flown in Saturday morning, and the look of love on their faces as they joined us for the celebration brought both Austin and me to tears.

And of course, Uncle Barnell was there with his wife, standing beside my mother, who stood beside my father, who stood beside Wick.

After I whispered, "I do," and Austin did the same, Austin leaned over and slipped the horseshoe-nail ring we'd removed from Nana Dale's charm bracelet onto my finger. And I slipped a similar looking one, fashioned by Barnell the day before, on his. We leaned across the space between Foxtrot and Jeep and kissed. And then we took off at a gallop around the ring, dodging the crater-like holes where Barnell had unearthed the horses' graves.

April 2020

Right after the wedding, Austin moved into my studio apartment with Maggie and me. It was in better shape than his bachelor pad, and Maggie only pouted for a few days before remembering her previous fondness for him.

"You were right," I said, standing behind where Austin sat at my kitchen table, my arms around his neck. "The whole world is shutting down because of the pandemic."

"Yep," he said, pulling me into his lap and planting a long, slow kiss on my lips. "And can I just say again that I am ecstatically grateful to be shut in with you?"

Just days before the scheduled implosion of Hickory Hills, much of the city of Atlanta closed down. Barnell's backhoe left the ring, and no other machinery showed up on March 28 to implode the house. Hickory Hills stood untouched as I watched from a distance, feeling a little awed.

And we never had the estate sale.

On April 2, Governor Kemp ordered all of Georgia to shelter in place, so I no longer drove to Nancy Creek Road to keep watch. However, almost daily, I called Nana Dale's next-door neighbor, Christy, a young mother who had moved in with her husband and two daughters a few years previously, to check on the status of the house.

"All clear today," she reported. "All I can see are mounds of red clay in the ring and a big ole house and barn across the way."

When I clicked off the call, I perched myself in Austin's lap and asked, "Why do you think he's waiting to destroy the house?"

Austin raised an eyebrow, kissed me on the cheek, and said, "Well, you never actually cleaned it out."

"I will, Austin. I promise, I will. As soon as . . ."

"We come out of confinement," we said in unison.

August 2020

"Allie, Ted Lorrider here. How are you and Dr. Andrews doing?"

"Well, we're doing great as a couple, but like everyone else in the world, we're figuring things out one day at a time."

"Yes, I imagine so." He cleared his throat. "I have some interesting news to report. As you may have suspected, Mr. Hightower has been unable to sell the Hickory Hills property with things so unsure."

"Yes, thankfully he hasn't imploded the house yet."

"Exactly. Now, most contractors would just wait out this virus until it blows over." He cleared his throat. "*If* it blows over."

"But nobody wants to buy land right now, and that wheeler-dealer has to build and sell to stay afloat. It seems that Hightower, much like his grandfather Weatherby, has overextended himself by a very large amount, and the banks are coming after him."

I gave a small gasp. "What do you mean?" I was afraid to breathe.

"In late July, Mr. Hightower's whole business went belly-up."

"So does that mean . . . ?"

"His business has imploded, instead of Hickory Hills. And next week, the bank will repossess the property." Mr. Lorrider let out a very uncharacteristic chortle. "And I've heard through the grapevine that you found your grandmother's cherrywood chest and a bunch of diamonds. So if you're interested—"

"Yes, oh yes. Yes!" I shouted into the phone, dislodging Maggie and causing Austin to turn from where he was staring at his computer screen while on a Zoom call with a client.

Four weeks later, when I sold some of the diamonds—very large and very fine diamonds—we had plenty of money to buy back my beloved barn from the bank and to bring our horses to the healing hotel at Hickory Hills. Then, on a muggy September evening, Austin and I moved into Hickory Hills, with lightning bugs just beginning to flare and mosquitoes nipping at my bare shoulders.

Arm in arm, Austin and I climbed the stairs to the Pink Room, where I set the cherrywood chest on top of the hope chest, and Maggie napped on top of the wedding-ring quilt tucked at the foot of the bed. With the windows open, the white canopy billowed above us as Tommy and Nana Dale kept watch, their faces smiling out of a black-and-white photo.

October 2020

Up in the riding ring, the beginning of a fence was being installed now that Barnell had filled in the graves, leaving the horses' bones inside. Mom and Tricia and I crunched through the fallen leaves with a cobalt blue autumn sky smiling down on us.

"Time for your first therapy session, Mom. And Tricia is going to lead you through it." I winked at my friend. "I will not repeat the mother-daughter dysfunction that's existed for several generations. I don't want you to blame me for making you try this. And you can quit any time you want. Deal?"

Mom nodded and strapped on the hard hat.

"You're our first client," Tricia said.

Mom smiled at me and shrugged. "Guess it's time to get started."

Angelfoot stood placidly as Mom gripped the pommel, placed her left foot in the stirrup, and pulled herself over the gelding's back. She landed gently in the seat of the saddle and stared in wonder. Then she began to laugh like a young girl who had just discovered the greatest pleasure in life.

On the tack room walls at Hickory Hills are narrow pieces of stained wood with these names burned into them: *Mr. Jinx, Krystal, Infinity, Essie, Nicky.* Barnell has attached the accompanying horseshoes to the correct plaque, and from each of those old, rusted horseshoes hangs a halter. But when the sun is shining through the window in the tack room at just the right time, or the moon is high and full, the light will catch the plaque with Essie's horseshoes on it in such a way that, if you squint, those shoes sparkle as if embedded with dozens and dozens of diamonds.

∩∩∩∩∩

Discussion Questions

1. Both Allie and Dale struggle with distinguishing between passion and obsession. Discuss the ways each woman becomes aware of having crossed the line from a healthy passion to an unhealthy obsession.

2. Can you identify a time in your life when something that was a positive dream, desire, or passion became an obsession? How long did it take for you to realize this, and what did you do next?

3. Discuss the theme of gratitude. Do you regularly practice gratitude? If so, what does that look like, and what have been some of the results?

4. Prayer plays a significant role in the novel. Husy reminds Dale not to forget her prayers. What do you think she means by this?

5. Both Allie and Dale witness someone close to them praying on her knees. At first Allie sees this as a posture of fear and weakness. Why? Later Allie finds herself on her knees.

Discuss different postures for prayer. Have any of these been important to you?

6. What is horse sense? How does Allie use her horse sense in the story, and when might it be a hindrance to her?

7. Were you familiar with the role civilians played during the Battle of the Atlantic? Had you ever heard of the merchant marines, Liberty ships, or Coast Guard Mounted Patrol? Discuss the acts of courage on display in America during WWII.

8. Near the end of the novel, Allie remembers one of her outbursts to Austin and reflects, "I loved *me*. Not *us*. *Me*." Have you ever had an aha moment that left you feeling like Allie? What was your response?

9. Nana Dale tells Allie, "In life, you often have to take the risk of being misunderstood. That's what I've done. I love my family, you know that. But I can't trust them with the money." How do you feel about taking the risk of being misunderstood? What have been the consequences when you or someone close to you has taken this risk?

10. Nana Dale tells Allie, "Life is paradox, Allie. When you learn to embrace it all, let it mix together like molasses in oats, well, the sweet fragrance comes out. Even when life stinks." Do you agree or disagree?

11. Which of the characters in the story can you most relate to and why?

12. Have you ever had someone like Husy who started as a caretaker when you were young and then became more

like a mentor to you? If so, share your experience and what the transition looked like.

13. After Mr. Jinx is put down, Dale remembers something Husy told her: "It'll break your heart, Dale. And you'll grieve. But loving an animal and losing it, watching it die, and then getting another, well, it teaches a person she can love again." Have you had the experience of losing a beloved pet and then finding love in another one? Do you agree with Husy's observation?

14. Before reading *By Way of the Moonlight*, were you familiar with equine therapy and its many derivatives? What is your impression of this type of therapy?

15. Nana Dale's estate, Hickory Hills, becomes like a character in the novel. What are your favorite homes, estates, or other places of residence in literature, movies, and television series? For example, the haunting charm of Manderley in *Rebecca*, the deep and pure beauty of Anne's Green Gables, and the elegance and extravagance of Tara in *Gone with the Wind*.

16. Discuss the theme of dysfunction between mothers and daughters. How does Allie seek to break this pattern?

Acknowledgments

A special thanks to the many people who made *By Way of the Moonlight* possible:

Jere W. Goldsmith IV, my precious and over-the-top generous daddy, who graduated to heaven a few months before this novel went into print, and Barbara Dale Butler Goldsmith, my feisty and devoted horse-loving mother, who predeceased Daddy by six years. The hoofprints of your remarkable lives are all over this story. I miss you both terribly but have a lifetime of wild and wonderful memories in the house and barn at Hickory Hills.

Petty Officer Keisha Kerr, who was kind enough to do a Zoom call with me while she was on duty in Guam. She also pointed me to the book *Prints in the Sand—the US Coast Guard Beach Patrol during WWII* by Eleanor Bishop.

Dr. George Cressman, docent historian, who provided me with formerly classified documents detailing the creation of the Coast Guard Mounted Patrol and the roles and results of the different stations along the coasts of the United States.

Gwen Hanna, whom I interviewed about her firsthand experience working in equine therapy.

Chip MacGregor, my agent and friend—*Et bien sûr—j'aime les chevaux!* I'm always thankful for your wise counsel, good humor, and unfailing support. *Merci, mon ami!*

Dave Horton, former vice president of editorial at Bethany House Publishers, with whom my publishing journey began back in 1994. You were the first to read my initial chapters of *By Way of the Moonlight* and gave me the green light to pursue this story. I miss your wisdom, humor, and encouragement, and I can still sense you peeking over my shoulder and saying, "*Chapeau*, Elizabeth."

The wonderful team at Bethany House Publishers—I am thankful to be working with such gifted people. A huge *merci* to Raela Schoenherr, Rochelle Gloege, and Kate Deppe, who have seamlessly transitioned to being my editors and cheerleaders after Dave and my longtime beloved editor, LB Norton, both retired. I'm grateful for the way you have embraced this story and made it so much better, expertly catching all my snafus. Also to Anne Van Solkema, Karen Steele, Brooke Vikla, and many others at BHP, *merci* for all you do behind the scenes. Your expertise is invaluable and reassuring.

Jori Hanna, my delightful, savvy marketing assistant, who does all things well and keeps my head on straight—as much as is humanly possible.

Doris Ann Musser, my energetic and lovely mother-in-law, who continues to model resilience, good humor, optimism, and courage in the face of aging. You have been a cheerleader and mentor to me for many years.

My brothers Jere Goldsmith V and Glenn Goldsmith—I'm so grateful for all the memories we have shared together for all of our lives at Nancy Creek. And to my sisters-in-law, Mary and Kim, true sisters in every sense of the word. You have prayed me through some really challenging times, and you love Nancy Creek every bit as much as I do.

All the others in the Goldsmith and Musser families—thank you for your support throughout our years on the mission field and my years in writing.

So many friends on both sides of the Atlantic pray for the work of my hands. I can't begin to name them all, but please be reminded that your prayers have been answered each time I birth a book.

My Transformational Fiction prayer partners: Lynn Austin, Sharon Garlough Brown, Robin Grant, Susan Meissner, and Deb Raney, we have prayed each other through so many joys and sorrows on this journey as writers and sisters in Christ. Thank you.

My family at One Collective—thank you for receiving what Paul and I have to offer with grace and for allowing me to pen my stories.

Andrew Musser, my firstborn son—I am constantly in awe of your beautiful mind, tender heart, subtle humor, patient endurance, deep love for your wife and kids and us, your parents. Thank you for helping me navigate my four worlds.

My daughter-in-law, Lacy Musser—I am grateful for your undying care for and support of your ever-expanding family and for your enthusiastic support of my writing career, even when it means I can't keep the grandkids for as long or as often as I want.

Jesse, Nadja'Lyn, Quinn, Lena, and baby Cori Lucille—thank you for listening to all the crazy bedtime stories your mamie tells you and for dreaming up others with me. Your love of life inspires me.

Chris Musser, my second-born son—your unique combination of wit, true diplomacy, optimization, and a kind heart are changing the lives of many. Thank you for speaking truth to me and helping me with all things business related for my writing career. Thank you for being such an amazing housemate for Granddaddy and making the last years of his life filled with such delight, and for marrying Ashlee, which was the absolute best gift to him and all of us.

My new daughter-in-law, Ashlee, you are one of my biggest cheerleaders, and your generous and loving heart helped me so much as I walked the final path with my father.

Paul Musser—always to you, my better half, my partner in love and life and the hidden hero in every one of my love stories. You care for and support my every endeavor and then take it all to the Lord. Thank you for loving me so well as our journey together twists and turns. *Je t'aime tant.*

My dear readers—you make my day over and over again with your comments and photos on social media and your heartfelt emails. And what a joy to get to meet some of you in person.

And finally, to Jesus, my Savior and Lord—thank You for calling me to Yourself when I was a little girl riding in the ring, playing with horse statues, and creating stories about horses, humans, and God. Day by day, You reveal more of Your mystery and holiness and extravagant love and grace to me. I owe everything to You—my life, my love, my all.

Author's Note

As a Southern girl, it's no secret that Atlanta is my favorite American city in which to spin my stories. But in this novel, I am not just focusing on Atlanta or even Buckhead, the neighborhood where I grew up. This time, I weave a fictional tale around my childhood home as I ask questions about the worth of land, faith, family history, memories, and shared dreams.

I grew up with a barn filled with horses and several of them buried in the riding ring. This property, which we affectionately call Nancy Creek, has been in the family since 1938, when my grandfather built a small house and a two-horse barn out on a dirt road for his only child (my mom) to indulge her love of riding and showing. My mother was a great equestrian, showing and jumping until she was seventy, and I rode and showed as a child and teen. Although Nancy Creek is not the magnificent estate I describe in the novel, it is beloved by the entire Goldsmith-Musser clan. My novels often touch on themes that mirror events and ruminations in my own life, and so I began to pen a novel about finding "dinosaur bones" in the backyard of a longtime family property.

I have many photos of the real Hickory Hills, silver platters, horse show ribbons, vintage photos of my mother showing her champion mares, and other fun memorabilia for your viewing pleasure available on Facebook, Instagram, Pinterest, and my blog.

As my family and friends know, I'm a sentimental girl. In this story, I've used proper names to honor those I love, but aside from Barbara Dale Butler, who resembles my mom, the names don't reflect on the personalities of the actual people, except when they do. So you can figure that out! And if you think I'm winking at you through a name or a phrase or a snippet of a story, be assured that I am and consider yourself hugged!

One of the great privileges of writing historical fiction is the wealth of new knowledge I gain as I do research. I hadn't heard of the Coast Guard Mounted Patrol until I began this novel. I serendipitously happened on a photo of a group of military men galloping their mounts along the beach of Hilton Head Island—my family's favorite vacation spot for the past fifty years—taken during the Battle of the Atlantic in WWII, when the island was still mostly deserted. I found myself cantering into the world of the Sand Pounders, and what a wild ride that was!

From there, I fell down many rabbit holes and learned about the two US tankers that were sunk by a German U-boat off the coast of St. Simons Island in 1942. My husband and I journeyed to the island and spent hours perusing the excellent displays at the World War II Homefront Museum. We also spent an afternoon on Hilton Head Island on the grounds of what was Camp McDougal, the training camp for the Coast Guard Mounted Patrol during WWII.

As I invested countless hours researching the Battle of the Atlantic, I was inspired by the heroism of so many Stateside civilians doing their part to construct Liberty ships and guard the coasts when the German threat was at its height. Although I could not find proof of any women being in the Coast Guard Mounted Patrol, Petty Officer Keisha Kerr believes that it was a real possibility, especially if there was a girl like Barbara Dale determined to join.

To understand more about equine therapy, I studied the different programs at the real Chastain Horse Park in Atlanta and read and watched different depictions of this type of therapy. Most interesting was learning the story of the Danish equestrian champion Lis Hartel, who overcame polio by using this therapy before it was well-known in the US. But of course, as a horse lover and a gal who grew up with ponies and horses as my best friends, I knew all about the healing power of horses from the time I was young.

If you would like more information about the Battle of the Atlantic, the Sand Pounders, and equine therapy, here are some suggestions.

The Battle of the Atlantic

All the U-boat sightings and sinkings in *By Way of the Moonlight* are true, and the dates accurate, although I added my fictional twist on how the civilians, Sand Pounders, and others dealt with the sightings.

Prints in the Sand: The U.S. Coast Guard Beach Patrol during World War II by Eleanor Bishop

Why Were the U-Boats Winning the Battle of the Atlantic? by Dr. George E. Cressman Jr.

The Beach Patrol and Corsair Fleet by Dennis Noble

The Coast Guard at War: Beach Patrol XVII prepared in the Historical Section Public Relations Division US Coast Guard Headquarters May 15, 1945 (was classified, now declassified)

April 8, 1942

Coastal Georgia Historical Society
World War II Home Front Museum
4201 1st Street
St. Simons Island, GA 31522
912-634-7085

"Close to Home" by Bill Hendrick
http://www.usmm.org/closetohome.html

"When War Torpedoed the Golden Isles" by Larry Hobbs
https://thebrunswicknews.com/news/local_news/when-war-torpedoed-the
-golden-isles/article_719cdfe4-bbc3-5a83-8e80-2913027428da.html

"U-Boat Attacks during World War II" by John P. Vanzo
https://www.georgiaencyclopedia.org/articles/history-archaeology/u-boat
-attacks-during-world-war-ii/

June 13, 1942

"When the Nazis Invaded the Hamptons" by Christopher Klein
https://www.history.com/news/when-the-nazis-invaded-the-hamptons

Hilton Head and Camp McDougal

"Our Islands" by Frank Coley, *Islander Magazine*, June 1989.

Merchant Marines

"The Merchant Marine Were the Unsung Heroes of World War II"
    by William Geroux
https://www.smithsonianmag.com/history/merchant-marine-were-unsung
-heroes-world-war-ii-180959253/

My Inspiration for the Mason Jar Treasure

"Nazis Fooled by Paris Diamond Merchant with Incredible Ploy during
    World War Two" by Warren Muggleton
https://www.dailystar.co.uk/news/world-news/nazi-art-plunder-fooled
-parisian-16799896

Equine Therapy

Chastain Horse Park
https://www.chastainhorsepark.org/

PATH International: Professional Association of Therapeutic Horsemanship
https://www.pathintl.org/

Temple Grandin (HBO Films, 2010)

Elizabeth Musser writes "entertainment with a soul" from her writing chalet—tool shed—outside Lyon, France. Elizabeth's award-winning, bestselling novel *The Swan House* was named one of Amazon's Top Christian Books of the Year and one of Georgia's Top Ten Novels of the Past 100 Years, and was awarded the Gold Illumination Book Award 2021 for Enduring Light Fiction. All of Elizabeth's novels have been translated into multiple languages and have been international bestsellers. *Two Destinies*, the final novel in THE SECRETS OF THE CROSS trilogy, was a finalist for the 2013 Christy Award. *The Long Highway Home* was a finalist for the 2018 Carol Award. Elizabeth's most recent novel, *The Promised Land*, won second place in Literary Fiction at the 2021 Georgia Author of the Year Awards and won the 2021 Carol Award for Contemporary Fiction.

For over thirty-five years, Elizabeth and her husband, Paul, have been involved in missions work in Europe with One Collective, formerly International Teams. The Mussers have two sons, two daughters-in-law, and five grandchildren. Find more about Elizabeth and her novels at www.elizabethmusser.com.

@ElizabethMusserAuthor

@elizabeth.musser

@EMusserAuthor

Sign Up for Elizabeth's Newsletter

Keep up to date with Elizabeth's news on book releases and events by signing up for her email list at elizabethmusser.com.

More from Elizabeth Musser

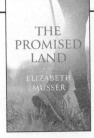

Desperate to mend her marriage and herself, Abbie Jowett joins her son in walking the famed Camino pilgrimage. During their journey, they encounter an Iranian working in secret to help refugees and a journalist searching for answers from her broken past—and everyone is called into a deep soul-searching that threatens all their best laid plans.

The Promised Land

You May Also Like . . .

Famous author Josephine Bourdillon is in a coma, her memories surfacing as her body fights to survive. But those around her are facing their own battles: Henry Hughes, who agreed to kill her for hire out of desperation, is uncertain how to finish the job now, and her teenage daughter, Paige, is overwhelmed by fear. Can grace bring them all into the light?

When I Close My Eyes by Elizabeth Musser
elizabethmusser.com

When Luke Dempsey's fellow inmate lay dying, Luke promised to protect the man's daughter, Finley, and help her find the treasure he had hidden. Upon Luke's release, he and Finley uncover the clues, and their reasons for resisting each other begin to crumble. Luke will shield her from unseen threats, but who's going to shield him from losing his heart?

Turn to Me by Becky Wade
A Misty River Romance
beckywade.com

Libby has been given a powerful gift: to live one life in 1774 Colonial Williamsburg and the other in 1914 Gilded Age New York City. When she falls asleep in one life, she wakes up in the other without any time passing. On her twenty-first birthday, Libby must choose one path and forfeit the other—but how can she possibly decide when she has so much to lose?

When the Day Comes by Gabrielle Meyer
Timeless #1
gabriellemeyer.com

◆ BETHANYHOUSE

More from Bethany House

When Cameron Lee's music career takes a nose dive, he reluctantly returns home, where he falls fast for single mom Lexie Walters. But fantasies only last so long, and soon they have to face the real world, one fraught with heartbreak and disappointment and questions that can only be answered on your knees.

Love and the Dream Come True by Tammy L. Gray
STATE OF GRACE
tammylgray.com

Natalia Blackstone relies on Count Dimitri Sokolov to oversee the construction of the Trans-Siberian Railway. Dimitri loses everything after witnessing a deadly tragedy and its cover-up, but he has an asset the czar knows nothing about: Natalia. Together they fight to save the railroad while exposing the truth, but can their love survive the ordeal?

Written on the Wind by Elizabeth Camden
THE BLACKSTONE LEGACY #2
elizabethcamden.com

After moving to Jerusalem, Aya expects to be bored in her role as wife to a Torah student but finds herself fascinated by her husband's studies. And when her brother Sha'ul makes a life-altering decision, she is faced with a troubling question: How can she remain true to all she's been taught since infancy and still love her blasphemous brother?

The Apostle's Sister by Angela Hunt
JERUSALEM ROAD #4
angelahuntbooks.com

◊ BETHANYHOUSE